A WATERY GRAVE

As Don gazed at his reflection in the water, something struck him as strange. With the moon behind him, and no other light source, he was surprised that he could still see his facial features.

Was reflected moonlight that strong? he wondered.

Closer he leaned, peering down at the marble-smooth water—still, placid. But then he saw something shift beneath the surface. A fish swimming below or a cloud drifting in front of the moon? He wasn't sure.

A scream burst from his mouth but was suddenly closed off when a hand suddenly shot up from the water and grabbed him by the throat. The viselike grip tightened, cutting off his air and threatening to crush his windpipe. The strong fingers clenched tighter—tighter, and Don could feel the points of the fingernails digging into his skin.

The only screams now were in his mind as he scrambled desperately to cling to the stream bank. The grip tightened like a coil, and then the thin arm began to draw him forward and down, down into the water.

The only thought in his *mind was, This is it! I'm going to drown!* With an i_____ _____ to the side, rolled over ont_____ grip on his throat.

Air roared into his lungs _____ scrambled up the bank, away _____ throat still felt as though a steel band were clamped around it as he ran up to the house and into the kitchen. Panting and shaking, he sat down at the kitchen table, trying to calm the hammering in his ears and chest.

It *couldn't* have been real! his mind kept repeating. But if it hadn't happened, what had . . . ?

TALES OF TERROR AND POSSESSION
from Zebra Books

HALLOWEEN II   (1080, $2.95)
by Jack Martin
The terror begins again when it is Halloween night in Haddon-field, Illinois. Six shots pierce the quiet of the normally peaceful town — and before night is over, Haddonfield will be the scene of yet another gruesome massacre!

MAMA   (1247, $3.50)
by Ruby Jean Jensen
Once upon a time there lived a sweet little dolly, but her one beaded glass eye gleamed with mischief and evil. If Dorrie could have read her doll's thoughts, she would have run for her life — for her dear little dolly only had killing on her mind.

ROCKINGHORSE   (1743, $3.95)
by William W. Johnstone
It was the most beautiful rockinghorse Jackie and Johnny had ever seen. But as they took turns riding it they didn't see its lips curve into a terrifying smile. They couldn't know that their own innocent eyes had taken on a strange new gleam.

JACK-IN-THE-BOX   (1892, $3.95)
by William W. Johnstone
Any other little girl would have cringed in horror at the sight of the clown with the insane eyes. But as Nora's wide eyes mirrored the grotesque wooden face her pink lips were curving into the same malicious smile.

Available wherever paperbacks are sold, or order direct from the Publisher. Send cover price plus 50¢ per copy for mailing and handling to Zebra Books, Dept. 1843, 475 Park Avenue South, New York, N.Y. 10016. Residents of New York, New Jersey and Pennsylvania must include sales tax. DO NOT SEND CASH.

NIGHT STONE

BY RICK HAUTALA

ZEBRA BOOKS
KENSINGTON PUBLISHING CORP.

ZEBRA BOOKS

are published by

Kensington Publishing Corp.
475 Park Avenue South
New York, NY 10016

First printing: October 1986

Printed in the United States of America

To my parents . . . for the sisu *and the* nisu.

Of course, the people who are *always* there—especially Bonnie—know that this book couldn't have been done without their help, encouragement, and patience. But for this time around, I want to thank four people who gave generously of their special knowledge:

—Bo Miller, of St. Mary's General Hospital in Lewiston, Maine, offered medical insight into the much-misunderstood disorder known as epilepsy;

—Arthur Spiess, Maine State Archaeologist in Augusta, Maine, directed me to the facts concerning Maine's rich archaeological heritage—which I then proceeded to distort;

—Russ Parker, musician and agriculturalist at the University of Maine in Orono, told me everything I needed to know about hay balers;

—And Dominick Abel, my agent, gave the suggestions and guidance I needed—*when* I needed them.

Thanks, everyone!

The Dreaming Stone

Prologue

January, 1921

. . . revere Spirits, but keep them at a distance.
                                        —Confucius

*I say this house is as dark as ignorance, though
ignorance were as dark as hell . . .*
                        Twelfth Night, IV, ii, 45–46
                                        —Shakespeare

The fiery brilliance of the Zebra Hologram Heart which you see on the cover is created by "laser holography." This is the revolutionary process in which a powerful laser beam records light waves in diamond-like facets so tiny that 9,000,000 fit in a square inch. No print or photograph can match the vibrant colors and radiant glow of a hologram.

So look for the Zebra Hologram Heart whenever you buy a historical romance. It is a shimmering reflection of our guarantee that you'll find consistent quality between the covers!

A Winter's Storm

I

With evening, the sky turned the color of thick soot. Toivo Kivinen shouldered open the door of his house, stepped inside, then swung the door firmly shut behind him. He stamped his feet on the braided rug, and most of the snow clinging to his woolen pants fell to the floor. Small puddles began to form and spread.

"You look cold," Aune, his wife, said, looking up from her knitting. She was propped on the couch beside the blazing fireplace and wrapped in a tattered afghan.

Toivo, a short, stocky Finn with blond hair and piercing blue eyes, nodded and grunted a reply as he took off first his *pussi lakki*, then his three-fingered mittens and let them drop. He bent over and began unlacing his boots.

"Has it stopped snowing yet?" Aune asked, keeping her voice low so she wouldn't disturb twelve-year-old Marie asleep beside her on the couch.

Toivo shook his head, still not saying anything intelligible. He knew she could see the thick flakes streaking past the living room window. Caught in the rectangle of light from the house, the snow made pencil-thin white lines against the dark night.

"It's beginning to break now," he muttered, kicking one boot off.

"And the animals?" Aune asked softly. "They're settled?"

"Yes. Yes. They're settled," Toivo said through his teeth. He kicked the other boot off, and it slammed into the wall. The sound made Marie stir. As Toivo started toward the living room, he stepped into a puddle of ice water and swore softly under his breath. *"Saatana! Saatana!"*

"Such language," Aune said sharply, not looking up.

Toivo shot her an angry glance, then paused. Another worse curse formed in his mouth, but he let it dissolve when he saw the haunted hollowness of his wife's face. With no curse permitted, words failed him, so he sat down in his armchair and grunted.

"Toivo," Aune said after a long silence broken only by the crackling of the fire and the steady click-click of her knitting needles. He looked at her, his hypnotized concentration on the fire broken. Aune's knitting needles were poised in midair like crossed swords.

"Toivo, the winter will be long and hard, and—"

"And night is dark. Snow is cold," Toivo snapped. He knew what was coming, what she would say next, and—just now—he didn't want to hear it.

Aune looked at her husband and sighed deeply as the knitting needles settled into her lap. Her thin lips drew back against her teeth, and she swallowed with difficulty before continuing.

"How long will it go on?" she asked. "How long will you work in that godforsaken quarry before you finally admit that it will never make any money?"

14

Toivo rumbled in his chest. "Such language," he said and turned his gaze back to the fire.

"How long before we all starve to death?" Aune said, her voice taking on a cutting edge that jabbed at his ears. "If we moved back to Lanesville now, you could find work in the quarries there. Urho, my uncle, will—"

"I don't care what your Uncle Urho can or can't do!" Toivo shouted, letting his fist drop like a hammer on the chair's arm. Marie rolled over in her sleep and dragged an edge of the quilt over her face. Toivo leaned forward and, lowering his voice, said, "I will not work for another man. Never again! Not when I have a quarry of my own!"

"But it's losing money," Aune said, pleading. "We haven't much food now, and winter's not even half over. We'll starve. We'll lose the house if we don't have money soon."

"We *will* have money soon. Come spring."

"Not next spring! Soon! Now! Look—look at Marie. Twelve years old and look at her—thin as a rail. If we moved back to Lanesville now, we'd be with family. We could all help each other."

Toivo hoisted himself to his feet and began pacing back and forth in front of the fireplace, slapping his fist repeatedly in his open hand. His bulky shadow swept like a dark wing across the room. Inside, his blood was raging; his stomach was tightening like a spring.

"I'm my own boss! My own person!" he said, slapping his chest solidly. "I don't need charity from anyone—not Urho, not anyone!"

"It isn't charity if it's family," Aune said, sounding desperate now. "And—and—"

She suddenly flung her knitting down and reached out to her husband, her hands folded and shaking as

15

though in fitful prayer. Her vision blurred as tears filled her eyes. "And I can't stay here anymore, Toivo. I can't! Not another winter! I saw him again, this evening—just before you came in."

Toivo turned to her, his fist clenched and raised as if to strike, but he held himself back, trembling. "You didn't see him, Aune! You didn't! Eino is dead!"

"I did! I saw him!" Aune screeched. Her eyes were wide and glistening, her face chalky.

"Your son is dead, Aune. *Dead!* And the sooner you accept that, the better off we'll all be." It took a massive effort for Toivo to keep his voice steady. The memory of his son's death rose in his mind like an acid-sharp etching. Eino's arm crushed beneath a three-ton granite block, his hand severed at the wrist and nothing more than a bloody, pulpy smear on the ground, he lay cradled in his father's arms as he bled to death. The company doctor arrived too late to do anything but pronounce him dead.

Aune looked up at his looming bulk, backlit by the fireplace, and a sudden terror flooded her as her vision of the man she loved shifted subtly into the shape of a monster poised to strike out at her. She choked back a pained sob and turned away, hoping the vision would pass, but when she saw a shadow shift outside the window, she screamed and fell to the floor.

"There he is! He's there!" she yelled, clawing her face with one hand and pointing frantically with the other. *"Outside! Look! There!* Let him come in out of the storm!"

Marie was startled awake and sat up blinking, looking back and forth between her mother and father. "Wha—? What is it?" she said, choking. She registered fear but not the source of the fear. Had papa been drinking again?

16

"He's outside! *He's outside!*" Aune yelled, pointing wildly at the window. "I saw him! I saw Eino! He wants to come in!"

Marie looked, horror-struck, at the window and saw nothing but reflected firelight and streaks of snow.

Toivo took four long strides to the window and, leaning on the sill with clenched fists, pressed his nose to the cold glass. Nothing. Nothing but the night and thick snowflakes, which always came at the tail end of a storm.

Marie knelt on the floor beside her mother, stroking her hair softly as she cooed in her ear. "It's all right, Mama. It's all right. Would you like some tea, Mama?"

Toivo turned, straightened himself, and placed both hands on his hips as he stared at his wife. One part of his mind questioned his wife's sanity, but, at least consciously, he thought her repeated claims of seeing Eino were nothing more than the aftereffects of the shock and grief of losing her first-born—something she *must* get over soon before it did drive her mad.

"There is nothing—no one—out there," he said firmly as though speaking to a child. "No one would be out there. Not on a night like this."

"I saw—him," Aune said, shaking with chest-deep sobs. "I saw—Eino . . . my boy." She buried her face in her hands, and warm tears filled the cups of her palms.

"No, woman," Toivo said. "There was no one there."

"I . . . *saw* . . . him."

With an angry huff, Toivo went to the door and began lacing on his boots. Hiking on his heavy coat, he swung the door open. A gust of wind carried a puff of snow into the house with a sharp, snakelike hiss.

17

"Get that tea for your mother," he growled at Marie, who immediately ran into the kitchen. "I'll go out and take a look, woman, if only to prove how foolish you are."

The frigid blast of air hit Aune, huddled on the floor; then the door slammed shut behind Toivo.

II

Outside, Toivo could see that the storm was breaking up. Thick, cottony clouds drifted pale blue against the inky sky. Sprinkles of stars shone through the rifts in the clouds, and the moon, almost full, cast wavering, eerie shadows under the eaves of the house. Toivo made his way slowly through the knee-deep snow to the side of the house.

"Damned woman," he muttered, his breath puffing plumes of steam. The night was filled with a bone-deep silence, broken only by the distant hissing of the wind racing over the snowy fields. The tang of wood smoke stung his nostrils, reminding him of the sauna back home in Finland, and a soft sense of loss, maybe homesickness, surged up in his chest. He plowed his way over to the rectangle of light cast through the window onto the snow.

What he saw there, beneath the window, made him jerk back a step or two in surprise. In the new-fallen snow, directly below the window, were the definite impressions of footprints. Toivo grunted, stepped forward, and bent low to study them. The light from the moon shifted under the passing clouds, filling the depressions in the snow with deep shadows.

"*Saatana!*" Toivo whispered, studying the footprints. They looked small, like a child's, and they pointed toward the house, clearly indicating that someone *had* been outside looking in. But who? Some

18

neighbor who needed help? Perhaps a practical joker or Peeping Tom. The tracks were fresh, he knew that much.

Toivo straightened up and, turning, scanned the snow-covered field down toward the road. He could just barely see the leaning stone gatepost at the end of the driveway, nearly lost in the tangle of shadows from the overhanging oak. But there were no footprints, other than his own, leading to the house. Just here, by the window—where Aune had said she had seen their dead son—was the snow cover broken.

"Papa . . . Papa," a voice called faintly.

"One minute, Marie," Toivo called. His voice echoed through the night as he scanned the unbroken snow. Confusion surged within him as he considered who might have been outside here, looking in on his family in the privacy of their home. He clenched his fists and shook them.

"Papa . . . Papa."

"Wait one minute, can't you!" he shouted. A sudden gust of wind blew a flurry of snow into his face, sending a chill down his back. He realized that he had come outside without his mittens and *pussi lakki*, and blew on his fists to warm them.

"Papa . . . I'm here," the voice said. There was a hollowness in the sound that made the chill reach deeper into Toivo's chest. He was about to yell once more to Marie to tell her that he'd be right in when he glanced into the living room. Aune sat hunched on the couch next to Marie, sipping tea as they both stared at the flickering fire.

Toivo frowned and looked around. Moon-cast shadows danced and wavered, and the low wind sounded almost like someone groaning. He looked back at his family, sitting warm and safe by the fire, and felt a chilly hand brush across the back of his

19

neck.

"Papa . . . Help me . . . Papa," the voice said, sounding strangely both distant and near at the same time. A surge of panic filled Toivo when he saw that neither Aune nor Marie had moved or spoken. The voice was here—outside—in the dark—*with him*!

Frantic, he turned and looked across the field, fear sinking like iron in his gut. And now he saw something looming black against the pure white of the snow in the field across the driveway. A huge dark block rose up out of the ground, casting a long, rectangular shadow that pointed directly at the house.

Toivo started through the snow toward the block. Moonlight wavered in and out, making the whole world shift sickeningly from side to side. The snow got deeper, and he struggled slowly, like a man wading through a ferocious riptide.

"Papa . . . Help me," the voice called.

As Toivo got nearer to the block, he realized what the block was: there, in the middle of his field where it had no business being, was a solid block of granite standing on one end.

"Papa . . . Please . . . I need you."

Panting like an overworked horse, Toivo plowed through the snow, nearer—nearer to the stone that shouldn't—*couldn't*—be there! The wind hissed, chilling his hands and stinging his face. His footprints behind him filled in as though he had never been there.

As he got closer, he saw that there was something in front of the stone. Squinting, he tried to make out what it was, but it wasn't until the voice came again, moaning in his ears, that he realized that it was a person standing there in the moon-cast shadow of the stone.

"Papa . . . Papa."

"Eino! No, not Eino! Not my boy!" Toivo shouted as the figure, head cocked to one side and hair streaming in the wind, drifted toward him with its arms open wide.

And then he saw with horror too shattering to comprehend that one of the arms the figure held out to him was handless, and it was *not* Eino. The face that leered out of the darkness and grinned at Toivo was rotten with decay. Papery flaps of decomposing skin hung loosely from a grinning skull face, and the stench of centuries-old death washed from its mouth.

Staggering backward, Toivo tried to fend off the approaching figure whose laughter mixed subtly with the groaning sound the wind made. But even as he backed away from the dark granite block, the black rectangle seemed to expand until it towered over Toivo. With a shuddering groan, Toivo hugged his chest as his heart nearly ripped itself apart. He lurched forward and was dead before his face broke the smooth surface of the new-fallen snow.

III

At first, when Toivo didn't return or answer their calls, Aune, only slightly calmed, figured that he'd gone to the barn to check on the animals once more. An hour later, when he still hadn't come back, she sent Marie out to look for him. After checking the barn, she finally found him, face down in the snow— dead, as the town doctor who arrived sometime after midnight determined.

Two weeks later, Aune put the house on the market and moved with Marie back to Massachusetts to be with her family.

Part One

June, 1986

Hark! the death owl loud doth sing
To the nightmares as they go.
                    —Chatterton

To such as note their nightly fantasies,
Some one in twenty may incur belief.
                    Arden of Feversham
                    —Anonymous

Chapter One

The House

I

"Are we there yet?" Beth asked from her balled-up position in the back seat of the family station wagon. Max, Beth's collie, lay curled beside her, his head lolling almost onto the floor. He had never liked car rides, even short ones, and this one had been too long. He and everyone else in the car were exhausted.

"Just 'bout, Pun'kin," Don Inman answered, glancing at his daughter in the rear view. He smiled, and she smiled back weakly. She had been carsick about an hour after they had left Jan's parents' house in Connecticut that morning, and even now, four hours later, she didn't have all of her color back.

Of course, Jan's parents had insisted that they swing by their house before they left for Maine, forget the two-hour detour! The commuter traffic into Hartford had eaten up more road time than Don had cared to consider, but he was no fool; the last thing he needed was to aggravate his in-laws. They had made good time after that, other than a little snarl just south of Boston. Joe Green's helicopter report said something about an overturned truck, but they hadn't seen it. Once they crossed the bridge into Kittery, things were a bit sluggish along Route One, but the summer tourist traffic wasn't in full swing yet, and *anything* was a relief after Hartford.

About fifteen miles past the state line, Don saw the sign he was looking for, slowed, and snapped on his left-turn signal. He nudged Jan from her half-sleepy daze. Straightening up, she yawned as she read the sign aloud. "*Mountain Road*. Hey! That's it!"

Don nodded and smiled, feeling an excited tingle in his gut. "We made it."

On Mountain Road, it was another two miles to the town of St. Ann's. When he saw the town-line marker and the first few buildings of downtown, Don shot a quick glance back at Beth. "This is it."

"Not really much of a downtown, is it?" Jan said, looking out her window at the small huddle of houses and shabby store fronts. Next to the brick fire barn was a small park with an octagonal bandstand and a well-worn baseball diamond.

"What do kids around here do?" Beth asked, trying not to sound too dismayed.

"The same things kids do everywhere, honey," Jan answered. She was smiling, but Don thought she seemed a bit put off by the town, too. Maybe it was just the reality of what they were doing finally sinking in—pulling up roots and moving from Rhode Island.

"It's nice here, Pun'kin. You'll see." He smiled at her in the mirror. "Much nicer—and quieter than Providence ever thought of being."

"But all of my friends *live* in Providence," Beth said, almost whining. Max looked at her, cocking his head to one side. In his own peculiar dog way, he sensed that the drive was almost over and began panting with relief. Beth reached over and started scratching him behind the ears, oblivious of the saliva stain he left on her pants leg.

At the center of town, marked only by a blinking yellow light, there was a triangular patch of grass surrounding a granite watering trough, used now as a planter for petunias. Don let out an excited whoop as he turned left onto Hunter Hill Road.

"We're close now!" he said, slapping the steering wheel.

"Good thing, too," Jan said, her face twisting, " 'cause I have to pee."

Max started to whine, and Beth shifted forward, leaning on the front seat. They passed the town hall on the right and an Episcopal church on the left as they started the gradual climb up the hill. The car sputtered once, threatening to conk out, but then it continued to churn steadily up the grade.

Around a long, graceful bend, Don saw it in the distance just above a screen of trees—the dark bulk of the house—but by the time he pointed it out to Jan and Beth, it had passed out of sight.

"Do you know why they call this Hunter Hill?" Jan asked. "Was that the name of a family around here?"

Don shrugged. "When we lived here with my mom, during the war, Susan used to tell me there was an Indian killed by a bear in our backyard and that he'd drag me off if I played too close to the woods."

"Who—the bear or the Indian?" Beth asked, snickering.

"Very funny," Don said.

The road dipped slightly where it crossed an alder-lined stream, and beyond the stream on the left, a vast, rolling hill edged up to the sky. The house and barn sat on the horizon line, almost creating the

27

illusion that they floated just above the ground. Don pulled over to the side of the road and let the engine idle.

"Well," he said, with obvious pride, "there it is. What do you think, Pun'kin?"

Beth stared up at the house, her mouth open and her eyebrows arched. Jan was silent for several seconds, then with a short breath said, "Well, it sure looks better than it did in the winter. Looks sorta like a Wyeth painting, don't you think?"

"Who?" Beth said. She glanced at Max, then back at the house. "Anyway, it sure looks old." There was a curious tone of awe in her voice.

"It *is* old," Don said. "Of *course* it's old. It's been in the family for over seventy-five years, but it's in—uh—darn good shape."

Jan's eyes tracked the rutted dirt driveway that led up to the house and barn, both of which looked sad and somehow brooding against the deep blue of the sky. The shingles had been weathered to a battleship gray, and a section of the roof on the barn had blown away. Two full maple trees stood like sentinels on either side of the colonial-red front door. At the foot of the driveway, a gnarled oak fluttered its leaves in the wind and shaded a tall, leaning stone gatepost.

"It looks smaller than I remember it," Jan said, glancing at Don.

"That's 'cause you saw it in winter. The trees full of leaves and the grass growing just make it look smaller."

"I suppose so."

"The barn sure looks big, though," Beth said, her eyes twinkling. "Probably more than big enough for a horse or something."

Don let out a slow sigh and looked over at Jan. "Beth—Pun'kin—we've been over this enough already."

"*Too* much!" Jan said.

"Yes, too much. Your mother and I told you that there's no way we can afford a horse. Not this summer, anyway. Maybe in the fall, after we see just how much money we're going to have to put into the house."

"One of the first things I want," Jan said. "is some hot top on this driveway. This looks like the Dust Bowl."

Don couldn't hold back his burst of laughter. "Pave the driveway! Do you have any idea how expensive that would be?"

"Probably more than a horse," Beth said under her breath, but Don heard her.

"You got that right, Pun'kin. *Much* more than a horse."

"Still, it might be cheaper than new shocks on the car every month," Jan said.

"You said the house didn't need that much work," Beth said. Her voice trailed up, making her statement a question, but Don could tell that she was calculating if the outside of the house looked as though it might need at least a horse's worth of paint.

"The inside's much better than the outside," Don said. "The people Aunt Susan was renting it to hadn't moved out yet when Mom and I were here in February for my teaching job interview, but we checked it out pretty good. A little Lysol and paint, and it'll be just fine. Much nicer than our house in Providence, believe me."

"I still can't figure out why Susan never got a buyer for the place," Jan said, still looking at the house. "I mean, the location's terrific. She must've been asking too much."

"I know she tried like a trooper," Don said with a

shrug. "She had it on the market, off and on, for over ten years. Lucky for us she never found a buyer, huh?"

"Yeah," Jan said. "Lucky for us."

"But then why doesn't Aunt Sue want Grammy Kivinen to know we're gonna be living here?" Beth asked. Her breath was warm on Don's ear, and he felt himself flush.

Don looked quickly at Jan, then said, "And what makes you think Grammy doesn't want us living here?" He hoped the quaver in his voice wasn't too obvious.

"I heard you guys talking one night," Beth answered with childish honesty. "You said something about, 'now that she was in the hospital, it wouldn't matter anymore,' but I—"

"That's just about enough," Jan snapped. "You shouldn't be eavesdropping on your parents."

"I wasn't eavesdropping," Beth said, blushing as she sank back into the seat. "I just heard."

Max gave her his best woebegone expression and dropped his head onto her lap.

"Look, Pun'kin, it's not that we don't care about Grammy being in the hospital . . ." Don said.

"I know that," Beth said, her voice low. She was scratching Max behind the ears again and staring absently out her window.

"It's just that—well, Grammy's very sick, and it's pretty obvious she won't live much longer. She'll be ninety-two on her next birthday, so Aunt Sue offered the place to us when I told her we were thinking of moving north."

"But why didn't she take the house," Beth asked, still sounding ornery.

"Because she and her family already have a house in Portsmouth; that's why," Jan said, obviously trying to cut this discussion short.

"But *we* had a house, too—in Providence."

"Look, Pun'kin, I don't want to get into this, but—well, when Grammy wasn't sick, she always said she didn't want anyone from the family living in the house. And—to be totally truthful—I don't think she even knew Aunt Sue was renting it out. But I've always wanted to move back to Maine, and when the job teaching shop at York High School opened up, your mother and I thought it was time to make the jump. Besides, I wanted desperately to get out of Rhode Island, if you want to know the truth."

"Sure," Beth said, "but the reason I never could have a horse was 'cause we lived in the city, 'n' I thought once we got—"

"Enough of *that*, young lady," Jan snapped. Frightened, Max pressed his face between the seat and Beth's back.

Don reached behind him and scuffed Beth's hair. "Pun'kin, I know—we *all* know—how much you want a horse, and I promise we'll try to see our way clear to get you one, but definitely *not* until after school starts—at the *soonest*."

"All right—I guess."

Don slipped the car into gear. From the back seat, Max let out a mournful whimper.

"Let's get up to the house and get unpacked. We could sit here gabbing until dark. We've got some cleaning to do and I, for one, need a good night's sleep before the movers come tomorrow with our furniture."

By force of habit from years of city driving, Don snapped on the turn signal. The car jostled onto the dirt driveway, past the oak shading the leaning stone post. The blinker had just clicked off when he heard an odd, strangled sound from the back seat. A deep-bellied grunt, as though—

—*someone's choking!*

An icy knot hit his stomach as he slammed on the brakes. The car hit a deep rut and bounced, then skidded to a stop. Jan was turning around in her seat.

"What the—? *Oh, my God!*" she screamed.

Don wrenched the shift into park and pulled on the emergency brake. Turning, he saw Beth, her face infused with blood and turning a horrid shade of purple. She was staring wide-eyed as she clawed at her throat and made feeble, strangled sounds. Just as he was reaching for her, her mouth opened and a warm cascade of vomit poured over the seat, splattering him and a good portion of the dashboard.

"Don! Help her!" Jan shouted close to his ear as they both struggled to reach Beth.

The tightness in Don's chest threatened to unravel as he watched Beth's eyes roll upward until all he could see were the whites. The stench of partially digested hamburger and strawberry milkshake made Don's stomach begin to rebel.

Beth took one deep, sputtering breath—which didn't sound like enough to Don—and then a second barrage shot out, thick and warm. Don thought crazily of Campbell's Chunky Soup as he turned and fumbled for his door latch.

Once outside, he thought he would just about pull the door off its hinges as he swung Beth's door open and scooped her up into his arms. Her breath came in short, ragged gulps that sounded like a baby's rattle. Still not enough air, Don thought, looking frantically at his daughter's purple-flushed face.

"Beth—Pun'kin—Come on, breathe. *Breathe!*" he said, as he rolled her over in his arms, hugged her from behind, and gripped his left wrist with his right hand just below her sternum. Closing his eyes to fight his panic, he gave her several, quick, controlled squeezes. She was stiff in his arms, her muscles knotting like taut cables, but after the fourth or fifth squeeze, a wad of trapped vomit shot out, and then air filled her lungs.

"Christ!"

"Is she all right?" Jan asked. She had come around the side of the car and was kneeling beside them in the grass, watching with agonized helplessness.

Beth wheezed, coughed, and sputtered, but when she inhaled, they could hear her lungs filling. The violent purple in her face was fading to a rashy red.

Gently, Don lowered Beth to her knees. She looked worn and strangely small as she moved into a sitting position slowly. Saliva and vomit stained the front of her blouse and jeans, but a trace of brave humor came to her eyes as she wiped her mouth with the back of her hand, sniffed her hand, and said, "Aww, *gross!*"

Max, who had jumped out of the car right behind them, came over to Beth and started licking her face until she shooed him away. Jan shifted over and started massaging Beth's shoulders. "Are you feeling all right now?"

Beth nodded. "Ummm. Kinda weak, though."

"I'll get the Handi-Wipes from the glove compartment," Don said. He dashed to the car and returned with the whole package. He handed them to Jan, who tore one of the foil packets open and spread out the alcohol-soaked paper. The foil wrapper fluttered to the ground.

"There—there, Beth. Take it easy now," Jan cooed as she wiped away the sheen of sweat from Beth's forehead. The red in her face was fading fast now and, if anything, she looked pale.

They were sitting in the grass near the leaning stone post. A cool breeze fluttered the oak leaves dappling them with shadows. Don felt a chill tingle between his shoulder blades.

"God, . . . you gave us a scare," Don said. "Whatever happened?"

Beth shrugged and looked at him, her eyes glistening. "I dunno. It happened all of a sudden."

"We'll get you cleaned up when we get up to the house, O.K.?" Jan said. She got up and then supported Beth as she stood up on wobbly legs.

Beth forced a smile and nodded. "Umm. I do feel kinda wrung out. Sorry 'bout the car," she said, looking at her father.

"Don't worry about that," Don said. "But do you have any idea how much you scared us? What happened?"

Beth shook her head as though dazed. "As soon as we turned into the driveway, I felt—I dunno—just woozy all over. Then, when I puked, I guess I swallowed some back, 'cause all of a sudden, I couldn't get my breath."

"It's a good thing they taught all of the teachers the Heimlich technique in that first-aid class last year, that's all I can say," Don said as he walked over to the car slowly. Jan cast him a "she's going to be all right, isn't she?" look, and he nodded.

"Do you want to rest a bit more before we head up to the house?" Jan asked.

Smacking her lips and wincing at the sour taste still clinging to the back of her throat, Beth said, "What I really need is something to drink." She took a couple of steps, still looking shaky.

"Well, you can have a drink if the water's been turned on, but if not, I'm afraid all we have is what's left of my root beer. I promise you, though, that I won't make you clean up the car." The humor seemed forced to Don, but Beth laughed.

34

"Thanks," Beth said, wrinkling her nose. "If it's all the same to you, I think I'd rather walk."

"I'll walk with you," Jan said, a bit too quickly Don thought.

Making a melodramatic, swooning gesture, Don added, "And I'll drive the Barf Mobile. See you there."

He got into the car and shut the door but immediately stuck his head out the window for a breath of fresh air. He watched as Jan and Beth ambled up toward the house with Max romping in wide circles around them. They were holding hands, mother and daughter, and leaning close together. The picture was almost idyllic, maybe even worthy of a Wyeth painting, but there was a dim echo of uneasiness that Don couldn't dispel.

He put the car into gear and went up the driveway slowly, stopping just by the side door. But even after joining Beth and Jan, who were sitting in the shade of the doorway, even after ribbing Beth about her "technicolor yawn," even after unlocking the door to their new home and entering the kitchen with its dust-furred floor, there was a faint pall over the day as if a thin cloud, barely visible, had sailed in front of the sun. Don wanted to ask Jan if she felt it too, but, whenever he looked at her, he didn't want to interrupt her silent, cautious inspection of the house.

Surprisingly, the water had been turned on. The kitchen faucet sputtered and ran brick-red water from the accumulated rust in the pipes. After a few minutes, it ran clear and tasted much better than Providence city water *ever* tasted. Beth finally got the drink she wanted to wash the sour taste from her mouth.

Ever the careful planner, Don had left a bag full of cleaning supplies within easy reach in the back of the station wagon. So, with a bucket of water and a handful of rags, he cleaned the car, leaving all four doors open to let it air. Beth got a change of clothes from her suitcase; then she and Jan took a quick inspection of the house except for the attic and cellar. Max was content to lap up the cold water Beth put out for him, dig a shallow hole in the dirt beside the barn, and go to sleep. There were plenty of interesting smells wafting on the gentle breeze, but he'd check them out and mark his territory later.

II

"Well, first things first," Don said when he was finished with the car. "I want to give my women a great big hug." Arms wide, he enfolded them both.

Beth shied away and, wrinkling her nose, said, "Yuck, Dad, you don't smell so good."

After planting a kiss on his cheek, Jan added, "Yeah, it's awfully stuffy in here. Let's get some windows open and air this place out before we all suffocate." She began to struggle with the window over the kitchen sink. "What *idiot*—would paint—a window shut—like this!" she said, grunting with the effort.

"The people who were renting moved out a week or so after we were up during the winter," Don said. "They must've thought painting was easier than washing."

Jan still hadn't gotten the window to budge, so he came over and added his leverage. Finally, after chipping the seam with the blade of a screwdriver, the window went up—and stuck halfway. The lead counterweight knocked inside the window frame with a dull drumming.

"They don't make windows like this anymore—thank God," Don said. He was bending low over the sink as he washed his hands, inhaling the sweet air that rustled the curtains. "A little silicon spray will probably take care of it."

"I'm surprised, though," Jan said, running her finger along the top of the doorjamb, checking for dust. "They left the place in pretty good shape. Still— we'll give it a good once-over."

"What d'yah think, Pun'kin?" Don asked, drying his hands on several paper towels.

"It's neat," Beth said, bouncing on her toes. "Mom and I took the tour, but what I *really* want to see is the barn."

"Cut it out, will yah?" Don said. "Why don't you keep yourself busy while your mom and I take a look around?"

Jan got a notepad from her purse, and together they began a careful inspection of the house, jotting down notes.

In the kitchen, it was fairly obvious that the old refrigerator would have to go. Even if it did work, Jan was convinced that she'd have to defrost it every week or two. There was some debate about replacing the stove, with its accumulated strata of cooking history, but Don maintained that the old Magee ("They don't make 'em like *this* anymore, either!") was still serviceable, and it had a built-in gas heater, too, in case of emergency. Jan finally agreed to keep it, as long as Don promised to do the first major cleaning. It went without saying that they would eventually repaper, but Jan said she could live with the rooster motif on the wall—for now.

There was one cracked window in the dining room, but other than that, the only work needed right off was repainting the ceiling, which had aged to a nicotine yellow. The wide pine floorboards had been painted a dull stone gray. Jan had plans to sand them down to the bare wood and then varnish them but—again—they could live with it as it was. There was some loose molding along one wall where Jan planned to put the china cabinet. When she mentioned that—maybe—they'd get a new table-and-chair set, Don rolled his eyes and ignoring both her and Beth, sauntered into the living room. Beth said from the kitchen that a dining room set would probably cost more than a horse.

"Well," Jan said, flicking the wall switch in the living room, "either every bulb in the house is blown or they haven't turned on the power."

Don shrugged. "I can give them a call from downtown when I go for groceries."

The living room obviously needed more work than did the dining room, but, still, it was not much more than cosmetics. The pile of ashes in the fireplace would have to be hauled, and the flue scraped. They planned to install an air-tight Jotul for their major source of heat, so Don intended to make sure the chimney was carefully cleaned and, if possible, re-lined. Don hoped the hairline crack in the masonry between the bricks didn't indicate a too serious shifting of the foundation. There were two more cracked windows, but the good news was that there were no water stains on the ceiling or walls; apparently there were no leaks or condensation problems. Jan insisted that she couldn't live with the wallpaper, and that they'd do this room first.

Back in the hallway, to the left of the stairs going up, was the downstairs bathroom. Jan said she wouldn't use the toilet until it was cleaned. "Who knows what's been breeding in here," she said, following it with an "evil scientist" cackling laugh.

Don had to agree with her; there was a close, rotting smell that reminded him of fresh-turned soil.

The claw-footed bathtub needed a good scouring, and the sink was stained from the dripping faucets. Don promised Jan that he'd give Beth the honor of cleaning the bathroom. Jan's only comment was that Beth would probably need shots when she was done.

Don took the cover off the toilet tank and wiggled the algae-covered chain several times. He stood back and watched as the water swirled down the bowl. A throaty gurgle came from the pipes below.

"At least it works," he said as the tank refilled. The sound of running water reminded Jan of the pressure in her bladder so, in spite of her initial complaints, she gave the toilet another test run while Don wandered upstairs.

The upstairs bathroom was no better than the one downstairs. The sink was crusted with dry, brown muck. Don figured someone must have washed mud-crusted boots there and not bothered to clean up afterward. The mirror above the sink was shattered, and the spider-web fragments made Don dizzy when he looked at his reflection. He left when he heard Jan's footsteps on the stairs.

In the master bedroom, Jan pointed out the three—or more—different shades of paint on the woodwork. The floor creaked underfoot, and Don saw gaps—some almost half an inch wide—between some of the boards. A little paint and caulk would take care of it all, he thought.

Walking over to the two windows that looked out over the driveway, he poked at each sill with his fingernail. "One of these days we'll have to replace them," he said, "but there's no sign of rot."

"Lucky us," Jan said from the other side of the room.

Don unlocked one of the windows and struggled to slide it up. When it was about halfway open and sweat stood out on his forehead, he sagged back with exaggerated exhaustion.

"A little sluggish, huh?" Jan said.

Don nodded, wiping his brow on the sleeve of his shirt.

"I'm beginning to accept the fact that *none* of the windows in this house go up more than halfway," Jan said.

"We'll see about that," Don replied, and renewed his struggle with no appreciable success. Finally, he gave up and looked out over the field. The dull green of the grass shimmered in the heat. He could see Max, asleep in the shade of the barn.

"Well," Jan said, walking in a wide circle in the room, "I suppose the bed will have to go here, against the wall. And the bureaus—here and here. My writing desk can go against the wall here, beside the closet door."

Don nodded approval, content to leave the planning to her.

"I hope this water stain's just from condensation," Don said as he rubbed his hand over a rippling bulge inside the dormer slant beside the window he had struggled to open.

"It looks sorta like South America," Jan said.

"You're so observant. Anyway, we'll be reroofing before winter."

Jan shook her head. "We probably shouldn't spend the money if we don't have to," Jan said.

Don stiffened. "We *have* the money from selling the house in Rhode Island, and I think it's pretty important that we make sure the roof's sturdy enough for winter *now*, and not wait until we have puddles all over the floor next spring."

"I suppose so," Jan said. She continued pacing around the room, studying the space and how she'd use it. Suddenly she stopped and hugged herself, shivering.

"What is it, hon?" Don asked, coming over and hugging her.

"I don't know." Her voice was barely a murmur. "I suddenly got cold. It's just that—the house is so—so . . ."

"I know," Don said, giving her shoulder a brisk rub. "It isn't anything out of one of your magazines, that's for sure." He chuckled, but Jan didn't respond.

"It all just looks—I dunno—so much *drabber* than I remember; that's all."

Don gave her shoulder a hearty shake. "When we were here last winter, there was those other people's furniture and stuff around still. The place looked lived in. Once our own stuff gets here, you'll see. We may make it to the pages of *House Beautiful* yet."

She smiled, but only weakly.

"And for crying out loud, stop worrying about the money. We have enough for the basics, and we've planned how we're going to spend the money we made selling the house. My teaching checks will start coming in soon enough and, besides, you'll have a job nailed down in a week or two—you'll see."

Jan's smile twisted wryly. "Yeah, sure. But maybe the job market up here isn't what we thought it'd be, either."

Don planted a soft, wet kiss on her lips and, bending to look her straight in the eyes, said, "Just wait. With your experience and charm, you'll be top dog in some real estate office before school starts. Who knows, you'll probably outearn me!"

"We'll see," Jan said, pulling away and going over to look inside the closet.

Don went back to the windows and tugged to get the other one open. With much less effort, it slid up

41

its track. Don stood back and looked at Jan with an expression of total satisfaction, but she still had her head inside the closet. A breeze wafted into the long-closed room, stirring dust in the corners.

"I guess it's just the reality of it all," Jan said, looking over her shoulder at Don. "You know—talking and thinking about it is one thing, but now that we're actually *doing* it, I—I guess I'm just feeling like we might've overstressed the good points, that's all."

"It's a dream house," Don said, beaming his best smile because he knew she needed it. "An honest-to-God *dream* house, but do you know what's strange?"

Jan cocked an eyebrow at him and walked up to encircle his waist.

"I still can't remember a single bit of this house from when I was a kid."

Jan shrugged. "Well, you were—what? Three years old when your mother moved out?"

"Almost four. She moved back to Massachusetts after she heard my dad had died. I told you about that—in Sicily—World War Two."

"You've told me! You've told me!"

"But I had the same feeling—or *lack* of feeling—when we were here in the winter. It's like—like the few bits of memories I have just—don't fit."

"I wouldn't worry about it," Jan said. She waved her hand in front of her nose and said, "Whew! We'll have to do something about airing out that closet! We ought to see what Beth's up to and then maybe head into town for some food."

"Umm," Don said. "I could eat a little something."

They went out and down the hall to one of the other bedrooms. Through the thick door, they heard a low buzzing, and it took them a moment to realize it was Beth, talking softly to herself in the closed room.

"When did she come upstairs?" Don asked. Jan shrugged and cocked her ear toward the closed door.

"That's not very nice," Beth said. She spoke louder, but her voice was still distorted by the heavy door.

Don knocked sharply on the door and called out, "Pun'kin? Can we come in?"

"Uh—yeah. Sure," Beth replied. She sounded startled and looked up at them, blinking her eyes rapidly as they entered the room. She was sitting cross-legged on the floor and had her hands behind her back.

"What's not very nice," Jan asked, taking in the small room with a sweeping, suspicious glance.

"The—uhh, the view from here—from the window," Beth replied. "I don't like that gnarly old apple tree out there."

Don looked out at the tree, it's ancient bark weathered to an oily sheen. "You don't have to have this room," he said. "The other one's much bigger, and I thought I'd use this one for—"

"No," Beth said, shaking her head. "I want this one. I like this one."

"Are you sure?" Jan asked. "It seems a bit dismal, don't you think?"

The wallpaper had all but lost whatever design it had once had, and tattered cobwebs drifted in the angles of the ceiling. Even the floorboards, scuffed to a dull shine with age, looked somehow older than the rest of the house.

"Wasn't this the room they used for storage?" Jan asked Don. "As I recall, it was full of old furniture and boxes and stuff."

"I thought it'd make a good office for me, and you could have—"

"No, really," Beth said. "I want this room—as long as you get rid of that old apple tree out there."

"No problem there, Pun'kin," Don said. "Apple-

43

wood's supposed to be the best for burning, and I think, with that tree gone, the afternoon light will brighten things up in here. Pun'kin, you can pick out whatever wallpaper and colors of paint you want, and who knows—maybe by Christmas we can get you a new bedroom set."

"You *know* what I want," Beth said softly, trying to avoid her mother's angry gaze.

Don noticed that Beth was sitting strangely, shielding something behind her back. "What've you got there, Punk'kin?" he asked, trying to look behind her.

Reluctantly, Beth held up a small wooden figure. She was clutching it so tightly her knuckles were turning white. "Nothin'—just an old doll I found in the closet here. Can I keep him?"

"Here," Don said, holding out his hand, "let me take a look at it."

"*Him!*" Beth said sharply, twisting to one side, protecting the doll with her body.

With forced patience, Don said, "Com' on, Pun-'kin, let me see—him."

Beth extended her hand slowly and let her father take the wooden doll. Don figured she had been playing with the doll and maybe was embarrassed at getting caught at her age.

"Oh, yeah. Sure, I can see he's a boy," Don said, frowning as he studied the rustic figure. The chiseled features of the wooden face had been highlighted with India ink, and there was a definite masculine cast to the lowering brow. The mouth was a dark, unsmiling slash, and the eyes, two intense pinpoints of black. The wooden body, arms and legs rigidly extended, was covered with yellowed cotton cloth. A small piece of something, either black string or aged leather, was wrapped around the left wrist.

"Can I keep him?" Beth asked again, her voice trembling slightly.

"I guess so," Don said, glancing at Jan, who merely shrugged. "I don't think whoever left it—I mean *him*—behind will be back for him, but—wait a minute. You know, I almost seem to remember this doll and—something my mother told me about . . . I dunno."

The whole time he spoke with Beth, there was something nagging at the back of his mind—like an important fact, glossed over but necessary—as if something just didn't fit right. It wasn't until he handed the doll back to Beth that it hit him: the doll was too heavy for its size! It was as if it were made of waterlogged wood or some other substance—lead or stone. He wanted to hold the object again to see if that was what it was, but Jan nudged him.

"Come on, hon, we really ought to get the car unpacked so we can get settled before dark."

Don agreed, and all three of them went downstairs to get the work started. While Jan and Beth started emptying the car, Don got a new lightbulb, screwed it into the kitchen socket, and flicked the switch several times. "Just dandy! No power," he muttered when nothing happened.

"I could've told you that," Beth said. "The dial on the power meter outside wasn't turning. I checked that when I went out to give Max his water."

"Of course. Leave it to me to not think of the *easy* way," Don said. "Well, if we have to survive one night with kerosene lamps, I guess we'll be all right."

"And *no TV*?" Beth wailed with mock terror. "I can't make it! *I can't make it!*"

"They do *have* television here in Maine, don't they?" Jan asked as she started putting away the few pots and pans they had packed.

"I don't know for sure," Don said, "but I hear tell the neighbors down the road a-piece have one of them newfangled wireless radios, 'n' we can visit 'em on Sunday nights to listen to 'I Love a Mystery' or whatever."

"Hey!" Beth suddenly called out. "Mom. Dad. Come here and take a look at this stuff."

She had been putting away a few things in the pantry, just off the kitchen, and was struggling to lift a bundle of tied-up newspapers. The string, rotten with age, suddenly snapped, and the papers fanned out across the kitchen floor. Yellow dust swirled up, making both Beth and Don sneeze.

"What've you got there?" Don asked, bending to pick up the paper nearest to him. The newsprint was yellowed and threatened to powder away in his hand. "Huh, look at this, hon. It's from 1921."

"Great," Jan said, leaning back against the counter and wiping her forehead. "Just what we need—more junk to throw away."

"That sure was a long time ago," Beth said, twisting to look at the paper her father held. Her eyes took on a brief, distant gaze.

"My grandparents—Grammy Kivinen—was living here then," Don said. His voice was tinged with awe as if he held a sacred relic. "I wonder why no one ever threw these out."

" 'Cause they're neat," Beth said excitedly. "Maybe I can use some of them for a school project or something."

"They probably just never felt like they wanted to tackle cleaning out that pantry," Jan said. "There's a lot of junk in there. It'd be nice if you could put some shelves in there after we hook up the washer and dryer."

"No problem," Don said. "I'll bet all of this stuff

has been here since my grandparents lived here." He opened the newspaper and scanned a few pages. "Huh! Look at these prices. Oranges were a nickel for three dozen. Coffee, ten cents a pound. And bread, five cents for two loaves. Incredible!"

"I sure wish we could have those prices now," Jan said, turning back to the work she had been doing.

"Are those prices real or made up?" Beth asked. "Stuff was really that cheap back then?"

"Sure was, Pun'kin," Don said. "But you have to remember, a really good salary back then was only a couple of dollars a week."

He picked up the newspapers and stacked them by the door while Beth continued rummaging through the assortment of old clothes, dented pots and pans, rusted tools (some of which, Don thought, might be valuable to an antique collector), and several large, decaying boxes.

"That does it. The car's empty," Jan said, backing into the kitchen, struggling with an armload of sleeping bags. She dropped them onto the floor, not caring where they rolled.

"Well, who wants to come into town with me to get groceries?" Don asked.

"I've got a better idea," Jan said. "Why don't we all get cleaned up and drive into Ogunquit for an honest-to-God Maine lobster feed. I think we owe it to ourselves, don't you?"

Everyone agreed, so after they had taken turns washing at the kitchen sink (Don teased Beth about her "extreme honor" in being appointed to do the bathtub) and Beth had tied Max out by the barn, they got into the car and drove off. They didn't get back until well after dark, full and satisfied. Using flashlights and kerosene lamps, they got their sleeping bags spread out on the living room floor. By ten o'clock they were all asleep.

For the first time in four months, the old Kivinen house on Hunter Hill Road was filled with the warm glow of family life.

Chapter Two

Bloodstone

I

The next morning the sky was overcast, and everyone overslept. Don was the first to awake, shifting stiffly in his sleeping bag on the hardwood floor. He stared out at the light mist pebbling the windows, then groaned when he glanced at his watch.

"Aww, shit! Nine o'clock," he mumbled, pushing down the sleeping bag as he sat up and swung his feet out. A chill raced up the backs of his knees when his bare feet hit the cold floor.

Jan rolled over and sighed but didn't open her eyes. In front of the fireplace, Beth gritted her teeth. Max, asleep at Beth's feet, opened his eyes, but even with the prospect of breakfast, he didn't seem all that anxious to move; the long drive had taken quite a toll on him.

Don considered the first order of business—coffee. He sat cross-legged for a moment on the sleeping bag, but it was only when Max padded over and jabbed the

49

cold, moist tip of his nose into Don's face that he got up.

"Come on. Rise and—uhh—shine," he whispered, gently shaking Jan's shoulder. Her eyes flickered open, focusing in and out, then dimmed again.

"Yeah," she grunted, burying her face into the puffy, down-filled bag.

"Time to get a move on," Don said as he pulled on his pants. "The movers will be here before noon."

"I know. *I know!*"

To set a good example, Don sauntered into the kitchen, filled Max's bowl with water and Gravy Train, then filled the teakettle. Taking two cups from the cupboard (most of their dishes would arrive with the movers), he dropped a rounded spoonful of Nescafé into each, then stared bleary-eyed out the kitchen window while he waited for the kettle to start singing. A few low grumbles came from the living room, then he heard the familiar scuff-scuff of Jan's slippers as she entered the kitchen.

Max was already at the door, waiting to be let out; it still amazed Don how fast that mutt could down his chow. He opened the door for the dog and paused to inhale the moist, fresh air deeply.

"Mornin'," he said cheerily. "Did yah sleep well enough?"

The sour expression on Jan's face said it all as she pressed both fists into the small of her back and stretched. "Most comfortable floor I've *ever* slept on," she said, walking over to the yellowed Frigidaire and opening the door. Her scowl deepened when the light failed to come on and she remembered that it was empty, anyway.

"Think the power company'll come out on a Saturday?" she asked. The kettle began to whistle, so she shut off the heat and filled both cups. "I'll tell you this; I'll get a motel room for the night if I have to stay here without electricity until Monday."

"The rustic life doesn't suit you, huh?" Don said, smiling. He quickly added, "They said they'd be here first thing." He accepted the steaming cup Jan held out to him, sipped, and winced.

"Are you going to let Beth sleep till noon, or—"

"Jesus, Don, will you let me at least wake up?"

"Sorry. Sorry," he said, and he began pacing the floor as he slurped his coffee. By the time Jan had drunk half of her cup, she was more civil. Don could hear Beth stirring in the living room.

"If we have a quick breakfast, we can get the walls washed before the movers come. No sense doing the floors until after they're gone," Don said.

"Just as well," Jan said. "Without electricity, we can't vacuum anyway." A look of despair came over her face, and she was unable to hide the sense of hopelessness she felt about the task ahead of them.

Don smiled. "You just need another cup to brighten your outlook, that's all. It won't take us long to make this house homey."

" 'Homey,' that sure is the word for it, all right."

"You're a bit discouraged by it all, huh?" Don said. He tried to keep the levity in his voice, but Jan's mood was making his own drop. The rainy day didn't help, either.

Jan shrugged and glanced around the kitchen. "Yeah—a little bit, I guess," she said, rubbing a spot between her eyebrows and shaking her head. "It's a little bit funny, I guess. I mean, if I was trying to sell this place to a client, I'd be bubbling over with praise,

51

pointing out how you could do this and that. But—well, now that *we* have to do all the cleaning and fixing and moving to realize the potential—it's just so formidable."

"It'll all be worth it, hon," Don said, moving beside her and wrapping one arm around her waist. "And it's how we planned it. I have the whole summer to get the repairs done. You can take as long as you need to find a job, and—"

"I know. I know," she said, the tension still in her voice. "It's just—I dunno. Forget it."

"No, let's *not* forget it," Don said, turning her and holding her firmly. "We talked and talked and *talked* about it. Now we're doing it. This is what you want, isn't it?"

She looked at him, her eyes still distant, but she nodded agreement. "Of course it is."

He gave her a long, slow kiss, their tongues darting back and forth, but they broke off when they heard Beth coming toward the kitchen.

"Mornin', Pun'kin," Don said, slightly embarrassed at having been caught necking. "Kinda hard to get up on a rainy morning, huh?"

Beth shrugged. "Least there's no school."

"Were you comfortable enough last night?" Jan asked. She rubbed the small of her back again.

"O.K., I guess," Beth answered, stifling a yawn. "But what was all that noise during the night."

Don and Jan glanced at each other. "What noise?" Don said. "I didn't hear any noise."

Beth shook her head, confused, and said, "I dunno—it sounded like someone hammering on something. It woke me up a couple of times."

"Might have been the water pipes," Jan offered.

"Maybe there were air pockets in them or something after not being used for a while."

"Maybe," Beth said, and that, apparently, was the end of that. She jumped up to sit on the countertop, letting her gaze wander out the window and over the field.

"Well," Don said, glancing at Jan, "it could have been mice in the walls or squirrels in the attic maybe. We'll have to check it out."

"Maybe it was that bear you were telling me about," Beth said, still gazing out over the field. "You know, the one that lives in the woods. Maybe we should check for paw prints outside the windows."

"I've got something more important than that to do, Punk. Why don't you come into town with me to pick up some stuff for breakfast."

Beth nodded agreement and slid down off the counter.

"I think I'll stay here and have that second cup of coffee you think I so desperately need," Jan said.

"We'll be back in a jiff," Don said as he shrugged into his raincoat. He patted the back pocket of his pants to make sure his wallet was there, then swung the door open. "Don't let the gray day get you down, O.K., hon?"

Jan smiled and nodded. "I just gotta wake up, that's all," she said. "The drive yesterday really took it out of me. I'll be all right."

"Don't get eaten by the bears, Mom," Beth said, laughing as she dashed out to the car.

II

Half an hour later, they were back, loaded with

groceries, and, shortly after that, they were sitting tailor-fashion on the floor, eating what proved to be a quite respectable spread—eggs (sunny side up), bacon, whole wheat toast (done in a frying pan because Don hadn't thought to bring the toaster), Tropicana orange juice, and more coffee.

A home-cooked meal did wonders for Jan's attitude too, and it took her prodding to get Don and Beth moving after the meal. They would have been content to laze around a bit longer, but once they got their respective tasks set, the time went pleasantly and fast. Except for Beth: under protest, she began cleaning the downstairs bathroom. She thought her mother's joke about her needing shots by the time she was through was so good she repeated it several times.

Jan started in with the kitchen cupboards, and by the time she was done with that job, Beth had finished with (or given up on) the bathroom. They then began washing the walls and floor in the kitchen. Meanwhile, Don gave the walls and woodwork in the dining room and living room a quick once-over with Pine-Sol.

When they took a quick lunch break at one-thirty, they were pleased and surprised that they had accomplished so much in so little time. The house reeked of pine-scented cleanser and ammonia. Except for the painting and papering and window replacements, the downstairs was done. They didn't get to start on the upstairs though because, just as they were cleaning up after lunch, Max's barking announced that an orange-and-brown van was lurching up the driveway and backing its way to the front door between the two maples.

Three men hopped out of the cab. The driver, a

thin, wiry, gray-haired man of about fifty, moved with surprising agility. Another man, probably thirty years old Don guessed, was beefy and smelled of sour sweat. The third mover was a boy of no more than nineteen. In spite of the cold drizzle, he stripped off his Van Halen T-shirt as soon as they had run out the ramp to the front door and begun off-loading.

Don helped as best he could, but he felt as if he were constantly underfoot as the men hefted and lugged into the house chests, chairs, tables, beds and mattresses, the couch, console TV, refrigerator, washer, dryer, and more boxes than either Jan or Don could remember packing. Jan stood inside the doorway—where she said the coat rack would go—and directed them to wherever each load was to go, but after a while the movers knew the layout of the house, so Jan just stood back with Beth and watched, keeping a hawkeye open for any damage to their possessions.

Don slipped the teen-ager an extra ten-dollar bill to help him wrestle the old Frigidaire out to the barn. After removing the refrigerator door, he spent close to an hour connecting and leveling the washer and fitting the outlet tubing for the dryer. Someone—God bless 'em—had put in a 220 line for the dryer and, miracle of miracles, the appliances fit into their places in the kitchen and pantry.

Four hours and two coffee breaks later, the van was empty and the house was filled with randomly placed furniture and pile after pile of boxes. The sky darkened with lowering clouds, and, just as the van rumbled down the driveway toward town, the rain that had been threatening all day finally came down in a torrent.

"See," Don said, standing in the living room with his arms around Jan looking out at the rain, "Murphy isn't *always* right."

Jan sniffed and said, "I'm beat!"

In the orange glow of kerosene lanterns—because the electric company *didn't* come out on a Saturday— Don and Jan set up Beth's and their own beds and put on fresh sheets and blankets. Jan repeated a variation of one of Lily Tomlin's classic lines: "We're the electric company—We don't care—We don't *have* to!" and they all laughed.

Finally, exhausted and sweaty from the day's work, they took turns in the shower, grateful that the hot-water heater was run by gas, not electricity. Then they drove into Ogunquit for supper. When Beth went to use the rest room, Don repeated a joke one of the movers had told him.

"What do you do if you drop your wallet on the beach at Ogunquit?"

Jan wrinkled her forehead. "I don't know. What?"

"Kick it to Wells Beach before you bend over to pick it up," Don answered, stifling a laugh.

Jan frowned. "I don't get it."

Don was going to explain, but then Beth came back, so he shook his head and whispered, "Never mind."

They were back at the house and asleep by ten-thirty, much too tired to celebrate what was officially their first night in their new house. The need for sleep was too demanding.

III

They spent the next three days sorting through

carton after carton of clothes, tools, cooking utensils, books and papers, and assorted junk. Don replaced all the broken and cracked windows one afternoon. On Monday, Central Maine Power Company came out and turned on the electricity, so that afternoon Jan drove to town to buy a week's supply of groceries. She said she never felt secure unless there was food in the refrigerator, and she was never gladder than when she could pack away the Coleman cooler, now needed only for picnics.

Don operated on the idea that you had to live in a house at least a full year before you found the right place for everything, but he was pleased with how fast they seemed to be settling into the old Kivinen house. It was, a little bit, like coming home for him, and he remarked several times how the house seemed to absorb their possessions. Within a day or two, the couch, easy chairs, and TV looked as though they had been bought expressly for the living room. "Homey" was the perfect word to describe how they felt, settled in their respective spots at night to watch "M*A*S*H" or "St. Elsewhere."

And day by day Jan was increasingly pleased with the house. At breakfast each morning, she'd leaf through several home decorating magazines and show dozens of alternative designs to Don. She fairly bubbled over with ideas and dashed off sketches of how they could rebuild the porch (or, better yet, add a deck out back), put a bay window in the living room, or take out a section of the wall between the kitchen and dining room so they could make a breakfast bar. Her ideas of what they could do grew in direct proportion to her excitement, and it was only Don's reminders that their funds weren't limitless that held

57

her in check. He was glad, though, to see her energy and enthusiasm on the increase.

Beth, too, seemed to be pleased with their move to Maine. She was happy with her bedroom, the smaller of the two she had to choose between. She *did* mention more than once that she wanted that "groody" apple tree outside her window cut down, but she seemed to be happy, if maybe a bit lonely for want of friends. Don kept reminding her that she'd meet plenty of kids once school started.

Don and Jan couldn't help but notice how much time she spent working in the barn, cleaning out years' worth (she jokingly said "centuries' " worth) of accumulated junk. They both knew what she was thinking about. Don was amazed one day when she asked for his hammer and saw and set about replacing some of the broken boards in one of the stalls. He didn't mind letting her do the work because he was so busy with other projects in the house, and, at least so far, Beth hadn't made friends with any of the local kids.

Beth did have one complaint, though: she said that night after night she still woke up at least once to the sound of scratching in the walls. One night, their fifth in the house, something happened that she didn't mention to her parents. She had woken up, convinced that the wooden doll she had found had moved from where she had left it. She had been positive she had placed the doll on her bureau, but when she had woken up, the doll had been on the window sill. Dusty moonlight had lit the doll's features, and the curtain had drifted back and forth in the breeze, covering and then uncovering the doll's face. It had taken her quite a while to get back to sleep that night.

Don wondered about the sounds Beth complained of, so he stayed up one night as late as he could, listening for anything unusual. Jan told him he was being ridiculous; the house was new to them and, like all old houses, it had its own peculiar sounds: floor joists settling, branches scratching the roof, whatever—all parts of the house's personality, you might say. He heard nothing that or any other night, but, in the morning when Beth complained again of hearing something, he decided it was time to check the attic for pests and, if necessary, call an exterminator.

With Jan close behind him and each of them carrying a flashlight, they went up the makeshift stairway to the attic. The old steps were extremely steep, and they creaked underfoot. When Don pressed his shoulder against the door, it gave reluctantly, the rusted hinges groaning like something out of a B horror flick. He couldn't resist turning to Jan and giving her his best ghoulish laugh.

She wasn't amused. "I just hope this hasn't turned into Rodent Haven," she said, wrinkling her nose as the stale air of the attic swirled out around them.

Don snapped on his flashlight and jabbed the beam at the dark slit of the doorway. Feeling a little bit like one of the Hardy Boys, with Nancy Drew close behind, he stepped up into the stifling air of the attic. Dust motes swirled in the cone of light, and just the slight disturbance of their entrance made long, black cobwebs wave gently like funeral lace.

"All right," Don said, looking around. "Not bad. Not bad at all." He had to bend over slightly as he walked the length of the attic, his fingers probing the roof supports, feeling for punkiness and rot. The two windows at either end of the attic were so thick with

59

goo, Don thought they had been painted over until he rubbed a spot clean. A solemn gray light just barely filtered in, casting a thick gloom that made the hairs on his arms prickle as though electrified.

"Cheery," Jan said. She was still standing in the doorway, watching Don.

"Well, we've got all summer to get the reroofing done, but by the looks of things, we don't have to worry about getting washed out by the first heavy rain." The swirling dust caught like sawdust in his throat, and he ended in a fit of coughing.

"Healthy for you, too," Jan said, covering her mouth and staying put. "There's a lot more garbage up here too that we'll have to get rid of." She played her flashlight beam over a pile of boxes beside the chimney.

Don made his way over to the boxes and stacks of old clothes. "The stuff's pretty old, whosever it is," he said, poking at it with his foot. The musty smell grew stronger as he lifted the coat that was on top. He cursed softly when he saw several mounds of cracked acorn shells and a matted nest. Fortunately, it was empty.

"Either squirrels or chipmunks have been up here," he said to Jan, "but that'll be no sweat—I hope. We can set a few traps and screen any holes we can see from outside. At least we've found out what's been making those noises Beth's been hearing at night."

"Great," Jan said, "Can we go downstairs now? We didn't have squirrels in the attic in Providence."

"Hey, you gotta expect these things in an old house. I must've told you about that friend of mine, Kenny Black. His family had a pre-Revolutionary War house in New Hampshire, and late at night you could hear mice scrambling in the walls. Kenny said there was a lot of room in there behind the walls. It was just in the winter, though; I guess the mice lived in the field behind the house during the summer."

"I don't need to hear this," Jan said. "I'm going down. You can do whatever you want up here."

"Hold on a sec," Don said as he cautiously opened one of the boxes, expecting a squirrel—maybe a *rabid* squirrel—to come flying out at him. Can squirrels carry rabies? he wondered. Cringing and glancing up at the dark-shrouded rafters, he half-expected to see a line of sleeping bats. A shiver ran up his back.

"There are some old books here," he said, beginning to sift through the box. A few silverfish skittered out of the light as he took out several books—some cheaply made novels, a leather-bound atlas, and a handful of old spellers.

"Some of these might be valuable to a collector," he said, turning again to Jan, who still waited in the doorway.

"I hope so," she replied, "because we're not hanging onto all this junk. Between what's here and in the barn, we'll need a dump truck to get it out of here. Have you checked the cellar yet?"

Don shook his head as he wedged the flashlight under one arm and began riffling through the books.

"I wonder how many years' worth of junk is down *there*," she said. "But you can take care of that, too. I'm going—"

"Jeez, look at this," he said, as though he hadn't heard a word she'd said. He picked up a leather-bound volume and brushed gray dust from the hand-printed title. He held the flashlight close, trying to read the title, but the light wasn't strong enough. He moved toward Jan, and in the light from the doorway, they both tried to read the faded handwriting on the small square of yellow paper pasted on the cover.

"In the corner—there—it looks like an *A* and a *K*," Jan said, leaning close.

"*A—K*. Hmmm, *A—K* . . ." Don's eyes got dreamy for a moment, then he said excitedly, "*A. K. Aune Kivinen!* Maybe this was my grandmother's!"

"Could be," Jan muttered.

The writing on the cover was a fragile, spidery scrawl. The faded ink and yellowed paper were almost the same color, but after studying it a few minutes Don mouthed the words written on the cover. "*Tama on Minun Uni Kirja.* Hmmm—It's got to be Finnish, but I have no idea what it means."

He closed his eyes, trying to dredge up the few words of Finnish he remembered from childhood. Mostly he could recall only a few curse words—the foundation of any good vocabulary.

"I'm not sure, but I think *uni* is the word for 'sleep'—maybe 'dream'. When I was tucked in at night, my mother sometimes said—Damn! I can't remember—something like *hyva uni* or *hyva ilta*. Damn! I wish I could remember!"

"It's not that important," Jan said, starting to edge toward the steps again.

"I know *hyva* means good, so she must have been saying 'good sleep,' or 'good dreams'—something like that. I wonder what the rest of this means."

Jan took the book from him and leafed through several pages. The paper crinkled, threatening to powder away to nothing in her hands. "These must be dates, here, at the top of each page. Do you know the Finnish for the months and days?"

Don shook his head. "I can't remember them. Besides, they look so different written out."

"Maybe it's a ledger—or a diary," Jan said.

"I'd bet it'd be fascinating to read," Don said, taking the book back from Jan. He couldn't explain it, but he felt an odd sort of protectiveness about the book—as though, because he was family, only *he* had the right to it. The diffused gray light of the attic and the stuffy air dampered every sound except the crinkling of the pages as Don flipped through the book. A sudden wash of dizziness swept over him, and he shook his head to clear it, convinced that he had almost fainted or fallen asleep on his feet. He looked quickly at Jan, but she seemed not to have noticed.

"Look at that last page," Jan said just as Don was closing the book.

He was about to suggest they go downstairs for a cup of coffee; he had to do *something* to get the muffled stuffiness out of his head. His ears kept whooshing with his pulse, and his breathing seemed shallow and dry.

"The last entry looks really weird," Jan said as Don slowly opened the book again. "Look." She pointed to the scrawling penmanship. "There's that one word repeated"—she counted silently, tapping each word on the page "—five, six, *seven.* Seven times."

She mouthed the words several times before attempting it aloud. "*Sur—man—loukku. Surman-loukku!*"

"Your Finnish is just about as good as mine," Don said. It was an effort to keep his voice steady because he still felt so disoriented. "But maybe we can con Susan into translating a bit of it for us."

"With all the trouble she and Tom have been

having? I can't imagine she'd find the time to—"
Jan's reply was cut off when Beth called frantically to
them from downstairs.

"Mom! Dad! I think we've got a problem!"

Her voice sounded incredibly distant to Don as he
and Jan started down the steep flight of stairs.

"What? What is it?" Jan shouted, her voice edged
with fright.

Don held Aune Kivinen's book tightly in his hand
as he followed Jan down to the first floor where Beth
stood, fidgeting and glancing over her shoulder toward the kitchen. He couldn't shake the subtle sensation he had of being half-asleep, of his head being
packed with cotton.

"What happened?" Jan asked as they followed
Beth into the kitchen. Then they saw the white,
bearded foam spilling out of the washing machine and
the puddle of sudsy water spreading out over the floor
from the pantry.

"For heaven's sake, Beth!" Jan shouted as she
splashed through the water and pulled the control
button on the washer. "You could at least have turned
it off!"

"I'm sorry," Beth said, and they could both see that
she was close to tears. "It started to overflow, and I
guess I must've panicked."

"No problem," Don said, still fighting his odd
sense of disorientation. "It's probably just the drain
pipe's plugged. I can fix it."

They all pitched in and mopped up the mess, which
didn't turn out to be as bad as it had looked. And Don
found that the problem was even simpler than a clog;
somehow, the drain tube had gotten crimped, pinch-
ing off the flow of water. Under his watchful eye, they

ran the load again without a hitch. Aune Kivinen's diary lay all but forgotten on top of the refrigerator where Don had left it during Beth's emergency.

IV

Even after supper, Beth seemed mopy and too quiet. It seemed to Don that her inability to react during an emergency was bothering her. In spite of his reassurances that it was "no big deal," she sat on the couch, listlessly watching TV. Then, a bit after ten, she gave her parents kisses and went up to bed, claiming she was "totally whipped" from almost a week of unpacking, cleaning, and arranging furniture.

"All work and no play makes *Jill* a dull girl, too, you know," she said, smiling weakly as she headed upstairs with Max at her heels.

What was bothering Don was his inability to talk to her about—whatever it was that was bugging her. Sitting back in his easy chair, taking small sips of a Pabst, he began to see that this gap, this distance between them, had started almost as soon as they had moved to Maine. At least he *thought* so. Maybe it had been there before, and the new surroundings just gave it a new background so he could see it more clearly.

He mentioned it to Jan, but she dismissed it as Beth's way of adjusting to the recent major changes in their lives—new home, new jobs (if, she repeated, she could *find* something!), new—everything. And, Jan added, if he hadn't noticed, Beth was no longer a "little" girl. Certain physical changes were happening.

Don couldn't deny that Beth was growing up faster

65

than he could keep track of—almost. He felt he understood her perfectly—yesterday. But now she was approaching adolescence, poised at that awkward age and just about to begin the grueling sprint across the scarred battlefield we call the "teenage years." It pained him to see her straddling the gap between being a kid and being an adult. If, like tonight, she had to be by herself to sort through her feelings, well, that's the way things were, and he, as a wise parent, had just better accept it. She'll talk to him, or her mother, when she's ready.

Jan started dozing not long into "The Best of Carson," so Don nudged her and snapped off the tube. After checking on Beth, Jan dropped into bed, having barely enough energy to get under the covers. She was asleep before Don finished brushing his teeth, so he slipped in beside her, careful not to touch her with his ice-cold feet, although he suspected that a shotgun blast at her ear wouldn't rouse her. He turned off the light and lay in the darkness, listening to Jan's sibilant breathing and the settling sounds the house made as he drifted . . . drifted off to sleep.

Suddenly, a knife edge of blue light filled the room, startling him to wakefulness. He sat bolt upright in bed, staring in confusion at the flickering darkness. The afterimage of the light burned bright vermilion on his retina. Then, just as his mind cleared enough so he knew they weren't in Providence, from far off came a throaty rumble of thunder.

With an uneasy sigh, he settled back onto the pillow, willing his taut nerves to untangle, telling himself it was just a summer thundershower sliding up over the horizon. Nothing more.

But as the storm drew closer, sleep pulled further

back. In the darkness of the room, illuminated now and again by hissing flashes of lightning, Don became intensely aware of the brooding alienness of the house. As if—as if they didn't quite belong . . .

It was their house, to be sure. They had clear title to the property so he didn't feel like an interloper exactly. It just must be the newness of it all, he thought—in spite of the house's age. The same things were bothering Beth in her way. Squinting his eyes so tightly shut that he saw whirlpools of light, he pressed his head back into the pillow, willing sleep.

"If only this house could talk," he thought—or said aloud—he wasn't sure. The idea that a house could store memories, much the way a battery takes a charge, was not new to him; he'd run across that idea in one of the Stephen King novels a student of his had recommended. As the hissing rain swept from the west and over the house, he thought about the other people who had lived here . . .

—His grandparents, who built the house in the early 1920s and lived here until shortly after Toivo Kivinen died, found dead in the field after a blizzard.

—His mother, who moved here with his sister, Susan, and himself, just before his father "bought the farm" in Sicily during World War II.

—The . . . how many other families who rented the house after all those years of being empty? Even Susan, who rented it without Aune's knowledge or consent, said there had been too many to keep track of. None of them stayed long.

If only this house could talk . . .

Lightning flashed with sharp bolts as rain pelted the roof and thunder crashed like tumbling boulders. From downstairs, Don heard a low whimpering and realized that it was Max, frightened, as usual, of the storm. No doubt cowering in the bathroom, too, he thought. The poor fool!

Jan slept on, undisturbed, but Don listened open-eyed between claps of thunder for an indication that Beth had woken up. Deciding that it'd be best to check on her—she might be scared or disoriented waking up in a strange bedroom—he swung his feet to the floor and tiptoed into the hallway.

At Beth's door, he pressed his ear to the wood and listened. With unusually sharp perception, he noticed that the wood of the door was cool against his face—actually cold. But there was no sound of activity in her room, and he decided not to chance waking her by opening the door.

The house will take some time getting used to, that's all, he thought, standing away from the door. Like making a new friend or breaking in a new pair of sneakers or—or . . .

Confused thoughts rushed in as he raised his hand slowly—too slowly! Look how it's shaking!—to the doorknob. What if she's awake in there, too frightened to call out even? The doorknob, too, was cold, sending a numbing chill up to his elbow.

Another low, pained whimper came from downstairs, so Don decided to leave well enough alone and go downstairs to check on Max—poor ol' Max.

The floorboards and stairs creaked underfoot, and even with the deep-throated rumble of thunder rattling the house, he was again surprised by the sharpness of his perceptions. He started thinking about how long ago, in college, he used to—as he called it—"drink himself sober." Whenever he was unable to sleep after a party and too much beer (or, at least while he dated one girl, too much scotch), he'd lie awake staring wide-eyed at the ceiling, not just remembering the party, but actually seeing and hearing swirls of activity around him. He'd sometimes start laughing aloud, convinced that the party really was continuing, everyone still enjoying themselves and completely oblivious of him sprawled out in bed. He'd realize the next day, usually not until sometime in the afternoon, that he had been too drunk to realize just how bad off he was.

Maybe that's what was happening now, in a way. The strain and pressures of moving, not to mention the new teaching job starting in the fall, had worn him down more than he realized. His awareness of the sounds he made as he went downstairs had that same eerie quality of being more memory than reality.

When he reached the foot of the stairs, Max scrambled down the hallway toward him, his claws clicking frantically on the hardwood floor. That same, crisp quality of sound, Don thought, bending down to scuff Max behind the ears. Whining, Max rubbed his head against Don's leg, almost knocking him over as he pressed his cold, wet nose into the cup of Don's hand.

Again the cold, Don thought, having to fight back a rush of uneasiness. Too cold!

"Hey, fella, let me get you a drink, O.K.?"

Don started for the kitchen, and Max came along, inches behind. Don switched on the kitchen light and, after filling the dog's bowl and placing it on the floor, leaned back against the counter and watched as Max lapped noisily. Then, just as he was turning to go back upstairs, a bolt of lightning exploded blue light across the field. Thunder rolled almost immediately after.

"Boy, that was close," Don said, glancing at Max. He flicked off the kitchen light and leaned over the sink, staring at the rain-swept night. Another fork of lightning cut the sky, and in the brief flash, Don saw something outside in the field. He was momentarily blinded by the flashbulb brilliance, but—*something* . . . was still a burning blue-purple afterimage on his retina.

He tried to bring back the fleeting image, but what he had seen—or thought he had seen—just didn't make sense. There was something out there in the field that shouldn't have been there!

Pressing his face closer to the glass, he stared out at the twisting black of the night. He waited, tension coiling in his stomach. His skin began to tingle, but whether from excitement or the static electricity in the air, he wasn't sure.

Just a trick of the light, he thought. Seeing things from the corner of my eye.

More thunder rumbled, rattling the window enough so Don backed away, fearful it might break. And the sound continued to build long after he thought it should have begun to fade. He could hear the cups and glasses in the cupboard beginning to vibrate, and something in the living room or dining room fell to the floor with a loud thump.

Then, catching him by surprise, another flash came, so sharp he would have sworn he heard a snakelike hiss. And in that blinding flash, he saw the thing again, outlined clearly against the night sky. Just on the crest of the hill, a little beyond where Jan planned to plant her garden, he saw tall, massive shapes—towering blocks of stone edged with lightning.

Impossible!

Don knew the field stretched unbroken from the barn, down the hill to the alder-lined stream. He ran to the pantry and hastily pulled on his boots and his slicker over his pajamas.

"Com' on, boy. Com' 'ere Max," he called as he opened the door. The wind and rain outside sounded like tearing paper. The last blast of thunder had sent Max scurrying under the kitchen table where he looked up at Don with fear-glazed eyes.

"You coming or not?" Don said, slapping his thighs.

Max stayed put and let out another shallow whimper to let Don know his final decision.

"Man's best friend, huh?"

Don shrugged and stepped out into the storm, closing the door behind him. Cold pinpricks of rain stung the back of his neck as he crossed the driveway and started across the field. The wet ground made soft sucking noises beneath his feet, and the mud almost succeeded in pulling off a boot. Holding his slicker tightly around his neck, he made his way toward where he had seen—*thought* he had seen—the large stones.

Impossible! . . . There can't be stones that big out here!

As he neared the crest, another bolt cast an eerie blue glow all around. Don saw that the field was clear. Of course it was! There were no towering standing stones!

Still, he slogged on, determined to stand where he thought he had seen the stones, if only to prove they weren't there. The storm twisted like an animal in pain, hissing around him with flickering light showing mountains of tumbling clouds overhead. When he reached the crest of the hill, he looked down toward the stream, satisfied.

Just a trick of the eye, he thought. That's all.

And then he saw them! Standing in the black slick of the stream they stood—tall blocks of stone outlined by sharp bursts of blue light as if they were the source of the storm's electricity. Don stared at them, amazed, trying to deny the testimony of his own eyes. Even after blinking several times and shaking his head, they were there—they were still there, standing and leaning in an odd arrangement that looked vaguely familiar.

Thunder sounded with the deafening concussion of a cannonade. With rain plastering his hair to his forehead and pelting his face, convincing him that he was not asleep, Don stared down the gentle grade toward the tall stones. The bite of ozone stung his nostrils, and prickling static electricity made his scalp tighten.

He suddenly started running down the slope toward the stones, his slicker flapping behind him like dark wings. Halfway to the stream, another flash showed him that the stones were still there, reaching up, their tops seemingly piercing and tearing the lowering clouds. He saw something oozing and bubbling over the stones, dripping down their sides in thick globs— something that looked like thick mud or, maybe, gouts of oil.

This is crazy! he thought as he ran and thunder ripped the night. The sound hit him like a wave, and he fell face first into the mud, sprawling and sliding another ten feet, finally stopping at the edge of the stream.

His pajama bottoms clung to his legs like cold, clammy fingers trying to hold him down, and panic rose from his gut as he scrambled to his hands and knees, eyes searching the inky night for another sight of the stones.

They're right there! his mind shrieked. Not ten feet from me in the darkness! Towering over me!

Panic flooded him when he thought that the stones might fall, crushing him, grinding him into the rain-soaked earth, his blood flowing into the sluggish black water, but when another bolt raced like a hot wire across the sky, he looked up and saw—nothing! Just the dark, lacy line of trees along the bank. No stones! No stones, tearing the storm clouds, oozing with . . .

He lurched to his feet and started running up the slope. His boots kept slipping in the mud and, when he floundered, low whimpers vibrated in his throat. Once he made it to the crest of the hill, he charged toward the house wheeling his arms like a drunkard fighting off a horde of demons.

His whole body, right to the bone, was chilled and tingling as he burst through the kitchen door and sprawled face down on the linoleum. Panting with exhaustion as foul-smelling rivulets of water ran from his hair onto the floor, he shut his eyes tightly, trying to blot out the image that still burned on his retina as though outlined with lightning.

At last he sat up slowly and stiffly and looked around the kitchen. He reached up for the light switch. He had to squint as the room filled with warm, yellow light. When he could focus his eyes, he found he was staring at his left hand on the floor in front of him. Horror mounted inside him as he saw

73

the thick, reddish brown smears that stained both his skin and the floor. He wondered if what he saw was—

—*No! Not blood!* he thought, struggling to keep from crying out. *Mud from the stream! Not blood! There were no stones in the field! And this was not blood! Not blood!*

He clenched his hand into a fist, and it made a sickening squishing sound.

No! Not blood!

His eyes stung and his body ached as he began to undress, letting his slicker and saturated pajamas fall into a sodden heap on the floor. Crouching in the doorway, Max whimpered softly but didn't come over when Don clicked his tongue and called.

"Com' 'ere, Max," Don whispered. The rasp of his voice surprised him; it sounded flat, lifeless as though transmitted through a long tube. Max whined but stayed where he was, perhaps not sure who Don was. Surely the sight and smell of him must be pretty horrendous.

"Should've been there, old buddy," Don said. He kicked his boots into the entryway, tossed his soaked and stained clothes into the washer, then got a towel and began mopping up the floor. He would have run the load in the washer, but he wanted all the hot water he could get for a shower.

After washing and letting nearly scalding water work on his aching muscles, Don towel-dried his hair and went back upstairs. First he checked on Beth, then he slid into bed beside Jan. She groaned and rolled over, eyelids flickering, but she didn't wake up.

Don lay in the darkness, listening to the storm fading in the distance, now nothing more than a low grumble. But sleep still didn't come as he considered

74

what had happened. Already there was an overcast of unreality that made him wonder just how much of it— any?—all?—had been a dream.

There were no tall standing stones in the field!—or in the stream!—no towering black stones, edged with lightning and oozing—

No! Not blood!

A night breeze stinging with ozone fluttered the curtains, and when sleep came, it was thin and disturbed.

Chapter Three

Summer Chills

I

Don overslept—not surprisingly—and by the time he dragged himself from bed, Jan and Beth had prepared a fantastically hearty breakfast. He moved stiffly, rotating his left shoulder as he came into the kitchen and greeted Jan with a cheery, if forced, "Hi yah, hon." He gave her a brushing kiss on the forehead and then plunked down in his chair.

Overnight, the storm had passed, and sunlight now streamed through the open kitchen window. The tangy fresh air mingled with the aromas of bacon, strawberry jam, and fried eggs. From where he sat, Don couldn't see out the window and over the field, and he had to fight back the impulse to stand and look out—just to make *sure* the stones weren't really there. He stabbed weakly at his fried eggs and chewed mechanically.

"My, my," Jan said, smiling. "Aren't we bright-eyed and bushy-tailed this morning." She walked over to the table with the coffeepot in hand and filled first his cup, then hers. The aroma swirled up into Don's face.

"What's the matter? Didn't you sleep well?"

Don grunted, looking first at Jan, then at Beth, and finally out at the deep blue sky. Again he had to resist getting up to check for the stones—just in case.

"Oh, and by the way," Jan continued, "what was with that mess I found in the washer this morning? Your p.j.s were covered with mud. When did you go out?"

He glanced at the pantry, for the first time aware of the churning washing machine. There were still faint streaks of mud on the floor—proof that at least *some* of what he remembered from last night had happened. It hadn't *all* been a nightmare!

He shook his head and took a sip of coffee before speaking. "Well, last night, I . . ."

His voice trailed off, leaving Jan hanging as he remembered the cold, slimy feel of the reddish mud on his hands.

Not blood!

"Yeah? What about last night?"

"I—umm—I went outside during the storm and I guess I took a tumble in the mud."

"I'll say you did. It looks more like you *wallowed* in it."

He tried to signal with his eyes and a subtle nod of his head that it was something he didn't want to talk about with Beth around, and on the second nod Jan got it and, rather awkwardly, stood up and began clearing the table. Don started to double-time it with his eggs, but all the while he was conscious of something looming behind him—as if those dark, leaning stones were still standing out there in the field.

Jan started running warm water into the sink and, turning, gave him a soft look. "You're feeling O.K., aren't you, hon?"

Don nodded and rubbed his forehead, trying to push back the sense of panic last night's memories brought to him. "I just couldn't get to sleep after the thunder woke me."

"Boy, not me," Beth said. "I never heard a thing." She scraped up her last bite of egg, then hopped up from her chair and brought her plate to her mother. Don noticed that she clutched the small wooden doll in one hand.

"I checked on both of you," Don said, "and you guys were sleeping like logs."

Beth tossed her head to one side, then turned, and ran off. Don and Jan listened to her footsteps as she went up to her room to change.

"So," Jan said, elbow deep in dishwater, "what's this all about?"

Don explained briefly, leaving out any mention of thinking his hand was covered with blood. That part was still too real, too scary to be dismissed although already most of what had happened had taken on a dreamy overcast.

"You mean you were sleepwalking," Jan said, half statement and half question.

Don shrugged. "I don't think so. I mean, I was conscious, and I remember everything, but—parts of it I remember more like they were a dream, not real. Most of it—like those stones—doesn't make *any* sense, and the way my hearing and seeing seemed so clear and sharp . . . I dunno."

"They were right out there?" Jan asked, tilting her

head toward the window over the sink.

Don nodded.

"How big were they? I mean, were they really big, like the stones at Stonehenge?"

Don jolted to his feet as the memory of the stones came into sharper focus. "That's it! That's it exactly! They looked like Stonehenge! Holy cow!"

Jan shook her head as she gazed out over the bulging green sweep of the field. Beyond the crest, she could see the tops of the alders, and beyond that, a few of the roofs of buildings in town.

"Sounds like a pretty wild dream to me," she said.

After a lengthy pause, Don sat back down slowly and took a sip of his coffee, now growing cold.

"But the sleepwalking," Jan said, again shaking her head. "I don't know. Do you think you should see someone about it?"

The idea that there might really be something wrong with him galled his insides, but—in spite of what had happened last night—he dismissed the idea of anything being seriously wrong.

"I don't think it's anything to worry about," he said, only half-convinced. "I'm just not sleeping that well 'cause of the move and everything." His hand was shaking as he took another swallow of coffee.

Jan nodded agreement, but there was a shadowed frown on her forehead as she turned back to the dishes.

Don was going to say more, but just then they heard Beth's footsteps on the stairs, and she burst into the kitchen, looking fresh and full of life, dressed in blue jeans and a red-and-white checkered blouse.

Swallowing his last mouthful of coffee, now completely cold, Don smiled widely and said, "You know what we need? We should pack ourselves a load of sandwiches and go out to the pit for a swim. It's such a beautiful day, and—"

The frown on Jan's face, which hadn't left, now deepened. "You mean the granite quarry Toivo used to work?"

"Yeah, my mother used to take us swimming there when we lived here. It's all right. It's on our property."

Jan shook her head. "Is it safe? I mean, it's all stone, right?"

"It's fantastic. Once you try it, you'll never want to get sandy and salty at the beach again."

"Can we, Mom? *Please?*"

"Don't you think we have enough to do around here without hacking off for a whole day?" Jan said. "I thought you told me you were going to start fixing the chimney today."

Don came over to the sink and dropped his empty cup into the sudsy water. "We can't get everything done in a day," he said, sliding one arm around her waist.

Beth bounced excitedly on her toes beside her mother. "Come on, Mom. I'm sick and tired of putzing around here."

" 'Putzing?' " Don said, giving her a grin.

Beth nodded. "Yeah, and besides, I thought one of the reasons we moved to Maine in the first place was for the fresh air and sunshine."

"Even *slaves* get a day off now and then," Don said. "We've been going nonstop for more than a week now."

"What d' yah say, Max?" Beth called, and as if on cue Max came skittering into the kitchen, his claws

80

clicking on the floor.

"I guess you're outvoted on this one, babe," Don said, tugging Jan closer.

Jan twisted out of his grasp, quickly rinsed out his coffee cup, and pulled the plug in the sink. The water made a throaty sucking sound as it drained away, and the sound reminded Don of something. He shivered when he made the connection—it was exactly like the sound his boots made in the muck down by the stream! Muck that, on his hands, had looked like—

—*Not blood!*

"It'll be good for all of us," Don said, hoping neither of them picked up the tightness in his voice. "We've got from now until September to get all the work done."

"You already said it; I've been outvoted," Jan said as she opened the cupboard and took down a can of Bumblebee tuna. She opened it on the electric can opener. With a whoop, Beth dashed upstairs to get her bathing suit on; Don set about digging out the Coleman cooler they had used their first few days in the house; then he went to find their beach towels.

Half an hour later, with sandwiches, chips, pickles, soda, and beer in the cooler, they started off across the field behind the house, looking for the path to the quarry. Don carried the cooler, and Jan carried their towels and sweatshirts just in case the day cooled off.

"You're sure you know the way, I hope," Jan said as they entered the woods and cool, green dappled shadows enfolded them. Don noticed that Beth cast an anxious glance back at the house before it was lost behind a screen of brush and trees. It had taken a bit of convincing to get her to leave her wooden doll behind, and Don thought—although it was impossible at this distance—that he could see the blank, wooden face in Beth's bedroom window staring out at them.

"Susan gave me good directions, and anyway I think I actually remember the way from when I was a kid."

"How could you?" Jan said, bending low to avoid an overhanging branch. "You weren't even four years old the last time you were out here."

Don shrugged and lifted the branch out of his way. "I don't know. Anyway—just follow Max; he seems to know the way."

Far ahead, out of sight, the dog barked; then they heard a wild scrambling in the brush and a deeper growl as he dashed off.

"Probably saw a squirrel or a rabbit," Don said.

"He's going to be surprised," Jan added. "They're probably not as slow and stupid as the pigeons in Rhode Island were."

"They won't hurt him, will they?" Beth asked.

Jan and Don both said, "Naw," simultaneously.

They followed the overgrown path for quite a distance into the woods. Jan led, followed by Beth; Don brought up the rear. All around them they heard the lilting songs of birds and the whisper of a warm breeze in the leaves. The fresh smell of damp soil after the rain was invigorating, and the trees gave some relief from the warmth of the sun. Now and again they heard Max up ahead, barking as he bolted after just about anything that moved in the brush."

"Why do you call it 'the pit'?" Beth asked. "I hope it isn't *the pits*!"

Both Don and Jan chuckled at that, and then Don began to explain that 'the pit' had been his grandfather's granite quarry in the early 1900s. As they took more and more stone out, it began to fill with water from underground springs. Once the water was deep enough, after Toivo died and the quarry was no longer worked, it made the best swimming spot you could ask for—clear, fresh water and always cool, even in August.

Don smiled as he walked along behind Beth, watching the smooth, youthful strength of her stride, and, seeing her in her bathing suit, he was suddenly conscious that her hips were definitely beginning to round out. Peace and quiet filtered through the shadows, and the tension he felt, the residue from last night, slowly uncoiled.

"This was the last of three quarries he tried to get going," Don said after drawing a deep breath. "They'd take out huge slabs of granite, load 'em onto oxcarts, and haul them down to York Harbor where they were shipped out on barges to Boston and New York. This trail should be crossing the old road soon—if we haven't gotten lost."

"Big 'if,' " Jan said, turning to look at him. She had her towel draped over her head like an Arab, and her face was glistening with sweat.

"Well, anyway, Pun'kin, Grampy Kivinen worked hard at it, but he never made a profit—or much of one anyway. Then, after their son died and after he died, Grammy Kivinen moved back to Lanesville to be with relatives."

"How'd their son die?" Beth asked.

Up ahead, Jan stumbled but saved herself from falling by grabbing onto a sapling. Beth and Don both jerked to a halt to avoid trampling on her. Don let the cooler drop to the ground, grateful for the brief break.

Jan looked sharply at Don. "I don't think we need to go into all this family history right now."

Beth glanced at her father and shrugged. "How'd he die, though," she asked once they'd started walking again.

"I guess Grammy didn't talk about it much. Her whole time living here was something she seemed to pretty much want to forget, and you'd understand why if you knew some of what she went through. The way I heard it from Susan—"

"Don! Really!" Jan said.

"There's no harm in telling her, for crying out loud," Don said. "The boy—his name was Eino—was up at the quarry, visiting his father. I guess what happened was somehow he got his hand under one of the big slabs of rock and the stone slid. It took his hand clean off, and he bled to death before they could get the doctor from town."

"Oh, yuck!"

"If you're trying to ruin my appetite, you're doing a great job," Jan said, not bothering to turn.

"So—like the stone just crushed it away to nothing?" Beth said. "Gross! I wonder how long before he died."

"Will you please stop it!" Jan shouted angrily. "I really don't think we need—"

She let out a scream when Max suddenly ripped through the underbrush like a bullet and almost knocked her over before dashing full speed up the trail. His wild barking echoed back hollowly.

"Damn dog," Jan muttered.

"Look! Up there!" Beth yelled, pointing ahead. "There's a clearing up ahead and I think I can see the old road."

"That's what we're looking for," Don said.

They scrambled up a steep, rock-strewn embankment and came out of the shade into the glaring heat of the sun. The road—two parallel dirt ruts with a Mohawk-haircut centerstrip of knee-high grass—cut obliquely across the path. Nailed to a tree beside the path was a rusted *No Trespassing* sign that had been riddled with quarter-sized bullet holes.

Once they were in the open, the sun blasted them and made the far ends of the dirt road shimmer. Don followed Jan's lead and draped his towel over his head. Shifting the cooler from one hand to the other, he walked along beside Jan, dragging his sneaker toes in the dirt with exaggerated exhaustion. Beth angrily snapped her towel at a deerfly, buzzing around her head.

"Hey, Sheik, how far to the oasis?" Jan asked, but nobody laughed.

"Not far now," Don replied although he was still just going on Susan's direction and his own vague sense of recognition. Each step made the cooler feel several pounds heavier, and sharp aches jabbed up to his shoulder.

They came around a shallow curve in the road and, up ahead, Don saw what he was looking for—a pile of stone stacked more than ten feet high, a tumbled mass of giant toy blocks. Scrawny birches circled the pile, and several saplings had managed to sprout up between the stones.

"That's it!" Don said. "That's the grout pile Susan said to look for, so we just have to follow the path around behind it and we're there."

"Fantastic," Jan said, "I'm sweating my butt off."

"What's a grout pile?" Beth asked.

Jan shot him a quick "no more stories about kids losing their hands" look, and he gave her a slight acknowledging nod.

"A grout pile's just the chipped and cracked stones they couldn't sell. They'd cart them a little way from the quarry and dump them."

As they came to the tumbled pile of stone, Don mentioned something he remembered his mother telling him: " 'Never play on those piles of rock,' she always told me, ' 'cause they could easily tumble down and crush you'—"

—and after what happened to Grammy Kivinen's son, Eino, he *knew* she wasn't just talking hogwash—

"—besides that, stone piles are favorite places for rattlesnakes to sun themselves."

"Are there really rattlesnakes?" Beth asked, hurrying her pace to get around the grout pile as fast as she could without bumping into her mother.

Don laughed. "I doubt it. She probably just said that to make sure I stayed away. Anyway, there aren't supposed to be any poisonous snakes in Maine."

"Tell *that* to the first one you meet, O.K., smarty-pants?" Jan said.

They circled the pile and continued on the down-sloping path. Up ahead, they heard Max barking, the sound oddly magnified. Don realized that the sound was echoing off the sheer stone cliffs of the quarry. As if that were her cue—or maybe to put some more distance between herself and the grout pile—Beth dodged around her mother and raced down the trail, her feet scuffing the pine needles that covered the ground.

Don sighed and readjusted his grip on the cooler.

As the trees thinned out and they caught a glimpse of sparkling blue water up ahead, Jan stopped and turned to Don.

"I want you to make *sure* she knows she's not to come out here alone, O.K?"

Don nodded. "I'm sure she realizes that, but judging by the number of bullet holes in the sign back there, I don't think this is exactly a private spot. There're probably people here all day, every day, in the summer."

"Still," Jan said, "I want you to make it clear to her: she's not to come out here alone."

"Sure. Sure. No problem."

From far off, Beth shouted, her voice ringing back from the stone cliffs. "Hey! Come on, you guys! Hurry up! I'm starving!"

Cupping his hands to his mouth, Don shouted back. "Wait up! I don't want you in that water until we get there!"

Max answered from far off with a burst of barking.

They quickened their pace and suddenly broke through into a clearing surrounded by stunted scrub pines. The smell of pine pitch filled the air and made Jan sneeze. Sunlight shimmered on the quarry water, and they could hear the slap-slap of Max as he swam happily in circles near the shore. Beth stood at the edge of a small cliff, looking over to the far shore. Sheer, slanting cliffs, streaked black by the underground springs that fed the quarry, angled down to the water. Some were more than thirty feet high, their surfaces almost alive with color and flecks of mica. Near the cliffs, the water was a deep marble black, and only out in the middle of the quarry did the water reflect the vaulting blue sky.

"Looks like we're the only ones after all," Jan said as she eyed the path leading down from the pine grove to where Beth waited at the water's edge. She could see that the flat shelves of ledge continued down beneath the surface and was glad that there was someplace to wade.

"We probably scared 'em all off with our yelling," Don said. He shifted the cooler again before starting the descent.

"This really is a beautiful spot," Jan said, looking around and trying to take it all in. "I'm surprised it's not *crawling* with people."

"I imagine on a hot August afternoon there might be a few locals around."

On the far side of the quarry, a crow called out its raucous song, then swooped up into the sky—a black, flapping mote against a blue that almost hurt the eyes to look at too long. High, tumbling clouds with flattened bottoms slid slowly across the horizon.

"I told you this was exactly what we *all* needed," Don said, inhaling deeply and smiling with satisfaction.

Jan looked at him, a wide smile splitting her face. "For the first time since we moved here, baby cakes, I think you're right." She came over to him and gave his buttocks a quick squeeze. He couldn't protect himself without dropping the cooler, so instead he glared at her and muttered, "Just wait—I'll get you for that!"

Adjusting the weight in his hand, Don started after Jan down the steep path, being careful not to trip over any of the exposed tree roots. His belly tingled with the anticipation of feeling the cold water sweep around him.

"Hmm, look," Jan said, casually nodding to the

left of the trail. "There's another grout pile."

Don glanced to where she indicated, then jolted to a stop. The hand holding the cooler went suddenly numb, but only because his hand was clamped tightly over the handle, he didn't drop it.

"Some pretty-good-sized ones, too," Jan went on, not noticing that Don had stopped in the path, staring open-mouthed at the grout pile in the woods. Huge, unevenly split gray stone slabs—some as large as a Volkswagen—had been dumped there.

Or purposely placed? Don wondered, shocked by the vague familiarity of the pile of stone.

Was it random? he wondered.

He was dimly aware that Jan was still walking down the slope. He stood there like a deer nailed by the glare of oncoming headlights, his eyes widening.

Damned if those stones didn't look just like—

Thunder rolled, and sharp tongues of lightning flickered in the darkness of his memory. And needle-sharp pain pelted him on the face and hands.

The stones in his dream last night!

The nightmare—it *had* to have been a nightmare—came back like the hissing intake of breath through clenched teeth.

Soft mud, sucking at his boots—tripping him—holding him. His wet pajamas, clinging to his legs like rotted hands. Shimmering globs of—something, oozing over the lightning-edged stones.

No! Not blood!

He stood in the needled shade of the pines, transfixed by the mound of abandoned granite. The sun shot through the foliage in misty bars of yellow light, casting shadows as black as the water at the edge of the cliffs.

89

The pattern is there! he thought, trying to fend off his rising panic.

"Don? Are you coming?" Jan called, looking up the incline at him.

Tall standing stones, dripping with—

"Don?" Her smile was fading as she registered the expression of mounting horror on his face. *"Don?"*

No! Not blood!

Don took a staggering step back, dropping the cooler. It sounded as if something inside had shattered. In his memory, dark tangled clouds were ripped—disemboweled by the towering black stones that leaned and teetered, threatening to fall over and crush him.

"Honey?" Jan said, starting back up the path toward him. "What's the matter?" She grabbed him by the shoulders and gave him a firm shake.

The frantic edge of her voice cut through Don's black memory, and he shook his head, trying to force away the images that gripped him like cold, steel bands.

"Mom! Dad! Are you coming?" Beth called, her voice was far away—almost another world away, Don thought.

"Come on, Don! Answer me! What is it?" Jan shouted, shaking him roughly.

"I—There was—"

No! Not blood!

Don closed his eyes and shook his head. Then, pressing both palms against his temples, he looked up at the sky, keeping his eyes wide open until they began to hurt—until he was *sure* he was awake.

"I saw—that grout pile over there. It looked like—" He cut himself off and, looking Jan squarely in the

90

eyes, took a deep, shuddering breath.

Jan glanced past him at the jumbled pile of stones. For an instant it looked as though they had shifted; but she quickly realized that it was the play of sunlight and shadow that had made the rocks appear to move. Her grip on Don's shoulders loosened into a caress.

"For a second there," Don said, his throat feeling scratchy, "I thought those stones looked like the ones in my dream last night," he said. His voice was still shaky but was now under control.

"Did you guys get lost or something?" Beth's voice rang out, echoing from the cliffs.

"We'll be right down," Jan yelled back, never taking her eyes away from Don. Then, more softly, she said, "Are you sure you're O.K.?"

Don nodded, feeling the flood of panic subside, but it was only with great effort that he could turn and look at the grout pile behind him and see it for what it was—just a pile of discarded stone.

"Yeah," he said, swallowing hard, "I guess so. I—" He laughed, but his laugh sounded forced and tight. "I guess I just let my imagination get carried away for a minute."

The pile of stones looked *nothing* like the stones in his dream.

If it had been a dream, he thought, and a shiver danced between his shoulder blades.

"Hey, come on," he said, bending to open the cooler and check inside. One of the glasses Jan had packed because they had run out of paper cups was shattered. "No problem. Let's not ruin the day, O.K? Let's get our butts down there before Beth has a bird."

II

Three hours later, with the heavy satisfaction of two tuna fish sandwiches, three Pabsts, and much too long a time in the sun pressing him down, Don rolled his head to the side and squinted at Jan, lying on a towel beside him.

"You know," he said sleepily, "after a while, you can actually almost get used to lying on stone instead of sand."

Without opening her eyes, Jan replied, "You've been in the sun too long, dear. The living room floor was softer. Next time, we'll try the beach, O.K.?"

"You've gotta admit, though, that the water's pretty damned fine, and you can't beat the privacy."

"I'm surprised no one else has been up here today. You'd think, hot as it is . . ." She let her voice drift away.

Don grunted a reply and was silent for a while; then he said, "You know, I've been thinking—"

"I *told* you you'd been in the sun too long," Jan said, snickering.

Don rolled onto his side and propped himself up on one elbow. The towel beneath him was saturated with sweat and Coppertone. He focused his eyes on Beth, sitting on a low ledge, dangling her feet in the water so fish would swim up close to investigate.

"I've been thinking of what we could get Beth for her birthday," Don said, softly enough so she wouldn't hear him.

"I thought we'd agreed on a stereo," Jan said, her eyes still closed.

"I know something she wants even more than that!" Don said softly, his voice tempting, teasing.

"Something she's wanted since she was—what? Four years old? And could never have—until now."

Jan suddenly jackknifed into a sitting position. Her towel clung to her back and then slowly peeled off, falling into a rumpled heap. The sudden brilliance of the sun made her eyes water as she looked at him, jaw firmly set. "You don't mean it! You're not really—"

"Yeah," Don said, shutting her off, "I am." He cast an anxious glance at Beth who, apparently, hadn't heard them or didn't care to listen.

"You're nuts," Jan said, her voice hissing like a burned-out match. "The sun's rattled your brains, is that it?"

"Maybe," Don said, his smile widening, "but I think it's a damned good idea. It's the only thing she *really* wants—and the last thing she'd ever suspect. I think we could at least check around."

"Be serious!"

He could tell by her tone that she meant it, but he pushed on. "I *am* serious. What could be better?"

"A stereo, like we said." Jan's mouth tightened as though she had bitten a lemon. "I hope I'm not going to have to listen to this horse nonsense from you, too."

Don glanced again at Beth, checked his watch, and said, "O.K., Pun'kin. It's been an hour, you can go swimming now."

After hearing the splash as Beth sliced into the water, he looked back at Jan. "Now, as I was saying— a horse would be—"

"An incredible expense, that's what it'd be," she snapped, eyeing him with a watery squint. "We've been over this too many times!"

"But I think we can swing it. Really."

"Well, I *don't*! Not when you consider what the

93

house needs." Jan kept her anger controlled but just barely.

"Needs? Or what *you* want?" Don said. He shifted to a sitting position, hugging his sweat-slick legs. "I think Beth's right when she says some of the ideas you've come up with would cost more."

"Maybe at first," Jan said defensively, "but in case you didn't realize it, you have to keep feeding a horse. I just don't think a salary teaching shop at York High School is enough to support a horse *and* a family."

Don stared at the widening circles of ripples that surrounded Beth as she swam to an outcropping stone on the far side of the quarry. The smooth, marble blackness of the water hid her below the surface, making her look strangely disembodied.

"She's going to need something like that to keep her busy," Don said, almost dreamily. "There isn't as much to do around here as there was in Providence, and besides building her confidence, I think having a horse will help her make friends."

Jan shook her head, disgusted. "She'll do just fine once she meets a few of the kids around town. And there's more than enough to do around the house to keep her busy."

Don snorted. "All work and no play . . ."

"Besides," Jan said, lancing him with a cool stare, "we just plain can't afford it. It's as simple as that."

"We'll see," Don said. He stood up and, shading his eyes from the reflection on the water, looked out to where Beth sat on the outcropping stone. Her hair was glistening like a mermaid's. She saw him and waved. He waved back and, even though lunch still weighed heavily in his stomach, dove in and swam out to her.

They passed the early afternoon in a shimmering heat haze of laziness, baking in the sun and luxuriating in the cool, dark water. There was a subtle tension between Don and Jan for the rest of the time at the quarry, but the day went by peacefully because each of them knew they would work it all out. Don was confident that Jan would see that, after all, it was a perfect surprise. Jan was just as positive that Don would see she was right—as soon as he got out of the sun.

A little after three o'clock, they collected their things and started back along the trail home. Going up the slope, Don was leery of seeing the grout pile again, but the day had fully relaxed him, and he saw it for what it was—just a pile of stones with no pattern at all.

They followed the path out past the other grout pile and were walking down the wheel-rutted road when Beth suddenly jerked to a stop, muttering under her breath.

"What's the matter, Pun'kin?" Don asked.

"My barrette. I think I must've left it back at the quarry." She looked back along the road with obvious longing.

"Is it that important?" Don asked.

Beth nodded. "It's my favorite."

Jan had her towel draped over her head again for the long walk in the sun. Already she looked sweaty. "Look, hon, I'll get you another," she said with an exasperated sigh. "It can't be all that important."

"I *really* like it," she said, still looking back along the road. "You guys keep walking; it won't take me long." Handing her towel to her mother, she took off down the road before either of them could say any-

95

thing. They heard her whistle between her teeth for Max just before she rounded a bend and disappeared from sight.

Beth pumped her arms like pistons as her feet slap-slapped the dusty earth, raising small puffs behind her. She turned off the path and, remembering what her father had said about rattlesnakes, put on a little extra steam when she went past the first grout pile.

She skittered down the path to the water's edge, feeling the moist air like a wall of coolness. On a ledge overlooking the water, the wet spot from her wet bathing suit still visible, she saw the barrette. Barely breaking her pace, she snapped it up, turned on one foot, and started back up the slope through the pine grove and toward the road. Exhaustion burned in her chest, and the backs of her legs were beginning to feel rubbery, but she pushed herself, determined not to make her parents wait too long.

When she was approaching the grout pile near the road, she was running awkwardly. Her arms had lost their piston stroking and now were pinwheeling. Sweat ran down her face and stung her eyes, making the slanting afternoon sunlight blur. As she rounded the grout pile, running closer to it this time, her foot snagged on a rock. Before she could register it consciously, she was pitching forward. A knife-edged block slammed into her knee, and pinpoints of light corkscrewed in her mind as she hit the ground with a dull thud. Her breath slammed out of her as though she had been hit between the shoulders by a sledge hammer.

"Beth! Are you coming?" she heard her father call. His voice sounded muffled as if by cotton, and from further off she heard a burst of barking from Max.

She struggled up onto her elbows, wanting to call out to her father, but her lungs were on fire and all that came out was a strangled groan. She crumpled to the ground totally, exhausted.

After a moment, she twisted to one side and looked at the blood clotting on her knee. Gingerly she touched the wound, wincing as a dull, chilling pain spread up from her knee. Then, before she knew what was happening, she felt a sharp pain burn like a hot needle on her neck. She cried out and tried to swat at it but missed. Then she heard and registered the angry buzzing of hornets as the swirling mass of enraged insects attacked her.

Beth opened her mouth to yell for help, but by the time she had enough air in her lungs, dozens of stingers had jabbed into her back, arms, legs, and face. Now frantic with pain, she twisted and tried to pull away, but the whirling mass spun around her, distorting the ground like a distant heat haze. The buzz-saw sound rose louder, filling her world with searing pain.

She struggled to move, to get up and run, but her foot was stuck. The hornets became a buzzing halo around her head, darting and stinging until every bite felt like a drop of scalding acid. She swatted furiously at the hornets, trying to protect her face, but the motion only riled them more. She pulled harder to free her leg but couldn't get it loose.

"Help! Help!" she screamed, her throat tearing like paper. "Oh, God! Help!"

Her vision blurred with tears and pain as she redoubled her efforts to get free, but it was no use—she was pinned.

Jerking up into a sitting position, she leaned forward, looking down at her trapped foot. When she saw what was holding her, her screams rose shrilly until her voice cracked and no more sound issued from her open mouth. Reaching out from beneath the grout pile was a thin, wrinkled hand, its bony fingers blackened with age, and pencil-thin tendons standing out in sharp relief. The yellowed, cracked fingernails dug into her ankle with a viselike grip, holding her down as the hornets swarmed over her.

This is crazy! her mind screamed through the pain and fear. This can't be happening!

She pulled frantically to free herself but didn't dare reach down toward that hand—*that hand*!

Nothing—no one living could be under all those rocks!

"Help!" she wailed, her voice wavering up and down like a siren.

It's gonna hold me here till I die, she thought.

"Help! Please! Help!" she yelled, her voice growing feeble.

The grip on her ankle tightened, and the hornets crawled over her until their stings merged into one incredible tormenting pain. She thought she was still screaming—she wasn't sure. Her world became one spiraling, throbbing buzzing sound that meant pain—fiery pain!

What she thought were her screams receded into a spinning pool of blackness, and she fell down . . . down . . . into the blackness because it was cool . . . cold . . . and in the cold blackness, there was no burning pain. There was . . . nothing.

She was unconscious and covered with stings and crusted blood when Don found her.

Don held the phone to his ear with his shoulder and held Jan's gaze as he spoke. "Yeah, Susan, she's sleeping now, but she's much better. The doctor gave her a shot of Benzedryl, and she's going to be a hurting trooper for a while, but she'll be O.K. Her knee's pretty banged up, though."

He wished he didn't feel as though it was his fault that this happened to Beth, but Susan never let him forget that he was her "little brother." He always felt a little bit on the defensive when he talked with her.

"Umm. Yeah. She fell right on top of a yellowjackets' nest. They really did a number on her face, but the doctor doesn't think there'll be any serious scarring. Just a lot of pain."

Jan raised her eyebrows and shook her head, irritated that Don had even mentioned what had happened to Beth.

"Yeah," Don said, turning away from Jan, "we're getting settled here, slow but sure."

"Don't invite them up," Jan whispered. "Not yet, anyway."

Don nodded his head in agreement, distracted for a moment. "Anyway, Sue, I just wanted to call and give you our number. Got a pencil? O.K." He had to repeat the number three times before she finally got it.

Tired of listening to a one-way conversation, Jan wandered over to the kitchen sink and looked out the window, over the field. Above the line of trees, she could see the faint glow of lights from town. The curtains wafted gently on the breeze.

"Umm. Yeah. I was thinking of coming down sometime soon to see Grammy. How's she been lately? . . . Hmmm. Too bad. Well, sure, maybe tomorrow."

He glanced at Jan, who merely shrugged.

"Yeah, I'll drive down tomorrow. Well, there's no point in running the phone bill sky high on the first call—'sides, I'll see you at the hospital tomorrow. Oh, one more thing before you hang up."

Holding the receiver down, he waved Jan over and said, "Get me that book off the refrigerator, would yah, hon?"

Jan reached for Aune's leather-bound diary and handed it to him.

"You know Finnish pretty well from taking care of Aune all this time. I was wondering if you could tell me what something means. It's—uh . . ." He carefully traced his finger under the title as he sounded out each word. *"Tama—on—minun—uni—kirja. The last word's kirja. K-I-R-J-A."*

After a short pause, he nodded and repeated Susan's translation. " 'This is my dream book.' That's it, huh? O.K., thanks. . . . Oh, nothing important . . . just something I saw written and was wondering about."

His fingers glided over the pebbled leather cover, and deep inside he felt the faint stirrings of excitement—of discovery.

"Hey, I'll talk to you tomorrow. I'll try to be there by eleven o'clock, but you know me—always late. O.K., 'bye. How are you and Tom doing?"

Don could feel Jan stiffen beside him.

"Hmm. Yeah, well, hang in there. Give my love to the boys. O.K. Bye."

He hung up the phone and stood there, feeling the leather-bound "dream book" heavy in his hand. A thorny irritation grew in him as he read and reread the Finnish title. He wished he knew some Finnish—*any* Finnish so he could begin reading what was in the book. It might be an incredibly interesting account of his grandmother's life here in the early 1900s.

"I always said she is too good for Tom," Jan said, shaking her head. "He always seems to want to spend more time hanging out with the guys than with his family."

"He's not all that bad," Don said, although he felt no great need to defend Tom.

"He'll never grow up," Jan said, sniffing. "I guess I'll go up and see how Beth's doing."

Don nodded, then replaced the "dream book" on the refrigerator. "Yeah, and we ought to hit the sack, too, if we're going to get an early start tomorrow."

Jan turned in the doorway and looked at him, her eyebrows raised like two dark commas. "What, do you have any ideas?" she asked, thrusting her hips out suggestively.

Don chuckled and followed her upstairs.

IV

The pungent smell of disinfectant stung Don's nose as he entered his grandmother's hospital room. He knew, even then, that the smell and its association with sickness would always be his most vivid memory of his grandmother.

Aune Kivinen was ninety-two years old and had survived both of her children. Eino, her only son, had died horribly in that accident at the quarry; her daughter Marie, Don's mother, had been dead more than ten years from cancer. But Aune was a survivor

101

and had outlived them all—husband and children. She had seen three great-grandchildren, so even though Don knew she wouldn't leave the hospital alive, he wasn't sad for her. All things considered, she'd had a long and, in spite of the tragedies that touch every life, a good life.

"Hi, Grammy," Don whispered as he glided silently to the edge of the bed and leaned over to give her pale cheek a kiss. Aune made such a small mound under the crisp hospital sheet he wondered if there was actually a whole person there in the bed. Certainly a portion of her mind wasn't there. Even prepared for that, Don was surprised to see how much she had failed since he'd last seen her, a year or so ago.

She's no bigger than Beth, he thought, taking the chair beside the bed and sitting down.

"How're you feeling today?" he asked, knowing that she little cared what day it was.

The old woman's head lolled to one side, crinkling the pillow. Milky eyes stared unblinkingly at him from the waxy, wrinkled face. Don smiled to himself, remembering the time Beth, when she was around three years old, questioned him about the "rattles" old people get on their faces.

"*Paivaa . . . paivaa,*" Aune croaked, and one side of her mouth twitched into a smile. Her feeble effort to raise a hand in greeting didn't last long. The ropy tendons on the back of her hand twitched uncontrollably.

"Good, Grammy," Don said softly. "I'm glad you're feeling good. They're taking good care of you here, I hope."

Behind him, Don heard the door open and, turning, saw Susan enter, holding a small bunch of wildflowers. She smiled, showing surprise that Don was actually on time—a bit early, even.

Don looked back at Aune and saw that her gaze had drifted to the acoustical tiles of the ceiling, but her focus seemed somewhere beyond. She mouthed words but too faintly for Don to understand.

"I'm glad you could come," Susan said as she took the wilted flowers from the vase on the windowsill. She filled the vase with fresh water and put in the fresh flowers. Then she sat down in the chair on the opposite side of the bed.

"It's been a while since you've seen her," Susan said, "but now that you live so close, maybe you can visit more often."

Don shrugged. "I don't think she even knows I'm here," he whispered, but when he glanced down at Aune, her eyes had locked on him. Her head made a quick, jerking motion.

"She catches more than you'd think," Susan said.

Unnerved by his grandmother's unblinking stare, Don turned back to his sister. "You're looking good," he said. "I like your hair long like that, and by the looks of that tan, I'd say you've been on the tennis courts quite a bit."

Susan shook her head. "Mostly yardwork, really," she said, and she went back to the flowers in the vase and busied herself arranging them. There was something dark and worried in her expression, but Don figured, if it had anything to do with the problems she and Tom were having, she'd tell him if she wanted him to know.

"Yeah," he said, "we've got quite a bit of work to do ourselves. But overall I'd say the house is in pretty good shape."

Susan shook her head sharply. "Don't mention it; we don't want to upset her."

Don cast an anxious glance at Aune. Susan came to the edge of the bed and, taking Aune's hand, began rubbing the back of it gently.

"How's Beth feeling this morning?" Susan asked.

Don shrugged. "Not bad—considering. Last night she had quite a fever, then the chills, but the worst, I think, is over. She's just irritated as hell that she has to stay in bed when the weather's so nice. Her ankle and knee are pretty banged up."

"Umm," Susan said, "I remember when Dale broke his leg when we got him his first two-wheeler. He was in a cast for most of July and all of August. It's tough on them to be cooped up like that."

Don nodded. "Tough on her, too, I'll bet."

"*Paivaa . . . paivaa . . .*" Aune muttered. For a moment, her eyes lost their distant focus, and her eyelids fluttered as she made a rattling, gasping sound deep in her throat.

"She's not doing very well, is she?" Don said.

Susan smiled weakly, the dark worry still in her eyes. "At ninety-two what can you expect? The doctors say she can't last more than a month or two, but they've been saying that for over two years now. She's tough—she's got what the Finns call *sisu*."

"Has it been much of a strain on you—and Tom?" Don asked, thinking he'd leave her the chance to talk about Tom if she wanted to.

Susan shrugged as she continued stroking the back of Aune's hand. "It's been a slow, steady decline going on ten years ever since she first moved in with us. I—we're doing what we *have* to do."

Don wasn't sure if she meant Aune or her marriage.

104

"She really was doing all right until Ma died, I think," Don said. "It hit her pretty hard, losing her only surviving child."

"Then, when she fell in the kitchen and broke her hip three winters ago—well, she just laid down and never got up—never will get up."

Deep, reedy breathing sounded in Aune's throat. In spite of her open eyes, she seemed to be asleep.

"At least she's alive—and loved," Susan said, pushing a strand of wispy gray hair back from Aune's forehead. "And she didn't spend those ten years in some nursing home."

"You can't call this *living*," Don said, irritated with himself for starting—again—the argument they had had for years. Susan had made the decision to care for Aune in her home and never would have considered sending her to a nursing home. It was only after Aune developed pneumonia that she had her admitted to the hospital. But if only she could see the toll it's taken, Don thought, on her—and her marriage.

"Anything—*anything* is better than a nursing home," Susan said sharply, and Don had sense enough to let it drop; it was too late, now, anyway.

"*Kivi . . . kivi . . .* " the old woman muttered as though talking in her sleep. Thick mucus stuck to her lips, making loud clicking sounds as she spoke. Her mouth reminded Don of a pale, bloodless wound.

"What'd she say?" Don asked, unnerved by the frantic edge in Aune's voice. She was staring up at the ceiling, her eyes bulging.

"*Kivi . . . kivi! . . . kuolema kivi!*" Aune wailed.

Susan leaned close to Aune and smiled down at her. "I'm here, *mumu*," she cooed. "I'm here."

The old woman's eyes fluttered, and she dropped

off to sleep again, her breath a hissing rattle.

"What did that mean?" Don asked.

Susan tucked the sheets up under Aune's chin, then stood up straight. "Well, *kivi* is Finnish for 'stone.' She says that a lot. I figure she's trying to say her name, Kivinen, but can't quite get enough air." Susan took a deep breath and let it out slowly. "And *kuolema* means—uh, 'death.'" She stabbed Don with a harsh look. "She knows she's dying."

He could tell by her reaction that Susan was bothered by the idea of Death. Christ! he thought, who isn't? Looking at Aune, he had to think that the longer someone lives, the more death they'll see, and Aune had seen more than her share of death. She had outlived her husband and both of her children—no doubt the *worst* human tragedy.

"Well, I guess I gotta head home," Don said as he stood and put the chair back where it was. "There's a lot of things Jan wants me to get done around the house."

Susan smiled and nodded, and Don had a quick impression that she was almost relieved he was leaving. Maybe she didn't want him to press any more about how she and Tom were doing.

"Say 'hi' to Jan from us," Susan said, "and tell Beth I hope she's up and around soon."

"O.K. See yah," Don said as he opened the door. "Oh, hey, I almost forgot. I found a book in the attic that I wanted you to take a look at. It's hers." He tilted his head toward Aune, who was peacefully sleeping. "It's her *'uni kirja'*."

"Hers?" Susan was unable to keep the surprise out of her voice.

"Yeah, a journal of some kind Jan and I found.

106

The penmanship's kind of scrawly, but because you know Finnish, I was hoping you'd translate some—or all of it for me."

Susan's eyes darkened. "Umm—yeah, I suppose I could if I can find the time."

"I'd really appreciate it," Don said. "The penmanship *can't* be as bad as my pronunciation. I'll leave it at the front desk for you."

"Kuolema! . . . KUOLEMA!" Aune shouted, suddenly catapulted out of her sleep. The power of her voice surprised both Don and Susan. He stood in the doorway, frozen, and she bent over her grandmother.

Aune's vacant eyes looked up at Susan with no apparent recognition. Fear twisted her face as she yelled, *"Kuolema! Kuolema kivi!"*

"Christ, is she always like this?" Don asked.

Without turning, Susan shook her head "no" as she peered into Aune's horror-filled eyes. "At least there's no fever," she said as she stroked Aune's forehead.

Aune thrashed on the bed, her thin arms beating futilely against the weight of the sheets. Susan pressed the button to summon a nurse, then did what she could to calm Aune, whose voice grew increasingly frantic.

"Kuolema kivi! Kuolema kivi!" she wailed, tossing her head from side to side and then lacing Don with a cold, milky stare.

"Varokaa kivia," she said, looking straight at him and making a mighty effort to raise her hand. She gasped, and then a gagging cough cut off her words.

A nurse brushed past Don and went over to the bedside. "It might be best if you left," she said over her shoulder to Don. Aune's mouth was still moving, but no sound came out.

"Yeah," Don said as he inched his way out the doorway. "I'll give you a call, Susan. We'll have you folks out to the house soon, O.K?"

Susan waved him a quick good-by, never taking her eyes away from the trembling old woman. As Don rode the elevator down to the first floor, he tried to sort out what he felt and thought. Fear—pity—disgust—all of these, yes, but there was more. Nibbling at the back of his mind was the question: What in the hell does *"varokaa kivia"* mean?

Chapter Four

The Hand

I

By mid afternoon, when Don arrived home from visiting Aune, rain came. It slanted in sporadic gusts against Beth's bedroom window. With effort, Beth opened her swollen eyes and looked out at the gnarled apple tree, its bark an oily, black wetness. A flock of drenched sparrows flashed past her window like blown leaves.

She started to rub her eyes, but the pain made her cry out. Settling her head into the well of the pillow, she gently touched the lumps on her forehead. Tears filled her eyes, but—at least to the touch—her fever seemed to have gone down. She remembered the chills she'd had in the night and hoped the fever didn't return tonight—with its delirium and dreams. She tried to think about the bracing chill of the quarry water and how refreshing that had been. The chill from the hornet stings was fiery and deep, and it scared her.

She was starting to drift back to sleep when she heard a soft tap on her door.

"Com' on in," she said with a rasp.

"How you feeling, there, Punk'kin?" Don asked as he tiptoed into the darkened room and sat on the edge of her bed. The view outside the window looked particularly depressing, but the doctor had told her to avoid bright light for a day or two.

"I'm O.K. . . . considering," she said, propping herself up on her elbows and forcing a smile.

"You must be getting pretty tired of lying around in bed, huh?"

Beth shrugged. "I don't really feel like doing much of anything else. I thought I heard a car drive off."

"Umm. Mom's gone to Ogunquit to apply for a job she saw in last night's paper. She figured I could take care of you 'cause I can't work on the roof in the rain."

"I'm all right," Beth said, sounding perturbed that he was treating her as though she were a baby.

"I'm sure you are," he said. He smiled and patted her leg. "You'll be up and around in a day or two. Maybe then you can finish putting this stuff away." He scanned the opened and half-empty boxes lining two of the walls and smiled. He had been shocked by how much her legs beneath the blankets had reminded him of Aune in her hospital bed. He patted Beth's legs again, hoping to feel the youthful strength there, not the brittleness of age.

"Ahhh! Watch it! That's my bad knee," Beth said.

He felt her leg twitch and drew his hand away, letting it rest on the bed beside her leg. She was growing up, he thought, and probably didn't want him touching her like that any more.

Beth shifted forward, and, when she saw her father's hand on the bed beside her, a frightful image rose unbidden in her mind. She stiffened and had to struggle to keep from screaming. She tried to push the image away, but it stayed there—a thin, blackened,

110

dried-out hand, reaching out from beneath the pile of stones, holding her, trapping her there while the hornets swarmed. Those dark, dizzying waves threatened again to engulf her.

"Something the matter, Punk?" Don asked, sensing her tension. "You know, Dr. Kimball said the medication might—"

"Daddy, I—" she began, but her voice choked off as the mental image of the hand intensified and its grip got stronger.

Don moved closer, gently holding her—

—the way Susan held Aune, he couldn't help but think.

Tears welled up in Beth's eyes and spilled down her enflamed cheeks.

"Hey now, Pun'kin, there's no reason to get upset. You'll be up soon, and then—"

"I—I saw something," she said, choking and wiping her tears away with the back of her hand in spite of the pain it caused.

"Take it easy there," Don said softly. He wanted to give her a tight hug—as he always did when she was frightened—but he was afraid of hurting her tender skin. "What's the matter? You can talk to me—You always have."

Beth sniffed loudly, her breath catching.

"You know," Don said, "if you're worried about your face, you know, not fully healing, just remember what Doc Kimball said."

"No—no, it's not that," Beth said. It hurt her face to do so, but she buried her face into her father's shoulder and let the tears flow unchecked.

"There. There," Don said, stroking her hair—

—like Susan stroked Aune's!

In his embrace, she seemed to diminish from an eleven year old to a five year old—to the husk of a

111

person that Aune was.

After a few minutes, she regained control and, leaning back, looked at her father. The release of emotion made her body shake, reminding her of the chills that came in the night.

"When I fell," she said, her voice congested, "when I banged my knee on the rocks and was getting stung, I—I *saw* something."

"The fall must've knocked it right out of you," Don said.

"No!" Beth's voice was suddenly loud and firm. She sat up, clenching her fists as she tried to dissolve the image rising again in her mind. "No! When I was on the ground with the hornets stinging me all over, I couldn't move! I couldn't get up."

"Hey, take it easy, Punk."

"My foot was caught, and, when I looked to see what was holding me, I saw a—a bony hand, reaching out from under the stones, holding me!" Shivers shook her body, but she shied away from her father when he made a move to hug her again; she had to deal with this herself, not melt into him!

A chill raced up Don's back when he heard Beth's words, and he stared at her, surprised to find that he had nothing to say. Beth trembled with the effort of telling him what she had seen.

"Right out from underneath that grout pile—that bony hand just held me there, wouldn't let go! And the hornets were all over me! Stinging!"

Don fought to control himself. "Pun'kin," he said evenly, "you *know* that's impossible. You were probably—you *had* to be freaking out with those hornets swarming you like that. When I found you, your foot was caught under a root."

He hoped she didn't hear the lie in his voice; her foot hadn't been caught under anything as far as he

112

could remember.

"That's all it was—just a root. Maybe it *looked* like something else, but—"

"I *know* what I saw," Beth said, shaking her head, her red cheeks glistening with tears. "I *didn't* imagine it!" Her face twisted with the tortured expression of someone seriously questioning her own sanity.

Don cleared his throat before talking, not wanting his concern about the trauma she's been through to show. "Anytime someone's in a situation like that—where they're panicking and in pain—their mind can play weird tricks on them."

Beth's gaze became distant as she replayed the memory, trying as bravely as she could to face the terror of that black, bony hand holding her ankle. She could feel its icy grip and the nipping heat of the hornet stings. A shiver racked her.

"It was bony—and old," she said, her voice fighting for control as she brought the image into clearer focus. By dealing with it head on, she hoped to blunt the power it had over her.

Don followed her gaze and saw that she was staring at her wooden doll propped up on the bureau.

"It was like it had been there hundreds—*thousands* of years, just waiting—waiting—for me."

Don sat on the edge of the bed, watching her. He knew—even then—that, no matter what had *really* happened, she was working it out—for herself. She wasn't the five year old he had imagined; she really *was* eleven, going on twelve, and for the first time, she had to deal with it on her own.

He took a Kleenex from the dispenser on her bedstand and handed it to her. She carefully dabbed away the tears that had spilled from her eyes. He felt a sadness, too, knowing that the gulf that separated them, no matter what happened, would continue to

113

grow simply because she was growing up.

"Look. Pun'kin," he said, standing up. Even using the nickname he had used since she was born sounded foreign now. "You need your rest. Why don't you try to get some shut-eye? Maybe this afternoon you could come downstairs and watch a bit of TV. Even Monty Hall's gotta be better than your bedroom wall."

Beth nodded, took another tissue, and blew her nose. "Umm, yeah. I'm pretty wiped out," she said as she settled back down onto the bed.

"Have a good rest," Don said. "And let me know if you need anything, O.K.?"

"O.K."

Don moved toward the door and stepped out into the hallway. He eased the door shut and then stood there a moment, trying to forget the last thing he saw in Beth's bedroom—that damned wooden doll, propped up on the bureau, looking at him . . . looking at him.

II

The next day was clear and bright with enough of a breeze so it didn't feel too hot. Not quarry weather. Don, huffing and straining with the relic of a wooden ladder he'd found in the barn, went around to the back of the house to go up onto the roof and, for starters, clean out the chimney. Max pranced around him in wide circles and almost got knocked down when Don swung the ladder around and leaned it against the peeling wooden gutter. He kicked two divots in the ground with his heel and jiggled the ladder into place.

"I promise myself a brand-new aluminum ladder when it comes time to reroof," he said, addressing Max, who had decided to sprawl out in the shade.

Shielding his eyes from the sun, he looked up at the weather-beaten chimney. Actually, he was surprised to see how well it had lasted. It would be a simple job to replace a few of the top courses of bricks and repoint the rest, down to the roofline. He decided to climb up and check the job out before getting the rope and length of chain he'd need. He started up, hand over hand.

Although it was still early morning, the roof was already warming up on the sun side. Moisture from the night steamed away in faint, smoky plumes. At gutter level, Don swung one foot, then the other onto the roof and, crouching low, started up the incline toward the chimney. Grit from the weathered tarpaper rolled underneath his feet like tiny ball bearings, and he almost slipped once or twice.

At last he straddled the peak of the roof and, clutching onto the chimney, looked out over his land. The field that rolled down away from the house toward the road still glistened with dew. It looked like a vast expanse of gray velvet shot through with spikes of green. In the alder woods beyond the stream, tatters of mist were shrinking away, ghostlike, as the day warmed. Several finches twittered in the maple trees by the front door.

Don took several minutes to enjoy the view before turning to the work at hand. He was in no rush; that, after all, was one of the reasons they'd moved to Maine.

Close up, the chimney looked no worse than he had expected. A few bricks had started to powder away, but the flashing, stained moss green, was undamaged. What surprised him most was the thick layer of creosote that lined the inside of the chimney. At least an inch thick, he guessed. Just *waiting* for a chimney fire come winter if he didn't take care of it now.

Leaning his face over the opening, he reached down inside and scraped with his fingertips. From deep inside, he heard chunks of soot and ash fall with faint, rustling sounds. The sound was distorted by the tubing effect of the chimney. He was just turning to go down, seal off the fireplace in the living room, and get started when someone inside the house let out a sharp scream.

"Jan?" he called down the chimney, his voice reverberating. Tension wound up his back.

Was it Beth? Hadn't she said she was going to lie on the couch and read for a while?

From inside the house, the screaming continued, rising higher. Cupping his hands to his mouth, Don yelled, "Hey! What is it?"

He turned and started toward the ladder in an awkward, crablike crawl down the slope of the roof. He was swinging his feet onto the top rung of the ladder when Beth burst out the back door. Max jumped up and started barking, thinking she had come out to play with him.

"What's going on?" he shouted as he took the ladder two steps at a time. Halfway down, he jumped the rest of the way, and the shock of landing sent a burning sting though his legs.

"What did you do up there, Daddy?" Beth asked. She had her hands to her mouth and was looking at him, eyes wide and hysterical. "God! It's gross!"

"What the hell is it?" he asked frantically. "Are you all right?"

Beth nodded her head, still staring at him, bug-eyed over her clenched fists. "It's gross! A whole bunch of bats came out of the chimney and into the living room!"

"Wha—?" He turned when he heard the back door slam open, and Jan ran out into the yard. Max started another round of barking.

"Jesus! Don," Jan said. Her face was chalky. "You must've knocked down a whole nest of them. They're all over the living room."

"I don't think bats have nests," Don said. He eyed the back door cautiously, then looked both at Jan and Beth. "Neither one of you got bit or anything, did you?"

They both shook their heads. "They scared me stiff," Beth said, still looking shaken and pale except for the inflamed hornet stings on her face and arms. The bright sunlight made her squint.

"But you're O.K.?" Don asked.

Beth nodded.

"What are you going to do?" Jan asked. She had her eyes fastened on the living room window, looking for any sign of the bats. "You've got to get rid of them."

"As long as nobody got bit," Don said as he started toward the door. "There's a broom in the kitchen I can use to swat 'em. How many were there?"

"I didn't stay around to count them," Jan said. "Maybe six or seven."

"Good thing Max wasn't inside," Don said, his hand resting on the door latch. "He would've gone nuts and tried to bite 'em." Looking at Jan, he added, "You want to come and help?"

Jan smiled and shook her head. "Not unless you've got a Louisville Slugger. This is your ball game."

"Thanks a lot," he said. He swung the door open and stepped into the kitchen. From the pantry he took Jan's brand-new broom and, gripping the handle, cautiously walked from the kitchen through the dining room and into the living room. The room received little of the morning sun, and the lights were off, so the only illumination was the TV's flickering blue glow. David Hartman was just concluding a chat with Carl Sagan.

For a moment, Don thought the whole thing was a put-on; he didn't see or hear anything as he scanned the dim shadows that filled the corners up at the ceiling. But then, as his eyes adjusted from the glaring sunlight, he caught glimpses of fluttering shadows, darting about the room. His ears prickled, listening, until he heard the high-pitched, chittering squeaks of the bats as they dove in crazy spirals.

Jan had followed him into the house and was crouching in the doorway. "Careful, hon. Don't let one of them bite you. Bats can have rabies."

"I know, I know," he said impatiently. "Why don't you go and wait outside with Beth?"

Jan grunted and, still keeping her low crouch, walked out, leaving Don alone with the bats. Don watched as they wheeled in erratic circles against the dingy ceiling, their wingtips slapping with a machine-gun rhythm he thought kept time with his own rapid pulse.

The broom handle was slippery in his hand as he waited, knees bent, poised to strike. When one of the bats—he still wasn't sure how many there were—fluttered by, he swung in a wide arc—and missed.

"Shit!" he muttered, adjusting his grip and stance. He edged along the wall, studying their flight and trying to estimate when to swing. Another bat swooped down, and Don watched—tensed and waiting—and then swung. The straw tips of the broom brushed against the bat and knocked it off balance enough to send it skittering to the floor.

Don darted forward and brought the broom edge first down hard. The first bat died with a short, rising squeal, and Don smiled with satisfaction.

It was more instinct than anything else that warned

him there was something behind him. He spun, bringing the broom up out of reflex. The bat glanced off the wooden handle just above Don's hands, and fell, stunned. Don looked at the animal, scrambling on the floor, its beady black eyes staring up at him. Its small mouth, a wrinkled parody of a human mouth, worked into a grimace, showing a row of pearly teeth.

Without thinking, Don stepped forward, bringing his foot down on the animal. The soft body exploded with a muffled pop and a curlicue of blood shot across the floor. This bat had no chance to squeal before it died.

Hunching his shoulders, Don backed up to the wall and watched the remaining bats, trying to get an accurate count. They moved so swiftly and erratically he couldn't be sure; he thought there were only three, maybe four more. The flickering light from the TV didn't help, but the wall switch was too far away.

Another bat fluttered overhead, and Don swung and missed. The bat, sensing the motion, banked sharply and darted back. Don dodged to the left, brought the broom around, and this time made solid contact. With another sickening squeal, the bat pinwheeled and then slammed into the wall where it left a dark red blot before it fell to the floor, dead.

By the time he had dropped the third bat, Don was seeing this as more of a game, and he crouched, broom poised, waiting for another swing. Unless there were bats resting somewhere—maybe clinging upside down to the curtains—there were only two left, flying high, their wings slap-slapping the ceiling.

Don eased over to the couch and waited until one was overhead, and then timed his swing perfectly. The broom whistled through the air and made solid contact. Don shouted, "Home run!" as the bat careened off the mantel and plopped to the floor. It tried to scramble away, dragging one useless wing and leaving a long streak of blood behind, but Don slammed the broom down, and the bat died.

When he looked up, he couldn't see the—hopefully—last bat. He tensed, listening for the flutter of wings over the sound of an ad for Tide, but there was nothing—nothing. From where he stood, he extended the broom handle and snapped off the TV. In the dimness, he saw—or *thought* he saw—something dart across his line of vision toward the window. Reaching behind him, he snapped on the overhead light and, broom braced like a battle-ax, strode over to the window.

"Come on, you little bastard," he said softly as he began to probe the curtains with the broom. He jumped back, surprised, when he saw it—the tiny winged mammal crawling its way head first down the curtain. He shivered involuntarily, watching the bat's lurching motion; then he brought the broom up over his head and swung down viciously. The bat squealed and dropped to the floor, and Don finished him off swiftly.

There were no more bats flying but, before calling Beth and Jan back in, Don circled the living room, probing behind furniture. At last, convinced there were no more, he dropped the bloody broom and collapsed onto the couch. His breath came in ragged gulps, and sweat ran down his forehead and into his eyes. He shivered when he looked at the small brown bodies and the bloody smears marking where each bat had died.

"Is it safe to come in now?" Jan asked, peering around the door jamb.

Don nodded and sighed deeply as he wiped his face with his shirt sleeve. "There's a bit of cleaning up to do, though."

Jan glanced at the carnage and wrinkled her nose. "I hope you didn't get blood on the sofa."

"It'll wash out if I did," he said.

"You ought to get right on it before it dries," Jan said.

Don looked at her, exasperated. "I'm the great white hunter, you don't expect me to—"

"Well," Jan said sharply, "you can't expect Beth to do it, and"—she glanced at her watch, and for the first time, Don noticed that she was dressed up— "I've got to get my make-up on. My appointment with Lower Bay Realty is less than an hour from now."

"Jeez, it looks like I'm having *all* the fun today, huh?" Don said. He looked at the splotches of blood covering the walls and floor and felt a wave of disgust.

"Really, Don," Jan said, "I'd help you if I didn't have this job interview."

"You aren't using this as an excuse to go downtown shopping, are you?"

One corner of Jan's mouth crinkled into a smile. "Well, I'll be in Ogunquit anyway, so I thought I might take a little time to look around."

"Sure. Sure," Don said, too wrung out to argue.

Jan turned to go but then added, "You know, you ought to block off the fireplace before you finish cleaning it. We don't want soot—or anything else— coming into the living room."

"Thanks for the advice," Don said, standing slowly and stretching his arms over his head. The muscles in his shoulders were beginning to bunch up from the tension he had felt, fighting the bats.

Jan went down the hallway toward the bathroom. "Oh, one other thing," she called to him. "I don't care how good she says she's feeling, I *don't* want Beth getting up there on the roof with you. O.K.?"

"Sure," Don replied as he bent to pick up the

121

broom. He was walking slowly toward the kitchen to get water and cleanser when Jan hustled past him and dashed out to the car.

"Have a good interview," he called from the kitchen doorway.

Jan waved, started up the car, and drove off, leaving a plume of dust along the driveway. Don saw Beth standing in the shadow of the barn and waved her over.

"You can come in now," he said, but she shook her head.

"If it's no problem, Dad, maybe you could get my book, and I could read a little outside."

"Sure. Sure," Don said.

III

"Why do I even bother?" Jan said aloud, slamming her fist on the steering wheel. She was driving along Route One heading toward home after one of the most humiliating experiences of her life.

She had sat in Mr. Howard P. Woodward's air-conditioned office for no more than two minutes before she realized the job she was applying for had already been filled. After another ten minutes of stumbling over questions—questions she knew the answers to but couldn't dredge up—she wanted nothing more than to see the last of Mr. Howard P. Woodward. The man chain-smoked cigars the size of cucumbers, and, air conditioning or not, she needed fresh air.

Rage boiled up within her as she drove past a seemingly endless array of motels, fast-food joints, flea markets, and yard sales. Sure, real estate in Rhode Island was just as competitive—maybe more competitive than it was in the Ogunquit area—and she'd been damned good at it. So why—*why* did she choke up and stumble on the most basic questions? The one lead she'd had was now down the drain and, just as well, as far as she cared.

She was more than halfway home when she decided that, maybe, it was too early to give up. There were plenty of other real estate offices. And, anyway, Ogunquit was a summer town. Who said she *had* to work in real estate again? There just might be an opening working in one of the clothing shops or something else. If college kids hadn't snapped up every job in town, she'd be content to work at something—anything—until the right job came along.

She snapped on her turn signal, slowed, and pulled to a stop in the gravel breakdown lane. She waited for a break in the traffic, then swung around in a U-turn, and headed back toward town. She drove slowly, glancing at both sides of the road, looking for someplace that looked interesting, something that would be a *fun* summer job. She didn't need the likes of Howard P. Woodward!

After a quick lunch in town and nearly four hours of writing her name and social security number on applications she knew would be in the wastebasket before she made it out to her car, Jan decided to go home. With a "We'll call you if something comes up" her best result at a classy build-your-own ice cream sundae shop, she started back down Route One toward St. Ann's, discouraged and angry.

Just on the Ogunquit town line, on the left, she saw a small restaurant. *The Rusty Anchor* read the pale red letters on the white sign over the door. There were rust streaks where the letters were nailed to the board. In the middle of the small patch of grass out front, with weeds growing where the lawn mower couldn't reach, was a large rusted anchor. How quaint. Jan was almost past the place when she saw the Help Wanted sign taped to the window. Without signaling, she cut across the road, pulled into the parking lot, and cut the engine.

"Last chance Texaco," she muttered under her breath as she dropped the keys into her purse and opened the car door. The parking lot was nearly full—a good sign, she thought, as she walked up the cracked pavement to the front door.

She swung open the door, and the thick smell of fried clams hit her like something solid. That alone almost made her walk back out, but then she saw the small knotty pine tables and booths, filled with people wearing Hawaiian shirts, tank tops, and Bermuda shorts. They all looked slick with suntan oil—or sweat. No air conditioning. The place must feel like hell on a humid August day! She figured it wouldn't hurt to ask about the job and walked up to the cash register.

A woman in a stained pink waitress uniform was rapidly totaling a bill. She moved her lips as she read each item and punched it into the machine. She looked completely bored and slightly hostile.

Jan thought again about leaving and almost turned to go, but the woman looked up and, indicating the far end of the counter, said, "There's a seat open down there."

"Hello. My name's Janis Inman." Jan held out her hand to the other woman, noticing that her nametag read *Carol*. "I saw the Help Wanted sign in the window and was wondering if I might speak to the manager."

"He ain't here," Carol said as she took a twenty-dollar bill from a customer and began counting back his change. Without looking at Jan, she added, "You can see we're pretty busy now."

"Will he be back soon?" Jan asked. "Or should I drop by tomorrow?"

She found herself hoping Carol would tell her to come back tomorrow because it'd be just as easy not to return. Looking at Carol's haggard expression, Jan was beginning to feel pretty wilted herself. When it seemed Carol was ignoring her, she turned to leave.

"I dunno, for sure," Carol said. She slammed the register drawer shut and held her hand out for the next customer's bill. "You can fill out an application I s'pose. He might be back in a bit."

"Sure," Jan said, placing her purse on the counter and beginning to dig for a pen. "I swear to heaven, this is the last time I'm writing my social security number today," she muttered to herself, but, when she looked up, Carol was smiling at her as she held out the single blue-printed application form.

"Why don't you sit over there?" Carol asked. "I'll get you a glass of water unless you want a Pepsi or somethin'." She went back to punching keys on the register.

"Water'll be fine," Jan said as she eased down the aisle toward the one open seat at the counter. She wanted to tear the application to shreds when she saw the space for her social security number, but she had to smile when Carol slid a glass of water to her and said, "There yah go, honey."

Jan downed the glass of water greedily and then began filling out the application. Just because she was so damned sick of filling in her previous jobs, she left off any mention of her last two positions as a real estate agent. She figured she'd just tell the manager of—what was the name? *Muddy Rudder*? No, *The Rusty Anchor*. She'd just tell him she'd been home with the kids for the last several years.

When she was finished and brought the application

back to the register, she was surprised to see another woman there. Carol was at the far end of the restaurant serving a table of Ratt and Ozzy T-shirted teenagers.

"You wanna talk with Dale?" the woman asked. Her nametag read *Sally*. She had short brown hair, and she didn't look nearly as dragged as Carol.

"He isn't in, is he?" Jan asked hopefully. The more she thought about it, the more she knew she had no intention of working here even if she was offered a job.

"Sure. He's out back," Sally said. "I'll buzz him." She reached under the edge of the counter and pressed a hidden button.

"Carol said he wasn't here," Jan said, still hopeful Sally was wrong.

Sally smiled, glanced over at Carol, and said under her breath, "One thing I gotta tell you, Carol's a nice lady, but more days than not, she ain't even sure *she's* here."

"Oh," Jan said. She stood back from the counter to let another customer come up to pay. Waiting for the manager, she took a moment to check the place over more carefully. Both Carol and Sally were kept busy, chasing back and forth between the tables, the central horseshoe counter, the kitchen, and the register. If there was a pattern to their movements, she couldn't discern it; it did look, though, that they were *where* they were needed *when* they were needed. Most of the customers seemed intent on eating—no frills here at *The Rusty Anchor*—but they seemed satisfied with the food and the service. Overall, Jan thought, the place wasn't *too* tacky. With air conditioning and a little less noise, it would be just fine.

The double doors leading to the kitchen swung open, and a man leaned out, looking around until he caught Jan's eye. He smiled, nodded, and walked around the counter over to her.

"Oh, Christ," Jan muttered. Thick, curly black hair framed a slightly plump but good-looking face. His eyes were a startling blue, and the deep cleft in his chin made Jan wonder how he shaved without cutting himself.

Maybe he cuts it deeper, she thought, to keep looking cute. He probably thinks it drives the women wild.

"Hello. I'm Dale Jackman," he said, extending one hand to her while the other hand toyed with the gold chain and small spoon hanging around his neck. His smile displayed a row of wide, pearly teeth. His light-blue silk shirt was opened halfway, exposing a thick mat of chest hair.

"My name's Jan. Jan Inman. Pleased to meet you." She let her hand drop to her side, then handed him the application.

"I own and operate this gorgeous tourist trap," Dale said, sweeping his well-muscled arm around to encompass the restaurant. "Now tell me—*honestly*— do you really want to work in a joint like this?"

It was a unique opening, Jan admitted to herself, and, even though she resisted it, she found herself thinking he did have some charm.

"I'm looking for something—just for the summer," Jan said, cursing herself for acting and sounding like a nervous schoolgirl. "If you had a—"

"An opening?" Dale said. He was silent as he quickly scanned Jan's application; then he smiled and nodded. "Well, we can't really say you've got a helluva lot of experience in the fast-food business, can we?"

Jan shrugged. "Well, I was pretty much tied down at home for the last few years."

"Kids?" Dale said, his eyebrows rising.

"One, a daughter. She's going on twelve."

127

Dale chuckled. "Well, I've got to say, you don't look like you're old enough to have a daughter who's almost a teen-ager."

Jan flushed and mumbled a weak, "Thanks," for the off-hand compliment. She was surprised at herself for letting herself be intimidated so easily, but her confidence grew as she began to realize that, beneath the cocky level, Dale was probably a quite insecure and vulnerable man.

"To tell you the truth, Jan, I'm not really looking for any help right now. And if I was, I'd be wanting someone who had a bit of experience in restaurant work, if you know what I mean."

Jan shrugged and almost said something about being too busy at home to work, but she thought better of it.

"I'm sorry I've wasted your time," she said, blushing.

"Of course," Dale continued, "something could come up—someone might quit or—to tell you the truth—the new kid I hired, college kid from Orono, she might not cut the mustard. There might be something in a week or so."

"Oh—"

Dale flashed her a wide grin, and a smoldering look came into his eyes. "I might be able to work you in on a part-time basis—least at first."

"Sure," Jan said, thinking she sounded just a wee bit *too* anxious and hoping Dale didn't take her wrong. "We just moved up from Rhode Island, and I really could use some extra money." She took a quick glance around the restaurant and added, "I think I'd like working here."

She was angry with herself for lying, and she wondered why she was acting like this; certainly she wasn't bowled over by Dale Jackman's too-slick charm!

"Does your husband have a job?" Dale asked. "Is that why you moved here?"

"He'll be teaching shop at York High this fall," Jan said. "We're fixing up an old house, first—old family property."

"I see," Dale said, nodding as he twiddled with the gold chain around his neck. His eyes narrowed to sleepy slits, and the tip of his tongue darted across his upper lip.

Is he coming on to me? Jan wondered, feeling almost frantic. It had been *years* since a man had looked at her like that, and it seemed so obvious he was playing a line out to her. She wasn't sure how seriously she should take the sexual undercurrent she thought was there.

—Thought? No, it was there. No doubt!

How much getting—and keeping—the job would depend on how receptive she was to Dale? Certainly, she wouldn't—had *never* even thought about—being unfaithful to Don. But the idea that a man like Dale, young, handsome, obviously experienced with women, would even play at coming on to her gave her an excited tingling in her stomach.

"Well, you'd be working evenings, and we're usually not out of here until eleven-thirty, sometimes midnight, on weekends. How do you think your husband would react to that?"

"If the money was good enough, I don't think he'd mind," Jan said, perhaps a bit too quickly, she thought. She didn't want to give Dale the impression that she and her husband had money, or any other, problems.

But do we? she wondered. Do we have problems? Not in the past, certainly, but ever since the move to Maine . . .

"As long as it's only a few nights a week," she added lamely, having to pull back her wandering thoughts.

Dale's smile widened even more, if that was possible, and he held his hand out to her. "Well, it's been real nice talking with you, Jan," he said, shaking her hand and, Jan noticed, holding it a bit longer than was necessary.

"Uhh, thank you . . . Dale," she said.

"I've got your number here, and I'll give you a buzz, maybe in a week or so, if something comes up, all right?"

"O.K. Great," Jan said. She clutched her purse tightly as she made her way to the door and out to her car. It wasn't until she was driving back up Route One toward St. Ann's that doubts began to assail her. How would she broach all of this to Don—that, instead of landing a spot with a real estate agency, she was probably going to spend the summer, at least, slinging hash at what, to be fair, was little better than a greasy-spoon restaurant. She *knew* he wouldn't want her working there, and she was going to have to force the issue.

"But why?" she asked herself aloud.

Sure, the extra money would be nice. She could sweeten it by saying that what she made at *The Rusty Anchor* would go toward getting Beth a horse. And, sure, getting out of the house a few nights a week would be good for her. But—and she didn't want to admit this to herself but, had to—the bottom line was, she *had* been charmed by Dale Jackman. It did the old ego, rounding the bend into thirty-eight years old, some good to have a man come on to her a bit. And certainly Dale didn't really mean anything by it . . . and even if he *did*, Jan knew she'd never, *never* cheat on Don. It just wasn't part of her constitution to do something like that.

But, she thought with a twinge of guilt, it was almost as if she had played along with Dale, *wanting* him to come on to her. The idea of actually following through terrified her, but she had to admit a certain thrill in the flirting game they had played.

"It'll never go any further than that," she told herself, gripping the steering wheel firmly, but a corner of her mind warned her that the tone of how she and Dale related had been set. If she *did* get the job there and if it *did* go any further . . .

"Naw," she said aloud, laughing; she'd heard all about Ogunquit. "He's probably gay, anyway."

IV

Don spent most of the next morning working in the cellar. He had finished cleaning the chimney the day before without further adventures with bats, but the time on the roof had convinced him that they had to get the reshingling done before winter.

He'd been a little upset when Jan announced she might be waitressing at *The Rusty Anchor*, but then he figured it would take her just a day or two to see that there was no glory working in a place like that. She'd quit within three days of starting, he was positive.

He leaned against the old workbench—maybe so old that Toivo Kivinen had made it—and the punky wooden legs wobbled whenever he shifted the chain saw he was oiling and sharpening. It was about time he cut down that apple tree outside Beth's window. After that he figured he'd head into town and check the prices for shingles.

Jan was outside, trying to get her garden planted. With Beth's help, although that didn't last long

131

because the sunlight still hurt her eyes, she laid out a small patch. It was late in the season so she figured she'd be lucky to get a few rows of beans and lettuce. Next year, she vowed, she'd do three or four times more.

Don kept his eyes on the dismantled chain saw and the repair manual, which he kept open with the weight of a large, rusted monkey wrench. Now and again, he noticed a shadow slide by the cellar window as Jan went to the house for something or other. He was concentrating on putting everything back together in the proper way.

He traced the words and diagrams in the book, his finger leaving a track of oily smudge. When he heard a faint tapping on the cellar window, he jumped, startled, and turned around, knocking a box of screws onto the floor.

"Hon?" Jan called, bending low to look through the filmy pane. The cheap glass distorted her features.

Cursing softly as he bent to scoop up the fallen screws, Don called out, "Yeah, what?"

"Honey, I can't get that ornery Rototiller started," Jan said. Her voice carried faintly through the glass, making it sound as though she were further away than she was.

Don muttered another curse and ran his oily fingers through his hair. "I'm kind of in the middle of things here."

"Couldn't you at least come out and help me get started?"

"I got the smallest one they had," Don said, hoping his irritation didn't show. "And we started it up at the Ag-Way. There shouldn't be any trouble." He was surprised how flat and muffled his voice sounded, and he cast a nervous glance around the cellar.

"Come on," Jan said, sounding so pitiful Don relented. He wiped his hands on an old cloth and went up the cellar steps and outside.

"Thanks a lot, hon," Jan said when she saw him walking across the field toward her. She had looked radiant and fresh, starting out this morning dressed in cut-off jeans, plaid shirt, and bandanna holding her hair back. Now she was looking a bit frazzled as she scrunched down, peering at the machine, pretending she could figure it out.

Don squinted up at the brilliant sun, grateful for a breath of fresh air after the dankness of the cellar. Beth was sitting in the shade of the barn, and Max was lolling in the hole he had dug at the end of the driveway. Don waved to Beth, but she seemed so intent on playing with her doll that she didn't notice.

"It's a real heavy beast if you ask me," Jan said. She wiped her forehead with her hand, leaving a muddy smear.

Without a word, Don placed his foot on the engine housing, gripped the pull cord, and gave it a hard tug. The Rototiller gave a congested cough but didn't start. After several tries, Don was sweating and muttering curses. Finally, after one last shoulder-wrenching yank, he stood back and gave the Rototiller's tire a savage kick.

"Goddamned thing! It started up nice and easy at the Ag-Way!"

"Don, watch your language," Jan cautioned, glancing in Beth's direction, but she seemed not to have noticed.

"Well, you'd think these things would—"

"Maybe there's just something loose," Jan said, looking at the Rototiller with grave concern.

Don unscrewed the gas cap and, bringing his eye close to the opening, peered inside. "Hey," he said, "I

133

can't see in here. You got a match?"

"Very funny," Jan said.

"You did fill it with gas, didn't you?"

Jan shook her head. "I—I thought you did."

"I told you," Don said, with sudden iron in his voice, "that this was your gig."

"I'll get some," Jan said, backing away. "There's some up in the barn, isn't there? For the lawn mower?"

Don nodded and reached out to slap her on the butt when she turned and dashed across the field.

Hands on his hips, Don watched her go, then he turned to Beth and called out, "Hi yah, Pun'kin."

Beth looked up and shifted uneasily as her father walked over to her. Her smile wavered and faded, and her hand closed tightly on her wooden doll as she rubbed out the pattern of concentric circles she had been drawing in the dirt.

"What are you doing there?" Don asked, looking down at the traces of lines still visible. "Writing love letters in the sand?"

"No . . . nothin'," Beth said. "Just playing." There was an odd tightness in her throat.

Don's smile froze when he saw the white-knuckled grip she had on her doll. Kneeling down beside her, he looked directly into her eyes, and it bothered him that she wasn't able to look back at him squarely for very long. There seemed to be an undercurrent of distrust that he wanted to get rid of.

"Pun'kin, are you feeling all right?" he asked, his voice soothing. Something was bothering her, that was for sure.

"I'm O.K., Daddy," she answered, but there was no conviction in her voice. She tried again to look at him, but her pale blue eyes flickered and drifted toward the open field.

"Well, you don't look so hot still," Don said. "You remember what the doctor said, that the medication might make you kind of woozy for a few days."

"I'm O.K. Really," Beth said.

"Hon, are we gonna get to work?" Jan called. She had returned and was standing beside the Rototiller, the heavy gas can pulling one shoulder down.

"*We*?" Don said. He stood up slowly, his eyes focusing on the circles Beth had drawn and partially erased. "Take it easy, Punk. You know, you shouldn't overdo it for a few days more."

""Yeah. Sure, Dad."

With the gas tank full, it took only two quick pulls to get the machine going. At first it sputtered and shot out little puffs of black smoke, but with a minor adjustment Don got it running smoothly.

"This lever here will put it in gear," Don instructed Jan. "This will make it go faster or slower." He held onto the handles as though they were motorcycle apehangers. "So hold the blades off the ground and—" He engaged the gears, and the spinning blades bit into the ground, turning up thick, rich loam. In seconds his feet were buried.

"Where're you headed, China?" Jan asked with a laugh.

Don dropped his weight onto the handlebars to free the blades. It took more effort than he thought it would to get the machine moving forward, but once he got the right amount of push, the blades folded the soil out nicely. The sound of metal grinding on buried stones set his teeth on edge. By the time he made it to the end of the garden, he thought he had the knack of it.

"Here you go," he said, shifting the gear into neutral and waving Jan over. "It handles nicely, once you get the feel for it."

"It looked to me like you were on a buckin' bronco," Jan said. She eased up to the machine and took the handles, the machine clattering and vibrating her arms. She turned around and headed the machine back along Don's initial furrow.

"Watch it now," Don warned her. "Don't let that horse run away with you."

Jan shifted the gears. The blades started turning, and she was off. The grim determination on her face made Don chuckle as he watched her jockey the mechanical beast down the length of the garden, turn, and head back.

"Not so bad—I guess," she called out over the sound of the machine.

Don started back up to the house, grateful to leave behind the churning of the Rototiller and the scraping sound of grinding rocks. Before he went inside to go back down cellar, he turned once more to look at Jan. He saw her mouth move as she yelled something to him, but he couldn't hear.

"I have my own work to do," he yelled as he pointed to the cellar window. He knew she didn't hear him.

V

As Don worked at the bench, the distant drone of the Rototiller lulled him. The tip of his file made quick, rasping sounds, like short, gasping breathing, as he ran it along the chain saw links. The gloom of the cellar was pierced only by the single sixty-watt bulb hanging from the ceiling by his left shoulder. Don whistled a lazy, tuneless song as he worked.

After a while, his eyelids began to feel heavy. A whooshing pulse sounded in his ears, and Don's head started to droop. Suddenly he jerked his head up and, blinking, looked around. A strange chill crept over him, and he felt vaguely as though he were dreaming. He tried to force himself to concentrate, but the monotony of sharpening each link and the numbing white noise of the Rototiller made the weird sense of dissociation continue.

Rising tension uncoiled like a cold snake in his stomach. With a deep breath that caught, he focused again on what he was doing.

—Standing by the old workbench . . .

—Oily rag . . . file . . . chain in hand . . .

—To cut down that apple tree that bothers Beth so much . . .

Suddenly he jumped and turned around, having felt a cold rush when he had heard a hissing whispering behind him. Staring into the dark corners of the cellar, he waited—tensed—for the sound to repeat. The chain rattled like a marble rolling down a metal tube as he slowly lowered it onto the workbench. The dreamlike quality prevailed as he walked across the cellar floor slowly, his head cocked to one side, listening.

First he went over to the cellar window, thinking it might have been a pane of loose glass vibrating from the sound of the Rototiller, but, as he stood there listening, the sound came again from behind him. This time, though, he thought he got a fix on it and headed over to the space under the stairs. Once he was there, the snakelike hiss seemed instead to come from behind him, from the other side of the cellar.

Brushing aside cobwebs, he prowled from one end of the cellar to the other, peering into the gloomy, dank corners. And every time he heard the sound—so faint, just on the edge of hearing—it seemed to be behind him. Under the workbench—from inside the old coal bin—behind the chimney—over by the ancient fuse box—like a will o' the wisp, it led him back and forth across the hard-packed dirt floor.

Again the sound came from over near the coal bin, and Don dashed over to it. For once, the sound didn't vanish or seem to move. As Don listened, the sound grew louder—cold hissing that seemed to take on the quality of words. Certainly not words Don could understand, but he thought there was a definite, almost chantlike pattern.

Don pressed his ear to the cold stone wall of the cellar and listened. He ran his fingers along the crumbling mortar joints of the granite block wall. The rocks Toivo Kivinen had used to make the foundation were a variety of shapes and sizes—probably scrap rock from the quarry, Don thought.

In the center of the wall directly above the coal bin, there was an opening at ground level. It had been used as a coal chute but now was boarded over. Don wedged his fingers under the topmost board and pulled. The rusted nails held so he gave up the effort, not wanting to make more work for himself.

The most curious aspect he noticed was that the sound increased in intensity whenever he touched the cellar wall. It was as if it somehow resonated through his hand, increasing in strength. One stone in particular caught his attention. It was a tall, narrow block—faintly familiar in shape—that went from the dirt floor to the ceiling joist above.

"Odd place for so much support," he said aloud. He touched the stone, running his fingers lightly over the surface, and the whispering sound suddenly crackled as though charged with electricity.

Don stood back, studying the stone. The shape . . . the shape. What did it remind him of?

When he touched the stone again, the sound increased until he was positive it was somebody talking. Had Beth left the TV on upstairs and the audio was, somehow, being transmitted through the foundation?

"Beth? Pun'kin? Are you up there?" he called out. Even yelling didn't completely drown out the hissing sound that now most definitely sounded like a foreign language or gibberish.

He realized he had been holding his breath and let it out slowly before taking a long pull of the cellar's cool air. A clammy sheen of sweat covered his face and neck.

He waited, listening, but the whispering sound was fading . . . fading . . . and then it suddenly stopped as though someone had thrown a switch. At that same moment, he noticed that the sound of the Rototiller had stopped, too.

"Pun'kin, are you up there?" he called. He kept his gaze fixed on the cellar ceiling, and a knot of tension tightened in his stomach.

Nothing—nothing at all. The sudden silence filled the cellar with a watery emptiness.

Cautiously, he eyed the dark recesses of the coal bin, thinking it would be a lovely place for a family of rats to nest. If there were bats in the chimney, there could be rats in the cellar. That was the most likely explanation for the sounds he'd heard. He made a mental note to put out a few boxes of D-con just in case the sound hadn't been something vibrating from the sound of the Rototiller.

He was turning back, determined to finish his work on the chain saw, when he heard Jan call out his name. Even with the muffling effect of distance and the cellar walls, he detected the edge in her voice. Sudden panic gripped him—not sure if he feared something had happened to Beth . . . or something worse. He took the cellar steps three at a time and raced outside.

The glare of the sun blinded him momentarily, but

he could see Beth, still sitting in the shade of the barn. He ran over to Jan and, panting heavily, asked, "What? What in blazes is it?"

"Look. Look at that," Jan said, pointing down at the Rototiller blades. Don saw a cream-colored bone sticking up out of the chopped turf. The end was broken off, leaving jagged splinters; thick streaks of loam had stained it the color of dried blood.

"Ah-hah!" Don said, stroking his chin thoughtfully as he leaned over and studied the find. "What we have here is a *bone* in the field!" He knelt down and, like drawing a sword from a sheath, slowly pulled the bone free.

"Don't you want to use my gloves?" Jan asked, wrinkling her nose.

Don shook his head, stood, and examined the bone closely. Holding it under his nose, he sniffed it noisily several times. "This bone is old," he said, nodding his head with pseudoseriousness. He pressed the bone between his thumb and forefinger, and it turned into a mushy paste.

Finally, looking at Jan, he said, "I can't *believe* you called me out here for something like this. All this is is a cow bone—or something."

"It looks too thin to be a cow's bone," Jan offered. She was wringing her hands in front of herself, suddenly embarrassed.

"Well, if it isn't a cow, it's a dog or maybe a deer. I don't know," Don said. "Whatever it is—or *was*, it makes great fertilizer."

"Don't you think it looks a little—quite a lot—like a human leg or arm bone?" Jan said. She leaned closer, inspecting it but then suddenly drew back. "Phew. It sure doesn't smell very good."

Don ran his hand along the length of the bone, watching as drying clumps of soil fell away, hitting the

140

ground with plopping, raindrop sounds.

"Don, remember Aune's son died here," Jan said, her voice suddenly tightening. "What if this is him? What if they buried him out here in the field?"

"Don't be ridiculous. Without a headstone?" Don shook his head but continued to examine the spongy bone.

"Well," Jan said, "do you know where he *is* buried?"

Don shrugged. "No, I don't. I never thought to ask, to tell you the truth."

"Well, maybe we should find out. There has to be some kind of record."

"I suppose Susan would know," Don asked. "Ask her the next time we talk with her."

Jan eased off her work gloves and silently examined the half-dollar-sized blisters rising up on her palms. "Well. What are you going to do with it?" she asked, making an attempt to sound offhand about it.

"I don't know. Maybe let Max gnaw on it a while."

Jan swatted at him with her gloves.

"Or maybe I could—give—it—back—to—who-ever—*owns*—*it!*" He pointed the splintered end at Jan and waved it at her menacingly. *"Give me back my bone. Give me back my b-o-n-e!"*

Jan backed away from him. When he came at her a second time, waving the moldering bone in front of her face, she sidestepped and then turned on him in a rage. "Will you please stop it! For God's sake!"

Don's playful smile suddenly faded. "Hon—I didn't mean—"

"If you're through playing," she said with controlled anger, "I'd like to get my work done before there's nothing left of my hands."

"Hey, you're the one who called me out here," he said. Still holding the bone and slapping it on his leg like a riding crop, he surveyed her work. "It looks like you're pretty much done there."

"I've got the blisters to prove it, too," she said as she bent and gave the starting rope several quick tugs. The machine sputtered but didn't start.

"I'll finish it up if you'd like," Don said.

Jan shook her head, gritted her teeth, and, placing her foot firmly on the Rototiller's housing, gave several more hard pulls. Finally in frustration, she stepped back and said, "Just get the beastly thing going for me and I'll be all set."

Don pulled once on the rope, and the Rototiller roared into life. Jan shook her head with exasperation and muttered, "Men" as she took the handles and popped it into gear. The Rototiller jerked forward, almost out of control, but she pulled it quickly back into line.

"Ride 'em, cowgirl," Don said. He walked along beside her, admiring the control she had. He was thinking about how sexy she looked with that grim set to her jaw when three things happened at once.

Don heard a dull chunking sound as the Rototiller struck a rock or something, and an ice-pick-sharp pain lanced his leg. At the same instant, just as Don dropped the bone and was reaching down to his shin, he heard Beth suddenly let out a scream that sliced razorlike through the deafening, rattling sound of the Rototiller.

He wanted to call out to her, but the only sound he made was a wounded gasp as he crumpled slowly to the ground. He craned his head around to look at Beth.

"Mommy! Mommy!" she cried hysterically, and she was scrambling to her feet, holding her wooden doll over her head. "*Mommy! Mommy!* My doll broke! His hand fell off!"

"Damn, damn, *damn*!" Don said, hissing between his teeth as he rolled over onto his hip and pulled up his pants leg. A purple bruise was already rising on his leg, and a thin line of blood ran down, staining the top of his sock.

Jan switched off the Rototiller and knelt beside him. "What in Christ did you do? Did the tiller blades cut you?"

Don shook his head, gritting his teeth. "It was something it kicked up."

"It looks pretty bad," Jan said, but she was splitting her attention between Don and Beth, who was standing in the shade of the barn, arms over her head and screaming.

"Yeah," Don said, "go see what's the matter with her. I'm all right."

Jan stood, hesitated, then ran across the field toward Beth, who was now walking slowly toward them, her wooden doll held out like an offering on her open hands. Tears were running down her face, but what sent a ripple of fear through Jan was Beth's expression. Beneath the angry red welts of the hornet stings, her face was papery white. Her eyes were wide, coined circles, and her lips paled to a sickly pink.

"He broke," she wailed. "He just broke! I was just sitting there, holding him, and he *broke*!"

"Hey, come on," Jan said as she came up beside her and ran her hand through Beth's hair. "Take it easy. I'm sure Dad can—"

"God almighty!" Don suddenly shouted. "Jan, come here! Quick!"

Jan held her hand up to acknowledge his call, but she took the time to untuck her blouse and gently dab away Beth's tears. Sharp, choking cries jerked Beth's chest.

"Jeez, Jan, will you get over here?"

Jan gave Beth a firm hug; then, with Beth following a pace or two behind, she went over to Don. He was on his knees, scraping furiously at something on the ground. At first, she thought it was a lump of dirt, but, when she looked closer, she saw he was holding something with a mud-caked wrapping.

"Will you take a look at this?" Don said, blinking up at her in amazement.

He carefully unfolded the flaps of the covering. Where dirt and moldy green had been scraped away, they could see glints of copper or bronze. As he unfolded the last flap of covering, they both gasped in astonishment. In the center was a twisted lump—at first, undistinguishable. Wrapped around it was a knot of beads made of what looked like tarnished copper.

Jan blinked and focused and finally registered what Don had found; it was a mummified human hand. It had decomposed to a dull ash black; the fingers were folded in on each other, making it look more like a hawk's talons than anything human. The string of copper beads were looped several times around the wrist bone, which looked as though it had been cut through in one, clean slice.

"Christ," Jan managed to say before she gagged.

"Can you believe this?" Don said with obvious excitement in his voice.

The sourness in Jan's stomach threatened to rush up into her throat, and she turned away, gulping air to fight down her need to vomit. Once she was under control, she looked back at Don's find. What nauseated her most was the way the fingernails—long, yellowed, stained with black streaks—curled back into the wrinkled palm.

"This is what hit me in the leg," Don said as he stood slowly, admiring the find. "The Rototiller dug it

144

up. Just look at it!"

"God, it grosses me out," Jan said, stepping back to keep her distance.

"It's so carefully wrapped, like it was ceremonial or something," Don said. He turned the hand over several times, studying it carefully.

Jan turned to Beth, who was standing at the edge of the garden, her cheeks glistening with tears. "Beth, honey," she said, "would you mind going up to the house?" Turning to Don, she whispered, "The last thing I want her to see is something like that!"

Don nodded agreement. "Pun'kin, we'll be right up." They watched as she went slowly across the field to the house. She called to Max, who pranced over to her, but, halfway there, she turned.

"But my doll! I want Dad to fix my doll," she said. She held out the wooden figure, and they could see the trembling of her lower lip.

The whining of her voice sounded more like a six year old's than an eleven year old's, and Jan completely lost her patience. "You do as I say, right now." She pointed toward the house, and Beth ran the rest of the distance. Max followed her inside.

"It looks like it might be Indian, don't you think?" Don asked, once the screen door had slammed shut behind Beth and Max. "I can't believe this. A human hand, for heaven's sake; and look at this—"

He carefully pried open the clenched fingers just enough to loosen their dead grasp on the beads. But as he pulled on them, the leather thong that held them broke. The beads spilled onto the ground like loose buckshot.

"Maybe you were right," Don said, bending to scoop them up. "Maybe that other bone you found *wasn't* a cow's leg bone after all." He picked up the bone from where he had dropped it when he fell.

Jan shivered and, hugging herself, looked anxiously around the field. "I wonder if there's anyone else buried around here," she said. Just then, a passing cloud covered the sun, plunging them into shadow. A light breeze whistled in the long grass.

Don glanced upward. "Hmm, looks like it might rain soon."

Jan found that her throat couldn't make a sound. She kept staring at the relic, trying to push away the roiling sense of dread it gave her.

"There may have been a graveyard here at one time," Don said.

"I—I'm not sure we should—you know—disturb anything," Jan said, voice trembling.

"You're probably right," Don replied. "We've got to get someone out here who can tell us what this is all about. Maybe we can contact someone at the University of Maine—someone in the anthropology department."

Jan grunted.

"Are you going to finish doing the garden?" Don asked.

Jan looked at him, wanting him to see and respond to her unsettledness, but he was too excited about his find to notice.

"I think it's probably too late, anyway," she said, shaking her head and pulling back a strand of hair. "Next year we can get a good, early start."

Don came closer to her. The desiccated hand rested on the unfolded copper sheet. "Just look at this, though," he said, "The arm bone was cut off—amputated." He held it out to her, and, as she looked at his own hand, she had a fleeting impression that it was stained, not with dirt, but with blood.

"I—I don't know," she said. "I can't tell. Hey, look; I think I'll go up to the house and see how

146

Beth's doing."

"Sure," Don replied as though he barely heard her.

Jan turned to go, then added, "Well, maybe you ought to come along, too. We should wash that cut so it won't get infected."

Don glanced down at his leg. The top of his sock had a thick collar of drying blood, and, looking at it, he suddenly felt the pain blossom.

"Yeah," he said as he carefully folded the copper wrapping back over the mummified hand. "I suppose we should." He limped as he followed Jan up to the house, and he carried his find as though it were a great treasure.

Chapter Five

First-Day Jobs

I

The thick-set, balding man leaned back onto his car, cringing away from Max. "His front end's barking, and his tail end's wagging. Which do I trust?"

"I'd believe the end that could bite," Don said; then he laughed and added, "You don't have to worry 'bout old Max here. Go on, Max. Go lie down!"

Max gave one last token snarl, then trotted off to find some shade. He didn't go far, though, and lay with his head on his paws, watching the strangers who had driven into the dooryard.

"M' name's Earl—Earl Remy. Wife's name's Lou," the man said, indicating the pregnant woman who had waddled around to stand by her husband once Max had pulled back.

Don nodded a greeting, and Jan held her hand out to Lou Remy.

"Krissy? Come on out here and meet our new

neighbors," Earl said, leaning down to shout—louder than necessary, Don thought—into the open car window. "She's kinda shy," Earl added, winking at Don and Jan.

"Krissy here's gotta be 'bout the age of your girl," Earl said. He squinted as he regarded Beth standing in the doorway, her figure indistinct through the screen door. " 'Course, we don't know who we got here in the oven." He patted Lou's watermelon stomach. "Our little surprise package."

"When's the baby due?" Jan asked.

"Not until September," Louise Remy answered in a tired voice.

"Beth will be twelve—tomorrow, actually," Jan said. She waved to Beth to come down and turned back to the Remys.

"Krissy just turned twelve last March," Earl said with obvious pride. "The two of them ought to hit it off just fine. They might's well, 'cause we're your nearest neighbors."

"Are you the folks who live in the red house just past ours?" Jan asked. "It's a nice place."

Earl and Lou both nodded.

"You and Beth'll get along just fine," Don said, "as long as you like horses." Bending down to meet Krissy at eye level, he smiled warmly. The mention of Beth's birthday reminded him that, as busy as he had been, he and Jan hadn't talked any more about getting Beth a horse. He glanced up at Jan to gauge her reaction, but she met him with a blank stare.

Beth came down the walkway slowly and stood between her mother and father while the introductions were made.

"Krissy here just *loves* horses. Don't 'cha, Krissy,"

Earl said, still using his too loud, good-buddy voice that already, in only a few minutes, was wearing thin on both Jan and Don.

"Every Saturday we take her out to Lakeside Ranch, down to North Berwick, for riding. Hey, why not next Saturday? Beth can come along. All 'a yah can, for that matter."

Jan shot Don a look he immediately understood and she said, "I don't know about that, Mr. Remy, we've—"

"Earl. Call me Earl. None of this *mister* shit— uh—stuff!"

"All right, Earl. Anyway, I was saying, we've got so much work to do around here, we hardly get a chance to sit."

Don was nodding rapid agreement. "We're hoping, though, that sometime—soon—we can get a horse. Now that we live in the country—"

"That's right," Earl said, "I heard you was from the city. Where? Connecticut was it?"

"Rhode Island," Jan said softly, not knowing—or caring—if Earl heard. She couldn't help but wonder how anyone in town could know anything about them.

"Well, there's no sense standing here in the hot sun," Don said. "How'd you like to come up to the house for some iced tea?"

"Beer'd be better," Earl said, and he clapped Don on the shoulder as if they'd been war buddies. As they all started up to the house, Earl continued talking, and Jan was beginning to wonder if maybe Lou Remy were mute. Any length of time listening to Earl would surely cause some nerve damage.

"Myself, now," Earl was saying to Don, "I'm a black-powder man. You ever shoot black powder?"

150

Don shook his head. "No, I'm not exactly sure what—"

"Black powder. You know, musket and ball. Gunpowder. Davy Crockett stuff."

"Oh, that," Don said, immediately pushing aside the thought that maybe Earl had been referring to some new form of drug or something. "I don't go in much for hunting. Of course, there wasn't much chance for it, living in Providence."

Jan held the kitchen door open as the Remys stomped into the house. Don could feel her harsh look searing his back. Beth made herself scarce, and Don was going to call her back, but then he figured, if she and Krissy were going to be friends, they'd have to work it out on their own terms.

Jan handed Don and Earl each a Pabst, then took out the pitcher that she'd filled that morning with Nestea. She poured a drink each for Lou and herself. They all sat at the kitchen table, except for Krissy, who said she'd be content with water and stood quietly beside her mother as she drank.

"I ain't talkin' 'bout huntin'," Earl said. "I'm talkin' target shootin'. Why, I have a Kentucky rifle—replica, actually—but it'll make your eyes water."

Don and Jan spent the next two hours listening to Earl Remy go on about most everything—whether he knew what he was talking about or not. Beth and Krissy finally connected, and they spent the time out in the yard, talking about horses mostly. By the time the Remys had left, Jan felt too wrung out to do more than slap together a few sandwiches for supper.

"Remind me," she said between chews of tuna fish, "never to ask them over again—at least not before I buy some cotton for my ears!"

151

II

The next morning—her birthday—Beth awoke early, even before Max, who was curled on the rug at the foot of her bed. Looking out her window, she was momentarily confused until she remembered that her father had—finally—cut down the gnarled apple tree after the Remys had left. The rectangle of clear, blue sky gladdened her, and she felt in some ways like a person who had at last recovered from a long illness.

It had always been a family tradition for her parents to leave her card and present on the kitchen table, so she could see it as soon as she was up. Of course, she had to wait until everyone was downstairs before she could open it. But half the fun—well, maybe a little less than half—was sitting there, looking at the package, and wondering what was inside. She gave Max a good morning pat and then tiptoed downstairs with him close at her heels.

She was surprised to see her father at the kitchen table, a half-empty cup of coffee in front of him.

"Hi, yah, Pun'kin. Happy birthday morning," he said. He was smiling, but Beth thought his eyes held a sleepy worry. He looked as though he hadn't slept all night.

"Hi, Daddy." She looked around, surprised to see that there was no present for her on the table. She was about to say something when he took out the package he had been hiding on his lap beneath the table. The present was wrapped in paper with pictures of horses. The bow, taped to one corner, had begun to unravel.

"I got a little something for you," he said, "but you know—"

"I know, I know," Beth said, nodding. "I have to wait for sleepyhead mom." She took the present from her father and felt an immediate wave of disappointment. She could tell just by the feel that it was a book. The only mystery now was what book was it?

Beth placed her present on the table, then went over to the counter to pop two slices of Wonder-Bread into the toaster. Don got up and refilled his cup while Beth poured herself a glass of orange juice.

"How are you feeling?" Don asked, glancing at her over his shoulder. "It looks like a lot more of the swelling has gone down."

A bit embarrassed, Beth grunted her reply. "Yeah—I feel O.K."

"You've been taking your medicine, haven't you?"

"Of course I have."

The toaster popped up, and Beth was beginning to slap globs of Teddie peanut butter onto it when they heard footsteps on the stairs, and Jan entered the kitchen.

"Mornin', hon," she mumbled, kissing Don on the cheek. "Happy birthday, Beth."

"Thanks. Can I open it now?" Beth asked, picking up the present and giving it an excited shake. It was too heavy to be a Nancy Drew, but all the while she was thinking, Is this all? She carefully undid the ribbon and slit the paper open where it had been taped.

"I might wanna save this," she said. "The pictures are pretty—Oh, wow!" She held up the book so her parents could see it, and this time her excitement was genuine. She read the title aloud, *Your First Horse.* Gee, thanks, Mom—Dad." She went over to them and gave each a hug and kiss.

153

"We thought you might like it," Jan said. She was leaning against the counter, still looking as though she were at least half-asleep.

"You might want to open the card, too," Don said. "Didn't your parents teach you any manners? You should always open the card first."

"Oops—sorry," Beth said. She had been flipping through the book, but now she picked up the envelope and opened it. Inside was a bland unoriginal card and greeting, but when she opened it and saw what was on the inside, she dropped back in her chair, astounded.

Taped to the inside was a cut-out picture of a horse and beneath that was written: "You better read this book fast because, in a week or two, we're going to buy you your *very own horse*! Love and Happy Birthday, Mom and Dad."

"Well—?" Don said, his grin widening.

"I think she's at a loss for words," Jan said, and Don couldn't help but remember last night when, after nearly two hours of discussing the idea, Jan had finally relented and given her O.K.

"I—I just can't believe it," Beth said. "I mean— Oh, I'm just so happy!"

Tears welled out of her eyes, and again she made the rounds, giving hugs and kisses, but this time they were breath-stopping embraces.

"I can't believe it! A horse! For *me*!"

"We figured there was really no reason to wait," Jan said. Only to Don did her voice sound false, but he knew how much convincing he had had to use.

"I just want you to remember one thing. A horse is going to be *a lot* of work. I can help you with the heavy stuff but, if your mother and I end up doing everything, we'll sell him right back. You under-

154

stand?"

Beth nodded in wide-eyed agreement.

"And you can start by taking care of Max, here. It looks like he needs some food and water."

"Don't worry," Beth said. She took a bite of toast and chewed it while she dumped Gravy Train into Max's bowl and then filled it with water. "I'll do everything—*everything*. I'll brush him every day and feed him and make sure he's always got water. Don't worry."

"I know you'll do a good job," Don said, "but slow down; we haven't got him yet. Here, finish your own breakfast."

Beth sat down to work on her toast and juice, but all the while she flipped through her new book, and, as soon as she finished eating, she went into the living room, curled up on the couch, and started reading.

"I'd say she was pretty excited," Don said once he and Jan were alone in the kitchen.

She nestled her cup of coffee in her hand, her gaze drifting out the window over the kitchen sink. "I'd be excited, too, if I were her age and were getting a horse."

"Well," Don said, "I'm just glad you—we decided to go ahead and do it."

"Even if it means I end up waitressing at that greasy spoon?" Jan asked.

Don shrugged. "It'll only be for a while—and only if you want to do it." He was still convinced that she'd last no more than a day or two at that job. He swigged down the last, cold gulp of coffee in his cup, then stood.

"Well, I guess I'll head up to Gorham," he said.

Jan looked at him, her eyebrows arched.

"I called a professor up there yesterday about that hand we found. He wants me to bring it up so he can have a look at it. I should be back by noon or so."

Jan shook her head and ran her hands over her face.

Don grabbed the folded copper sheet, took his car keys from the hook by the door, and went out. The screen door banged shut behind him, cutting off Jan's shouted, "Drive carefully!"

III

Don was nervous as he limped down the corridor of Bailey Hall. The cut on his leg was still hurting; it seemed to hurt more now than it did the day before. To conserve electricity during the summer session, the lights had been turned off in the hallway, so what little illumination there was came from the few open class-room doors. He held the bag containing the folded copper sheet and its contents flat in one hand as he waited outside the door marked *Dr. Roger Mitchell—Anthropology.*

Through the translucent glass he could see a blurred figure moving up and down the length of the room. The sound of Mitchell's telephone conversation was an indistinct buzz; it reminded Don of the time when, as a child, he caught bees in Band-Aid boxes and pretended they were radios.

Several times, he opened the bag and looked in at the twisted mass of copper. The thought crossed his mind that perhaps he should have contacted the state police first. The hand might not be as old as it looked, and it *was* human. But on consideration, the copper beads on the leather string indicated the relic was quite old, and the leathery black skin of the hand *couldn't* be less than several hundred years old.

The conversation in the office stopped suddenly, and Don was about to rap on the window when the door swung open.

"Oh!" Dr. Mitchell said, taken by surprise, "you must be Donald Inman."

"I am," Don said, shaking hands with the professor. Mitchell was a stocky, balding man, dressed in khakis and a forest-green Izod shirt. He wore wire-rimmed glasses that, Don soon noticed, continually slid down the bridge of his nose. His voice had a pleasing resonance like that of a TV newscaster.

"Do you have your find in that bag?" Mitchell asked.

Don nodded.

"Good." Mitchell stepped back into the office, waving to Don to follow him in. "Have a seat—if you can find one."

The office was strewn with books, magazines, pamphlets, and a wild assortment of artifacts—including what looked like a genuine human skull. On the desk, a stack of term papers leaned with more of an incline than Pisa's. Mitchell hastily cleared off one chair for Don and then sat down behind his desk.

"So," Mitchell said—and he sounded to Don more than a little skeptical—"what is it that you want me to take a look at?" He placed an unlit pipe in his mouth and began chewing on the stem, making watery noises.

"Just this," Don said, hoping for a bit of drama as he withdrew the folded copper from the bag and leaned forward to place it on the desk. Mitchell shifted forward and placed his pipe on the desk as

157

Don gingerly began to unfold the flaps, exposing the gnarled hand.

"I found it while I was Rototilling the garden," Don said. Once the hand was completely exposed, Don sat back in the chair, smiling with satisfaction.

"My goodness," Mitchell said. He let his breath out slowly as he studied the relic from several angles. "This is quite—unusual."

Don reached down and rubbed the cut on his leg. The skin around the wound had turned a vicious purple, and his leg itched as though it were in a cast.

"My goodness," Mitchell repeated. His breathing was slow and deep, but there was excitement in his eyes. He picked up a small, pointed instrument and probed the mummified hand, carefully inspecting the leather thong and copper beads.

"The leather was pretty rotten—probably from being in the ground for so long. It broke, but I think I got all of the beads."

"Hmm, yes," Mitchell said. Gently, he lifted the hand and hefted it. After turning it over several times, he replaced it on the copper sheet and sat back. The unlit pipe went back into his mouth, and he took several useless pulls as he pondered Don's find. The pipestem went click-click on Mitchell's teeth.

"I figure it *has* to be Indian. At first, I thought I should call the police."

Mitchell chuckled. "Whoever severed this hand from its owner did so quite a while ago." He looked at Don with a furrowed brow and said, "I want you to tell me exactly how and where you found this. You said you lived—where?"

"St. Ann's—just outside of York."

Mitchell nodded. "I know where that is."

"We just moved here; I'll be teaching at the high school this fall."

For the next fifteen minutes, Mitchell was silent as Don filled in the details as fully as possible. When he had finished, Mitchell sat, scratching his chin.

"Tell me, Mr. Inman, is there a stream or river near where you found this?"

Don nodded. "Yeah, just down the hill there's a stream. Now much of one, really."

"But it could have been a river a thousand or more years ago," Mitchell said.

"Sure," Don said. "I suppose so."

"I'll tell you right now, Mr. Inman," Mitchell said, making no attempt to disguise the excitement he felt, "I'd like to have a colleague and myself come out to your place and take a look around. If it's all right with you, that is?"

"I don't see any problem there," Don said.

"If this is not a hoax—I don't mean to accuse you of any wrongdoing, something like this could have been planted years ago as some kind of macabre joke—but if it *isn't* a hoax, you have made a remarkable archaeological discovery."

"How so?" Don asked, wanting to share some of the professor's excitement.

"It's not so much the condition of the hand—which in itself is remarkable—but the way it was preserved and what we might be able to speculate about the religious rites involved."

"Does the copper sheet mean anything?"

"I'll repeat: if this is not a hoax, you may have just found the first physical remains of a prehistoric Indian. You see, the soil in Maine is far too acidic for human remains to last more than, say, five hundred years or so. The chemical composition of the soil, mostly from the pine forests, rapidly decomposes flesh and bone. What little we have of prehistoric remains, and that has never included human remains, has been found primarily in shell heaps, usually near a river."

"So the chances are," Don said, a bit crestfallen, "that this isn't all that old."

"We could guess all day, but, until we run some tests on it, we have no way of knowing. Archaeology is as precise a science as nuclear physics."

"So what's your nearest 'scientific' estimate?" Don asked.

Mitchell's frown deepened, and he brought his face close to the hand again. "I'd say, on the basis of the beadwork, that we should think in terms of—at least a thousand years old—maybe more. The copper sheet apparently preserved the hand from the acidity of the soil. I'd like to do some spectrographs of the copper sheet to see if there are any inscriptions."

"As far as I'm concerned, the thing is yours," Don said. "My gift to the university."

"I want to thank you," Mitchell said, nodding his head contentedly. "But what I'm trying to tell you is, if there are more artifacts in the area where you found this—well, this could be a discovery on the order of King Tut's tomb."

"You're kidding," Don said, but, even as he said it, he knew from Mitchell's face that he wasn't.

"We have absolutely no human remains of the Maine Indians before historic times. And what excites me more and more as I think about it is the condition of the hand itself. Look at it, Mr. Inman. Tell me what you see."

Don shifted forward and regarded the hand until he

began to feel uncomfortable.

"Well—?" Mitchell said.

"I don't know," Don replied. "It's old, leathery—wrinkled sort of like a prune. It looks like what I'd guess a mummy looks like."

"Exactly!" Mitchell said, pounding his fist onto the desk. "Mummified!" He took a long pull on his pipe, and the stem made a slushy, sucking sound. "Tell me, Mr. Inman. Have you ever heard of a man named Barry Fell?"

"I teach high school shop," Don said with a chuckle.

"Well, Prof. Fell teaches at Harvard," Mitchell began, assuming the tone of the lecturer. "Some years ago he proposed a theory—which, I might add, is most heatedly debated when not entirely dismissed—that, prior to Columbus, a variety of Europeans, Celts and Vikings primarily, visited the New World. Of course, much of Prof. Fell's conclusions are open to debate, but much of his work deserves attention.

"One of his ideas is that ancient Egyptians made contact with Indians in Maine, particularly with the Micmac and Wabanaki."

Don let out a slow gasp and, staring at the hand, said softly, "Egyptian mummies?"

Mitchell shrugged. "It's one man's idea, but, if this hand is as old as the beadwork suggests, I'd say it's in a remarkable state of preservation, wouldn't you?"

Don grunted agreement.

"You must understand, Mr. Inman, that this is extremely speculative. I find Prof. Fell's ideas interesting, but—until I saw this . . ." He let his voice trail off as his glance wandered back to the hand, resting on the copper sheet. "But I don't want to get too far

161

afield. At this point, I'll merely speculate that there might be a very valuable archaeological site on your property."

"What makes you think there could be anything else?" Don asked. He was beginning to feel like the dedicated graduate student, whose sole function was to pump the professor so he could expound.

"The wrist, Mr. Inman, the wrist," Mitchell said, using his pipe stem as a pointer. "We know next to nothing—make that *absolutely* nothing—about how the Indians lived over a thousand years ago. The clean cut through the wrist bone here, the string of copper beads wrapped around the hand, and the carefully folded copper sheet all suggest a ceremonial nature. We have no evidence that the Indians in this area practiced human sacrifice; we don't have evidence they *didn't*, either. Quite possibly, there could be an ancient burial site on your land."

Don shook with a sudden, unaccountable chill, and he reached down to rub the bruised cut on his leg. "Well," he said, aware that his voice trembled slightly, "you're more than welcome to come out and have a look around." He wasn't sure why but, as soon as he had said it, he found himself regretting the offer.

Mitchell produced a notepad and pen from the confusion on his desk and slid them over to Don. "Why don't you jot down your address and phone number. I'll give you a call in a week or two."

Don started to write on the pad, and his elbow bumped the mummified hand on the desk. He jerked away, startled, and then finished scribbling down the information.

"And if you wouldn't mind," Mitchell said, "I would like to hang onto this for a while." He indicated

162

the hand. "I'd like to show it to my colleague. I'd also like to get it dated, but that could take several months—depending on how booked up the dating equipment is."

"I told you, you can keep it," Don said. He felt a measure of relief, knowing the mummified hand would no longer be in his possession. He stood hastily and started for the door. The throbbing in his leg intensified, and he wanted to get walking, to get the circulation going.

"I want to thank you for bringing this to my attention," Mitchell said, rising and holding out his hand to shake Don's. "This is the kind of thing that only drops into one's lap once in a lifetime—if that."

"Just let me know when you want to come out," Don said, realizing he was too far committed to go back on his word. He left the office and, turning to close the door behind him, saw Mitchell, his head flat on the desk as he peered at the twisted copper sheet and the gnarled, mummified hand.

IV

"I thought you said you weren't going to do the garden this year," Don called out, after parking the car in the shade of the barn. He started over to Jan, who was on her hands and knees in the turned-up soil, carefully rolling peas into the furrow she'd dug.

She looked up at him, smiled, and shrugged. "Like you said, any bones down there are probably good fertilizer." She snickered and rubbed her forehead with the back of her work glove. It left a thick muddy streak. "This getting back to nature is tough work, though."

Don folded his arms across his chest and watched silently as she finished filling the furrow, then began covering the line of seeds. The smell of fresh-turned soil filled his nose. She packed the earth down firmly, grunting with each push. Beads of sweat rolled down her forehead and neck and dropped to the ground.

Briefly, Don filled her in on what Mitchell had said about the hand they'd found. Jan didn't react until he got to the part about Mitchell and another professor coming out to the property.

"I can't believe you said they could do that!" she said, her anger suddenly uncoiling. "It may be late in the season, but I'll be damned before I let them come out here and start digging up my garden. Not after the work I've put in!"

"They just want to have a look around. That's all," Don said mildly. He decided it was best not to mention that she might have planted her garden near or *on* an ancient burial site.

"Well, that better be *all* they do!" she said with a huff. Picking up the hose, she pointed the nozzle into the watering can and gave it a twist. A loud, metallic sound rose gradually up the scale as the can filled. She cut off the water and then walked slowly down the line, dowsing the newly planted row until it ran in wide, muddy rivulets.

After an awkward silence, Don asked, "Where's Beth hanging out—still inside reading her horse book?"

Jan shook her head and, squinting at him, pointed over toward the house. Don turned and saw Beth, slouched with her back against one of the maple trees out front. The book was open in her lap, and she was staring blankly at the page. Sun and shadow danced

164

across her face, giving it a curiously pale cast. He was surprised that he hadn't noticed her there when he drove up, and now—thinking about it—he was surprised that she hadn't come running up to greet him as she usually did.

"She's pretty excited about getting a horse, isn't she?" Don said.

Jan nodded, then picked up her hoe, and began chopping up another row, grunting with each swing. Don couldn't tell if it was their getting the horse or his promising to let the university people come out to the house that was bothering her. Maybe it was just that she'd been out in the sun too long.

Don looked again at Beth, and he noticed with a sudden, sinking sensation that she hadn't moved; he could easily have mistaken her for a statue. Keeping his eyes fixed on her, he started in her direction— slowly at first—but, as he got nearer, his pace increased with his panic.

"Don? What is it?" he heard Jan yell from behind.

He was breathing hard when he drew up beside Beth and saw that she was apparently asleep. He felt suddenly very foolish—spooked and jumping at shadows like that. Then he saw the wooden doll—its left hand missing—lying on the ground beside Beth, and he couldn't deny the belly-deep jolt he got looking at its faded, painted face, its vacant smile glaring up at him.

"Is something the matter?" Jan called from across the field. Don saw that she had started toward them.

"Beth—Pun'kin—" he said in a whisper. Kneeling, he drew his face close to hers, listening to the sound of her breathing. At first he heard nothing—or thought what he heard was the wind sighing in the branches overhead. An icy chill spread from his groin. Only when he held his hand beneath her nose did he feel the unmistakable wash of breath. He sat back on his heels, faintly relieved, but still struggling with the sensation that—somehow—she had reminded him of Aune Kivinen in her hospital bed.

Why was she so immobile—so still?

"She's just sleeping," he said, looking back at Jan, who was standing in the spotted shadow of the tree.

With a sudden shake of her head, Beth took a rattling inhale and opened her eyes. She jumped, her hand clutching her doll, when she saw her father kneeling so closely.

"Oh—hi, Daddy," she said. There was a flat cheerlessness in her voice, a sad distance.

"Hey, Pun'kin. What 'cha doing?"

"Nothing," Beth replied, "just playing with my doll."

V

The elements conspired against him—Don was sure of that. After several days of good weather, spent doing other things, it rained on the morning he was ready to get back on the roof and begin reshingling. He and Jan spent most of the morning sorting through the trash that had accumulated in the pantry. The old newspapers Beth had found the first day proved to be the most interesting; everything else was rotted, rusted, or broken.

"You know one way we could make some money?" Jan said. She was wrestling with the flaps on an Italian Swiss Colony Wine box filled with old dishes. "We should clean out all this junk and have a yard

166

sale. We'd probably make a bundle, selling this authentic down-home, useless trash to out-of-staters."

"You're forgetting, hon; we *are* the out-of-staters."

"Well," Jan said, finally giving up and leaving the flaps open, "we can at least store it somewhere out in the barn. I can't function with all this around. Here—look at this. What *is* this?" She held up a rusty length of metal with a curved wooden handle.

Don shrugged, and Jan wedged the whatever-it-was into the box of dishes and slid the box out onto the kitchen floor. Max sauntered in, noisily lapped up some water, sniffed the box, then went to the door, and gave it a scratch.

"You can go out," Don said, after getting up to open the door, "but don't get yourself all muddy again or you'll sleep in the barn."

"This can go, too," Jan said, giving another box a hearty shove that got it more than halfway to Don. "Pile this stuff up by the door for now."

"I don't want to put too much stuff out there, either," Don said. "After all, we are going to have to clean the stall out before we get the horse."

Jan let out a noisy exhalation that flapped the hair hanging over her forehead. "Just promise me we'll name the horse Hayburner, all right?"

"Not funny," Don said.

The jangling of the telephone interrupted them, and Jan stood, lunging forward to scoop up the receiver. "Yeah—hello."

After a slight pause, Jan's eyebrows rose. "Oh, hello, Mr. Jackman."

Don had to think a moment, then the name registered—Jackman, the man who owned *The Rusty Anchor*. He shook his head with disgust and resumed picking through the trash in the pantry. Of course, he couldn't help but overhear everything Jan said to Jackman.

Jack-off's more like it, Don thought.

"I don't have one, but I'm sure I could pick something up. By tomorrow? O.K., sure. I'll go out this afternoon and buy one—No, really; it's no problem. O.K.—Tomorrow at nine o'clock. Fine. Bye."

She replaced the phone and stood in the pantry doorway, looking down at Don. "I suppose you figured out what that was all about."

"You know," Don said, "I think your problem is you watched too many episodes of *Alice*. Waitressing at *The Rusty Anchor* isn't going to be like Mel's Diner, you know."

Exasperated, Jan merely shook her head. Maybe it was the rainy day and his frustration at not getting to do what he wanted to do, but something made Don want to hang on to it—not let it go quite yet.

"I can't believe you'd do something like this!" he said. "You're one of the best real estate agents in Rhode Island, and now you're going to be a waitress—a confounded waitress in a dump like that! If it weren't so pitiful, I'd be laughing."

"Well then, you're *really* gonna bust a gut when I get back from town, 'cause Mr. Jackman wants me to buy a waitress's uniform before I start tomorrow."

"Pink, no doubt," Don said. He rose to his feet and came slowly out of the pantry, slapping his hands together several times.

"Actually, he said I could pick whatever color I want as long as it's pastel."

Don let out a barking laugh. He turned to her, standing close. "And you're *really* going to go through with this?"

Biting her lower lip, Jan nodded. "Yeah, I am. What do you want me to do, not take the job?"

"You're damned right," Don yelled. He brought his fist down hard on the table. The sugar bowl jumped and almost spilled. "You call him right back and tell him that, as things turn out, you don't need the damned job. You're the one always bitching to me about how much work there is to do around here."

Jan shook her head sadly as though she were watching the sad remnants of a wasted life. "Can't you just lighten up on this for one minute? I want to do something besides staying at home all the time. Ever since Beth's been in school, I've been used to having my own job—something to get me out of the house. If you've got some delusions about my staying home, being some kind of country kitchen wife, well, then—"

"I never said that," Don shouted. His anger had passed the boiling point, and he was ready to let the argument rip. "I'm just saying that I don't want you doing something like this—waitressing, for Christ's sake!"

"We can use the money," Jan said, trying to keep herself calm, but she couldn't pass up one last dig. "Besides, we *need* the money now that you've promised Beth a horse."

"We agreed on that!" Don yelled. His face flushed, and he was pacing rapidly back and forth across the kitchen floor. "And besides, what'll you get paid there? Seventy-five cents? A buck an hour plus tips?" He looked up at the ceiling and let out a gasp.

Shaking her head, Jan stood by the sink, looking out over the field. The rain had beaten the grass

169

down, and everything had an oily look to it. Torn clouds scudded across the horizon. A closed-in pressure began to build around her, making her want to scream, but she took several deep breaths before turning to face Don.

"Honey," she said. "you're just not looking at it from my point of view. Look at it like this: it's just something I'm doing for the hell of it. Look, I can't stand here arguing all day. I've got to go into town and get that uniform."

Don looked at her and was filled with the thought that he had no idea who this woman he was talking to was. Almost seventeen years together, and she felt like a stranger to him. The thought that Jan—like Beth— had drifted away from him so subtly and so far hit him like the hollow concussion of a shotgun blast close to his ear.

He shook his head and forced a smile. "I'll say this once, and I hope to hell a week from now I can say: 'I told you so.' You probably won't last more than two days there. I'll lug these boxes out to the barn and maybe get a start fixing up one of the stalls. The work Beth did out there wasn't exactly professional level. If you're heading into town, you better get started."

He took a glass down from the cupboard and filled it with water. Jan mumbled something about asking Beth if she wanted to come along for the ride and disappeared upstairs to change her clothes.

He got the boxes of junk out to the barn, in spite of the rain, and was renailing some boards on the stall door when Jan and Beth came out and got into the car. He waited, listening for her customary toot on the horn as she drove off and, when it didn't come, a dry emptiness filled his stomach. Swinging wildly with

170

the hammer at a bent nail, he missed and walloped his thumb. When Jan and Beth got home nearly three hours later, he had a blood blister the size of a dime on the end of his thumb.

VI

The next day was as rainy as the day before, so Don planned to spend several hours in the barn, working on repairing the stall. He left Jan ironing her new waitress's uniform; Beth had been asked over to Krissy Remy's to play.

He was surprised at how fast the work in the barn went. After pulling and replacing all the rusty nails, he planned to shovel the stall floor down to the hard-packed soil. By asking around downtown, he got the name of Frank Herman, a local man who sold baled hay, who had agreed to bring out a load on the next sunny day.

Don was busy replacing the broken hinge on the Dutch door of the stall when he heard the side door squeak open. Glancing up, he saw Jan, an indistinct silhouette in the diffuse light. He had a feeling of immense distance between them as though several inches of plate glass separated them.

"So, you're heading to work, huh?" he asked, putting down the hammer and standing slowly.

Jan remained silent and unmoving.

"Beth didn't say anything about coming out to help, did she?"

Still, Jan neither moved nor spoke, and Don had a brief, unnerving impression that it wasn't Jan at all standing in the doorway. Tension began to crackle like spit on a hot grill.

"So . . ." Don said. He looked nervously around, first at the work he'd been doing, then at the figure in the doorway. "I'm having a tough time with this hinge. You might want to tell her, since it *is* her horse, that I could use an extra pair of hands." He bent down and picked up his hammer, but, when he looked back up, the figure in the doorway was gone.

He muttered a low curse, dropped the hammer, and went to the barn door. Looking across the driveway, he saw that Jan was just opening the kitchen door. She had on her raincoat and a clear plastic rainhat. Below the hem of her raincoat, he could see the pink edge of her waitress's uniform.

"I'm going to be late if I don't get a move on," she called as she jerked the car door open, jumped inside, and started the motor.

"Better hurry then," Don called back over the sound of the car as she backed around. He was wondering how she got from the barn door back into the kitchen so fast—if that *had* been her in the doorway.

But if it hadn't been her, who *had* it been?

Jan drew up next to him and rolled down the window. He could barely hear her above the slap-slap of the wipers. "The Remys will be over to pick Beth up in a half-hour of so."

Don nodded, still wondering whom he had seen in the doorway. He shivered, remembering the weird sense of distance he had felt between himself and— whoever that had been.

"Just make sure you don't get jawing with Earl; you won't get a darn thing done all day," Jan said with a laugh.

She sat there a moment longer, with the car idling,

172

and finally said to Don, "Well, aren't you going to wish me good luck on my first day of work?"

"Yeah," Don said hollowly, "have a good day."

"Try to dampen your enthusiasm," Jan said. She rolled up the window and popped the car into gear. Don stood in the shelter of the barn, watching stupidly as Jan went down the driveway and turned onto the main road. When she was gone, he shook his head like a man emerging from a dream and went back to working on the stall door.

As it turned out, Beth didn't make it out to help him before the Remys came to pick her up. Once she was gone, Don worked without interruption, but every time he glanced over to the doorway, he half expected to see someone standing there. Right into the afternoon, he couldn't shake the sensation that he was being watched.

VII

Jan was only five minutes late for work, but Dale met her at the back door and made a point of tapping his watch. He was wearing a silk shirt with a splatter design that looked like a painter's dropcloth. Jan didn't feel half so bad once she realized *The Rusty Anchor* didn't open until ten-thirty.

First, Dale had her sign a W-4 form; then he gave her a tour of the place, showing her where dishes, silverware, napkins, and other supplies were kept. He gave her an order pad, showed her where to put the order and where to pick it up. He often touched the crook of her arm as he directed her from one end of the kitchen to the other and explained what would be expected of her.

173

He introduced her formally to Carol Parker—whom she'd met the day she had applied—Will Conway and Brian Noyes, the dishwashers, and Bill Jacobson, the burly, black cook. Bill had a yellowed smile that perfectly matched his stained apron and a ready laugh that seemed to boom from his guts.

"Dale m' man, you probably been runnin' this young girl all over th' place," Bill said. "Why don't you go t' yah office and keep yahself busy. Jan, how'd you like a coffee 'fore we all get crazy 'round here?"

"That'd be nice," Jan said. Then glancing at Dale, she added, "I think I've got a pretty good idea of what to do." She took a seat at the counter, already wondering how her feet would ever hold up to all the walking she'd be doing.

Bill went to the coffeepot, poured mugs for her and himself, then came back, and sat down next to her. The cups looked like doll's toys in his beefy hands, and his rump hung out a considerable distance on both sides of the stool.

"So," Bill said, taking a sip of coffee, "tell me a bit 'bout yahself."

But before Jan could say anything, a face, moving so fast it was a blur at the order window, yelled out, "Tell Brian I want those plates out on the double! Is he in the men's room, tokin' up already?"

" 'Scuse me," Bill said mildly, Then looking at the order window, he bellowed, "Carol, will you just hold yah ass. I'm tryin' t' be sociable." Then, turning back to Jan, Bill said, "You was sayin'—"

But before Jan had more than two words out, Dale burst through the swinging doors. "O.K., enough chatting. Jan, did you punch in yet?"

Flustered, Jan shook her head. "Ahhh, no. I didn't

know I was supposed to."

Bill heaved himself to his feet, draining his cup as he did. "Well, I 'spose I'll get started on th' coleslaw."

Jan followed Dale to his office where he snatched a manila card from his desk and handed it to her. "Over by the storeroom," he said. "Make sure the Social Security number's right."

He busied himself at his desk while Jan went over to the machine and slid the card into the slot at the bottom. With a loud clang, the machine stamped 9:48 A.M. on the top. It wasn't lined up perfectly, but she slid the card into the box where she saw all the other employee's cards.

When she went back to the office, she was wondering whether or not to ask if she'd be paid for the first hour, but she decided not to push.

Dale looked up and handed her a piece of paper. "This is a schedule for the next two weeks. I hope you can work the times I have you down for."

Jan glanced at the paper and shrugged. "Sure. I don't see why not."

She slid the paper into her purse. While Dale was scanning through a stack of bills, Jan took a few moments to get a second impression of him. With a tingle of guilt, she realized that she was happy to see him again—maybe a bit too happy, she thought. She liked the way he stroked the tips of his mustache when he was thinking. There was still that aura of unapproachable cool, but she was impressed at how obviously he was in control of himself and his restaurant.

"It's too bad Sally's off today," Dale said, pushing back his chair and coming around the corner of the desk. "She's the only one who *really* knows what goes on around here. You can ask Carol, but I'd take anything she says with a couple of grains of salt. Any questions before you start?"

He went over to the floor safe, spun the tumbler left, right, and left, and took out the bag of money for the register.

Jan swallowed, and her stomach made a deep rumbling sound. "Hundreds. I hope you'll be patient with me, but I think I'll catch on."

"Good," Dale said. "We open"—he glanced at his watch—"three minutes ago. You've got tables sixteen through thirty. Go give 'em hell!"

Jan took a deep breath as though she were about to dive into the ocean and walked out onto the floor.

The lunch crowd came and went, and after four hours of literally running between tables, the kitchen, and the register—with only one fifteen-minute break—Jan saw with relief that the crowd was starting to thin out. By two-thirty, there were only five tables with customers, and two of the three that were Jan's had already been served. With the happy feeling that she had *really* earned it, Jan jingled the considerable amount of tip money in her apron pocket as she approached the last table—a family of five.

"Another minute or two if you don't mind," the father said, glaring at her. His face and balding head had the complexion of a lobster, and his voice had a reedy, Southern twang.

The mother, a mousy-brown-haired woman with a perpetual frown, was tapping the menu with her fingertip and repeating, "The hamburger looks great, Billy. Have a hamburger."

The oldest boy pushed a flag of hair from his eyes as he slouched back in the booth. "We shudda gone to MacDonald's."

Jan smiled and moved away from their table; she was still glowing with the heady feeling of success. Of course, she didn't move half as fast as Carol did, but she hadn't once confused or forgotten an order. Bill told her several times through the early afternoon what a great job she was doing. She joined Carol, who was sitting at the counter, smoking a cigarette.

"I'm going to have calf muscles like Arnold Schwarzenegger at this rate," Jan said.

"You don't need a health spa with a job like this, that's for sure," Carol said, letting smoke waft from her mouth. She held the pack out to Jan, who shook her head, no.

The father at the table waved at Jan to come over, and she approached with her pencil poised over her order pad.

"Would you be so kind as to get us some *clean* glasses for water?" he asked, his voice a thick, lazy drawl. He held one glass up to the light of the window and slowly turned it around. "This isn't, by chance, someone's science project, is it?"

The mother was looking out the window at the slow-moving traffic, as though she weren't involved.

Jan took the glass, which had—at most—a water spot or two, and got five glasses just out of the dishwasher. When she returned, the mother was still looking out the window, the children all sat in sullen silence, and the father was polishing his fork with the napkin. Jan almost asked him how he *dared* assume the napkin was clean.

"Are you ready now?" she asked, putting more pep into her voice than she really felt. She scribbled their order down, then rang the order bell as she spindled the tab.

177

Bill's meaty black hand shot out and grabbed the slip of paper, then his face appeared with a smile and a wink. "Got yahself a real turkey there, I see."

It amazed Jan how Bill, isolated in the kitchen, could pick up on something like that so fast. She shrugged and waited for the order.

Fifteen minutes later—the expression on the father's face telling her she was fourteen minutes late—Jan brought the order to the table. She daintily slid the plates onto the table, shocking herself by actually getting the correct orders to each person. After filling the water glasses—thinking curses at the man as she did—she was turning to leave when she was brought to a halt by the rattling sound of the man clearing his throat.

"Is everything all right?" she asked, forcing a smile and internally regretting ever setting eyes on these people.

"You seem to have things a bit confused here," the father said. He held the tuna roll aloft and shook it. "The tuna roll is warm and the French fries are cold. Isn't it supposed to be the other way around? And this tomato—this pathetic little *pink* thing—looks like it died of anemia."

Jan had to bite off a snappy reply. Instead, she said sweetly, "Well, if you're not satisfied, I can get you something else."

"You most *certainly* will," the man said huskily. "I'll have a hamburger—rare."

Try raw, Jan wanted to say, but she turned and, handing Bill the offending tuna roll, said through gritted teeth, "The *gentleman* will have a hamburger—rare."

"Jus' a minute there, honey. I'll see if ah can find

178

ma powdered glass."

"Hey, don't chuck that. I ain't had lunch yet," she heard Brian yell. He came around the side of the dishwasher and made a grab for the plate before Bill could scoop it clean.

"Well, 'least *someone* 'round here ain't particular," Bill said.

"Does that guy think he's in the Waldorf of something?" Jan asked, and the laughter genuinely relieved the tension that had been building.

"Jus' be grateful you didn't get him at the beginnin' of yah shift," Bill said. He slapped a patty onto the grill, and hissing steam rose to the vent.

Jan waited at the window for the hamburger, then carried it over to the table and placed it in front of the man. "I hope this is better," she said brightly.

The man grunted a reply and began to eat, taking a huge bite. A stream of hot juices ran down his chin, but he seemed not to notice. The children, who had been waiting hungrily for their father's meal to come before they could eat, made sudden grabs for their plates.

Throughout their stay, the family kept Jan hopping—racing back and forth for new spoons, an unopened bottle of ketchup, more napkins. Finally, when the youngest's bowl of Jello was sent back half-eaten because it was the wrong flavor, Jan exploded.

"Why are you trying to make things so difficult for me?" she shouted. Her hands holding the dessert bowl shook. Jello danced like it had never danced before. "This is my first day on the job, and I'm doing the best I can. But nothing—*nothing*—I do is right."

It was after three o'clock, and the *Anchor* was

mostly empty, but a preternatural silence fell onto the place. Customers at other tables glanced in the direction of the disturbance. Bill peeked out through the order window and shook his head, but Jan didn't see him.

Completely unruffled, the father looked at her. His eyes didn't blink, and he had a curious toadlike expression. "My dear," he said, shifting back in the seat, "I believe it is your job to see that your customers are satisifed. I've merely been pointing out to you that your service and the menu here leave something to be desired."

"Your Goddamned *attitude* leaves something to be desired, too!" Jan shouted. She knew she was blowing it, and she was telling herself to stop, but she couldn't— not now. This jerk was going to get both barrels now.

"I don't think it's fair that you come into a place like this, looking to give people a hard time. If that's your idea of summer fun, you can stay the Christ in Georgia or wherever the fuck you come from!"

"Well I *never*," the mother said. The first time she had spoken since they came in, as far as Jan knew.

The man balled up his napkin and tossed it to the center of the table. "I'm unaccustomed to being insulted when I eat," he said, "And I *certainly* don't expect to hear vulgarity! Come on, dear—children. We're leaving. And I *certainly* have no intention of paying for a meal when I have to put up with such— such *vulgarity*." He struggled to his feet, snapping his fingers to hurry the family along.

"Wait a minute," Jan said softly. She knew she had blown it—blown it in a big way. "I'm sorry. This is my—"

"Listen to me, young lady," the man said, wheeling

on her and jabbing a finger at her. "You may think you can get away with such mistreatment of your customers, but you're wrong—*dead* wrong! You're lucky I don't call the manager and get you fired."

"Get me fired?" Jan said, and her laughter surprised even herself. "I wouldn't want to work here if I have to deal with assholes like *you* all day. Please, make it a point *never* to come back here again."

"You can be sure of that," the man said, and he marched his family out to their car in single file.

Jan stood by the window, watching as they pulled out of the driveway and onto Route One. Then, slowly, she picked up a plate, covered with limp French fries and smeared ketchup, and slammed it onto the table. Tooth-shaped shards skittered onto the floor, and she turned and ran into the back room, crying.

One customer at the counter stood up and applauded.

VIII

Fifteen minutes later, still sobbing and wiping her nose with a piece of toilet paper, Jan was sitting on a case of tomatoes in the supply room. Dale had shut the door and was pacing back and forth, his hands clasped behind his back.

"You know," he said gruffly, "I should fire you on the spot."

Jan nodded as a burning, tingling sensation went up her spine. "I know," she said meekly.

"I mean, you just can't talk to customers like that—*ever*!"

"What can I say?" Jan asked, sniffing. "That I'm

181

sorry? That it was stupid? I know that—I *knew* it when I was doing it, but that . . . that . . ."

"Asshole," Dale said evenly. "I think you referred to him as an *asshole*."

Forcing a weak smile, Jan nodded. "Yeah—I think I did, but that asshole was deliberately baiting me. I wouldn't be surprised if he does that every time he takes his family out; it's a nice way to eat for free."

Dale laughed, and, when she looked up at him, she knew, in spite of her screw-up, that she was off the hook.

"I've owned the *Anchor* for almost ten years," Dale said, "and I've got to admit, that guy was up there in the top ten of assholes." He stopped pacing and looked at her. "And *you're* right up there, too. I've never seen anyone take it and then throw it back so well. Hell, you were *great!*"

"He made me so *angry!*" Jan sputtered, shaking her clenched fists.

"But seriously, Jan," Dale said, coming closer, "you're going to have to learn to control your temper. Some days—and it happens more than you think— you could get a whole string of jerks like that, and you've just got to handle it. Come back into the kitchen. Swear and kick over a trash can. Kick Brian in *his* can! Anything! But don't let them see that they're getting to you, 'cause if they know that, they'll put it on all the more."

"I know—I know," Jan said meekly. She relaxed her clenched fists and wiped her nose again. With a sigh, she leaned back and closed her eyes.

"You know, one other thing," Dale said. He gently placed his hand under her chin and tilted her head up. "You look beautiful when you're angry."

Jan's eyes opened, shocked. Good grief, she thought, the oldest line in the book.

She looked anxiously at the closed storeroom door and then twisted away from Dale's touch. Now she began to suspect the real reason Dale hadn't fired her on the spot.

After a too long moment of silence while the tension in the room sang like a tight wire, Jan sighed and said, "I guess I better get back out there, don't you think?"

Dale was silently studying her face, then he dropped his hand to his side and reached for the doorknob.

"Yeah, you better," he said, and Jan felt relief wash through her like a tide as the door swung open slowly.

Chapter Six

Night Dance

I

Two days later the rain finally lifted. When Don came downstairs for breakfast, he was surprised to see just Beth, sitting at the table. She was trying to stare down her few remaining Cheerios.

"Hey, Punk. How're you feeling?" he asked as he poured himself a cup of coffee and then dropped two slices of bread into the toaster.

"I'm all right," she answered, her voice sleepy.

Although he wouldn't comment on it, Don noticed that the inflammation from the hornet stings was just about gone, and—just as Dr. Kimball had said—it didn't look as though there'd be any scarring.

"Where's Mom?" Don asked. "She didn't have to work today, did she?"

For answer, he heard a dull clunk-clunk sound coming from outside, and, looking out the kitchen window, he saw Jan on her hands and knees in the garden, tossing stones off to one side. He watched her for a while, wishing the tension he felt between them—ever since she took that damned waitressing job—would disappear as the rain had. The bright blue of the sky almost hurt his eyes.

"When are we gonna get my horse?" Beth asked. She was sitting back in her chair now, her feet barely touching the floor. One hand at her side was gripping the stiff wooden figure of the doll.

Don stirred sugar and milk into his coffee, then, when his toast popped, he spread grape jelly on it. As he sat down in his chair, he gave Beth a little chuck under the chin. "I don't know for sure. Maybe, if you helped me some out in the barn, we'd get ready sooner."

Beth cringed. "I know I should," she said softly, "but I still haven't been feeling all that good." She ran her lower lip under her teeth. "Anyway, though, I've been reading the book you guys gave me."

"Well, that's at least something," Don replied. He wondered at what point he and Jan had become *you guys* to her. "But you know, we can't do anything until the stall's ready."

His expression suddenly froze when he noticed the wooden doll again. The handless left arm seemed almost to point up at him in accusation. He shivered and had to look away before concentrating on his breakfast.

"You know, Pun'kin, I've been so darned busy lately, I forgot all about your doll breaking," he said. "Do you still have the piece so I can fix it?"

"Him," Beth said, as she twisted away from her father, holding the doll protectively to her side. "No. He's O.K."

"I'll fix—uh—him if you want." Don was still holding out his hand for the doll, and now he shook his hand with slight impatience. He suddenly felt a compulsion to hold the figure as though he *had* to feel the thing to—to what? He wasn't sure. To make sure

185

that's *all* it was? Just a doll?

"I can't fix it if I can't see what's wrong," he said mildly.

"He's just a little bit broken," Beth said. Her tone was defensive, almost aggrieved. "He's O.K.—really! Besides, I lost the piece that broke off."

"That's too bad," Don said. "Maybe I could make him a new hand—" He suddenly cut himself off when he realized what he had said: the doll was missing a *hand*!

The kitchen door slammed open and vibrated on the rebound, and both Beth and Don jumped with surprise. Jan came into the kitchen, her hands and knees caked with dirt. She didn't seem to notice their reactions as she went over to the sink and started to wash up.

"I live with a couple of lazybones. Here it is after nine o'clock, and I've already put in two hours in the garden." She dried her hands, then filled a glass with water, and gulped it greedily. "It's going to be a scorcher today."

"I can't believe how hard you're working on that garden after you said it wasn't worth doing this year," Don said. He hoped he successfully hid the nervousness in his voice. "You got home from the restaurant so late last night, I thought you'd sleep till noon."

Jan sat down with them at the table and took a nibble of Don's toast. "I was hoping to get some more seeds in, but the ground's too wet after all that rain. I think the seed would rot. Maybe later today."

Don drained his cup, leaving about half a piece of toast on his plate for Jan to finish. He was just rinsing the cup out at the sink when he heard wooden side slats rattling and a bad muffler backfiring as a rust-red truck started up the driveway.

"Looks like that guy's here with the load of hay," he

186

said, glancing at Jan. He noted the lack of enthusiasm in her expression.

"Sounds like man's work to me," she said, stuffing some toast into her mouth.

The truck looked like the spearhead to a swirling screen of dust and flying hayseed as Don walked out to meet it. He waved them over toward the barn and ran to open the front barn doors. He could barely hear the grating of the door wheels along the rusted track above the sputtering truck.

The driver slowed, turned, and started to back up to the barn. Don was prepared to give the driver directions, but a shirtless, long-haired teen-ager leaped off the back of the truck and started signalling to the driver. The old man at the wheel squinted and brought his face close enough to the side-mounted rear view to fog the mirror with his breath. He eased the rattling truck up to the barn doors, then jolted to a stop when the boy whistled shrilly.

The motor died with a chattering gasp. With a dull pop, a cloud of black exhaust kicked out of the loose tailpipe. Don waved the smoke away from his face, thinking it smelled like burned hair.

"G' mornin'," the man said as he stepped out onto the driveway. He walked over to Don, his head cocked to one side like a chicken about to peck a choice grub. Drawing a blue bandanna from the back pocket of his bib overalls, he wiped the back of his neck. The boy, whose black hair was peppered with hay chaff, edged nervously to one side.

"Hot 'nough for yah?" Don asked, smiling inwardly at his attempt to sound local.

The old man's face turned into a scowl of wrinkles as he shook a Lucky Strike from a crumpled pack, lit a wooden match with his thumbnail, and then lit his cigarette.

"It'll be beastly hot 'fore long," the man said, his breath a blue haze of smoke. "M' name's Frank Herman. My boy here's Mark. Got you that load of hay you wanted."

Don was about to introduce himself and shake hands when the man turned and snarled at the boy. "Wha' cha waitin' for. Get on up they-ah."

Without a word, Mark scurried up over the stacked hay and began loosening the ropes that held the bales in place. Don thought the whole thing was going to collapse, but it stayed in place.

"Where d' yah want it?" Frank asked. He picked the rope up from the ground and began winding it up on his arm. "Up in t'loft, I suppose."

"If you want to leave it in the doorway here, I can haul it up later," Don said.

The old man snickered, shaking his head slowly from side to side. The laugh blended into a low cough that rumbled in his chest. He hawked and spat, and Don watched the glob of spit roll up into a dirt-coated pellet.

"No sense handlin' in twice," he said. "Mark'll get it up there for yah. Won't yah, boy?"

Mark, who stood beside the truck, looked like hauling the hay into the loft was about the last thing he wanted to do, but he nodded his head.

"Uhh, sure," Don said walking toward the barn. "I'd appreciate that. I'll go up and open the loft door."

Frank laughed again and said, "I guess that'd be as good a way to start as any."

Don went into the barn, grateful for the sudden, dark coolness. He quickly climbed the steep ladder leading up into the loft, wondering if the old winch would still work. He had seen it up there but hadn't bothered to give it a try.

The iron bolt locking the loft doors opened easily enough, but the rusted hinges shrieked and gave only an inch or two when Don pushed out on the doors. Leaning back he gave the door a firm shove with his foot, and finally the doors swung wide, hitting the side of the barn with a loud shotgun report. The sudden blast of sunlight stung Don's eyes, and he was momentarily dizzy.

"I doubt that winch there will work," Frank said. "Looks to me like it's been unused quite some time." Hands on hips, he was looking up at Don, his cigarette trailing blue smoke over his left shoulder.

The triangular wooden support stuck out from the barn like a gallows. Don reached out from the opening and gave the structure a firm shake. "It seems pretty solid to me," he said.

"We might as well give it a try," Mark said, squinting up at Don. "It'll beat tossing all them bales up."

"Lazy asshole," Frank said, glaring at his son. He shook his head disgustedly, coughed again, and sent a marble-sized wad of spit in Mark's general direction.

Don found the rusty hay hooks and stiff rope lying on the loft floor. The smell of rotten hemp almost choked him as he shook out a length of the rope. He went to the doorway and, leaning out, carefully threaded one end through the pulley. Then he fastened the hook and lowered the end to Mark, who was now waiting on top of the bales.

"This hay's from last year," Frank said. "I ain't cut yet this year—won't till the first of July. This'll get you by for bedding and such till I can get you some new."

"No problem," Don said, not daring to look at Frank because he was afraid he might lose his balance. He steadied the rope as Mark secured the first bale.

"O.K.," Mark called, "haul away." He stood back as Don wrapped the rope around his arm a few loops and began pulling. There was a gentle tug on the rope as the bale swung free and began to rise. The pulley let out a squeal that sounded like a cat caught under a car wheel. The sound set Don's teeth on edge.

Be much easier on the nerves to toss them up, he thought.

Pulling back, Don realized he was almost ten feet from the doorway when the bale rose into view. He freed his arm and, hand over hand, worked his way forward. Watching the swaying yellow bale, he was just allowing himself a feeling of pleasure at doing honest, hard work when there came a sharp cracking sound followed by a slow, tearing groan.

Sweat broke out on Don's forehead when he realized that the bolts holding the pulley were giving way. Loosening his grip on the rope, he made a frantic grab for the bale.

"Heads up," he yelled. The rope whipped through his hands, burning until he let it go.

"Aww, fuck!" he heard Mark yell. Don dashed to the doorway and was just in time to see the boy dive from the truck as the bale landed. It hit the tailgate and broke open on the ground, spreading out like an accordion. The hay hooks swung wildly, hitting and breaking one of the truck's taillights. Don looked up at the pulley and crossbars. One or two bolts still held, and the whole apparatus lay flat against the barn, useless.

"Darn yah, boy!" Frank bellowed. "Now look at wha' cha done!"

Don looked down and saw jagged pieces of red plastic on the ground. They caught the sunlight, casting wickedly bright reflections.

Frank was pacing back and forth, angrily waving

the flying dust away from his face.

"Damn yah! Don't think this ain't comin outta your wages, boy," he yelled. "You're damned lucky I don't take it outta your hide!"

"It wasn't *my* fault," Mark said, but he quickly shut up when his father glared at him.

"Don't worry about it," Don called down from the loft. "I'll pay for the taillight. As long as nobody's hurt—"

Frank grumbled in his chest and spat viciously. "That ain't no way to teach 'um a lesson." He nailed Mark with an angry look.

"It was my fault, really," Don said, feeling sorry for the boy who was trying his best to look unfazed by the whole thing. "I really should have tested the pulley before we tried it."

"Yeah," Frank said. He took another cigarette out and lit it. "Well, git tossin' them bales."

Mark took hold of a bale and hefted it. Then he started swinging it back and forth in a widening arc. Looking up, he asked, "Ready?" He increased the swing, then let the bale go. It tumbled end over and then landed with a thud in the doorway. Don had to scramble to get a hold on it and keep it from falling. By the time he had dragged it across the floor to the back of the loft, Mark was swinging another bale.

They worked without talking. The only sounds were Mark's huffing as he swung up the hay and Frank's chest-rattling cough. When the tenth bale had been stacked and a thick cloud of chaff hung in the air, Don called for a break. Mark vaulted down from the truck, landing heavily beside his father. He reached into the truck, got a cigarette, and lit it the same way his father had.

Don leaned out as far as he could over the edge of the loft door. The humid air hit his face like a sheet of ice after the close heat of the loft. His face dripped sweat, and the hay chaff made his skin itch like it was on fire.

Glancing up at the house, Don was startled to see a face peering out from his bedroom window. At first he thought it was Jan, but then he saw her carrying a bucket of garbage for the compost heap she had started. What on earth's Beth doing in our bedroom? he wondered but, when he looked again, the face was gone.

"Get yer ass in gear, boy," Don heard Frank say. "Time's a-wasting."

Mark ground his half-smoked cigarette out in the dirt and, exhaling a thin cloud of blue smoke, called up to Don, "Ready for round two?"

Don rubbed and rolled his shoulder, already feeling stiff, and nodded. Mark grabbed a bale and began his steadily increasing swing until he arced the bale up to the loft. They worked like this a while longer—Mark as steady as clockwork, Don scrambling and pushing the hay to the back of the loft. Don had lost exact count when Mark sent another bale sailing up; he grabbed at it and missed. The twisted end of the baling wire ran up the inside length of his arm.

"Hold it! Hold it!" he shouted.

Mark gently slowed his swing and lowered the next bale in his hand back onto the truck. "What's the matter?"

Don pumped his fist several times and watched as blood beaded up on the length of the gash.

"Wire caught me," he said. A drop of blood hit the loft floor with a plop and mixed with the chaff. The cut didn't look all that deep except right at the heel of his hand. Don took his handkerchief from his pocket and wrapped it around the wound. Blood soaked through almost immediately.

"You want I should come up there?" Frank asked.

The question genuinely surprised Don. He shook his head and said, "I can manage. Let's get the rest of this load up here."

They got the rest of the twenty-five bales up, but the last weren't stacked properly. The cut on Don's arm was beginning to throb, and, much as he hated to admit defeat, he asked Mark to come up and stack them while he went up to the house to get something for the cut. He told Frank he'd bring back the check he owed him, too.

Mark jumped up from the truck bed, grabbed the loft doorjamb, and boosted himself up and in. He began shifting the bales silently as Don made his way down the ladder.

When Don came back from the house, his arm wrapped in gauze, Mark was still up in the loft. Don could see him, looking out the small, dirt-coated window toward the house. Frank was leaning against the truck's fender, looking up at the loft with an expression of satisfaction that, if Don didn't know better, would have made him think Frank had done all the work himself.

"Here's what we agreed on," Don said, handing a check to Frank. "The extra five dollars is to pay for your taillight."

Don was wondering if he had gotten a good deal or if he had been skinned. Frank's expression never wavered as he glanced at the check, then folded it, and tucked it into his wallet.

"Like I told yah," Frank said, "new hay'll be ready in a coupla weeks. Just give me a holler when you want some."

"Sure thing," Don said.

"Hey, boy. You fall asleep up there or somethin'? Let's get a move on."

193

Mark appeared in the doorway, looking down at them as though dazed. He jumped down, hitting the ground hard. "You outta do something with that pulley rig," he said, and then he hopped into the truck cab as his father started gunning the engine.

As they rattled down the driveway, leaving a swirling trail of dust and hay, Don noticed that Mark was looking back up at the house. His eyes seemed to search each window as though looking for something that eluded him. Don glanced up at the house too but was unable to see anything until Jan appeared in the doorway and called out that lunch was ready.

The last thought he had as he watched the truck turn onto Hunter Hill Road was how much the truck's sputtering muffler reminded him of Frank Herman's hacking cough.

II

Jan had the morning off, and she decided to spend it in the garden while Don drove in to the Village Trustworthy store in York to pick up some hardware supplies. He figured he'd get better prices there than he'd been getting in St. Ann's. Beth said she felt like having a nap, so she didn't come with him, either.

As he walked across the parking lot to the store, the sun hammered down onto the tar and rebounded into his face. The pain in his arm was a bit less, but between that, the rope burn on his hands, and the cut on his leg, he was beginning to think that he just might not survive this "living the good life" in Maine. The air conditioning in the store came as blessed relief.

"Can I help you with something?" a voice said from behind a seed display.

Don came around and saw a young man, perhaps

194

in his mid thirties, kneeling on the floor, sorting through a drawer of assorted washers. He had a stocky build, and the muscles in his forearms rippled, making his shirt sleeves bulge. His long, black hair was tied into a small ponytail, and his skin had the dark, almost olive green of a Native American. His brown eyes glistened with an intelligence Don felt was both sharp and deep.

Don unfolded the piece of paper he was holding, scanned it, and said, "Yeah, I need a little bit of stuff—working on fixing up my house."

The young man rose to his feet, brushing off his backside. "And where might that be? I can tell you're new around here."

"Uh, yeah," Don said, taken aback. "I live out on Hunter Hill Road, in St. Ann's. My name's Don Inman." He held out his hand, and they shook. Don noticed the man had a firm, cool grip.

"My name's Billy Blackshoe," the man said, smiling as they shook. "So you're the new fella living out there. I was wondering when I'd finally meet you."

"You—uhh—you live out that way?" Don asked, feeling a bit confused.

Billy nodded. "I don't exactly live in St. Ann's, but I drive through on my way to work every day. I live out on Mountain Road, out past the town dump."

"Oh—O.K.," Don said, still feeling confused; there was something about Billy Blackshoe that—well—didn't exactly *bother* him, but there was a feeling of having met him sometime before, almost as if they had once, long ago, been good friends.

"So you're planning a few repairs on the place, huh? Nice spot you've got there. It'll be good to see that place get a bit of the attention it deserves," Billy said. He took the list from Don, glanced at it, and shook his head. "I'd say you're planning more than a

195

few repairs. Sure, we can fix you up with this. No sweat."

He started toward the back of the store, and Don trailed along behind. They said little, beyond comments on prices and value of materials, as Billy selected the shingles, nails, felt, tar, and other supplies Don had listed. Half an hour later, there was quite a pile at the register.

"I don't think you're going to get even half of this into your car," Billy said, leaning against the register and stroking his chin. "You know, it'll be no sweat for me to drop it off tonight, on my way home. I've got a truck."

Don, who had been intimidated by both the amount of stuff and the price he'd be paying, agreed. "If it's no problem—" he said.

"No sweat."

"Hey, Wingnut," the woman at the register said, "I'm due for a break, so why don't you ring this stuff up, O.K.?"

Billy nodded, and Don found it impossible to disguise his smile.

"Wingnut?" he said as Billy vaulted over the counter and began ringing up prices.

Billy nodded. "Just sort of a nickname around here," he said. He was frowning as he glanced over at the retreating form of the cashier. "I get a bit of ribbing around here because I read about—you know—psychic stuff—UFOs and stuff. One of the store wits came up with that name for me."

Don didn't know what to say, so he was silent as Billy rang up and totaled his bill. It came to almost double what he had planned to spend, but one of his handyman rules of thumb was just that: whatever you plan to spend, double it!

He wrote out a check and handed it to Billy, who

accepted it without checking any I.D. "So you don't mind," Don said, "dropping this off later?"

Billy shook his head. "No sweat. I drive by the place every day. I noticed someone had moved in, but I'd never seen anyone up there. I figured—no, never mind."

It was obvious to Don that there was something Billy wanted to say, but he wasn't sure if he should prod him or not. He slipped his checkbook into his pocket and reached for his keys.

"How long have you been living there?" Billy asked so suddenly it caught Don off guard.

"Huh?" He shook his head and shrugged. "Must be going on three weeks now." He did a rapid mental calculation and nodded. "Yeah, just three weeks."

Billy nodded his head sagely, and his dark brown eyes seemed to increase their intensity. "Three weeks, huh? Hmm."

Don felt a dancing line of cold rush up his spine. "Why do you ask?"

Billy's reaction wasn't at all what Don expected; he thought Billy would just dismiss it as, perhaps, his being too nosy, but he leaned closer to Don, his eyebrows beetling over his intense eyes. "You—ah, you haven't—" He suddenly laughed and shook his head at his foolishness. "Never mind. It was just something I—never mind."

"No, what," Don said, feeling Billy's intensity even when he tried to dismiss it. "Why'd you ask me that?"

Billy's expression clouded again, and Don knew he wanted to say whatever it was on his mind, but he was weighing both sides.

"Is there something about it I should know?" Don asked.

Billy shrugged. "No—I don't know. It's just that

197

that house is, well, kind of special. I used to go out there when I was in high school."

"Really?"

"It was one of the favorite spots kids went to go parking," Billy said. He paused, still apparently weighing the matter over in his mind; then he leaned closer to Don, lowering his voice. "Do you want to hear some small-town talk about the place? Hear some of the rumors about it?"

Before Don could answer, an older man, sitting at the central desk, called out, "Hey, Wingnut! You gonna jawbone all day or are you gonna get that stuff loaded onto your truck?"

"Come on," Billy said, leading Don through the door and into the blistering heat outside. As they tossed Don's roofing supplies into the bed of Billy's truck, Billy filled Don in on a bit of the history of the Kivinen house.

"When I was a kid—before I was old enough or interested in going parking with a chick—that house was special to me. All of us kids said the place was haunted." He suddenly nailed Don with that intense stare of his and asked, "You haven't seen or heard anything since you've been there, have you?"

Don shook his head. "No. No transparent figures. No hollow moaning sounds," he said with a laugh, but he felt another shiver as he remembered the nightmare he had had—the tall, standing stones in the stream, dripping with—

—Not blood!

"Of course," Billy went on, "I remember my grandfather telling me about the house from way back. I don't remember exactly how or when, but he said something about that place burning down. He thought it was the best thing in the world that could happen to that house. I don't know why. But then he

198

said, sometime in the early 1900s, somebody rebuilt it. He was about my age, I guess, when that happened."

"That was probably when my grandfather, Toivo Kivinen, bought the place," Don said.

"When I was a kid, we used to use that house as part of the initiation to get into our club," Billy said. "Because we were positive it was haunted, each of us had to go into the house—alone—look out from the attic window, and then come back down." He paused, staring into the distance as his memories grew stronger.

"Did anyone ever *really* see anything in there?" Don asked. He could feel the goose flesh rising on his arms in spite of the heat outside.

Billy shrugged and looked at Don, but his eyes still held their long-distance stare. "Course we *said* we saw something, or heard something, but I suppose most of us—at least I said it just to scare the new kid who was going in. And there have always been the usual stories everyone tells about an empty house—someone saw a light in one of the windows or a figure walking up to the front door or something. I never saw anything there, but I've always had some—I don't know—some weird feeling about the place."

"Like what?" Don asked, and he was debating whether or not to tell Billy about the mummified hand he had found in the garden. The professor at the University of Southern Maine had said it was probably an Indian artifact. Billy was Indian; maybe he knew more than he was telling, Don thought. Even if he didn't, maybe he should know about the hand.

"When I used to take a chick up there. Wow, remember those days?" Billy said, shaking his head from side to side. Sweat from loading the truck made his skin sparkle. "Back in those days, we'd just about

199

pass out if we got to French kiss a little. None of this heavy stuff on the first date that kids do today."

Don tried to smile, but he was thinking how soon it would be before Beth started dating. "I can see why that was a popular spot," he said. "I mean, there's a nice view of the town, and it's so quiet. My wife and I could hardly sleep the first few nights because there weren't any police sirens going by every half-hour."

"You know," Billy said, "I never really liked going up there. Maybe it was because we used to play at haunted house, or maybe it was something more, but whenever I was up there I always felt as though I was being watched."

Again shivers ran up Don's spine. Everything Billy was saying seemed to strike some deep, dark note within Don, and several things that had happened since they had moved in—the wooden doll Beth had found; the sounds he had heard in the cellar; the buried hand he'd found; even, now that he thought about it, his seeming accident proneness, what with cutting his leg and arm—all of these began to at least *feel* somehow connected.

"Well, I haven't heard anything about this before now," Don said. "Then again, people have been pretty stand-offish so far, but my sister's been renting the place out for quite some time, and, as far as I know, she's never had any complaints."

Billy's smile widened. "Yeah, but have you ever heard of anyone staying there for long? I don't know of anyone staying more than a few months. Driving to work, I've seen them moving in and, not long after that, moving out."

Don shrugged, trying to dismiss it all, but Billy had planted suggestions, and now his mind was beginning to make some tenuous connections.

Billy laughed aloud. "If I keep going on like this

you're going to start calling me Wingnut, too. I dunno. I'm, you know, sort of interested in this kind of thing. I don't suppose we should take it seriously. Every town has a house like that, especially if it's been empty for any stretch of time."

They had finished loading Billy's truck, and now Don started toward his car. "I suppose next you'll be telling me that old whopper about the escaped convict, or lunatic, who has a hook for a hand, and it gets ripped off and is found hanging from the car door." He laughed, but as soon as he mentioned a missing hand he wished he hadn't.

Billy shook his head and laughed along with him, but there was something in Billy's laugh, too, that made Don think he was still holding something back.

Don opened the car door and sat down, but before he closed the door, he said to Billy, "You know, you seem to have everything I need here for building, but I was wondering if you could suggest some place local where I could get feed and equipment for a horse. We're thinking of buying my daughter a horse."

Billy scratched his chin thoughtfully. "Hogan's Supply here in town is good—expensive, but good. If you want to bother with a bit of a drive, there's a discount warehouse for feeds down in Kittery. It's just off Route One after the rotary."

"I think I remember it," Don said. He shut the door, started the motor, and rolled the window down to shake hands again with Billy. "Well, anyway, it's been nice talking with you, and I'll see you later on this afternoon."

"Some time after five," Billy said. "I'd enjoy meeting your wife and Beth, too. Take care."

"Sure thing," Don said, slipping the car into gear and backing out of the parking lot. It didn't hit him until he was halfway home that Billy had mentioned

Beth by name, and, try as he might, he just couldn't remember telling him his daughter's name.

III

As he waited, hating it whenever he was put "on hold," Prof. Roger Mitchell braced the phone to his ear with his shoulder and leaned back in his padded chair to watch the brisk Frisbee game being played outside in the quad. He sucked noisily on his unlit pipe and was beginning to lose his patience when the receiver clicked and a gruff voice said, "Hello, Roger? Thanks for waiting."

"Hello, Desmond," Mitchell said. He placed his unlit pipe on his desk and leaned forward, but his eyes still tracked the floating Frisbee. "It's been a while. How they treating you up there in Augusta?"

"Same as always," Patterson replied, his voice sounding congested as it always did, but also very tired. "More work; less budget. What else is new? I can't help but wonder how on earth they expect me to preserve Maine's archaeological heritage on a budget slightly less than what my kid gets on his paper route."

"I've always told you," Mitchell said, "we should have gotten into computers when we had the chance."

"Bah!" Patterson replied. Neither one of them felt like laughing when they considered the realities of what recent budget cuts had done to their profession.

Mitchell let his gaze drift over to the mummified hand Don Inman had delivered to him the day before. It was lying there in front of him on the spread-out copper sheet, its black skin looking closer to a raisin than a human.

"I think I've got something to spark up your day," Mitchell said. "I've got a lead on a site that—well, maybe you have to see what I've got to believe it."

"Roger, my boy, don't you think I've got enough interesting sites already? My problem is financing the digs I've already got lined up. Now, if you'd be willing to take this find of yours—whatever it is—on down to Washington and convince Mr. Reagan to toss a few thousand bucks our way, I might take a second to listen to you."

Mitchell cleared his throat; he always had to clear his throat when he listened to Patterson speak. "Just hear me out. A fellow from the York area—St. Ann's, I think he said—has found a skeletal hand that, frankly, has me baffled."

"What kind of hand?" Patterson asked.

Mitchell couldn't miss the genuine irritation in Patterson's voice. He felt a flush creep along the back of his neck as he continued. "Actually it's a mummified hand, and it apparently—"

"Roger, I don't see why you're bothering me with this," Patterson cut in. "No human remains can possibly be old enough to interest me."

"I know, I know," Mitchell said quickly, but he was thinking there were more surprises and discoveries made—even in a field such as archaeology—by ignoring such "accepted" facts than he cared to contemplate.

"But this was found wrapped in a sheet of beaten copper, and the beadwork found with it definitely suggests a prehistoric origin. My speculation is that the copper sheet protected the hand, preserved it from decay. I honestly think we might have a prehistoric human remain."

"Or a hoax more than likely," Patterson said, his throat rumbling.

Mitchell stared at the hand, its wrinkled, black fingers curled into a clawlike ball that suggested a hawk's talons grasping a perch. There was something about the artifact that made him distinctly uneasy. A closer examination of the copper sheet had revealed several swirling patterns etched into the metal. In all he had found five whirlpool designs, but the copper was grossly twisted and dented out of shape, and he wanted to run a few spectrographs to be certain.

"It's not a hoax, Des," he said, and he knew he believed that. Now it was just a matter of convincing Patterson. "I want you to come down and have a look at the thing. I'd also like to drive out to this man's property with you and take a look around. If I have to lure you with the promise of one of Mary's home-cooked meals, I will."

"The last thing we need," Patterson said, "in this woeful time of budget cuts is our own little Piltdown Man episode, Roger."

"I'm not asking for a dig," Mitchell said, and he knew he sounded too desperate. "I want you to come down and have a look. That's all. I know it sounds unlikely, but, believe me, I think we've got something significant here. I've got a gut feeling about it."

Patterson snorted loud enough to make Mitchell pull the receiver away from his ear. "Roger, my budget doesn't get approved on gut feelings!"

Mitchell had known Patterson would be difficult, and he now wished he had sent him some photographs before making the call. But, hoax or no hoax, there was definitely something strange about this hand, and he knew that, with or without Patterson, he was going to investigate further.

"Besides," Patterson continued, "my calendar's extremely full. There's the conference in Denver in two weeks, and after that I have to present a paper in Buffalo. And I thought you were finalizing plans for that dig in England this September."

"Yes, yes," Mitchell said impatiently. "I am, and this probably is nothing." He didn't really feel that, but he thought it might help pacify Patterson, the stubborn goat.

"But I don't want to take a chance of missing out on it if this is legitimate, and I don't think you want to take that chance, either."

There was a delay of several seconds, broken only by Patterson's raspy breathing.

"And Mary's been doing quite a bit of Mexican cooking lately . . ." Mitchell said, his voice dangling temptingly. He could hear Patterson flipping the pages of his calendar.

"I suppose I could shoot down there on the—let me see. Yes, I'm free July seventeenth and eighteenth. That's Thursday and Friday. Will that suit you?"

Without checking his calendar, Mitchell said, "The seventeenth is fine." He felt a wave of elation, but that quickly subsided when he looked again at the hand. It had to have been his imagination, but he was convinced the fingers were clenched more tightly than they had been, making a ball of the fist.

"I'll, uh, just jot that down," he said, conscious of the tautness in his voice.

It had to have been his imagination!

"Tell Mary, by the way, to go easy on the hot sauce," Patterson said. "Doctor's orders. I'll be anxious to see this Piltdown Man's hand of yours."

"See you then," Mitchell said and hung up. For the next several minutes, he sat staring at the mummified hand, trying to convince himself that it was *impossible* for the fist to have tightened—unless the tendons were drying out and shrinking.

"Yes," he muttered, "that's it."

With a start he noticed that he was late for class, and he gathered his books and hurried from the office, grateful to leave that mummified hand behind.

IV

Don got home just before noon. Beth was over at the Remys' again. After a quick lunch with Jan, who had to hurry off to the *Anchor*, he spent the rest of the day on the roof, tearing up old shingles with a pinch bar. The work went fast and well, and before long he was dripping with sweat.

Toward late afternoon, Billy drove up in his battered pickup truck and, as he watched from the roof, Don had the curious sensation of having seen the truck, having *known* that truck before—not just today at the hardware store, but from some other time. As he climbed down the ladder and came over to Billy, the sense of dé jà vu continued. He dismissed the idea, finally concluding that probably he had just noticed Billy driving by the house on his way to work.

They unloaded the roofing materials into the doorway of the barn, just in case the good weather didn't hold until the job was done. Then, for the next hour or so, they sat in the shade, drinking beer and talking. Little mention was made of what they had talked about that morning, but Don found himself studying Billy's reactions, trying to pick up if the man still was uneasy, felt "watched" while he was on the property. If he was feeling anything, he didn't let it show. They passed the time talking about anything *but* the reputed history of the old Kivinen house.

Billy left after two beers and, feeling a bit logy, Don went back up onto the roof, hoping to get back the swing he'd felt earlier with the work. At one point the phone rang, and he scrambled down to answer it. It was Beth, asking if it'd be O.K. for her to stay and have supper with Krissy. Don figured there was no

206

problem with that; he'd get as much work done as he could.

Toward evening, as the night sounds filled the gathering darkness, Don climbed down to the ground, exhausted but satisfied. He had stripped off almost one entire slope of the roof. It would be a good job for Beth, he decided, to collect the fallen shingles into a pile so he could haul them away. He picked up a few of the broken pieces and skimmed them off into the dark, waiting to hear them cut through the trees. Bats circled overhead, dodging and darting after insects.

"Honey, get the Doan's, will yah?" he called to the empty house as he lurched into the kitchen, rotating his aching shoulder. Max was sleeping on the floor, his head lolling to one side. Smiling, Don went upstairs. He had a long hot shower, then came back down and fixed a light supper of soup and a grilled cheese sandwich.

After that, he walked downtown, enjoying the cool evening and the chance to stretch his legs after kneeling on a hot roof all day. He picked up a copy of the *Evening Express* and actually got a friendly greeting from the clerk in the corner store. Beth was home, planted in front of the TV by the time he got back.

They spent the rest of the evening pretty much in silence; he was too exhausted to talk, and Beth apparently wanted to say little more than, "We just messed around." After watching "Simon and Simon," Beth said she was beat and went up to bed. Don lay back on the couch, trying to concentrate on the baseball scores, but his eyes kept blinking, threatening to close. The newsprint blurred, and at last he drifted off to sleep until—

—until a faint, fluttering sound awoke him.

He rolled over on the couch, momentarily disoriented. He glanced at his watch—

—quarter of twelve. Shouldn't Jan be home by now?

As he stood up, he heard the click-click of Max's paws on the kitchen linoleum.

"Quarter of twelve," he said aloud, his throat raw. He wiped the bit of drool from his chin and scratched his head. Max looked into the living room, a woebegone expression on his face.

"Wanna go out, huh?" Don asked, rising and starting for the kitchen. Max followed him to the door but then held back when Don swung the screen door open.

"What's the matter? Don't be such a pain!"

He was about to let the door swing shut when he saw that he and Billy had left the barn door open. He reached for a flashlight and went outside. The moon was low, casting a dull, blue dusting of light over the land. Don crossed the driveway to the barn door, but, as soon as he got there, he stopped, nerves tingling.

Had he heard something inside the barn?

He directed the flashlight beam into the darkness and skimmed the circle of light over the stalls and the pile of building supplies.

Nothing. Or if anything, probably just a mouse or something equally harmless, he thought. Still, the sense that there was something wrong swept through him, and Don entered the barn, constantly sweeping the flashlight beam around as he went.

Everything seemed in order. Nothing had fallen from the pile of building supplies and, as far as he could see, nothing had fallen from the wall pegs or shelves on the far wall. *Imagination*, he thought, swinging the light up and down the barn walls. *Nothing but—*

And then he froze. There in the circle of light, he saw it: Beth's handless, wooden doll. It was perched on the edge of the stall he had been fixing for the horse they had promised Beth. The painted black eyes seemed deeper and blacker than the surrounding darkness—as if they might start swirling, like a whirlpool, and suck him in.

Panic raged in Don, and he stood frozen, unable to move forward or backward. He wanted to go up to the figure, take it, and smash it or get out of there, away from it. The smile on its painted wooden face—*that smile!*

Slowly, keeping the flashlight directly on the figure, Don began to approach the figure.

What the devil is happening? his mind was screaming. Why was he so afraid of this thing? It was just a simple doll!

But the closer he got to it, the more his fear grew, and—as he held out his hand, willing it to reach out and pick up the wooden figure—the more vivid and violent the images that filled his mind.

The doll would suddenly leap from the stall edge and, grasping him tightly, sink ratlike, needle-sharp teeth into his flesh, he thought.

It almost seemed he could feel the numbing sting as the teeth clamped down, grinding, severing veins and arteries.

With a muffled groan, Don began to back away from the figure. "This is ridiculous," he whispered, but he kept his eyes on the doll, waiting, waiting for the impossible. He bumped into the barn wall and, suddenly turning, he dashed out of the barn. He was halfway across the driveway to the house when he again noticed the faint rustling sound that had awoken him.

The flood of panic rose as he listened for the sound to be repeated, and, when it was, he recognized it. It was an owl, hooting in the night-stained woods across the field.

"The stream," Don said, his voice grating in his throat as though it violated the night sounds. A bone-deep chill raced up his legs with each slow step he took around the side of the barn. Moonlight washed the grass with a silvery sheen, and cold currents of air swirled around him.

The owl's hoot came again, distant and hollow, like the tail end of a dream. A low grunt of surprise came from Don when he rounded the barn and saw some-one standing in the middle of the field. Shimmering and immobile, outlined sharply against the star-sprin-kled sky, the figure stood with arms raised, palms up to the night. It took several seconds for him to realize it was Beth.

He opened his mouth to call to her, but only a strangled, choking sound came out. He moved, drifted toward her, watching fascinated. The panic he had felt in the barn now shifted subtle into a rising, electric tension.

Beth stood stock still, her head tilted back as she looked up at the stars. Don groaned when, momentar-ily, he had the impression that he could see the dark line of trees not only beyond, but directly *through* Beth's body. She looked translucent with the moon-light washing her with glowing powder. Again, he tried to call to her, but no sound came from his throat.

The owl hooted, louder, closer; and Don felt a numbness twining through him as Beth began to sway gently from side to side. Her motion at first reminded him of a child in a school play, representing a tree blowing in the wind. The sleeves of her gauzy night-gown fell back in fluttering folds at her elbows. Her fingers opened and closed, opened and closed, sug-gesting a gentle, watery motion, as though she were beckoning to someone.

The owl hooted still louder, still closer. Beth's swaying gradually increased its tempo. From side to side she waved, seeming almost to sweep the ground on each side as she bent one way, then the other. The breeze picked up strength and began whipping Beth's nightgown back, flapping it wildly. The contours of her body were outlined with sharp definition.

The owl's hooting increased in frequency and volume, and Beth started to walk slowly sideways in a wide, counterclockwise circle. Don shook his head, fighting the strange rush of dreamlike disorientation as Beth began to run and skip faster in wide circles on the moonlit field. The dark outline of her body was now vague, indistinct between the fluttering nightgown that wrapped her like a milky cloud.

Beth ran, faster, *faster*, and the owl hooted louder, filling the dark hollow of night with its mournful wail. Motion and sound merged, blending until Don couldn't be sure what was sight and what was sound. He was sure though of his fear for both himself and for Beth, but he was unable to move or call out to her.

She ran in the track of her circle faster, ever *faster*! And then something happened, so subtly at first that Don didn't credit the evidence of his own eyes. In the diffused light of the moon it looked as though Beth's feet were skimming off the ground as she ran. She wasn't jumping or leaping. Her feet just seemed to drift above the ground, floating behind her as she gracefully rose into the air. Don shook his head, watching but not believing. As though suspended from an invisible wire, Beth drifted, spiraling like a wind-tossed leaf, ever higher above the ground where she had been running.

Don heard a low, strangled sound. He thought, at first, it was Max; it was the sound Max made in his sleep. But then he realized the sound came from his

211

own throat. And still the moonlight throbbed and vibrated with the fluttery hooting of the owl.

Beth spun around, faster, higher, her gauzy night-gown whipping in the wind. Her arms were spread out like a diver at the beginning of a swan dive. Still, she rose higher, higher!

Don got dizzy watching; the ground seemed to pitch crazily, and he grabbed at the side of the barn for support. Other than the hooting of the owl, the night was still with a haunting quiet.

He wanted to call out, but the only sound he could make was a tangled groan. He licked his parched lips and watched as Beth floated, now more than twenty feet above the ground, twisting, spinning, helpless in the swirl of night.

With a loud shout that nearly tore his vocal cords, Don lurched forward, his arms outstretched as if he could catch her. The only thought that filled his mind was that he had to save her, *save her!* He *had* to stop her crazy, gravity-defying dance!

He started to run, and his foot snagged, pitching him forward. The dark ground rushed up at him like a wave, and like Beth's wild dance, darkness swirled up, engulfing him. When his head hit the ground, he was curiously dissociated from the pain; it was as if it were happening to someone else. The ground under his ear reverberated like a drumbeat with sound. Then darkness, thicker than the night, exploded in his head with a muffled, ruffling sound—

—like an owl hooting in the night.

V

At ten-thirty that night, exhausted from a hectic eight-hour shift, Jan sank onto one of the stools and leaned her head on the counter. Sally and Bill had already left: Bill to go to his one-room apartment for a few—or several—nightcaps; Sally to a late-night date with—her words—a "hot stud." Dale was in the office tallying the day's receipts while Brian mopped the kitchen floor. Even through the thickness of the kitchen door, the clattering of the mop bucket made Jan's temples throb. She wanted nothing more than to go home and get some sleep, but Dale had said he wanted to talk to her about something. She just hoped she wasn't getting canned already. At least there had been no repeat performances of the disaster of her first day.

The kitchen door swung open, and Brian poked his head out. His John Lennon glasses caught the red light of the revolving Budweiser sign. "G'night, Missus Inman," he said and was gone before she could reply. She heard the back door slam and then the grumble of his motorcycle as he revved up and drove off.

As if waiting for his cue, Dale sauntered into the restaurant and slid onto the stool beside her. "What're you drinking?" he asked.

Jan, with her head resting on her folded arms, considered for a moment. "I don't care—anything. Rosé, I guess." She sat up and rubbed her temples with her palms.

Dale went behind the counter, put out two glasses, and got a gallon jug of Gallo from the cooler. He poured two generous servings. A few drops spilled onto the counter, looking like cheap red plastic beads.

"Here I go, drinking up the profits again," Dale said as he rounded the counter and sat back down beside Jan. He took a sip and waited for her to drink before saying, "Tough night, huh?"

Jan nodded. "I've never worked this hard in my life and, no offense, but some of these customers couldn't tip me enough."

"It takes some getting used to, for sure," Dale said. He leaned one elbow onto the counter, bringing his face level with hers. Tipping his glass, he clinked the edge of her glass and said, "Here's to another day and another dollar."

Jan snorted and took another sip. "Is it always this busy?"

Dale shifted in his seat, and his knee brushed against her leg. She drew back, trying to ignore the "accidental" contact.

"Right through August and into September it is," he said. He ran his fingers over his mustache, keeping her pinned with his steady look.

Jan looked away, holding her glass to the light and studying the rich ruby color. She didn't like the way he was looking at her so intently; it made her squirm.

"So tell me, Jan," he said after a while, "are you happy?"

"You mean with the job?"

Dale shrugged. "With everything—working here, living in Maine, your life."

Jan considered his question as she took a sip of wine. It sloshed in the glass, and a trickle ran down her chin until she wiped it away. She cursed herself for acting as nervous as a schoolgirl.

"Well," she said, shaking her head, "things certainly are different. I grew up and spent most of my life in Connecticut and Rhode Island. It's a little hard, getting used to the—the—"

"Boondocks?" Dale said.

Jan shook her head. "No, not exactly. I guess it'll just take us a while to feel settled."

"And how are things between you and your husband?" Dale asked.

Jan made a face, thinking the only surprise here

214

was how fast Dale moved—if, she warned herself, he was making a move. He might really just be making small talk.

"We're doing O.K., I guess," she answered and, as soon as she said it, she wondered why she was playing along with him. Why not tell him things between her and Don were perfect, or at least as good as could be expected?

"Maybe I've been reading you wrong, then," Dale said. He leaned closer, studying her face. "I had you pegged as someone who was pretty unhappy at home. Maybe not divorce time, but certainly thinking about it. I mean, why ever would someone like you want to work in a joint like this?"

"Oh, you mean what's a nice girl like me doing in a place like this?" Jan said, and she couldn't help but laugh.

But Dale remained serious. "Yeah—sort of. I mean, I'm a pretty intuitive guy, and I saw you wanting to work here as kind of a desperate measure. You *had* to get out of the house and do something— even be a waitress in a greasy spoon."

Jan had to break eye contact with him. She felt a blush rise to her face as she considered what he had said. Sure, to a degree, she wanted to get out of the house and *do* something. In Providence she had had a full-time job ever since Beth was in kindergarten. She had never been the stay-at-home type. But now . . .

"And I thought *for sure* it was because you and your husband weren't getting along," Dale said.

"I don't know," Jan said with a shrug. "I mean, we have our differences and stuff, but I'd say, on the whole, we're doing all right."

"And you really did take this job just because you wanted a little extra money?" he said, astounded.

"Material for a novel I'm writing," Jan said, chuckling. "A *roman a clef* about the tourist trade in Ogunquit."

Dale laughed and raised his glass to his lips. "Be a damned short book," he said and drank. "Anyway, I just wanted to take a minute or two and shoot the breeze with you. Make sure everything was going all right for you."

"Sure," Jan replied. Again she flushed, but this time at her own embarrassment for thinking Dale would even consider putting the make on her. With his looks and money, the last thing he needed was to whip up a frenzied affair with a thirty-eight-year-old housewife. The thought stung her like a wasp.

She looked at him, and his face suddenly shifted. The gleam in his eyes intensified, and his features seemed to soften. Must be the wine, she thought as a swirling sensation surrounded her, seeming to lift her up by the stomach. Too much work and now wine on an empty stomach.

Jan stood and was going to say it was time for her to be heading home, but suddenly she had to reach out to the counter to keep from falling. Waves of dizziness crashed over her.

"Hey—Jan. Are you all right?" Dale asked. He grabbed her, his strong hands gripping her shoulders. She felt like a limp ragdoll collapsing in on itself as he steadied her with one arm and pressed his hand against her forehead. It was warm but certainly not hot to the touch.

"Here, sit down," he said, easing her back onto the stool. "I'll get you some water."

Still fighting the waves of nausea, Jan leaned her head onto the counter. Its slick coolness was like ice. Dale went to the sink and filled a glass after letting the water run to get cold. He gave it to her, and she sat up and took several huge gulps.

"Wow," she said. She took the water glass and rolled it over her forehead. "I don't know what came over me." She looked at him, and the genuine concern in his expression made her feel suddenly foolish.

"Are you feeling better?" he asked.

Jan nodded. The waves of dizziness were receding like the tide, still there but fainter, weaker.

"You probably have just been overexerting yourself," Dale said. "And that wine probably didn't help any."

Jan glanced at her watch. "Darn, it's getting late. I've got to get home."

"Are you feeling well enough to drive?" Dale asked. "I can drop you off if you'd like."

Jan shook her head, thinking how good *that* would look—having to get a ride home with the boss because she drank too much after work. "I'll be fine," she said. She stood up, fished her car keys from her purse, and started for the door.

"You're sure you're O.K.?"

She nodded. "Fine. Don't worry."

"You're not in for the next—what—two or three days? Take it easy. Get some rest, will you?"

"I will," Jan said, and she went out into the cool night air. As she drove home, making sure she stayed well under the speed limit, the wine buzzed like an insect in her brain.

She felt guilty and full of embarrassment for even thinking that Dale might try to hustle her. And getting dizzy like that! Like a schoolgirl, she thought, getting drunk just sniffing the bottle cap! She wondered if she hadn't let that happen just so Dale would *have* to make a grab at her!

God! she thought. How will I ever be able to face him again?

VI

A flood of light suddenly blinded him, and as he rolled over and sat up, Don recognized the squealing sound of car brakes. Dust and gravel swirled into the air, making the headlight beams two wide cones of light fixed directly on him.

"Don? Don!" he heard a voice—Jan—call out. "What on earth are you doing out here?"

He got up stiffly, brushing the seat of his pants as he came up to the driver's window.

"Whatever happened out here?" Jan shouted at him through the open window.

Don shook his head, confused, and images of what he had seen came flooding back into his mind.

—Beth's wooden doll, sitting on the edge of the stall, glaring, smiling at him.

—Beth running in the field until she drifted up, spiraling into the sky.

"I—umm—I came outside to check something in the barn, and I slipped on the gravel here," he said, awkwardly pointing to the driveway. "Something on the ground tripped me."

"Christ! I could have run you over," Jan said angrily. "It's a good thing I saw you there!"

Don shook his head and rubbed where he had banged his elbow on the ground. "Yeah—"

Jan peered up at him, trying to see his face, not sure if the smear she saw on his forehead was dirt or blood. "Well, let me park the car and we'll go inside. I had a heck of a day at work."

"Umm, me too," Don said. He stepped back, and Jan drove up to the barn and killed the engine. As he walked up to meet her, Don wondered how much he should tell her of what he had seen, and how much of what he had seen had been real.

It had to have been a dream, he thought. *Had* to have been!

Jan was getting out of the car and coming to meet him. "You're getting to be quite the clumsy ox around here, you know that?" she said. "In the past few days, you've cut your arm and leg, banged your head. You're a wreck!"

"I feel it, too," Don said as he eased his arm around her shoulder and they walked up to the house.

Beth is sleeping in her bed, safe, he told himself as he swung the kitchen door open and Max came to them, whining a greeting. She hadn't even been out here!

Jan headed straight for the stairway. "I'm beat. You coming up?"

"Yeah," Don replied, but he stood there in the kitchen for a moment, listening to Jan's tread up the stairs and into their bedroom.

It *had* to have been a dream!

Chapter Seven

Goblin

I

Don was up on the roof early the next morning. The slump-shouldered piles of discarded shingles that had collected around the house were slick with dew, but the roof dried off as soon as the sun hit it. He could tell it was going to be another hot day, so he stripped off his shirt before pulling up the old roof. Most of the nails were rusted down snugly, and he had to use the hammer to get the pinch bar under the nail heads.

His hammering echoed over the field like gunshots, and, as he worked on the front side of the house, he looked out past the garden, over the field toward town. He found it difficult—no, impossible—to believe that what he had seen last night was anything more than a dream, but it had been so vivid, so weird, it remained in his mind like a bad aftertaste.

In the kitchen, the sounds of his working disturbed Jan and Beth as they ate their breakfast. Max paced back and forth in front of the door until Beth let him out. Once outside, he bolted across the yard and out of sight.

Jan thought Beth looked particularly drawn, with darkening circles under her eyes. But when Jan asked if she was sleeping all right, Beth said she was—that she was probably just getting a reaction from the medication she was still taking for the hornet stings.

"So, what are your plans for today?" Jan asked her.

Beth shifted in her chair and took a sip of orange juice. "Krissy Remy's mom asked me to go to the Maine Mall with them today. I already asked Dad, and he said it was O.K."

"Do you have any money?"

Beth shrugged. "A little, I guess."

Jan fished in her purse and took out a ten-dollar bill. Handing it to Beth, who slid it into her jeans pocket, she said, "That's just a little extra so Mrs. Remy won't have to pay for your lunch, too."

"Gee. Thanks."

"So you and Krissy are getting to be pretty good friends, huh?" Jan asked. She took a seat opposite Beth and looked at her, smiling.

Beth shrugged, her thin shoulders making twin peaks of her blouse. "I dunno. I suppose so. Sometimes, though, I think she just wants to be friends 'cause I'm gonna be getting a horse."

Not knowing Krissy Remy well enough, Jan didn't know what to say to that.

"Then again," Beth said, "I only like her 'cause they've got cable and I can watch MTV." She laughed, and Jan was glad to see pleasure in her face.

But the steady hammering overhead vibrated the timbers and seemed to drive deep into Jan's skull, which still hadn't entirely cleared from last night's dizzy spell. She forced a smile, stood, and went to the sink, piled high with dirty dishes.

"You just be nice to her, and mind your manners while you're at the mall."

"I will," Beth replied, looking down at the floor. She had just left to go to the bathroom to brush her teeth when Louise and Krissy Remy drove up.

Jan leaned over the sink and called out to them. "Beth'll be right out." Then she turned and shouted, "They're here."

Beth left the house at a run and jumped into the Remys' station wagon. "Have a good time," Jan yelled as the car turned and went down the driveway, swirling just in its wake.

Once Beth was gone and Don had moved so the hammering at least wasn't directly overhead, Jan filled the sink and started doing the dishes. She stared vacantly as her hands mechanically did the work. The sudsy water circled her arms, making them both look cut off just above the wrists. Her mind wandered back over what she had said and done with Dale last night.

In the clear light of day, with at least a half-decent night's sleep behind her, she felt even more foolish than ever for thinking that Dale was at all sexually attracted to her. She realized and tried to accept that she had probably been projecting onto him what she herself was feeling. And as she considered that, she started wondering—again—how well she and Don were getting along.

Sure, the move to Maine and the abrupt change in their lifestyle had put a few pressures on all of them, but, Jan wondered as she slowly washed and rinsed each plate, was that any reason to start questioning

222

their relationship? Christ! Their seventeenth anniversary was coming up! If she was going to get a bit itchy, well, she was ten years too late for the seven-year itch.

The rapping of Don's hammer on the roof created a numbing white noise that lulled Jan into a shallow trance as she washed the dishes. She had that curious light sensation in the pit of her stomach—the same feeling she had had last night, only less. She found herself almost dozing as she mulled in her mind what *had* been said and what she thought *might* have been said.

Would she? she wondered. Would she *ever* have the—what? *nerve? stupidity?* to cheat on Don?

She shook her head, trying to dispel the fantasy of what she and Dale *might* have done. Maybe the opportunity had been there. Maybe it had been, and that was why she had gotten so dizzy.

"But why?" she said aloud. "Why now?"

Sure, the romance with Don was gone. How could it not be? After seventeen years, it was at least blunted.

—When you know how many times your husband will sneeze, and wait for the second one like waiting for the second shoe to drop.

—When you know how often he changes his underwear.

—When you know—exactly—what he'll say to you first thing in the morning . . .

Well, the exciting moments of discovery you felt in the first few years together just don't come any more. Plain fact, and no surprise there. That was when you started what dime-store psychologists on Merv Griffin and in their self-help books call "building your life together."

Beautiful concept, Jan thought, but after seventeen years, is it too much to expect a little—just a tiny bit— of excitement, of romance? Maybe the little gaps, the small differences they had always acknowledged, had imperceptibly widened into a dry gulch.

And maybe, bottom line, that's all it was. What she was feeling—or *thought* she was feeling—about Dale was just the need to find, maybe for one last time before she fully accepted that she wasn't eighteen anymore, that she was still attractive to men and that she needed that sense of discovery and, yes, *romance*.

Jan smiled feebly at her distorted reflection in one of her squeaky clean dishes—

So clean you can see yourself!

"Janis, my girl," she said, addressing her wavering reflection, "you is sufferin' from a midlife crisis. Yes, suh!" She laughed, both at her imitation of Bill's accent and the ridiculousness of such glib phrases, more geared for Merv's show than the experiences of real people.

Suddenly she was overwhelmed by the feeling of being watched. Slowly she turned around, expected to see someone—or something—standing by the door.

"God! What's come over me?" she said aloud. She pulled the drain and watched as the dirty water sucked down the drain.

The sound of the sink draining overshadowed for a moment the noise Don was making on the roof. It was while she was rubbing Pond's hand cream over her knuckles that she became aware of another sound. She struggled to recall how long it had been playing there, on the edge of her awareness—*how long*?

It was a faint, faraway scratching that reminded her

of something—someone shaping her fingernails on an emery board, or a cat clawing on the family sofa, or maybe a metal rasp dragging slowly over a stone.

She scrinched her eyes shut, concentrating on the sound, but every image she got didn't quite work. The sound suggested something deeper—darker—

She put the bottle of Pond's down gently and, cocking her head from side to side, tried to get a fix on the sound. Suddenly, with a jolt of surprise, she realized that it was coming up from the floor, from down in the cellar.

Beth and Max weren't in the house, so they couldn't be making the sound. Perhaps Don's hammering on the roof had started something vibrating. An old house like this would have its share of quirks—creaking timbers and snapping floor joists—but this was different. This was . . .

She went to the cupboard and got the flashlight. At the cellar door she hesitated. She had never liked cellars and, actually, hadn't been down there since they had moved in. Why not let Don check it out when he took a break from the work on the roof?

But the vibrating sound continued, and Jan swung open the cellar door. She was surprised by the cool, moist fingers of air that rushed up from below. There was a strong, almost overpowering smell of mold, and she had the sensation of descending into tepid water as she went down the cellar stairs slowly.

Halfway down, when a sprinkle of goose flesh crept up her arm, she snapped on the light and scanned as much as she could see. The weak beam of light seemed compressed in the dank gloom, further suggesting being under water.

The sound of Don's hammering grew fainter as she

225

went down the creaking steps and finally stood on the hard-packed earth floor. She listened, nerves stretched and tingling, and—yes, she heard it louder now.

"Better not be any rats or mice," she said aloud to bolster her courage. She knew she'd scream if she saw a rodent glaring beady-eyed at her, but that's what it sounded like now—a rat clawing from behind a wall. She moved toward the old coal bin slowly, still fighting the odd sensation of trying to walk under water.

The oval of light leaped across the broken wooden slats of the bin and danced over the rough stonework of the wall. Her gaze suddenly froze on one stone, next to the bin. Amazed, she went up to it.

"My God," she muttered, running her fingers along one edge of the stone. "Don never mentioned this."

There didn't seem to be any two stones of the same size in the cellar wall, but this stone was huge. It went from the earthen floor right up to the ceiling joist and stood over six feet tall, not counting what was buried below floor level. Approximately four feet wide at the bottom, the stone tapered gently toward the top and, at the very top where the floor joist rested, it flared out again. Jan gasped, immediately recognizing the rough-cut phallic shape of the stone.

Is that what's it's supposed to look like? she wondered, standing back and looking at the stone, or was she just imagining that's what it looked like because of the things she had been thinking about Dale?

And there was something else about the stone that struck a note of recognition, something she couldn't quite pin down. Jan swung the beam of light over the other walls but didn't see any other stone even half as big as the phallic stone by the coal bin. Her breath caught with a sharp hitch in her throat when she heard the sound again, the dull, rasping sound, and there was no doubt this time. It was coming from behind the stone in the wall—steady, deliberate scratches, as though something were behind the stone, trying to claw its way out!

A small whimper came from Jan's throat when she saw a small piece of mortar on the edge of the stone suddenly drop and shatter into dust on the cellar floor.

I just loosened it when I touched it, she told herself, but there was no denying the sound, which became louder. Frantic, Jan turned and ran up the stairs, taking them three at a time. She didn't stop running until she was in the kitchen, leaning over the sink and splashing cold water on her face. Her pulse hammered in her temples, and she was sure she was going to vomit.

After splashing her face several more times, she regained her composure and forced herself to keep busy with simple housework. Her mind kept turning over what she had seen and heard down in the cellar, and she felt a compulsion to go down to check if that piece of mortar had *really* fallen out. But before long, she convinced herself that, at worst, there were mice down there, and Don had better set out some D-con before things got out of hand.

An hour later, when Don came down from the roof for lunch, Jan wanted to tell him about what had happened to her, but she felt suddenly embarrassed, especially if she mentioned the phallic-shaped stone, so she just said something about mice down there, and Don said he'd take care of it, and that was it. Just the memory of the cold, clammy air in the cellar sent waves of nausea through her.

After lunch and a leisurely glass of iced tea in the shade, Don went back up onto the roof. Jan was upstairs, changing the sheets on Beth's bed when she made the connection that had been nibbling at the edge of her mind all through lunch. The stone, that phallic-shaped stone in the cellar wall, it looked like the leaning gatepost stone at the foot of the driveway!

II

The Remys dropped Beth off at the door a bit after three o'clock, and she came into the house, loaded with a new blouse, three paperback books, and the new album by Tears for Fears.

"If you had lunch, too, I want you to teach me how to stretch ten dollars this far," Jan said, inspecting the pile Beth put on the kitchen table.

"I told you, I had a bit of money already," Beth said, and then she dashed off to the living room and put the new record on the turntable. As the opening bars wailed out, Jan wished—again—that they had bought her her own stereo system for her birthday, preferably one with headphones, so they wouldn't have to hear her music.

That evening, while they were eating supper, Don got a call from Jack Stewart, a horse trainer who lived about three miles out of town on Mountain Road. He said he had heard from Billy Blackshoe that they were thinking of buying a horse for their daughter, and, if they wanted to come out after supper and have a look, he thought he might have just the animal for them.

Beth was too excited to finish eating, and she stood, fidgeting by the door while Jan and Don finished and cleared the table. Leaving Max tied to the barn so he wouldn't follow, the three of them got into the car and drove over to Stewart's farm.

From the road, only the wrought-iron weathercock on the barn cupola was visible, but, as they drove into the dooryard, both Jan and Don exclaimed how beautiful the sprawling, newly painted barn and house looked. What impressed Jan the most, and she wished aloud that their house had one, was the porch that ran the length of three sides of the house. Morning-glory-covered trellises over the back steps exploded with deep-blue flowers.

Stewart's wife, who introduced herself as Bessie, met them and walked with them out to the paddock behind the barn. Don took a deep breath of air tinged with the aroma of manure. "Our place'll look like this, someday," he said.

Jan wrinkled her nose and said dryly, "Will it have to *smell* like this, too?"

Turning to Beth, Don said, "Better get used to the smell, though, because you're going to be shoveling most of it."

"Who cares," Beth said as she dashed up the fence, stretching to look over the top rail.

"Is that him?" she asked. "Is that going to be my horse?" She watched an elderly man, dressed in a white shirt and brown trousers held up with green suspenders, as he exercised a frisky brown stallion on the end of a long tether.

Concern washed over Jan's features as she studied the bunches of taut muscles sliding beneath the horses' sweat-slick coat. The animal looked frighteningly large, and Jan thought a horse that big would never do for Beth.

229

"I—uh—I don't think so," Don said, catching Jan's anxious glance. "Mr. Stewart said something about a gray horse over the phone."

Stewart waved to them with his free hand. Bessie cupped her hands to her mouth and called out, "These here are the Inmans." Don picked a long stem of grass and stuck it into the corner of his mouth.

Drawing the horse in, Stewart unclipped the bridle and, with a slap on the rump, set the horse loose. The stallion kicked his hind feet into the air when he felt his freedom, then galloped to the far end of the paddock, kicking up puffs of dust. Jan felt a moment of panic, thinking the man might get trampled, but with an air of total unconcern Stewart walked over to them.

Beth found it difficult not to laugh aloud at the man. He was tall and hefty and had a bulbous nose, lined with dozens of broken blood vessels—what her dad had once told her were "drinker's tattoos." His ambling walk reminded her more of a bear than a man.

"Pleased to meet you," he said, sticking his hand between the fence rails to shake with Don. He winked at Jan and reached through the rails to give Beth's shoulder a hearty shake. She pulled away from him.

"Billy said you was looking to buy a horse," he said.

"Looking," Don said, not wanting to appear too anxious; he was learning how to deal with Yankees. "My name's Don. This is my wife, Jan, and daughter, Beth." He gazed across the paddock at the stallion, still rearing up, kicking his hoofs. "That's a nice-looking horse you've got there, Mr. Stewart."

"First off," he said, smiling, "call me Hoss. Every-

230

one does—you know, like on 'Bonanza'."

"On what?" Beth said, scrinching up her nose.

Don shook his head. "A character from an old TV show," he said.

"Yeah, back in the days when they had *good* shows, none of that sex and power stuff, or cars that talk to you, like today," Hoss added.

"There was 'My Mother the Car'," Jan said softly as if she didn't want anyone to hear her.

"Well, I tell yah," Hoss said. He climbed to the top of the fence with remarkable agility, then jumped to the ground bending to brush the dust from his pants legs. "I think I got just the horse you're looking for."

"I hope you don't mean *that* horse," Jan said, nodding toward the stallion.

Hoss burst out laughing. "Course I don't! If you're gettin' a horse for your daughter, here, you sure as sh—uh—sure as heck don't want no stallion." He lowered his voice and leaned close to Don. "Not when she comes around to her—uh—if you know what I mean. Drives a stallion wild!"

"Really?" Don replied, wondering if that was a fact or if Hoss was putting him on.

" 'Sides," Hoss continued, "this here horse's too frisky for a girl. Wouldn't do for a kid's first horse. He's young and ain't been broke proper. You can see where they got the expression, 'feelin' your oats' just watchin' him." He laughed deeply and heartily, and his nose turned a darker shade of purple.

Beth found that she couldn't take her eyes off Hoss's nose, and she wondered if it hurt or if it just looked as though it did.

"No, ma'am," Hoss said, tapping the side of his nose like Santa. "But this here old schnozzola helps me out. With it, I can sniff out a damn—uh—a darn good horse."

Or whiskey bottle, Don thought, giving in to the old prejudice that most horsetrainers—*all* of the good ones—are rummies. Besides helping Hoss sniff out a good horse, it might also help him find a whiskey bottle in the dark. He had to fight back a low chuckle, but Jan seemed to be the only one who noticed.

"Come 'round here," Hoss said as he started toward the barn. Beth walked beside him, still keeping a short but safe distance away; Jan and Don followed. "Soon's Billy mentioned you new folks wanted a horse, I knew I had the ticket for you."

He swung the barn door open, and the full-strength smell of manure hit them. "Ahhh, whew," Beth said, holding her nose, and even Don was a bit taken aback by the smell.

Before following Hoss into the barn, Jan turned and gulped one last, deep breath of fresh air, thinking she'd just as soon have gone up to the house with Bessie. After a minute or two inside though, she didn't notice the smell.

"This way," Hoss said, walking down a line of stall doors. Don's eyes were still adjusting to the dimness of the barn after the brilliant sunshine outside, but from behind the doors he could hear soft nickering and the sounds of animals feeding.

At the last stall door, Hoss stopped and swung open the top half of a Dutch door. "This here's the nicest, gentlest mare you're ever likely to meet. Here," he said to Beth, "let me boost you up."

Even though he still made her a bit nervous, Beth's curiosity and excitement were too much. She let Hoss grip her around the waist and lift her.

"Oh, my Gawd!" she said, low and admiring. Don chuckled, not having heard her use that expression in years. Inside the stall, a sleek, black mare—*my horse*, she thought—lifted her head from the manger and, chewing oats noisily, regarded the faces in the doorway. Her moist, brown eyes fixed on Beth, and Beth felt an immediate attraction arcing between them like an electrical impulse.

"Best—uh—darn horse you'll find," Hoss repeated. He lowered Beth to the floor and stood back so Jan and Don could also look in at her.

"Gentler than a kitten," Hoss said behind them. "Saddle-broke, easy going. I hate to sound like a used-car salesman, but it's as simple as that: take 'er home, saddle 'er up, and ride." He laughed out loud, and Don could have sworn Hoss's nose emitted a dull light.

Jan cast an inquiring look at Don, who stood, arms folded, straw hanging from his mouth as he studied the horse.

"She's—she's *beautiful*," Beth said with true awe in her voice. Hoss knew right then that he had to convince only two people. Don had to admit that, as little as he knew about horses, this one looked good— sleek, alert, healthy, certainly no sway-backed old mare!

"I wouldn't 'spect you to buy a used car without a test drive; I can't 'spect you to buy a horse without a test ride. D' you want to saddle 'er up?"

Beth's eyes widened, and she started bouncing on her toes. "You bet I do!"

Hoss went over to where he kept several bridles and saddles and grabbed one of each. "Grab that blanket there, Beth, and I'll help you saddle 'er up."

"Can I, Dad? Huh?" She was shaking, holding her clenched fists at chest level.

"Like the man says," Don replied, "you can't tell until you ride her." He could feel Jan's eyes boring into the back of his skull, and he turned to her and said, "She'll be fine. She's ridden a lot."

"There's no better horse to learn from than ol' Dobbin here," Hoss said, hefting the saddle onto his shoulder.

"Dobbin?" Beth said.

"A horse can't be three years old and not have a name," Hoss said. "I'll grant, it ain't the most original name goin', but Dobbin's her name. Right ol' girl?"

As if in answer, Dobbin nickered softly. Don thought it was a bit too pat and figured she was just reacting from hearing the saddle cinches clinking.

With the saddle on his shoulder, Hoss said, "I'll drop this outside. Just give me a second to get that stallion inside."

When he was gone, Jan and Don faced each other. Beth stood on tiptoe, watching the horse she just *knew* had to be hers.

"So what do you think?" Don asked Jan.

Jan shrugged and shook her head. "You know I'm not nuts about all this. Don't you think we should take our time and look around?" Again she shook her head. "I mean, it's an awfully large horse."

"I went with her when she went riding all last summer," Don said. "I've seen her; I know she's a good rider. And any horse looks big at first. We can't very well get her a pony. She wants a *horse*."

"I know. I know," Jan said "but—" She leaned close to Don's ear and whispered, "Those horses at

234

the stables that she rode, they were all plugs. I don't know. This one looks so—"

She cut herself off when the barn door swung open. They watched as Hoss led the stallion, still prancing and kicking, into his stall. The clatter of hoofs started the other horses stamping and whinnying.

"Let's just see how she does on this one," Don whispered to Jan. "There's plenty of time to decide."

Hoss put fresh water and an armload of hay into the stallion's stall, then rejoined them. "We'll saddle 'er up outside," he said and swung open the stall door so he and Beth could enter. "Now, do you know how to gentle a horse?"

They walked up to Dobbin slowly. Hoss held one hand out and softly clicked his tongue. "You know, gentlin' a horse is 'bout the most important thing in the world. You've gotta give her the attention and trust she needs. Here you go." He took Dobbin by the halter and pulled her to face Beth.

"Hi yah, Dobbin," Beth said tentatively, and Don couldn't help but chuckle; she was doing a fair imitation of Hoss. "How yah doin', girl?"

Dobbin made a low, blubbery sound and nudged her nose against Beth's shoulder.

"See there?" Hoss said. "She likes you already. You're doing good. Let's take her out outside."

Beth held the halter as Hoss swung the outside door open. Dobbin whinnied and stamped her feet, but still she stayed close to Beth. Beth looked back at her parents, beaming proudly.

"Don—" Jan said, an edge in her voice.

"She's fine. She's fine."

Gently but firmly, Beth led Dobbin out into the warm sunlight, all the while murmuring soft, cooing sounds. The animal, Don noted with surprise, actually seemed to respond to her with loving gentleness, and he wondered for a moment who was really leading whom. He and Jan went out the other door and watched from behind the fence as Beth saddled the horse, under Hoss's direction.

Once Dobbin was ready, Hoss tugged at the cinch and stood close by as Beth placed her foot in the stirrup and swung up into the saddle. She bounced up and down a few times to get the feel.

"Like a real pro," Hoss said admiringly.

She held the reins loosely, arching her shoulders back. Hoss smiled up at her as he stroked Dobbin's neck. When he stepped back, Beth clicked her tongue and gently kicked Dobbin's sides. The horse started off at a slow walk.

Jan glanced at Don and saw the proud smile on his face; she didn't feel half as confident. Backing up to keep his eye on her, Hoss came over to where Jan and Don were standing. Shielding his eyes from the sun, he nodded, saying, "She's a purty good rider. Got a good way with horses, too. I can tell."

Don grunted agreement.

Beth made several slow circuits of the paddock, then, clicking her tongue, said, "Git up!"

Dobbin took off at a brisk canter with Beth bouncing in the saddle, her face split by a grin.

"What d' yah think?" Hoss said.

"That's one fine horse you've got there," Don replied, trying to ignore the soft hissing sound Jan was making.

Don really had no idea what to look for in a horse. He could imagine himself stretching back Dobbin's lips to check her teeth, lifting each hoof to inspect for wear, but he figured he'd probably just get bitten and stomped. The best gauge he had was how much Beth seemed to be in control of the horse, so he watched her carefully as she urged the horse to go faster. She looked confident and in control, as if riding the horse gave her a self-assurance she didn't otherwise have.

"So d' you think we can start talkin' business?" Hoss said. "I'd say that horse and your girl were a match made in heaven."

Hoss climbed over the fence again, and he and Don wandered off around the barn, all set to bicker about the price. Don thought it was pretty much like setting the price on a used car—the seller always asked for more than he would settle for and the buyer always offered less than he was willing to pay. But Hoss was different. Even though he seemed genuinely anxious to sell, he didn't budge on the asking price. No matter how many times he repeated that Beth and Dobbin seemed made for each other, he'd say, "Take it or leave it," when Don tried to talk him down.

"Tell you what," Hoss said at last. "We could— literally—go around the barn all day on this. If you give me my askin' price, I'll include the saddle and bridle. You don't have the tackle, do you?"

"No," Don said.

"Then you ain't gonna do any better anywhere else. Can we call it a deal? Horse, saddle, bridle, and blanket." Hoss held out his hand, and Don took it, shaking firmly.

"It's a deal."

Walking back toward Jan, Don could tell by the sour expression on her face that she had seen them shake. He nodded, smiling, and said, "It's settled."

"How much?" Jan asked.

Don didn't like the tightness in her voice. He looked out at Beth, who was now leading Dobbin in a wide figure eight. He mentioned the sale price, and Jan's eyes widened. "We wouldn't get a better deal anywhere else," he said, echoing Hoss.

Beth came galloping over to them, her face flushed with excitement, and drew Dobbin up short at the fence. "She's the best horse in the world," she said, her voice blending admiration and desire.

"Well, Pun'kin, we won't be taking her home with us today," Don said.

Her smile dropped so fast Don half-expected to hear it plop in the paddock's dust. Her face paled, and her eyes started to tear up.

"I think we need another day or so to get her stall ready," Don said. "So if Mr. Stewart's willing to keep her till tomorrow and bring her by when he's got the time—"

"Oh, Daddy!" Beth squealed. She made a move to jump down and give her father a hug, but Dobbin made a nervous side step. Beth quickly drew back on the reins and, gently coaxing the horse, led her in a tight circle before dismounting and coming up to her father. "Thanks a whole bunch, Dad—and Mom."

The reins trailed loosely in her hand, and Jan wondered frantically how she dared turn her back on such a large animal.

"You're a darn good rider," Hoss said. He reached through the fence rails and ruffled her hair. "God's honest truth, I'm glad you'll be owning Dobbin. I knew you two'd get along as soon as Billy Blackshoe said you were wanting a horse."

"Billy Blackshoe?" Jan said, frowning.

"The guy at the hardware store I told you about,"

Don said. "You know, Wingnut."

"Oh," Jan said, nodding.

Beth looped the reins through the railing, then climbed over the fence to give hugs to both of her parents. She squeezed her father until her face started to turn red. "Thanks a whole lot," she gasped. "This is wicked neat!"

Don looked at Hoss, who seemed genuinely pleased with the deal, and said, "So if it's all right with you, I'll give you a check when you drop the horse off."

Hoss nodded. "I think I might be able to tear myself away from my pressing business to drop her by sometime tomorrow."

Jan and Don went back on their car and waited while Hoss brought Beth into the barn with him to show her how to unsaddle the horse and brush her down.

My horse, she kept thinking, nearly exploding with joy.

It took some doing to separate Beth from Dobbin, but Jan kept reminding them that it was getting late. Don caught the agitation in her voice and the frequent angry looks she shot at him.

As they drove home, Don wondered why Beth wasn't filling the car with her excited chatter. Maybe she was sensitive to her mother's reluctance to the whole idea. She just sat, staring out the window, lost in thought.

As they turned into the driveway, past the leaning stone gatepost, her eyes flickered rapidly. "You know," she said, her voice dreamy, "I'm not sure I like her name. I think I'll change it."

"Can you do that?" Don asked. "I mean, after being called one thing for three years, you can't expect her to respond to a new name, just like that." He snapped his fingers.

"Maybe if I pick a name that sounds sort of like the one she has now," Beth said. "I know! I'll call her *Goblin*. That sounds enough like Dobbin. That's what it'll be—*Goblin*!"

III

Early the next morning, Don took Beth into York with him to pick up a few supplies for the horse—combs, brushes, salt blocks, an extra blanket, and a hefty supply of Powder Pak. When they got back to the house, they spent the rest of the morning in the barn, making sure everything was ready for Goblin. Don had been a little on edge, thinking Beth would bring her wooden doll to the barn, and if she perched it—*him*, Beth would correct him whenever he mentioned the doll as *it*—up on the edge of the stall . . .

But the wooden doll was forgotten, for now, in the excitement of getting the stall ready. Now that it was a reality, not just a promise, Beth pitched in, working feverishly to spread straw and organize the tackle.

After a hasty lunch, Beth went down to the end of the driveway and sat, back against the gatepost, waiting for Hoss and Goblin to arrive. From the kitchen window, Don and Jan could see her, but at that distance, they didn't see that, in her lap, she was clutching the stiff wooden doll figure. They couldn't see that her knuckles had turned white and her hand was shaking from holding it so tightly. They couldn't see that her eyes had rolled back in her head and only the milky whites were showing.

Jan was just finishing putting away the lunch

dishes.

"She's pretty excited about all of this," she said, trying to sound happy for Beth. She and Don had talked it through the night before, after Beth was asleep; and Jan had resigned herself to the idea of owning a horse. Bottom line, she had to agree that it was good to give Beth such a clear, exciting focus. Other than Krissy Remy, she hadn't met any other children in their new hometown, and it looked as though it would stay that way until school started in September.

Don sat at the table, scratching Max behind the ears and laughing at the pleased grunting sound the dog made. "Wouldn't you be excited, too?" he said. "How many kids her age have their own horse?"

Jan sniffed. "Not many. I hope we're not spoiling her."

"I think she and Goblin will be just fine," Don said.

Jan shook her head. "I don't like that name!"

Don stopped scratching Max's ears, and Max let out a faint whimper as he padded off into the living room. "I'm going to go out and see how she's doing down there," Don said. "There's no sense in her wasting the whole afternoon sitting around."

He got up and was just opening the door when the telephone rang. Snapping it up in midring, he said, "Hello." Then, holding the receiver out to Jan, he said, "For you."

"I hope it isn't work," Jan said. "Hello?"

At the door, Don turned when he heard a loud shriek and, looking down the driveway, saw Beth jumping up and down, her arms spinning like pinwheels. There was something in her motion that

241

suggested the dream Don had had of Beth running in the grass, gently floating up into the night sky. He shivered and stepped outside.

"Here she comes! Here she comes!" Beth was yelling, her voice shrill as she followed the truck pulling a horse trailer up the driveway.

Don ducked his head back into the house and said to Jan, "Hoss is here. I'm going out. Make sure Max stays inside, O.K.?"

Jan nodded, cupping the receiver with her hand.

In the dooryard, Hoss's truck pulled to a stop. Beth raced to the back of the trailer and, standing up on tiptoe but keeping a respectful distance, looked in at Goblin. Her hands covered her mouth and her eyes flashed wild excitement as Hoss eased out of the truck and walked back to the tailgate.

Don came over and stood behind Beth, his hands resting on her shoulders as Hoss unfastened the latch, ran out the ramp, and backed Goblin out into the sunshine. The horse whinnied and stamped, raising puffs of dust.

"She's just gonna love it here," Beth said, her voice an excited squeak. "I just *know* she is!"

"I think so, Pun'kin," Don replied.

Hoss held Goblin by the halter and led her around in a wide circle, letting her adjust to the freedom and sunlight. Nodding toward the truck, Hoss said, "The saddle and stuff is in the back there, if you wanna get it into the barn. 'Less, of course, Beth here wants to take ol' Dobbin for a ride."

"Goblin is what she's going to call her," Don said.

Hoss shrugged. "It makes no difference to me. Not anymore."

Don knew there was no way around letting Beth

242

take a ride, so he hefted the blanket, saddle, and bridle over to the shade of the barn and called to Beth to lead the horse over. "She's your horse, now, so saddle her up."

Beth got to work while they watched. Once Goblin was ready, Beth swung up into the saddle and took off across the field. Her hair bouncing back in the wind, Don noticed, was almost the exact color of Goblin's mane and tail.

Jan came down from the house toward them, a deep scowl lining her face. Don hoped she wasn't going to start in again, about not thinking this was such a great idea.

"That idiot Jackman," she said, cheeks puffing. "Sally called in sick today and he wants me to cover her shift tonight. Darn it! She's probably got another date, but Dale insists he needs me to help cover the weekend crowd."

"It's only Thursday, if you don't mind me saying," Hoss said. He kept his eyes fastened on the distant horse and rider.

"Weekends start early, I guess, when you're on vacation," Jan said. "That really gets my goat, though. There was a lot of work I wanted to get done around the house today."

"The extra money won't hurt though," Don said. He winced as soon as the words were out of his mouth because he knew she wouldn't take it as a joke.

But Jan's expression didn't change; she was looking across the field at Beth, who had turned and was shouting and waving back at her parents. Her words didn't carry over the distance, but they would see the wide white gleam of her smile.

Jan waved back, then sighing, said, "He wants me

in there as soon as I can make it." She went back up to the house to change for work, grumbling as she went.

"I'll have to give you a check," Don said to Hoss.

"No problem."

"Would you like to come up, maybe have a cool one in the shade?" Don asked.

Hoss shook his head. "Thanks, no," he said. "I haven't had a drop of liquor in—going on twenty years, now. 'Sides, I've gotta get back to the farm. Bessie wanted me to string up a new clothesline for her."

Whistling shrilly, Don signaled for Beth to come back. She had ridden to the edge of the forest, and he didn't want her riding off any further. She started toward them at a good clip and, when she reined up beside them, Don told her to unsaddle Goblin in the stone corral behind the barn while he went up to the house for the checkbook. Hoss offered to help her brush Goblin down.

Jan was in the kitchen blow-drying her hair while the iron heated up. Her pink uniform was a rumpled heap on the back of a chair.

"This job might turn into something full-time if this keeps up," Don said.

"Very funny," Jan said over the whine of the blow-dryer. She watched, saying nothing as he took the checkbook from her pocketbook and wrote out the check to Hoss.

Don signed the check and put the checkbook back into her purse. He was heading out the doorway when Jan said, her voice barely loud enough for him to hear, "And who knows. Maybe that's *exactly* what I need—a full-time job."

He wasn't sure if he was supposed to hear her

comment or not.

IV

By evening, Don was exhausted. Beth had spent the rest of the afternoon until well after dusk riding Goblin. He had spent the rest of the day on the roof, laying down a few courses of shingles just so he wouldn't feel as though the day was entirely blown. After dark, with bats whispering in the sky overhead, he helped Beth get Goblin fed and settled in the stall. They had a supper of hot dogs and beans, and then Beth planted herself on the couch, reading her horse book while Don watched TV.

Once Beth had kissed him good-night, Don took one of the folding chairs and went outside, setting himself up with a cold Pabst by the kitchen door. He sat back, looking up at the sprinkling of stars as he scratched Max behind the ears. Night sounds filled the air.

"You know it don't get any better than this," he said, addressing the panting lump at his side. He took a noisy swig and leaned back.

Only the hiss of a passing car interrupted the sounds of crickets and whippoorwills. There was the occasional buzz of a mosquito on a strafing run, but they weren't bad, considering the breeding ground they had in the swamp just below the stream. After living so many years in Providence, he had begun to think that such a night as this was just a fantasy, and he breathed deeply of the night air, savoring his new life.

"So what d' yah think, old boy?" he asked, leaning forward to take another sip.

Max made a low, contented sound that was almost like purring; then he let out a sneezing whoof before settling his head on his paws.

"I know just what you mean," Don said, laughing. He leaned back again and closed his eyes, letting the cool breeze lull him. When he dropped his hand to pat Max again, he was surprised to find that the dog was gone. He hadn't heard him get up and walk away, but when he whistled, Max didn't show up. Don glanced at his watch and was shocked; it was after eleven o'clock already.

"Damn, I must've fallen asleep," he said, but even as he did, he slid further back in the chair.

Jan'll be home soon, he thought, drifting with the soothing night. The steady chirring of the crickets pulled him drowsily down like cushioned weights. His hand dropped down beside him and knocked over the beer can, spilling what beer remained. He realized that he was drifting to sleep again and that he should go inside before he got a stiff neck, but he didn't move; he let himself drop . . . drop. He didn't—or couldn't resist.

But he didn't sleep—not completely. He fluttered between waking and sleeping like a stone skipping on water. Images—vague, dark, and disturbing—began to stir, and he had the sensation of floating with liquid ease up, above his body sprawled on the lawn chair.

He found the drifting sensation curious because, although he was aware of motion, he also felt his limbs locked in a viselike grip. A tight, tingling sensation spread lazy numbness through his body, and with it came a feeling of threat.

What was that? he thought. He had heard something or *thought* he heard something; the memory of it had the remnants of color.

Did I see something?

No—It was—a sound. . . .

He tried to focus his attention and found the effort staggeringly difficult. There was a distant drumming sound with an echo that reverberated like a shot in a long tunnel. Confusion blanketed his mind, but the dull, steady beating sound continued.

A drum! That's it! Soft, muffled, steady. A drum beat that thumped like . . .

Maybe Beth's playing her new album, he thought. The idea pierced his paralysis like a bolt of lightning. He wanted to open his eyes, turn, and look at the house to see if the lights were on, but a swirling gray mist pulled at him, separating him from . . .

Everything!

Panic flooded him, and he struggled against the cold grip that held him. The drumming sound continued, rising and fading with a dizzying Doppler effect. What had started as a pleasant floating sensation turned increasingly into a nauseating spiral. He poured every ounce of strength into trying to move, into turning his head around.

What was that sound?

His ears throbbed and hammered as the sound became clearer.

Not a drum. Thunder!—No, not thunder! Hoof-beats!—Horse's hoofbeats!

As soon as he recognized the sound, the paralysis holding him broke with a gut-kicking jolt. He fell forward onto the ground as if suddenly released from some incredible tension. Snapping his head up, he took in a long pull of air.

He heard, beyond the drumming, another sound—

247

a dog, barking.

Max!

"Max!" he shouted, scrambling to his feet. His knees were soaked with spilled beer as he stood, looking anxiously around. "Max! Here boy! Where are you?"

He was disoriented for only a moment. He got a fix on the sounds; they were coming from behind the barn. Fighting to keep his balance, he ran across the driveway and around the barn to the stone corral. He saw that Goblin's stall door leading outside was open.

"Max! No!" he yelled as he climbed the stone wall. Inside the corral, Goblin was darting back and forth, trying to break clear of the dog barking at her feet. In the dim moonlight, the horse's eyes gleamed wildly as she darted first one way, then the other. But Max stayed with her, dodging between the hoofs that flashed in the moonlight and drummed the ground.

"Jesus, Max! Stop it!" Don yelled from the top of the fence. He didn't quite dare to jump down inside. Goblin was a gentle horse, but there was no telling what she'd do, panicked like this.

Dust swirled up, thick and cottony, obscuring the dimly lit scene. The sound of Max's barking and Goblin's running filled the night. A dizzying wave swept over Don, but it broke suddenly on the wind when he heard one sharp yelp. Then silence, punctuated only the heavy stamping of Goblin's hoofs, filled the night. The dust slowly settled.

"Oh, no! Max, are you all right, boy?" Don called. He listened for the dog but heard only the horse's fear-filled nickering. Then he saw, in the far corner of the corral, a dark, motionless lump. He watched it intently, waiting for signs of life, but even as he

248

lowered himself into the corral, he knew. Max was dead.

"You poor dumb dog!" he muttered, glancing over at Max. Goblin snorted once, then, head lowered, came slowly toward Don. Her mouth was still flecked with foam, but her eyes had lost their fire. He took her firmly by the halter and rubbed her flank; it was slick with sweat.

"Easy there, girl," he said as he stroked her. "Take it easy now." But she was completely docile, her panic having subsided like the calm after a storm. Don felt an edge of fear that perhaps the animal would start again.

Hoofbeats like drums!

"Hey, whatever's going on out here?" a voice— Jan's—suddenly called out of the darkness.

Both Don and Goblin jumped with surprise. Turning, Don saw Jan, standing at the gate.

"Hon! Someone—either me or Beth—left the stall door open. Goblin got loose."

Jan unhitched the gate and started to swing it open, but when Goblin snorted and stamped her hoof, Jan let the latch fall back into place.

"Max got in here," Don said, his voice starting to break, "and—and the horse trampled him."

"Oh, shit! Is he hurt bad?"

"I think he's dead," Don answered. "I haven't had time to check him yet." Tears stung his eyes as the reality of it sank in.

Once he got Goblin back into the stall—making sure the door was latched—he went over to Max, lying like a rumpled sheet in the dust. Jan came into the corral and stood over him, shaking her head from side to side.

"I *knew* we shouldn't have gotten that animal," she said between sniffles. "But I never thought something—something like *this* would happen."

Don looked down at Max. His eyes were protruding, the whites glistening with silver. With his final yelp, Max had bitten through his tongue, and blood ran from his nose, soaking into the ground. His side was caved in, almost flattened by the pounding it took from Goblin. When he tried to lift the dog, Don thought it felt more like hefting a sack of feed. Too many bones were broken, pulverized. Don was grateful, at least, that Max hadn't lingered in pain.

Slowly, with Jan following, he carried Max out into the field. The tears in his eyes made the circling stars blur as he looked up and shook his head sadly.

"That goddamned horse!" Jan said behind him. When Don laid the dog down on the dewy grass, Jan knelt beside him and scratched Max behind the ear for one last time.

"We're going to get rid of that horse," she said, her voice low and even. Don could tell she was fighting for control. "We'll take him back to Stewart. Tell him it just isn't going to work out. Oh, my! How do you think Beth's gonna feel about Max?"

"Wait a minute, Jan. You can't tell me you're—"

"That horse is a killer. She didn't have to trample Max." Tears streamed down her cheeks, and her shoulders shook. "Poor old Max!"

"It wasn't exactly the horse's fault, you know?" Don said. "She was terrified! What was she supposed to do, let the dog bite her?"

"Max probably thought it was just fun."

Don snorted. "Some fun. If it was anybody's fault, it was mine. I should have made sure the stall was

250

closed for the night. I thought I *had*. And I certainly shouldn't have let Max out loose—not until he got used to having Goblin around, anyway." His voice continually broke, and tears coursed down his cheeks.

"All of this isn't going to bring Max back to life," Jan said.

"And neither will getting rid of Goblin," Don countered. "It'll break Beth's heart all the more."

He stood up, pressing his hand into the small of his back. Then, wiping his eyes on his shirt sleeve, he said, "Well, I'll get a shovel from the barn and bury him. Beth didn't wake up, did she?"

Jan shrugged weakly, still kneeling beside Max and scratching his ear. "I don't think so. I had just driven up when I heard the commotion out back here. I didn't see any lights on in the house."

"Good," Don said. He took Jan by the shoulders and lifted her to her feet. "I want you to promise me one thing," he said. "Promise."

"What?"

"That you won't tell Beth that Goblin killed Max."

"You're not serious," Jan said.

"I sure as hell am," Don replied. His grip on her shoulders tightened. "It'll break her heart if she knew what happened. We can tell her Max got hit by a car. I don't want her to think anything bad about her horse. Promise me that!"

"But that horse is a killer!"

Don shook his head. "You saw her when I was in there with her. Gentle as a lamb. How she got out in the first place and how Max got in there, I don't know. But she was terrified and she protected herself the only way she knew how."

"You don't mean to tell me you're planning on

251

keeping that animal? After she killed Max?"

"I sure am," Don said. "Why don't you go up to the house. It won't take me long to bury him."

Jan turned and went inside and Don got a shovel. As he started to dig Max's grave, he began to wonder why he was defending Goblin so strongly. It bothered him that he had actually taken sides against Max, but Max was dead, and there was no point in taking it out on Goblin or Beth. Still, it bothered him; his tears were testimony to that.

He dug down about four feet, gently slid Max into the hole, and began covering him. He had to stop his work now and again to dry his eyes, but he smoothed the soil on top and replaced the sod. In the morning, if they decided to, he would make a grave marker.

When the work was done and Don stood there in the chilled night, looking at the mounded heap of earth, a low ruffling sound filtered across the field from the distant line of trees. It was the soft hooting of an owl.

Part Two

July, 1986

How long will a man lie i' th' earth
ere he rot?

Hamlet, V, i, 153
—Shakespeare

I sleep—I sleep long.
I do not know it—it is without name—it is a
word unsaid.

Song of Myself

—Whitman

Chapter Eight

The Fourth

I

Beth let out a squeal and cupped both hands over her ears as the first firetruck rolled by, its siren wailing. Standing behind her, his hands on her shoulders, Don smiled, feeling a rush of boyhood memories. When he was a boy, growing up in Lanesville, Massachusetts, the Fourth of July parade in Rockport had seemed just as good—no, *better*—than Macy's parade. The quaintness of the St. Ann's parade made him start wondering just how impressive those parades really had been.

"It's too *loud*!" Beth screamed. Don could barely hear her voice above the wavering siren. She cringed back, hugging her father's leg.

"Let's move back a little," Jan said, tugging at Don's belt loop.

Don looked at the wall of people behind him and shook his head. "It'll be by in a minute, anyway," he said.

Jan pulled harder on the belt loop as a line of slick, blackcoated firemen marched by. "It looks like it's said "Are you feeling O.K., Pun'kin?" He thought she looked a bit pale, and, down at her level, the press of the crowd seemed particularly stifling.

"It's just—just so loud," she said, wincing. "It hurts my ears." Her lips were thin and pale, and, as he held her, he could feel a trembling in her body.

He stood up, brushing the grit from his knees, and, holding Beth's hand, directed them back, away from the crowd. "Come on. Let's get a soda or something. I don't want you punking out on me before the fireworks."

They moved through the mass of people—he didn't know this many people lived in St. Ann's—over toward one of the pushcarts, where an overweight man was selling candy apples, cotton candy, and soda. Solid American health food. Behind them, the sound of the siren dropped, only to be replaced by the belly-thumping bass drum of the Kittery High School marching band.

Don was still smiling to himself, inhaling childhood memories with the mixed smells of hot dogs, popcorn, spent gunpowder from fireworks, and hot tar. He asked Beth if she wanted a drink but, just as he spoke, a blast of trumpets drowned out his voice. At the cart Beth pointed to the cotton candy, so he got that for her and two Pepsis for himself and Jan.

The parade was wending its way down Main Street, past the stone watering trough, covered with red, white, and blue streamers, toward the park where the town band would play until the official fireworks began. The unofficial fireworks had been exploding and flashing all day.

Don, Jan, and Beth all sat down on a clear patch of grass and started to eat. They couldn't see the parade from where they sat, but just hearing it was enough for now. Someone let off a string of ladyfingers nearby, and Don jumped, sloshing Pepsi onto his shirt. Jan laughed and offered to get him some napkins, but he told her not to bother; she could suck it out later if she wanted.

"Boy, remember how much firecrackers used to bother . . . Max," Beth said. She looked at her father, and he saw tears in the corners of her eyes.

He nodded and said, "Yeah, Punk."

When they had finished their treats, they stood to watch the parade some more. A line of horses from Whispering Pines Stables was going by, and Beth waved wildly to Krissy Remy, who was riding in the lead. Everyone laughed at how the pack of Cub Scouts marching behind didn't miss a step as they avoided the steaming piles the horses dropped in the street. The last official part of the parade went by—the St. Ann's volunteer firemen with a large tarp for people to toss money onto. The tarp snapped with each step they took, jingling and jumping the pile of change they had already collected.

Behind the firemen came a group of teen-agers, laughing and pretending to be marching. Most of them, the boys anyway, had cigarettes hanging from their lower lips. The girls, Don thought, shouldn't be dressed as they were unless they were looking for trouble.

Applauding and laughing, the crowd started to shift toward the town park. The bonfire and fireworks weren't scheduled to start until nine o'clock, but there were rides set up for the little kids and plenty of huckster booths, sucking up people's quarters and dollars. At the bandstand—a white gazebo-shaped building on a granite base—the town band was setting up, getting ready to deliver on the Sousa.

"I don't know about anyone else," Don said, "but I'm getting hungry. You want me to get a couple of slices of pizza or something?"

"Nothing for me, thanks," Beth said.

Jan considered a moment and said, "I know I shouldn't, but the pizza smells pretty good."

"You guys wait right here, or I'll never find you," Don said and then disappeared into the crowd to get a slice for each of them, figuring Beth would want one once she saw how good it was. He was edging his way through the press of people when he heard someone call his name. He was surprised when he turned to see Billy Blackshoe sitting behind a rickety card table. On the table was spread an assortment of what looked to Don like cheap costume jewelry.

Authentic Indian Charms—Real Magic—Strong Medicine, the hand-painted sign proclaimed.

"How are you doing on that roof of yours?" Billy asked, smiling widely. His black hair glistened from the row of light bulbs strung up over his table. In spite of the heat, he was wearing a fur-lined vest, and around his neck was a round beaded design picturing a bear.

Don shrugged, tossing his hands into the air. "Haven't tackled too much of it yet," he said. "Been busy."

Billy nodded. "Too hot for roofwork, too," he said. He took a moment to make eye contact with someone else at the table, then turned back to Don. "And Beth, how's she liking the horse?" he asked.

"Fine. Just fine," Don answered. He wondered how he knew they had gotten one.

"Hoss told me he'd made a deal with you folks," Billy said.

Don was surprised that he seemed to be answering his thoughts. "Well, I've gotta get something to eat," he said, backing away.

Billy looked at him, still smiling. "Tell Beth I'm

258

sorry 'bout her dog, O.K?" he said.

How the hell'd he know about that? Don wondered, but before he could ask Billy, the crowd pulled him away from the table. Confused, Don waited in line for his pizza, then rejoined his family. He was going to mention seeing Billy to Jan but then decided against it.

The sky was turning the color of soot, and dark rafts of clouds pointed like fingers to the northeast. Mosquitoes hummed in the twilight, enjoying the abundance of warm-blooded things. Dusty-winged moths darted crazy spirals around the concession lights. The ground was littered with crushed paper cups, crumpled hot dog holders, and the tatters of exploded firecrackers.

"I hope it doesn't start to rain," Jan said, looking up at the dark line of clouds closing in.

"We'll be all right," Don replied. On the bandstand, the leader tapped his baton on his music stand, and the band blared out a slightly off-key march. Don couldn't remember the name of it, but it was familiar.

"They're going to start the bonfire in a half-hour or so," Don said. "Why don't we go out in the field there for a bit? The crowd's kind of getting to me. What d' you say, Pun'kin?"

They both looked at Beth, who stood there, watching the band. Her eyes were wide and moist, reflecting the lights and swirl of activity. Her mouth was a thin, harsh line that, with a sudden sinking feeling, Don thought looked like the black painted mouth on her wooden doll.

"Beth?" Jan said, nudging her shoulder. She moved, surprisingly loose-jointed, but still kept her gaze fixed on the bandstand. "Beth? Are you coming with us?"

"Huh?" she said, looking up glassy-eyed at her

parents.

"Are you feeling O.K.?" Don asked, and tension edged his voice. Something was galling at him—maybe it was the noise and the crowd, maybe it was too much junk food since they got there, or maybe it was talking to Billy Blackshoe—but whatever it was, it cast a sense of unease over the evening like a drifting, settling cloud.

"Yeah—sure," she replied, but her voice had a strange flatness. Don wasn't sure if it was the deadening sounds of the crowd around them or a quality in Beth's voice. A panicked sense of disorientation swept through him as the band wound into a sprightly rendition of *Stars and Stripes Forever.*

"Your mother wants to move over into the field before the bonfire starts," Don said, leaning down and cupping his hands to her ears so she could hear.

"I want to listen to the band some more," she said. "Can I go over?"

Don glanced at Jan, frowning, but Jan shrugged and said, "Why not?"

"Why don't you pick out a spot over there by the baseball dugout?" Don said, pointing across the field. "We'll find you in half an hour or so."

"O.K.," Jan said. She gave Don a little kiss on the cheek and started off, soon swallowed by the crowd. When Don turned back around, Beth wasn't there. He got angry, thinking she should have waited or at least had permission to go off alone. Craning his neck to see above the crowd, he started toward the bandstand, figuring that's where she was headed.

As he got closer to the music, the steady thump-thump of the bass drum hit his stomach like soft hammer blows.

Distant drums! Hoofbeats! he thought, and another wave of panic rippled through him like chilled water. Trying not to get nervous, he began to circle through the crowd, looking for Beth.

Beth had moved toward the bandstand with a dreamy, slow motion, bouncing harmlessly off people, almost unnoticed in the general push and shove. The lights on the bandstand, reflecting from polished brass instruments and silver uniform ornaments, swirled like a view from under water. The lights moved from side to side, leaving long, yellow tails. The colors of peoples' clothes and faces mixed and ran like watercolors left out in the rain. The music—slow and steady—wound out like a dangling rope, and that rope pulled Beth closer and closer to the bandstand.

But it wasn't just the color and the sound that drew her. Something else, something cool, dark, and nearly lifeless pulled her, called her closer—closer to the solid granite blocks of the bandstand's foundation.

The closer she got, the more the sounds of music and people deadened as though her ears were packed with cotton. Everything became flat and gray, lost beneath another sound that grew louder. Beth stood in the shadows beneath the bandstand, searching the dark stone base for the source of what she heard.

The march ended, and applause burst out from the crowd, but it was lost to Beth as she searched the edge of the foundation, sure that this was the source of the dull, hollow scratching sound she heard. Everything—lights, music, firecrackers, and people—faded.

I know that sound, she thought, listening intently to the frantic scratching sound coming from the darkness.

Where have I heard that before?

She wished she hadn't listened to her father and left Bear, her wooden doll, at home.

He'd tell me what it was! He'd know what was

making that sound!

Bending down, almost on hands and knees, she scoured the darkness that ringed the thick stone blocks supporting the bandstand. She was convinced the sound came from there, from the ground, but where—*where*?

And as she circled the bandstand, lost in the darkness, ignored by the crowd, she saw something— a blur of motion. As she came up close to it, the scratching sound intensified.

The bright lights surrounding her made the darkness all the deeper. It was nearly impossible to see, but there was—*something*. She could see it moving there between two of the granite blocks.

Sudden fear knotted her stomach as she remembered that day in the woods—the yellowjackets swarming, stinging—her foot caught, held so she couldn't move, couldn't get away—the bony hand, reaching out from the grout pile, death-black fingernails cutting into her ankle, holding her—*holding her*!

She saw a gap, a slash of inkiness appear between two of the stones as the scratching sound filled her ears, rough clawing like a metal rasp grinding against stone. Cold steel closed around her throat when she saw thin, bone-white fingers picking away at the cement that held the granite blocks together.

Beth staggered back, choking and gasping for air. A tingling jolt raced up her spine, and her hands and feet were coldly numb. She tried to look away but couldn't, and the shriveled hand clawed the cement to dust as it tried to push its way out from under the bandstand.

Her eyes stinging and her vision clouding, the cold spread up her arms and legs, and the sudden fear that when it reached her heart she would die filled Beth with anguish. She fell, trembling to the ground and curled up into a quivering fetal ball. Flecks of foam flew from between her chattering teeth.

"Beth! Pun'kin!" Don shouted when he saw her fall. The crowd stepped back, ringing Beth; and the music died away when someone shrieked.

"Ooh, Beth!" Don cried, holding her tightly in his arms as she shook. Tears stung his eyes, and the pressing smell of the crowd made him want to vomit.

"For Christ's sake, stand back," he shouted, waving wildly at them. "Give her room to breathe!"

Before the bandmaster had a chance to ask for assistance over the P.A. system, a young man, a physician's assistant from Westbrook, came forward and, together with Don, carried Beth away from the crowd. They laid her down on the grass in front of the post office, and, while the young man stayed with her, Don ran over to the baseball field to get Jan.

When Beth came to, she complained only of a slight headache, probably from falling. The young man gave her a quick check-over. He suggested she had just fainted from the crowd and excitement but they could bring her to the emergency room at York Hospital if they'd feel better. But they didn't. Instead Don carried Beth home with Jan walking along beside them. At the top of Hunter Hill Road, as they walked up their driveway, the skyline toward town suddenly flared an angry orange. The bonfire licked up at the darkening clouds, and flowers of exploding fireworks popped, muffled by the distance.

II

The clouds that had threatened to spoil the Fourth of July celebration finally opened up sometime after midnight, saving the local firemen the trouble of hosing down the last embers of the bonfire. In the morning, the rain was blowing in sheets off the ocean when Don dropped Jan off at *The Rusty Anchor*'s back door.

"I'll pick you up right here at five o'clock, O.K.?" he said, leaning to give her a kiss. He watched her dash to the door, then pulled out slowly onto Route One.

"Mornin'," Bill called, waving a spatula at her as she hung her raincoat beside the time clock. She could hear the snap of bacon and eggs on the grill.

"Great weather, huh?" she said, and then she ducked into the ladies' room to check her make-up. The rain had wilted her freshly ironed uniform.

When she came out, Bill was leaning against the salad bar, chowing down a breakfast that looked large enough to fuel two, maybe three, teen-agers. He smiled, using his napkin to dab egg yolk from his chin before speaking. "Oh—ah, Dale's in the office."

"This early?" Jan said.

"Yeah," Bill said. He scooped up egg yolk with a piece of toast and slid it into his mouth. "Said he wants t' see yah soon's you came in. You ain't in trouble wit' him, are yah?"

Jan shrugged. "Not that I know of." She straightened her shoulders, went to the door, and knocked softly.

"Come on in," Dale said, and Jan swung the door open.

The blue haze of tobacco smoke in the office was enough to stifle her as she went over to the chair beside the desk and sat down.

"Morning," she said, smoothing her dress and putting on her best "rainy-Monday" smile. "What's up?"

Dale looked up from his paperwork and said,

"Depends." He lit another cigarette, and Jan could see his hand tremble slightly. He exhaled noisily, his left hand twirling the silver chain that was tangled in his chest hairs. He was wearing a white shirt and white pants—to show off his tan, no doubt.

As she watched him, waiting for him to begin, Jan was amused by the duality she felt. On the surface he was so self-confident, so conceited it almost nauseated her; but below the surface there was still something about him that—she hated to admit it—attracted her.

"So, what did you want to see me about?"

Dale flicked the lengthening ash and cleared his throat. "You see, Jan, it's like this. You've been here a couple of weeks now, and—well—frankly, your work just isn't up to par."

"You're not firing me, are you?" she asked. There was a cold, sinking feeling in her stomach; and, as much as she hated it, her first thought was that she would never see him again.

"Not exactly," Dale said, inhaling on the cigarette. "But come on. You've got to admit that Sally and Carol can run circles around you."

Flushing, Jan looked him directly in the eyes, noticing that he couldn't hold eye contact. "But you knew I didn't have any waitressing experience when you hired me. I thought I was doing a good job."

"Good enough," Dale said, "but that's the point right there: the amount of work. The way this summer's been going so far, it looks as though I just might not be needing you. Not as much as I thought, anyway."

Jan was angry, but with the anger was another feeling—one of rejection. She began to wonder if Dale had picked up on what she had been thinking about him and, for whatever reason, was turned off or intimidated by her.

265

Or maybe, she thought, he's thinking about *me* what I've thought about *him*.

But she dismissed all that as foolish fantasies.

"The point is, the Fourth of July weekend was supposed to be one of our best weekends, and you were here for a bit of it. You saw that we weren't *that* busy."

"What are you talking about?" Jan said, not caring that her anger showed. "I was running my feet off!"

Dale shrugged. "That's only because you don't know what you're doing yet. I—"

"So what you're telling me is that I'm just not working out. Is that it?"

Dale paused, and that pause spoke more than anything he could have said.

"Is that it?" Jan asked.

"No. Not really," Dale replied. "But at least for now, I'd like to leave it at that you're just on call. You know, to cover for sick days and things. I'll keep your number handy and give you a call if I need you."

Biting her knuckle, Jan nodded. "Sure. I mean, you know, it's not like I was planning on making waitressing a career or something." She stood to leave. Dale snubbed out his cigarette and immediately lit another.

"Do you want me to work out the day?" she asked.

Dale turned, nodding his head toward the rain-streaked window and the tossing gray sea beyond. "On a day like this, it isn't going to be busy. So if you can get a ride—"

"Yeah," Jan said, turning, "I can get a ride." She was reviewing in her mind everything she had said and done since she started working for Dale, trying to find something she could pin this on. Maybe that night they had shared a drink after work. Maybe then Dale had come on to her and she just hadn't read it right.

266

Maybe—the idea made her chuckle as she swung the office door open—maybe she was being canned because she hadn't played up to the boss. These days, anything was possible.

She swung the door firmly shut on him, leaving him sitting there at his desk, hazy smoke rafting around him. She stomped over to Bill, who had started cutting up the day's salad ingredients.

"So," Bill said, looking up but not breaking the rhythm of his chopping, "what's what?"

"I'm—I guess you'd call it a 'temporary layoff.' "

Bill's thin eyebrows curled into two tiny Os. "What you talkin' 'bout?"

"Dale says it hasn't been really busy enough to need three waitresses, so I'm pretty much out of a job."

"Ain't been busy?" Bill said, his voice rising close to laughter. "We ain't been busy, 'n' a hound dog don't have fleas! She-it! Beggin' your pardon, but we sho *have* been busy!"

Jan felt her blush deepen, and she was heading for the phone to call Don for a ride home when the back door sprang open, and in walked a young girl—no more than twenty, Jan guessed—with a pink waitress's uniform on underneath her raincoat.

"Excuse me," Jan said when the girl almost knocked into her.

"Hi," the girl said, her voice a high-pitched whine that, with that one word, set Jan's nerves on edge. "My name's Betty. Betty Coleman. Sorry I'm a little late."

Bill and Jan exchanged glances but said nothing.

"Is Dale in?" Betty asked. Her eyelids fluttered as she looked around the kitchen. "I'm supposed to start work today."

"No fooling," Bill said, and then he looked over at

Jan. "What the hell did you do?" he asked her.

Jan shrugged, then reached for the telephone and started dialing. "I don't know," she replied, "maybe it's what *I didn't* do."

III

Don picked her up an hour later in front of the pinball arcade. On the drive home, they talked it over, and probably the worst part of it all for Jan was Don's smug "I told you so." He never came right out and said it, but it was there all the same.

As they drove up the driveway, Don noticed—again—how much he missed Max. It had become such a part of his life, having the old guy come bounding up to the car whenever they got home, Don thought he'd never get used to missing him. This hollow sense of loss for the dog, compounded with the rain and the lackluster greeting from Beth, was enough to cast a complete gloom over the day. After lunch, Don decided he'd feel better alone, so he went out to the barn to putter around for a few hours.

By late afternoon, the rain seemed about to clear off, but then purple clouds began to gather in the west. Lightning veined the thunderheads, and dull rumblings of thunder made the barn windows rattle. Don had been replacing a few weak rungs in the loft ladder when Jan called him for supper. After making sure Goblin was settled in and her stall doors were locked, he went up to the house.

The sky opened up again as they were sitting down to eat. Don tried to joke about the lousy weather, but it didn't help raise anyone's spirits. At ten o'clock, Beth headed upstairs to bed, carrying her horse book and wooden doll with her. Jan was still moping about her interaction with Dale that day, wishing she could just get enough of a handle on it so she could forget all about it. Don had told her several times that he'd just as soon she never went back there, even if Dale *did* call her.

They decided to stay up and watch Johnny Carson, so Don left to go downtown to the local Big Apple for a six-pack.

Mark Herman was standing at the foot of the driveway as Don drove out. He dropped to the ground behind the leaning gatepost and craned his neck to watch the taillights disappear. Excitement tingled in his belly—and lower.

Ever since that day he and his father had delivered the load of hay to the Inmans, he had wanted to come back. After Don had cut his arm and Mark had finished stacking the bales for him, he had noticed something about the barn that had given him an idea—an idea he hadn't had a chance to try until tonight because his rummy father had kept him so busy at home.

But tonight—tonight he had his chance. He'd told his father he was going to the AC/DC concert in Portland and gotten out of the house right after supper. So what if it rained; he'd be dry.

The window up in the loft, Mark had noticed, was directly across the driveway from the house, and, when he looked out, he could see right into the Inmans' bedroom. He figured it had to be theirs from what he could see of the bedroom furniture. If they didn't draw their curtains, and if they left the light on, he thought he just might get one hell of a show! It was worth the try.

Silently he started up across the lawn. Thunder grumbled in the distance. All of the lights except the one in the living room were off, and through the curtains he could see the flickering glow of the TV.

Keeping in the shadows as much as he could, he went up to the side of the house, sneaking his way toward the living room, where he could hear the local weather report.

Suddenly he heard the sound of a car approaching, and he froze. The car turned into the driveway, and as it did its headlights swept over him. He thought for sure he'd been spotted and dropped to the ground, panting. The car lurched to a stop, and the driver—Mr. Inman—got out and went into the house.

"Stupid asshole. Never saw me!" he whispered, getting up slowly and brushing himself off. His clothes were wet from the damp ground, but he didn't care.

The light in the kitchen came on, casting a yellow rectangle onto the lawn, and Mark heard Don call out, asking his wife if she wanted a Coors. She said, "Yes," then he heard Don as he walked into the living room. Mark slowly raised his head up to the sill level, then eased up until he could see them. Both were sitting on the couch sipping beer.

The old lady uses a glass for hers, he thought, sneering.

Mark stood outside, watching and listening for about half an hour, but when nothing more interesting developed in the living room, he started to think about getting up into the loft, just to be ready. The storm seemed to be dropping back behind the horizon, rumbling in its retreat.

Edging along the side of the house, Mark moved down, past the kitchen window, and in a dash raced across the driveway to the barn door.

He stood for a moment in the doorway, safe in the shadows, and listened. He wondered why their damned dog hadn't started barking by now, but he wasn't about to question his luck. He flattened himself against the barn wall when the light in the kitchen was suddenly blocked off. Someone—it looked like Mr. Inman—was leaning up to the window, looking outside.

Did he see me after all? Mark wondered, but then he saw Don go to the refrigerator and take out another beer.

Just as Mark ducked inside the doorway, he heard from the woods behind the house the soft hooting of an owl. It sounded like someone blowing over the top of an empty Coke bottle.

The tingling he had felt in his stomach ever since he had hidden behind the gatepost increased as he felt more than saw his way over to the loft ladder. In the dark, he kicked something over. It sounded like a water bucket as it rolled with a clatter across the barn floor and stopped. Mark stood frozen, waiting to bolt if he heard activity from the house.

"Yes, sir," he whispered, rubbing his hands together. Just as he gripped the first rung, the horse nickered softly in the darkness. It sounded right up next to his ear. Quickly, he went up the ladder, each rung groaning under his weight, and into the loft. The warm air surrounded him, so thick with the smell of hay it made him want to puke. It smelled just like his stupid hayseed old man!

He was dragging his legs up through the trap door into the loft when he heard the Inman's kitchen door spring open. Footsteps crunched the gravel in the driveway, approaching the barn.

A beam of light suddenly lanced the darkness below Mark, who crouched, breath burning in his lungs, waiting to be discovered as Don walked over to the horse's stall.

"Honest to God, Goblin!" Don said, "I'm beginning to think you have hands. How'd you get this door open?

And what's this doing way over here? Huh?"

Mark was peeking over the edge of the trap door, keeping Don in sight. He could see the beam of light, focused on the water bucket he had kicked over. Don snapped the latch on the stall door, jiggling it several times to make sure it was secure. Then he picked up the fallen bucket and placed it in front of the stall door. After rubbing the horse's nose, he scanned the barn once, then went back to the house.

Mark sagged back, letting out the breath he had been holding since he had heard the kitchen door open and then bang shut.

Safe!

He made his way carefully over to the rectangle of dirty glass. As far as he knew, there wasn't anything on the floor, but he didn't relish the thought of stepping on an up-turned pitchfork. He was sweating, more with excitement than anything else, as he dragged a bale of hay over to the window, positioned it just right, and sat down, looking at the house. He huffed onto the glass and, using his shirttail, wiped a small circle clean.

"All the better to watch you," he said, laughing softly.

He waited and waited. The minutes dragged on as his expectation grew and more than once he wished he dared to chance lighting a cigarette. If only he had been able to nab a bottle of his father's whiskey, but the old coot kept *that* as close to himself as wet underwear.

He waited, his impatience growing, and with the passing minutes he grew sleepy from watching. More than an hour went by, and he was close to giving the whole venture up, but then a light snapped on in the bedroom, and Mark let out a delighted squeal when he saw both of them enter the bedroom.

"All right!" he said, rubbing his hands together and adjusting his seat. "Holy shit! Here we go!"

They were talking as they moved around the bedroom. Of course Mark couldn't hear what they said, but it looked as though Mr. Inman, at least, was agitated about something.

Probably can't get it up, Mark thought, and he's tired of her complaining about it.

Mark watched as Don walked toward the window and, stretching his arms over his head, took off his T-shirt. Jan was sitting on the bed, back to the window as she unbuttoned her blouse, slid that off, and then unhooked her bra.

"Turn around, bitch!" Mark hissed. "Turn around!"

Don unloosened his belt and let his pants drop to his ankles. Sitting on the edge of the bed, his back to Jan, he kicked the pants off into the corner. He stood again and rolled his underpants off, and Mark could clearly see the dark beard of pubic hair.

"Come on, man," Mark chanted lowly. "Come on. Do it to her!" He brought his face close to the window, his breath fogging the glass.

Don sat back down on the bed and, half turning, put both hands on his wife's shoulders and slowly drew her backward. A hard lump formed in Mark's throat when he saw Jan rest her head on her husband's thigh. Her breasts folded together as she leaned onto her side and slowly slid her hand up Don's leg.

"All right!" Mark whispered, licking the sweat on his upper lip. "Better than the State Theater any day!"

Don leaned down and kissed his wife; her arms twined up around him, pulling him close. When they broke off their kiss, Jan's hand finally reached for Don's already rigid flesh and began to massage it gently. Mark felt himself harden as he watched Don grow stiff under his wife's touch.

"Come on, baby! Use your mouth," Mark said. And as if in answer, Jan slid down lower on the bed to comply.

Mark swallowed with difficulty, feeling his erection grow until it was a near-painful throb as he watched Jan's head bobbing up and down. Before he realized he was doing it, Mark's hand started rubbing the bulge of his crotch. The scene in the bedroom across the driveway held his unblinking gaze just as a magnet holds iron.

"Sweet Jesus," Mark said, more a moan than anything else as Jan's head moved up and down faster and faster. Don continued massaging her breasts, but he tossed his head back, eyes closed in ecstasy. Quickly, Mark stood and unfastened his pants, letting them bunch at his ankles as he knelt on the floor.

"Oh, sweet Jesus!" he said, grabbing himself once more while keeping his eyes fixed on the bedroom scene. Just when he thought Don and he were about to explode, Don twisted his hips around, spread his wife's knees with his legs, and plunged into her. Mark's hand slid up and down faster, his eyes fluttering as his orgasm threatened to explode. Gyrating his hips back and forth, he paced himself with Don's thrusts. And the expression of pleasure on Jan's face made him picture himself on top of her thrusting deeper . . . *deeper*!

He stroked almost with anger and suddenly exploded, his sperm shooting out and splattering against the dusty glass.

"Hot stuff," Mark said with a quivering sigh as he dropped back onto his heels. He was satisfied, satisfied and incredibly thirsty as he stood and hitched up his pants.

Still watching the love-making going on in the bedroom, Mark wiped the sweat from his forehead, his breath burning in his lungs. He wondered if his buddies would ever believe him when he told them—*if* he told them. Something like this might be too good a thing to reveal, for now. He decided to wait and see.

Jan and Don slowly finished their love-making. As soon as they were done, Jan rolled over and snapped out the light on the nightstand. Disappointed that the show was over, Mark stood there, face pressed to the barn window, watching the dark rectangle of the window across the driveway. His flaccid penis throbbed as it shrank.

His pulse was still hammering in his ears as he sat back down on the bale of hay, but after a while it slowed to a faint, fluttering sound. Again, he wished he dared light a cigarette. "I always have a cig after sex," he said to himself, laughing.

Suddenly jerking to his feet, he swatted the air over his head. "What the hell?" he said. The fluttering sound he had thought was his heartbeat was something else, something unseen in the dark of the loft.

He thought it might have been his imagination, but then he swung out blindly when it came again. A soft whickering sound like—like *wings*!

He knew what it was when he heard the high-pitched chitter of a bat. So it hadn't been his imagination after all.

"Stupid bastard," Mark snarled as he tried to track the invisible spiral of the bat. Crouching low and shielding his head with one arm, he started crawling toward the loft trap door. The gray light of the night through the window wasn't enough to see by, and he suddenly sprawled forward when his hand reached through the opening. Feeling blindly for the top rung, he cringed when the bat's squeaking suddenly got louder, and something soft and furry grazed his ear.

"You *bastard*!" he yelled, not caring if the Inmans

heard. He swung his arm overhead and was surprised when he connected with the furry body. For a second the animal fluttered at the window, beating futilely at the glass. Its size surprised Mark, and he hurried to swing his legs into the opening.

The dark wings flickered past him again. This time, when Mark swung, he rammed his elbow onto the loft floor, sending shooting pains up his arm to his shoulder.

Momentarily disoriented, Mark lurched to the side trying to protect himself. His footing slipped, and his knee smashed into the ladder. He maintained his grip but maybe not so luckily because again the bat swooped down at him, and this time Mark felt tiny points of pain in his scalp as the bat clung to his hair.

The leathery wings beat on his head, and all he could think about was the chance of rabies if it tangled in his hair and bit him. Mark grabbed the bat with one hand and let go of the ladder with the other. With a groan of pain he slammed onto the floor, surprised to find his hand wrapped tightly around the struggling bat. Close to his ears, he heard the high frequency of a "morning after" buzz as he tried to pull the bat free.

The animal's body seemed uncommonly large in his hand and he gripped it tighter, squeezing.

"You rotten little bastard!" he said, and he squeezed until he felt something warm and sticky gush down over his face. The bat went suddenly limp, and he yanked it away from his head, removing a large clump of hair as he did.

He threw the dead bat into a corner of the barn, satisfied with the splat it made when it hit. Staggering backward, he hit the other barn wall, and pinpoints of light exploded in his vision. He spun around, gasping for breath, and lurched forward into something else.

This is insane! his mind screamed, but blind panic swept him away. His arms pinwheeled as he careened about in the darkness, searching for the door out. Sweat and blood from the bat stung his eyes, but through his raging fear he heard another sound. The clouds in his head cleared enough for him to recognize the fear-filled neighing of the horse.

"Shut the fuck up! You bastard!" Mark screamed, and somehow his anger helped him to focus. He was no longer in the loft; the bat wasn't still attacking him—

—Attacking! Yes, the bat had attacked!

He saw the slate of night through the window beside the door and, plunging forward, grabbed the latch and nearly ripped the door off its hinges as he flung it open. He pitched forward, spread-eagle onto the ground, and was just thinking, *Run! Get the hell outta here!* when the horse lunged at him through the open door.

Mark turned and saw the bone-white flash of teeth bearing down on him. He felt the heated animal's breath wash over his face as he turned and tried to scramble away. Pain from the fall from the loft raced up his leg like a hot needle. The horse reared back, hoofs flashing, catching the moonlight, then slashing down like wicked knives inches from his face.

"Go on!" he shouted, frantically waving his hands. "Go on! Get!"

From the corner of his eye, he saw the light beside the kitchen door wink on. He rolled to one side, leaped to his feet, and sprinted down the driveway.

"What the hell?" he heard Don shout, his voice carrying on the night; but Mark never looked back to see if he was being followed. Whether Inman knew he had been there or not, he sure wasn't about to get caught!

As he went racing down Hunter Hill Road, Mark heard Don call out, "I don't know how but goddammit! Goblin's loose again!"

There was more yelling from the Inman house, but it faded into the night as Mark raced for home.

At least, he told himself as he ran blindly through the night. *I've got the memory of what I saw!*

IV

It took Don until almost two o'clock to catch Goblin. In the excitement, neither Jan nor Don thought to check on Beth. She was a pretty sound sleeper, so they figured she would sleep through the noise. Once Goblin was in her stall and the door latch was locked, Don poked his head into Beth's room. As he had thought, she was sleeping soundly, her hand clutching her wooden doll. Her breathing was deep and regular but, as he watched her, her shoulder began to tremble as though she were chilled.

"Shouldn't—shouldn't do—that," she muttered as she rolled onto her side, facing her father. He couldn't tell for sure, but it looked as though Beth's eyes were wide open and rolled back, exposing only the whites. He attributed it to a trick of the dim light from the hallway and went back to bed where Jan was already soundly asleep.

Don snapped off the light and lay in bed, watching the gauzy curtains belly in and out with the night breeze, carrying the smell of wet earth and the sting of ozone.

"Fresh air, one of the reasons we moved here," he said, wishing his nerves would untangle.

He peeled back the covers and let the cool breeze wash over him as he tried to unwind. But lying there, trying to force himself to fall asleep, he just couldn't do it! Sleep seemed increasingly distant.

"Varokaa kivia," he whispered softly, and immediately sat up in bed, shocked.

What the hell made me say that? he wondered, unaccountably shivering in the dark. The words Aune Kivinen had said—had *screamed*—at him in the hospital came unbidden to his mind.

Jan stirred in her sleep and rolled over, dragging the covers with her. She smacked her lips and then sighed. The cool breeze chilled his nipples to two hard buttons and, acknowledging that sleep wasn't yet in sight, he slipped quietly out of bed, put on his shirt and jeans, and started downstairs for a glass of milk.

Halfway down the stairway though, he felt overwhelmed by a sudden disorientation. He had to grip the banister with both hands to keep from tumbling forward. Shouting in his mind to calm down, he went down slowly, step by step. When he finally reached the bottom, feeling safe at last, he let go of the railing. It was as if he were suddenly transplanted to the pitching deck of a ship at sea. He pressed his back to the wall, hoping, praying for the feeling to pass.

It was as if—as if—

He fought back the idea, but it intruded into his mind like a rusty blade.

—As if he didn't belong here—As if the house didn't want him!

That was the first way he thought to describe the feeling. The idea twisted in his mind, becoming more frightening until he was convinced that, if he went back upstairs and looked into the bedrooms, the people he found sleeping there would not be Jan and Beth, his wife and daughter. He was consumed by the fantasy that what he would find was corpses—dozens—hundred of centuries-rotted corpses!

He wanted to cry out, but his throat felt filled with

sand. Not knowing which way to go, he finally forced his feet forward, slap-slap on the wooden floor. Sweat beaded up on his forehead as he walked zombielike through the dining room and into the kitchen. And when he snapped on the overhead light in the kitchen, he felt only a slight measure of relief. Everything looked all right. Just as it should be.

—*Except for Max. Max isn't here!*

—*Max should have come running now for me to scratch him behind the ears!*

Don's hand was shaking as he filled a glass with cold milk and gulped it down. It hit his stomach like a stone. Leaning over the sink, past his pale reflection in the window, he saw billowy clouds scudding past the nearly full moon. Cottony, black shadows slid silently over the contours of the field.

"*Varokaa kivia,*" he whispered again, watching his reflected lips move. "What in the hell does that *mean*?

He had another gulp of milk, wiped his mouth on his sleeve, opened the door, and stepped outside. He stood in the driveway for a moment, looking up as the clouds sped by, making the moonlight waver. The air was strangely still, and the subtly shifting moonlight was disorienting but not nearly as bad as what he had felt on the stairway.

Not enough sleep, that's the problem, he thought, but you can't force sleep to come. A wiry apprehension began to build up inside him, and he looked around the yard, trying to pin down something. Something seemed just plain wrong.

The moon!

Don looked up and shivered. The moon was nearly full. Shaking his head, he thought back, trying to remember. He was positive it had been just two or three nights ago he had noticed that the moon was a fingernail in the east—nowhere near full! But that wasn't all, he suddenly realized—

—The moon! It's in the wrong place!

He had seen it from the kitchen as he looked out over the field toward town, but now it was behind the house and barn. He couldn't possibly have seen it from the window over the sink!

Looking down, he saw the inkstain shadow of the barn cupola at his feet. The shadow seemed to be pointing something out to him—giving him direction. With the moon at his back, he looked out again over the field, down the slope to the alder-lined stream.

The stones! he thought with a shudder. *Those tall, black stones!*

He started slowly across the field and past the garden. His own shadow in front of him ripplied like a black silk banner on the ground. Up the crest he went and, looking down at the stream, he more than half-expected to see the black stones, towering up out of the water, dripping with—

—No! Not blood!

But they weren't there. There was nothing but the open stretch of field down by the stream, a dull curl of gray speckled with moonlight.

But the moon! The moon shouldn't be behind me! he thought, and the words *varokaa kivia* came to mind with a whoosh like dark wings flapping. He started down the hill, feeling compelled to follow the direction indicated by the shadow.

At the edge of the stream, he paused and scanned the distant line of trees. Softly, from far away, came the hooting of an owl, and Don shivered. Then he looked down at the water, at his reflection.

"No goddamned stones tonight!" he said softly as he got down on one knee and leaned over the silent water. The night was close, pressing his words back on him. The pale disk of the moon glowed over his left shoulder and made the water look a textured gray. Again, from further off, came the hooting of an owl.

But as he gazed at his reflection in the water, something struck him as strange. With the moon behind him and with no other light source, he was surprised that he could see his facial features.

Was reflected moonlight that strong? he wondered.

Closer he leaned, peering down at the marble-smooth water—still, placid. But then he saw something shift beneath the surface. A fish swimming below or a cloud drifting in front of the moon? He wasn't sure.

A scream burst from his mouth but was suddenly closed off when a hand suddenly shot up from the water and grabbed him by the throat. The viselike grip tightened, cutting off his air and threatening to crush his windpipe. The strong fingers clenched tighter—tighter, and Don could feel the points of the fingernails digging into his skin.

The only screams now were in his mind as he scrambled desperately to cling to the stream bank. The grip tightened like a coil, and then the thin arm began to draw him forward and down—down to the water.

Razor-sharp panic filled Don as he struggled against the pull of the hand. A dank, rotten stench filled his nose. Stagnant water? Or something worse?

Closer—closer, the hand drew him. The icy grip numbed his throat. Rocks and soil plopped into the water from his efforts to avoid being pulled in.

My God! he thought frantically. *I'm going to drown!*

He focused on the water, watching the foam that ringed the upthrust arm. He could see pencil-thin muscles and tendons working to hold him. As the fingers cut off air and blood to his brain, a dull, leathery sound hammered in his ears.

Closer—closer, his face came to the water, now rippling with activity. With no voice to cry out, he felt his chin touch the water. Cold pain, steely and sharp, jabbed into the back of his skull, and everything turned swirling gray as he was drawn inexorably down.

The only thought in his mind was, *This is it!* But with an incredible effort he twisted to one side, rolled over onto his back, and broke the grip on his throat.

Air roared into his lungs with a strangled cry, and he scrambled up the bank away from the water. His throat still felt as though a steel band were clamped around it as he ran to the house and into the kitchen. Panting and shaking, he sat down at the kitchen table and tried to calm the hammering in his ears and chest.

It *couldn't* have been real! his mind kept repeating, but, if it hadn't happened, what had? Had he been sleepwalking? Dreaming with his eyes open? Maybe—somehow—a hallucinogenic had gotten into his food. It certainly couldn't have been just the two beers he had had that evening or the lack of sleep from chasing Goblin after midnight!

After a half-hour or so, he stood up, every muscle in his body aching from the effort of resisting the hand. He made his way to the downstairs bathroom and splashed cold water over his face. As he looked at his bleary-eyed reflection—not at all like the face he had seen reflected in the stream!—he noticed marks on his neck. Looking closely, he could see that red welts circled his throat—welts the size and shape of fingers!

"It's impossible!" he said, studying the marks. But if he hadn't almost been pulled into the water by that hand, how had he gotten those marks?

He remembered something about the Salem witch trials where children had accused witches of tormenting them, and the trial testimony indicated that the children had actually gotten bruises and cuts from, apparently, unseen hands.

Maybe, Don wondered, fighting down his fear with great effort, those witch marks—and the ones on his neck—were psychosomatic, produced by hysteria.

As he stood looking in the mirror, he became aware of motion behind him. Neck hairs prickled as he turned around slowly and saw a figure standing in the doorway.

"Jeez, Beth!" he said shakily. "You scared the crap out of me!"

"Daddy?" Beth said, her voice strangely flat.

"Huh? Beth, what is it?" He started toward her, and she dropped back, gliding smoothly over the floor. Her nightgown drifted lazily, as though a subtle breeze had caught it. Out in the hallway, she turned and over her shoulder beckoned to him.

"Come on, Punk. What the hell are you doing?" His voice was edged with fear, and he unconsciously rubbed the bruises on his neck.

With fluid ease, Beth went down the corridor to the cellar door and then stopped. Holding out one hand and pointing it at the door, she said softly, "Daddy. Listen!"

The light from the bathroom cast dimly on the cellar door as Don came up to it and stood beside Beth. She stepped to one side, still pointing at the door.

"Listen! Down there!" she whispered. Her voice sounded gritty.

Don felt a cold chill in his groin—a cold deeper than the chill of the stream, deeper that anything he had ever felt before. His hand shook as he reached for the doorknob and turned it. Stepping back, he watched as the door swung open—slowly but steadily—as though someone were pushing it from the inside. There was no creaking of rusted hinges, just the smoothly opening door revealing the blackness of the cellar.

"Listen! Can you hear it?" Beth whispered, her voice close to her father's ear. Her finger pointed down the steps into the well of blackness.

Don leaned into the cellar, feeling the moisture rising up the stairway. His hand fumbled for the light switch, but he couldn't seem to find it.

"Can't you hear?" Beth whispered sharply. Her voice raised the goose flesh on Don's arms.

"No—I, ahh—I don't hear anything."

"Listen! *Down there!*"

He still groped for the light switch, and, when he found it, the sudden blast of light stung his eyes. At that same instant, he heard a loud rumbling. It sounded like a roll of thunder, issuing from the cellar.

"What the hell was that?" he asked, turning to Beth. He was astounded to see that she wasn't there. He looked up and down the hallway. "Beth? Pun-'kin?"

But she wasn't there. Somehow she had gotten past him and had probably gone back up to bed. Don stood in the cellar doorway for a moment longer, but then he decided that tomorrow was soon enough to go down there and see what had made that sound. Probably something just fell off the workbench, he thought, and he snapped the light off and closed the door.

When he went upstairs to bed, he checked on Beth. She was sleeping soundly, curled with one arm hanging over the edge of the bed. Hoping he wouldn't disturb Jan, he eased back under the sheets in his own bed and, finally, sleep claimed him.

V

The next morning, Don finished breakfast and went out to the stone corral where Beth was brushing Goblin. He stood in the shade, watching her for a while, and he was pleased to see that she was doing a good job. She kept both hands moving, pulling the currycombs in long, even strokes along the horse's flank. After a while she saw him and smiled.

"You're doing a good job of that," he said, walking over to her.

"Thank, but it's *killing* my arms!"

Don reached out and rubbed Goblin's muzzle, and Goblin regarded him with her moist, brown eyes. She nickered softly.

"So what am I going to do with you?" he asked addressing the horse. "That's two times now you've gotten out of the stall at night. At this rate, I won't get enough sleep to keep me going."

Beth laughed and said, "Oh, Daddy, you get enough sleep 'cause you're in bed until almost noon."

"Well, that's the second time it's happened, Beth. We have to make sure it doesn't happen again."

"I know," Beth said, sounding defeated and a bit worried that, if it happened much more, her father might start thinking about getting rid of her horse.

"It's upsetting, you know." Don said. "I suppose Mom told you I was up till after midnight, chasing her."

"I'm sorry," Beth said. "It won't happen again even if we have to nail her stall door shut every night."

Don nodded. "O.K." He looked at his daughter. Dressed in jeans and a yellow sleeveless shirt with a picture of Bruce Springsteen on the front, she looked for all the world like a stereotyped farm girl bursting with health. As he looked at her, he tried to see the frail girlish figure he had followed last night to the cellar door, the same girl who, nightgown flapping like wings, had danced in the field until she slowly drifted into the air.

"All just a dream," he said softly, and Beth, who had resumed brushing Goblin, looked at him questioningly.

"You say something to me?" she asked.

He shook his head, perplexed. "Oh, nothing. It's just that—my sleep's been so disturbed lately, I've been having some pretty weird dreams."

He sighed deeply and rubbed his neck, which was still pretty sore. One thing that made him think it had all been a dream was that, looking in the mirror this morning, he had been unable to find the slightest trace of the bruises on his neck. They were gone, vanished with the night—like the nightmare he had had.

But where, he wondered, had the nightmare started—or ended, for that matter?

Had Goblin getting out of the stall been part of it?

Had the hand, reaching out of the stream to pull him into the water, been part of it?

Had Beth, standing at the cellar door, whispering "Listen," been part of it?

He had no way of knowing.

"Last night," he said, considering each word before saying it. "Last night, did you hear—or do anything? You know, after you went to bed?"

Beth squinted and shook her head. "No. I slept right through everything."

"Did you have any—you know—kind of funny—strange dreams last night?"

Beth stopped brushing Goblin, letting her hands

287

drop limply to her side. The posture suggested the figure he had seen in the dimly lit hallway last night. She shook her head, her ponytail swishing from side to side. "Nothing," she said. "I was out like a light."

Don sighed. "I had a dream—I *guess* it was a dream—that you told me you had heard something down in the cellar."

Beth wrinkled her nose. "Ugh! You know I'd never go down there! I can't stand all the spiders and stuff."

"Well, in my dream, you kept telling me to listen to—whatever it was down there. You don't remember anything—hearing anything last night?"

Beth regarded him for a moment, and Don was struck by the subtle shade of "womanness" he saw in her face. "Daddy," she said with a giggle, "Is this some kind of joke? How could I remember something if it happened in one of *your* dreams?"

"I'm not making a joke," Don said seriously. "It's just that this dream was so—so *real*, I thought it *was* real."

"Sometimes I have dreams like that," Beth said, "but I didn't have one last night. How about you?"

Don thought she meant him, but, when he followed her gaze, he saw that she was looking past him. He turned and felt a dash of chills when he saw her wooden doll propped up on the top of the stone corral. The doll's unblinking, pinpoint eyes seemed to stare right through him.

Chapter Nine

Wingnut

I

The next four days Don tried to get the roof done. Goblin hadn't broken out of her stall in all that time so Don was well-rested at least. He finished stripping off and hauling away the old shingles, nailed down new tarpaper, and then ran up the courses of new shingles. The weather was hot, and Jan spent several days at Wells Beach with Beth. Whenever Jan mentioned going back to the quarry, even if just to rinse off the sand after a day at the beach, Beth resisted the idea.

Don finished the roof on a Sunday morning, so after lunch he gave Billy Blackshoe—Wingnut—a call to ask if he could drop by for a visit. Billy said he'd be home all day, and Don could come over any time. Working on the roof had given Don a lot of time to think about what had been happening around the house. He suspected Billy might know more—maybe a lot more—than he was saying, and Don wanted to ask him a few questions.

He drove up Hunter Hill Road, away from town, took a left on Albion Road and then a right onto Mountain Road. He drove past the Remys's house, and just beyond the dump on the left he saw Billy's house—the only red ranch and practically the only house on the road. A peeling sign out front read, "Blackshoe's Small Engine Repair."

As Don came up the driveway, he saw Billy, sprawled in a lawn chair in the shade of the open garage door, a green felt hat pulled down over his eyes. He appeared to be sleeping.

Don pulled into the turnaround and got out of his car. Billy, alerted by the noise, shifted his hat up and sat a little straighter in his chair as Don walked over to him.

"You've got a nice spot here," Don said, turning and looking at the view across the road. A flower-filled field rolled down to a line of trees, and in the distance was a range of low mountains, receding into hazy blue.

"Like it like this," Billy said, drawling. "Nice and private."

"And you do lawn mower repairs?"

"Snow blowers and boat motors, too," Billy said.

Don chuckled. "Boy, between that, working at the store, and selling Indian jewelry, you keep yourself pretty busy."

"I like it like that," Billy said. He reached down beside his chair, picked up a can of Budweiser, and drained it off. "I'm about due for another cold one. How about you?"

"Sure," Don said.

"Grab yourself a chair from the garage there, and have a seat," Billy said, and then he disappeared into the house. Don unfolded one of Zayre's special lawn chairs and sat. The cheap strapping of the chair creaked beneath his weight. The field across the street was hazy with slanting sunlight and buzzing with crickets, creating a dreamy feeling.

Billy came back out, handed Don a beer, and then sat back down. He snapped the top and took a healthy slug. "So, what's on your mind?" he asked. "Got a question about the roofing?"

Don sipped his beer, shaking his head. "No. Not that." He didn't want to dive right into it, but Billy didn't seem all that intent on small talk.

"After I talked with you at the store the other day, well, what you said got me thinking," Don said. He took another sip and went on. "You see, I guess it was two or three weeks ago, my wife and I were plowing up the garden."

"Kind of late for gardening, ain't it?"

Don shrugged. "We thought we'd see what we could get. Anyway, while I was running the Rototiller, I dug up—" He suddenly stopped as a shiver coursed through his body.

"Somebody just walked over your grave," Billy said solemnly.

"Huh?"

"My grandfather always said that. Whenever you shiver like that, it means someone's walked over the spot where you'll be buried."

"What a pleasant thought," Don replied, looking out at the receding line of hazy mountains. "But as I was saying, while we were getting the garden ready, I found a severed hand buried in the ground."

Billy's eyebrows suddenly shot up, and he leaned forward, showing a spark of interest for the first time. His ponytail swished over the collar of his blue workshirt.

"This hand was wrapped in a copper sheet and,

when I opened it, inside there was all this beadwork."

"No fooling!" Billy said, and Don registered the genuine amazement in his voice.

"I took it to U.S.M. in Gorham, had a professor check it out."

"And—?" Billy said, but before Don could continue, he finished for him. "And this professor said it was Indian, right?"

Don nodded.

"Do you still have it? The hand, I mean?" Billy asked.

"I left it with the professor. I guess he wants to show it to someone else, but he said he'd want to come down and take a look at my property. Actually, he said there was a possibility there was an ancient Indian burial site on my land." As he related all of this, Don's throat felt incredibly parched, and he had downed the whole beer without realizing it.

Billy was sitting there, shaking his head slowly, his ponytail swinging from side to side. "I'll be a son of a gun!" he muttered. "Hey, you're dry. Let me get you another beer." He stood and went into the house before Don could respond.

While Billy was gone, Don mulled over what else he wanted to tell him. How much of all that had happened was connected and how much was just—what, he wondered—coincidence? Should he mention the dreams he had been having? And what about Beth's wooden doll?

Billy interrupted his thoughts by slapping a cold can into Don's hand before sitting down. He left his own beer untouched on the ground beside him. "So you want me to give you all the answers, huh?" he said.

Don looked at him, locking onto the steady brown eyes. Billy sat for several seconds, silently looking back at Don. His face was impassive, but Don knew he was mulling over what he had said.

"Another thing," Don said suddenly. He felt guilty for intruding on Billy's thoughts, but he felt sure it had to be said. He wasn't sure why, but for some reason he felt he could trust Billy, so he started to tell him about the series of nightmares he'd had ever since they moved into the Kivinen house.

When Don was finished relating several of the dreams, Billy puffed out his cheeks and sat back, closing his eyes. "I always knew there was something about that place," he said at last. "I think ever since I recognized the actual glee in my grandfather's voice when he told me about the time the house burned down. And the way he got so angry when he talked about when the house was rebuilt."

"When my grandfather rebuilt it," Don said.

Billy snorted. "I guess so. My grandfather said all palefaces look alike to him."

They both laughed at that and then sat silently for a moment. Then Don said, "So, what do you think? Is there something to all this, or is it a bunch of nonsense?"

"Curious thing, ain't it?" Billy said. "But I think—I dunno. Look, Don, I have an interest in this kind of thing, all this occult stuff, but I don't—at least I *try* not to take it seriously. But what you've been telling me pretty much connects with—some other things."

"Like what?" Don snapped.

Billy shook his head and reached for his beer. "Might be connected, might not be."

"You know, you're not being much of a help," Don said, suddenly angry at him. "I mean, at the store, you tease me with these vague stories about people seeing 'something' in the house and all. If you know something, I think you have an obligation to tell me. Especially if my family and I could be in some kind of danger."

Billy's lip curled. Nailing Don with a harsh glance, he said softly yet sternly, "The way I look at it I don't owe anyone anything—especially a paleface."

Don blushed and made a move to stand, but Billy held his hand out and pushed him back down. "Don't get all huffy, now," he said. "I know some things, things my grandfather told me, but, hell, I was born in 1950, not the Middle Ages. I—I guess you could say I only *half* believe some of it."

"Some of what?"

"I'll tell you this much, for starters," Billy said firmly. "That professor you gave the hand to. If he ever wants to start digging around on your property, I wouldn't let him."

"Why not?"

Billy sniffed. "Because if there *is* an Indian burial ground there, you wouldn't want to go messing with it, that's why! To an Indian, the burial ground was sacred. The absolute worst thing one tribe could do to another was to desecrate their graveyard. There's strong medicine in a burial site."

"But what would be the problem?" Don asked. "If the graves are so old, maybe it's a good thing to dig them up, to learn more about how people lived back then."

Billy's eyes hardened, and his voice sounded like metal. "Burial ground is sacred ground, and a tribe would do all it could to protect it. The Great Spirit would make sure nobody messed with it."

"How?" Don asked, aware that his voice sounded as awe-filled as a ten-year-old camper at the campfire.

"Each tribe had its own ways," Billy answered. "My grandfather told me some—certainly not all—

but some of the ways our tribe did it."

"Did your tribe live in this area?"

Billy nodded. "You bet. In all fairness, you could say your land belongs to me more than to you." He laughed, shaking his head. "But you won't see me in court on that account."

"But what were some of the ways they did it?" Don asked. He was becoming convinced that somehow the skeletal hand was part of this "strong medicine" Billy had mentioned.

"Guardian spirits, that's how," Billy said. "If a tribe thought a piece of land was sacred, they'd protect it—both in this world with warriors, and in the next world with spirits. Sometimes a certain talisman would be used." He gave Don a harsh stare. "They'd use certain magical implements—certain kinds of jewelry, paintings, carved figures—or maybe the severed hand of a sacrificial victim."

Don shivered and watched Billy's face for signs that he was putting him on, but Billy was intensely serious.

"My grandfather knew a lot more than he ever told me, I'm sure," Billy said. "But after everything you've said, I sure wouldn't let anyone go poking around there. If there is a grave and there are sacred relics in it, tradition at least says tampering with it could reanimate the corpse buried there. Curious thing, though, ain't it?"

Don didn't know what to say. If Billy wasn't handing him a line of high-grade nonsense . . . But this was absurd! What he was talking about was magic—guardian spirits and sacrificial victims. Maybe all of this was good for stories told after lights out at summer camp or in a horror novel, but this was 1986!

"And you honestly think there might be something

295

to this?" Don asked.

Billy threw his head back and laughed. "Look, when I was a kid, I heard all this stuff from my grandfather. I can see now that he was a pretty strange old coot. I mean, Christ, he clung to what he called the 'old ways' as if, somehow, you whites were going to give us all our land back and we could live in peace. He told me things when I was a kid that either I didn't believe or that scared the piss out of me. But if there *is* something going on here, there are ways we can check it out."

"How? What ways?" Don asked, leaning closer to Billy, like a conspirator.

"We need something a little more positive, more concrete, right? Now, we can dig around there, hit or miss, and maybe we'll find something; maybe we won't. Better still, maybe we should let that professor do the digging, so if the shit hits the fan, maybe we won't get splattered. There might be an Indian grave-yard there—or something else."

Don's mind immediately filled with the memory of the tall stones, standing in the dark, swirling water. The words *varokaa kivia* sprang into his mind.

"What did you say?" Billy asked.

Don shook his head, confused. "I didn't say anything. I—" He broke off, not daring to repeat the Finnish words aloud, as though they had taken on some kind of power that he didn't want to touch.

"Anyway," Billy went on, "we can do a little investigating without causing too much trouble. We can dowse your property."

"We can *what*? You mean, with a bent stick and all?"

Billy nodded. "That's one way; there are other ways to dowse."

"I thought that was only used for, you know, like

finding water."

"Oh, sure. People 'round here call it 'water witching,' and it's good for that, like most people think. I have a friend, he's chief engineer of a town's water department, and he always dowses to find leaks in pipes, but that ain't all you can do with it," Billy said. "You can use it to find—anything you want. I don't use a willow twig, like most. I have my own, specially designed dowsing rod. I've found lost wedding rings, important papers, even a lost kid once by dowsing a map of the area he was lost in. My average ain't quite one hundred percent, but I've beat the odds by a damn sight."

"Come on. I thought you said you didn't believe in psychic powers," Don said. He tried not to laugh and took a sip of beer to try to cover up. His image of Billy Blackstone was getting much too complicated: hardware-store clerk, small-engine repairman, Indian-jewelry dealer, and now dowser! Maybe he did rain dances, too, when the wells ran dry.

Billy didn't miss the smirk on his face. "I told you, I have an interest in them, but dowsing is different. If something works—consistently and predictably—I think it deserves the name of science, rather than magic. Dowsing works!"

"And you're saying we could dowse on my property and maybe locate—well, whatever might be there?" Don asked, and then he laughed aloud. He could tell his reaction bothered Billy, maybe hurt his feelings a bit, but he couldn't accept this—not on face value.

"We don't even need to walk your land," Billy said sagely. "We can get a map of the property and do it with a pendulum on that. Tell you what—"

"Wait a minute," Don said, holding up his hand to silence Billy. "You know, my—he would have been my uncle, my mother's brother, Eino. He died at the quarry my grandfather tried to get going."

"Ledgemere," Billy said. "That's where we used to go skinny-dipping as kids."

"He died and—now this may be wild coincidence or not—he died when a block of granite—"

"Crushed his hand and he bled to death," Billy said. "I know the story. It was something else that seemed to have pleased my grandfather no end."

"Well, my wife thought maybe that hand we found was his, Eino's, that maybe what the Rototiller turned up was his grave, not some prehistoric Indian's."

"Except for the copper sheet and the beadwork," Billy said, looking wistfully at the mountains. "I wish I could see that beadwork."

"But do you think you could, you know, dowse and find Eino Kivinen's grave?"

Billy shrugged. "If it's on the property, I suppose so. I do prefer a trail that's a little hotter than—what—sixty years old? But we could give it a whack. Do you have a map of the land?"

"Sure," Don said. "My sister had one that went with the deed when she sold the house to us."

"So there we are," Billy said, clapping his hands together. "All I'll need is that map and my pendulum."

"And what do you think we'll find?" Don asked, trying to keep the skepticism out of his voice.

"What do you think you lost?" Billy said. "Could be your grandparents buried their boy on the property. You might want to drop by the library and check the old newspaper files. There might be a report about his death. See if it mentions where he was buried. If you could do that 'fore I come by to dowse, it might save a bit of effort."

"No problem," Don said. "I'll stop by Standley Memorial on my way home. Oh, no. It wouldn't be

298

open on Sunday."

"Just as well. I'm kinda busy today and, besides, I'm a bit superstitious about dowsing on Sunday."

Don smiled. "*Superstitious?* All right, how about tomorrow evening?"

"Don't see why not?" Billy said.

He might have said he was busy today, Don thought, but he sure as hell wasn't bolting up out of the lawn chair to get working!

"Well, I suppose I ought to get on home. Thanks for the beers."

Billy waved him away. "Ahh, don't mention it. And if worse comes to worse, it won't be a total waste of time. I'll get to see how you did on the roofing."

"Tomorrow, then," Don said, and he walked to his car, got in, and drove off. He felt a measure of relief, having talked to Billy, but also a bit foolish. He could just imagine Jan's reaction when he told her he had invited an Indian over to dowse the land, looking for—what? Eino Kivinen's grave—or something else?

But he also felt a genuine friendship beginning between him and Billy, and he found himself looking forward to spending more time with him. Probably all of this nonsense with the mummified hand and his nightmares and all was just that—nonsense. He was probably pulling things together that had absolutely no connection at all, and it really might not be the best—for him or Billy—to pursue it any further.

One other thing bothered him as he drove home, although he didn't have it clearly in his mind until he turned into the driveway and saw the house. Billy had said something about checking out the work he had done on the roof. When—if at all—Don wondered, had he mentioned that he had actually finished the job?

"Curious thing, though, ain't it?" he said. He

pulled up into the shade of the barn and then backed the car around. After killing the engine, he sat for several minutes, staring blankly out across the field and wondering what secrets it held—and how long it had held them.

II

"To seventeen years," Don said, clinking his glass of champagne on the rim of Jan's glass. He watched her over the rim of his glass as she sipped and smiled, but there was something bothering her—something not quite right. Ever since he had gotten home from his visit with Wingnut, the whole time they were dressing to go out Jan had seemed—distant, edgy.

"You know," Don said, easing back in the padded chair, "after seventeen years, we ought to consider the trial period is over. What do you say, do we renew the contract for another year?"

Jan's eyelids flickered for a moment as she cast a glance at the ceiling. "Why not," she said, all the while thinking that, after all these years, some of his standard jokes had worn paper thin.

Don tried to ignore the chilly response as he scanned *Michel's* menu by the feeble candlelight at their table. This place had been recommended by the Remys, for what that was worth, but Don's first impression of the place had been good.

"Just be grateful I didn't insist on going to *The Rusty Anchor*, you know—for old time's sake."

"You're *so* funny," Jan muttered, looking away.

Don picked up a celery stick and bit into it, trying to tell himself the tension he was feeling wasn't really between them. They had hung in there—beat the odds, as he was fond of saying. The few strains they had felt in their marriage had been eased because they

300

had one hell of a solid relationship. No, it wasn't something between them that was the problem; it was other things.

"We both sure needed this tonight, huh?" he said. "Get away from the house and the kid." He put the menu down and reached for her hand. She didn't respond; she just let him rub her knuckles until he awkwardly reached for his champagne glass again and sipped.

Jan sat manikin-still, and it actually surprised him when she spoke. "Don't you think we should stop kidding ourselves and clear the air?" Her voice was huskier than usual.

Don froze, the champagne glass halfway down to the table. "What—what do you mean?"

Jan sighed. "I mean that, after seventeen years, we can cut through the smoke screen and stop pretending nothing's wrong."

Shaking his head, Don leaned back and took a deep breath. *So here it comes*, he thought, trying to fight down the panicked rush in his stomach.

"I think, considering everything that's happened lately, we're hanging in there pretty well," he said, his voice tightening.

Jan shook her head and sneered, "Oh, Don. Come on!" She pierced him with an angry look, but he could see tears welling in her eyes.

"Jan—hon, come on; it's our anniversary. Let's not get all—all—whatever. I'll grant you, I haven't been exactly Mr. Relaxation lately, but with everything I've had to do around the house and—the roof, and getting the barn finished off, and all—"

He shrugged, looking at her with a silent plea for understanding. His stomach felt like he had swallowed a bag of ice. *Seventeen years!*

"Look, Jan, if there's something bothering you, out

301

with it." He reached for her hand again and held it. It was clammy and limp in his grasp.

"Out with it?" Jan said, snorting with laughter. "Out with what? I don't know what's bugging me. It's you, me, Beth, the house—*everything!*"

"You're sore because I went over to Billy Blackshoe's house this afternoon instead of being with you, right?"

Jan shrugged. "That—but not just that. It's everything—the way you've been acting ever since you found that goddamned hand in the garden! It's like—like you haven't been yourself."

"I don't know what to say. I mean, O.K., sure I may have been putting a little too much attention into that thing, but— What do you want me to say?"

The tears spilled down Jan's cheek, and she wiped at them with the back of her hand until Don handed her his napkin.

"I realize we've been under some pressure lately, I'll grant you that," he said. "What with moving, and you not finding the job you wanted, Max getting killed—"

"But that goddamned horse!" Jan snapped. "I never wanted to get that goddamned horse!"

Don clenched one fist under the table but struggled to keep his voice calm. "Sure, sure. I might have pushed a bit too hard on that, but that's no reason to get upset tonight. We're supposed to have fun tonight."

"It's not any one thing. Don't you understand that? It's *everything. Everything!*"

"Everything?" Don repeated.

Jan nodded, and a strangled sound tried to escape from her throat.

"Now wait a minute," Don said. He leaned forward, clasping his hands on the table. "You're not—you know—thinking anything about splitting up, are you?"

He found it curious that, like the words *cancer* and *death*, he couldn't quite bring himself to say the word *divorce*. It had such a finality to it.

Jan's shoulders shuddered, and, as she looked at her husband, she wished to heaven she could stop the nagging corner of her mind that was wondering what she'd be thinking and saying if it were Dale Jackman sitting across from her.

The long pause before she answered gnawed at him like a rat on a grain bag, but at last she shook her head slowly from side to side. "No—At least I don't think so. I don't know."

"O.K., so maybe I've become a little bit—"

"Obsessed!"

"Obsessed?" Don looked at her, amazed.

"Yeah," Jan said, dabbing at her eyes with Don's napkin. The waiter made a move to come over to their table to take their order, but he sensed something was going on and went to the kitchen instead.

"Honey, if we don't pull together, we're going to pull apart," Don said earnestly.

Jan snorted. "Is that all you can offer? Platitudes?"

Don looked down at the table, stung.

"Sometimes I do think about it," Jan said, gaining control of her voice. "I think about striking out on my own—what it would be like on my own."

"For God's sake, Jan, just listen to yourself," Don said, throwing his hands up in dismay. He sat back, shaking his head from side to side, and, lowering his voice, said, "I just can't believe your timing. I mean, you aren't going to believe me, but I've been looking forward to tonight for a long time, and now here you are, blowing it."

"I'm not the one blowing it," Jan said sternly. "You

are, what with all this nonsense about that mummified hand and all. And now you're having that *Wingnut* guy over to do what? Dowse the field? I think you both need a good dowsing with a bucket of cold water to bring you to your senses."

Don shook his fists in frustration but kept his voice low. "What in the hell is bothering you? Look at where we are compared to where we were just a few months ago. We've gotten out of Providence. You *hated* living in the city. We're living in the country where people are just dying to move. We've got money in the bank. I've got a good job lined up for the fall. In God's name, we've got a situation most people would envy."

"Well, the grass is always greener, maybe."

"Who's talking platitudes now?" Don said. "Come on, honey, let's enjoy ourselves."

Jan sat back, finding it difficult to make eye contact with him. Finally, though, she sighed and straightened up. Reaching across the table, she took Don's hand into hers. Her touch was warmer now, he noticed.

"Just promise me that you won't mention that damned hand or dowsing once tonight, O.K.?"

"I never mentioned them in the first place."

"O.K.!" Jan snapped. "Don't start now." She looked over her shoulder, got the waiter's attention, then asked Don, "What are you going to get?"

Don chuckled under his breath and said, "I was thinking of having the swordfish."

"Umm," Jan said. "That looks good."

During the meal, Jan did loosen up, and by the time they had dessert, she was actually laughing. In a way, Don was grateful that the discussion had come up in the restaurant rather than at home because, by having to keep their voices low, they had actually addressed the problem, instead of resorting to a high-volume argument.

Don was glad, too, that Jan had confronted him on a few things. It was that kind of honesty, he thought, that they needed between themselves even after seventeen years. It showed they weren't just taking each other for granted.

After supper, they debated going to a movie, but there were only horror movies or half-baked college comedies playing, so they went dancing, instead, at the Holiday Inn in Portland.

The only time during the rest of the evening that Jan dredged up some of her bad feeling was when, while dancing, she found herself wondering if this was the kind of place Dale Jackman took a date to. She doubted it.

III

Jan didn't want to be around on Monday evening when Billy Blackshoe dropped by, so she drove to the Maine Mall to do some shopping. Beth had wanted to go but, tired from having ridden Goblin all day, stayed home. She even offered to do the dishes after supper and was at the sink, scrubbing a pan, when she announced that a Ranchero station wagon was bouncing up the driveway.

"Must be Wingnut," Beth said, snickering.

Don gave her an angry look. "Don't you go calling him that when he's here. I didn't tell you; Mr. Blackshoe is an Indian, so, if you make fun of him, I might not be able to stop him from scalping you."

"Oh, Daddy," Beth said, giggling. She dried her hands on a dishtowel and went with her father to the door. They saw Billy coming up the walkway with a battered wooden box under his arm. He had undone his ponytail, and his black hair flopped at his shoulders.

"He really *is* an Indian," Beth whispered.

"Full-blooded," Don said to her, then to Billy, "Nice evening, isn't it?" He held the screen door open and stood back so Billy could enter.

Billy shifted his wooden box to his other arm and shook hands with Don. "Sure is," he said. Then, glancing at Beth, he held his hand out to her. "And good evening to you, Beth. How's old Goblin treating you?"

Caught by surprise, Don almost asked him how he knew the horse's name, but he let it pass. He was beginning to accept this kind of thing from Billy.

"I'll let you get back to your dishes," Billy said. "Your dad and I have some work to do."

One thing Don was beginning to admire about Billy was his no-nonsense approach even to something as— well—strange as dowsing. He didn't waste time socializing.

"We can set up on the dining room table," Don said. "There'll be more room there."

"Whatever you say," Billy said. He followed Don into the dining room and gently placed his wooden box on the table. He glanced out the dining room window and frowned. "It's going to be dark soon, but if we've got time, maybe we can take a stroll around the property later. I always like to get the 'feel' of the area, too."

"I thought you told me, when you were a kid, you never liked to come up here."

Billy gave him a dark look and, squinting his eyes, seemed to be trying to remember back to his childhood. "Probably I was all worked up because all the kids around said the house was haunted," he said. "But even today, coming out, I felt—well, I don't

306

want to get you or me hyped up. Let's just do the dowsing."

Don got the surveyor's map from the top of the china closet and gave it to Billy, who unfolded it, studied it for a moment, and then spread it out on the table.

"You don't mind if I mark this do you?" Billy asked.

"I don't see why not."

He unsnapped the box he had brought and, without looking, took out a wooden ruler. Nodding and grunting he took a few rough measurements, the ruler clicking and snapping on the table as he worked.

"Would you like coffee or tea? Maybe a beer," Don offered, not wanting to break Billy's concentration.

Billy was silent for several seconds, then, exhaling, he straightened up. His face was creased with an expression of confusion—or worry. "Ahh, do you have any herbal tea?"

Don shook his head. "Just Salada."

Billy shrugged. "Salada will be fine," he said. His brow was still furrowed, and, as Don was leaving to go to the kitchen, Billy said, "You know, just as I turned off the road into your driveway tonight, I had the most—curious sensation."

"Really?"

Billy nodded and tugged at the hair hanging at his shoulder. "Yeah, and the thing of it is, I just can't pin it down. It was like—I don't know. The closest thing I can think of was how I used to feel as a kid on Christmas morning—all tingling with excitement."

He chuckled softly and made as though he had dismissed the whole thing, but his brow was still wrinkled. His brown eyes seemed to glaze over as if he were trying to remember something.

"Take some more time with the map," Don said.

307

"I'll get the tea."

When Don returned several minutes later with a pot of tea, cups, sugar, and milk, he almost laughed aloud when he saw what Billy was doing. From his wooden box, he had taken out several colored pens, assorted rulers, and an elaborate tripod device with a small lead weight dangling from a thick black thread. He was mumbling to himself as he adjusted the length of the string and looked up, startled, when Don slid the tray onto the table.

"There's something damned peculiar here," Billy said, scratching his head. He glanced past Don and saw Beth standing in the doorway. The overhead light caught his face just right, emphasizing the hard line of his cheekbones. Don thought his face looked almost skull-like.

Billy looked back at the tripod, tied another loop in the string, and then let the plumb bob go. The lead weight swung back and forth—back and forth. Everyone watched until it gradually slowed—slowed—and finally stopped.

"So?" Don said, wondering what was supposed to happen. "What's so peculiar?"

Billy pointed at the tripod. "Look at that—the string."

Don bent down and studied the length of black line. Standing up, he shrugged. "You've got me."

"Look at the plumb line," Billy said, an edge of irritation in his voice. "It ain't hanging straight down. Look again."

Don looked again, and he had to admit that yes, the string looked—well, maybe a little bit off, no more than a fraction of an inch. "Maybe it just looks that way because of the tripod or something, an optical illusion." In the back of his mind was the suspicion that Billy was playing an elaborate practical joke. But if so, why?

"Curious thing, though, ain't it?" Billy said. He knelt on the floor, bringing his eyes to table level, and sighted the tripod.

"Could be a trick of the eye," he said. He lifted the tripod, checking to see that each leg was equally extended; then he placed it back down, allowing the lead weight to swing.

Don found he was holding his breath as he waited for the weight to stop swinging, and, when it finally did, both he and Billy leaned down to examine it.

"Looks O.K. to me now," Don said tentatively.

He looked at Billy, who nodded agreement, then straightened up. His mouth slowly widened into a smile, exposing wide, white teeth. "It sure beats me," he said. "How about that tea before we get started?"

They sat at the dining room table for their tea, and Don noticed another thing about Billy. He seemed always to enjoy relaxing and talking, but only after the business at hand had been taken care of—or at least started. They spent fifteen minutes in casual conversation, just superficial, getting-to-know-you stuff. Then Billy brought the conversation around to what he was trying to do with the pendulum and map. Speaking in clipped sentences, he gave a brief overview of dowsing, its uses and a sketchy theory of how it might work.

"Primarily," Billy said, staring into the bottom of his teacup, as though reading a fortune, "it's thought to have something to do with the electromagnetic fields generated by—whatever the dowser is looking for. They're supposedly as individual as fingerprints. These fields cause the dowsing rod or pendulum to react."

"But what you're talking about, at least if you do it on a map of the area, is what they call—what, sympathetic magic? Isn't that the term? The idea that a representation of the thing will react just like the real thing. The same thing makes sticking pins into a voodoo doll have an effect on the actual person."

Billy shrugged. "Curious thing, though, ain't it?"

"So when you dowse a map, like this, say, what you're actually doing is a kind of long-distance dowsing. It sounds like *magic* to me."

"You can call it whatever you want," Billy said. "Have you ever heard of Clarke's Third Law?"

Don shook his head.

"The law says that 'any sufficiently advanced technology is indistinguishable from magic.' All I know is that it works because it *works*. Scientists with degrees can think about it and try to figure it out. Meanwhile, us dowsers are out in the field getting results!"

"And what kind of results do you think you might get around here?" Don asked, indicating the map. "At least right now, we don't even know what we're looking for."

Billy put his empty teacup back on the saucer and, leaning forward, picked up the tripod and pendulum. "I didn't even have this sucker set down on the map, and the pendulum seemed to respond to—something. There's some kind of attraction here. But if you noticed, the plumb didn't point toward the map, it pointed toward the kitchen doorway."

They both glanced at the doorway and saw that Beth was still standing there, watching them. She held one hand behind her back as though hiding something from them.

"Hey, Pun'kin. Have you settled Goblin for the night?" Don asked.

Beth looked at him, cocking her head to one side. "Uh-uh, not yet."

"Well, why don't you go out there before it gets too dark?" He glanced at the graying sky outside, then turned to Billy, and said, "Well, let's give it a whirl."

As Billy prepared his things, smoothing out the map and carefully placing the tripod, Don had the impression this was like a seance—dimmed lights, an awed, mystical silence as they waited and waited for the pendulum to swing. In the back of his mind, he again suspected Billy of carefully staging a hoax, but why? to what, or whose advantage?

"What I want you to do," Billy said, once he seemed satisfied that the tripod was set, "is watch while I close my eyes and move the tripod over the map. After the plumb bob stops swinging, watch to see if it moves. If you notice anything, put a mark and try to indicate the direction of the swing. O.K, ready?"

Don swallowed and nodded. "Yeah, ready." He picked up a red felt-tipped marker, snapped off the cover, and sat poised as Billy closed his eyes, felt for the map, and gently placed the tripod down. The pendulum swung back and forth, slowly, slowly, and finally came to rest over the rectangle on the map marking the barn.

Several times, Billy moved the tripod randomly over the map and waited, eyes closed, as the pendulum swung slowly, slowly. Don grew impatient, waiting for it to stop, but when he asked Billy if he could slow the swing by hand, Billy said that would only confuse the reading—whatever *that* meant.

The mapping went slowly. Beth came back from the barn and watched for a while, but soon she lost interest and went upstairs to read. Don noticed that she was carrying her wooden doll with her, and it almost seemed as if the plumb bob accelerated its swing as she walked past the table.

Every time the pendulum stopped swinging, Don leaned forward, wishing the damned thing would do something, *anything* so he could do more than put a small red dot on the map where the pendulum pointed.

It took them more than an hour to locate about ten or twelve spots on the map. Billy sat the whole time with his eyes closed, and, if he hadn't kept his hands moving, Don would have thought he was sleeping.

During this time, Don had plenty of opportunity to think about how foolish this whole situation was. He asked himself over and over what the hell he was doing. He had told Billy that his research at the local library had turned up only a short notice of Eino Kivinen's death. No mention had been made of where he had been buried. So he still didn't know what they were looking for! His grandmother's son's grave? An Indian burial site? Maybe the other hand of whoever *had* been buried out there in the field. It struck him increasingly as complete nonsense.

"Still nothing," he said after staring at the motionless weight until his eyes began to hurt. He was convinced that, if he saw any reaction in the pendulum now, it would be the result of eyestrain and fatigue.

"Patience," Billy whispered. "These things can't be hurried. There's something here, I know it, I *feel* it." He was just reaching for the tripod to place it on another part of the map when Don grunted.

"What? You got something?" Billy asked, still keeping his eyes closed.

"Maybe," Don said. He watched the lead weight swing back and forth, and it looked to him—if it weren't just an illusion—as though the swing was increasing rather than decreasing. He noted that the pendulum was centered over the field just down the hill from where Jan had planted her garden.

He watched intently, and the weight increased the tempo of its swing until there was no mistaking it. Somehow it was generating its own motion, swinging back and forth in a widening arc.

Suspicion blossomed in him, and he glanced under the table to see if Billy was manipulating the weight with a magnet. Billy's hands were folded in his lap, and his feet were firmly planted on the floor. Again, Don looked at the swinging pendulum.

"This is incredible," he said softly, hoping his voice wouldn't shatter the fragile magic. "It keeps swinging faster and faster."

By now, the pendulum was swinging almost a hundred and eighty degrees. The legs of the tripod seemed almost to lift off the map with each pass.

"Mark the center of the swing and the direction," Billy said, opening his eyes and glancing at the map. "Then you can stop the pendulum."

Don grasped the thin black string near the top and ran his fingers down to the lead weight. His fingertips tingled, and he had a fleeting sensation of rubbing something alive. It was impossible, but it felt as though the thread had given him a mild jolt of electricity.

He let go of the weight and was marking the point at which the stilled pendulum pointed when something curious happened. On its own, the pendulum started swinging back and forth again.

"You've really got something there, don't you? I can feel it," Billy said. He was sitting back in the chair, eyes closed.

"I don't believe this!" Don said, astonished. He slowly drew his hand back and watched as the pendulum swung wider and wider. He held his hand out to stop the motion of the pendulum and it hit the cup of his palm with surprising force. As the weight bounced off his hand, he thought he heard a low, thrumming sound as though the cord vibrated like a plucked violin string.

"It's right over the field where—"

"Sh-sh," Billy said, waving his finger. "Don't tell me. I want to move the tripod over the map at random." He reached blindly for the tripod and repositioned it on the map.

Another hour quickly passed with more interest on Don's part. Outside, the sky darkened to a deep blue. Although they got some minor motion from the pendulum, which Don dutifully noted on the map, they didn't get any more dramatic results. After they had tried fifteen more random locations, Don's frustration began to build again.

"One more, and then we'll take a break," Billy said, as if anticipating Don's reaction. He took the tripod and put it down on the map only an inch or so from the spot that had shown the most activity, Don noticed. When the weight started moving on its own again, Don let out a gasp.

"There it goes," he whispered, and Billy nodded.

"Watch the direction carefully."

"This one's different though," Don said. "It's moving in a circle."

"What?" Billy said, opening his eyes and suddenly leaning forward.

The lead weight was swinging around, inscribing a wide circle that almost perfectly bisected the red line Don had drawn the only other time the pendulum had reacted. Again, Don thought he heard a low humming sound. This time it sounded like a hollow winter wind moaning in the trees. Haunting—and frightening.

"I've never seen it react like that before," Billy said, and Don realized Billy was genuinely surprised. "Just keep an eye on it."

Don stood up and looked directly down at the tripod, trying to see the design the pendulum was making. It appeared to be more an oval than a perfect circle, but the pendulum moved so fast, he couldn't be sure. The bulge of the oval seemed to be in the direction of the garden.

The pendulum swung—faster, faster, so fast it became a blur, and the humming sound grew louder until there was no mistaking the sharp whistling. Don was so concentrated on the whizzing pendulum that he didn't notice what happened to Billy until he heard him groan. There was a heavy thump when he fell forward from his chair and hit the floor.

"Wha—?" Don shouted. He turned and saw Billy staring up at him. His eyes were rolled back, and a heated purple rushed over his cheeks. The tendons in his neck stood out like cables, and it looked to Don as though invisible hands were holding Billy from behind and were pulling his head back. Billy clawed at his throat, jerking spasmodically. Thin, white foam spewed over his lips and ran down his chin and neck.

"Billy! Jesus Christ, Billy!" Don shouted. He knocked his chair over as he rushed to lean over the fallen man. When he grabbed Billy by the shoulders, he could feel the violent tremors racking his body. Every opposing muscle seemed to have contracted, twisting Billy's body grotesquely out of shape. Don had the sudden horrifying thought that his friend's body was changing into something different.

Billy's mouth moved, and he seemed to be trying to form words, but all that came out was a strangled, watery sound. Foam gushed now from his mouth, staining his shirt and the rug.

"Oh, *my God*! Beth! *Beth!* Come down here! I need help!" Don shouted.

He tried to remember what to do when someone had an epileptic seizure. There was no doubt in his mind this was what was happening to Billy. His fingers fumbled to loosen Billy's collar, and he stared helplessly as Billy's eyes rolled back and forth, vacant and unfocused. Don didn't need a doctor there to tell him this was a full-tilt boogie *grand-mal* seizure.

He reached for his wallet in his back pocket and tried to get it into Billy's mouth. That was the one thing he remembered; you had to stop the person from biting off his tongue! But Billy's teeth were clenched so tightly they seemed wired shut. The trembling in his body increased in intensity, and panic rose like phlegm in Don's throat.

"Hurry, Beth! Come down here!" he shouted. "I need help!"

As he leaned over Billy, supporting his head so he wouldn't bang it as he thrashed about on the floor, Don became aware of a sharp whistling sound. At first he thought it was the sound of air rushing between Billy's clenched teeth, but then he realized that the sound didn't correspond to the rapid rise and fall of Billy's chest. He glanced up and saw what was making the sound. It was the pendulum.

"For Christ's sake!" Don said, and he followed that with a low moan.

The pendulum was swinging around, lost in a blur of speed. The sound it made reminded Don of the whickering sound of arrows flying overhead, only louder, and beneath that sound was another, lower, steadier humming sound. The legs of the tripod rattled and swayed with the wild motion of the pendulum.

Don looked frantically down at Billy, trying to block out the vibrating sound that seemed to pluck and vibrate his spine. The seizure was still intensifying. Even the skin on Billy's face looked stretched, pulled back against his skull.

Suddenly there was a loud twang followed by the sound of exploding glass. Don glanced over his shoulder and saw the dining room window curtain was jammed out through a hole in the glass. The lead weight of the pendulum was hanging outside the broken window in the nest of curtain. Making a quick estimate, Don figured the flying lead weight had missed his head by mere inches. He was positive it would have split his skull if it had hit him.

After five frantic minutes, the seizure gradually subsided. Billy's arms and legs lost their brittle stiffness. Billy looked up at Don with glazed eyes as Don lifted him up and directed him into a chair.

As his breathing got more regular, the purple faded from his face. At last, Billy's eyes cleared and focused on Don with a dazed expression. Don stayed with him for another five minutes before he dared leave him to run to the kitchen for a glass of water.

When he returned seconds later, Billy's color was almost back to normal, except for a few splotches of red from broken blood vessels. His eyes had regained a bit of their usual sparkle.

"Sorry to trouble you," he said, his voice rumbling with mucus as he reached for the glass of water in Don's hand. He took a sip and coughed it out as soon as he tried to swallow.

"Take it easy there," Don said, giving him a gentle slap on the back.

Billy sat slouched in the chair, totally sapped of strength. "Well," he said, after taking another sip and swallowing successfully, "I can guarantee you *that* doesn't happen very often."

Don shook his head and whistled between his teeth. "I should hope not! You scared the be-Jesus out of me!"

Billy smacked his lips and took another sip of water. His head lolled against the back of the chair, and he stared up at the ceiling light. "Christ, I'm sore. Was it a bad one?"

Don nodded. "It was a bad one. Not that I'm any expert."

Billy shook his head. "I didn't break anything, did I?"

"No," Don said tightly.

Billy blinked his eyes rapidly and focused on Don. "Don't get all panicky on me, now. I'll admit it, I have epilepsy. It's happened before. Not in quite a while, though. It happened once when I was dowsing a field, but—jeez!—never when I was map dowsing!"

"Do you take medication for it?" Don asked.

Billy nodded, wiping his mouth with his shirt sleeve. "Yeah. Usually, though I don't actually have a seizure like that. More often than not, I just sort of black out."

"Not this time," Don said. "Here, let me get you something so you can clean up." He went into the bathroom and wet a washcloth with warm water. Returning to the dining room, he gave it to Billy, who leaned back in the chair and wiped his forehead.

"Boy, that one was a doozy," Billy said. "My ears are still ringing."

Don didn't like the way Billy's eyelids kept fluttering. Several times he would momentarily lose focus. The whites of his eyes were now totally pink from bloodshot.

"I'd say we've done enough map dowsing for tonight, wouldn't you?" Don said. He picked up the fallen tripod and began folding up the map.

Billy reached out and stopped him. "Hold it. I want to take a look at what we got. Hey, where's the pendulum?"

Don went over to the broken window and, pulling the curtain out, let the lead weight drop into his hand.

"What the hell happened?" Billy asked.

Don tossed the weight in his hand several times. "You said it was a doozy, and it was. This damned thing shot right off the tripod and through the window. I don't know how far it would have gone outside if the curtain hadn't stopped it. I *do* know it missed hitting me by inches."

He handed the weight to Billy, who turned it over in his hand a few times before dropping it into the wooden box. "Curious thing ain't it?"

"It could've killed me," Don said. "And then where would *you* have been?"

Billy shrugged. "I was afraid something like this was going to happen because of what I felt as soon as I drove in this afternoon," he said. "I should have known better."

Reaching for the tripod, he collapsed the legs, scooped up his colored markers, and put them away. He snapped the wooden box shut and then pulled the map close so he could study it.

Don began pacing back and forth behind his chair, angry at himself for allowing any of this to happen. He wondered if Billy's seizure had somehow been triggered by their dowsing—maybe not from anything the pendulum had responded to, but just from the excitement of the situation. Again, he felt foolish for allowing himself to get sucked into this. Maybe the hardware-store wit was right; Billy *was* a Wingnut.

"I want you to give Doc Kimball a call tomorrow and make an appointment. I want him to check you over. Maybe the medication you're on isn't strong enough or something," Don said.

"I'll be all right. Don't worry. Indians have strong

medicine."

While Billy put his things away, Don kept after him until he promised to see the doctor, and he privately determined to give Dr. Kimball a call in a day or two just to make sure Billy had seen him.

"I don't see much of a pattern there," Billy said, slapping his hand onto the map.

"I don't think you're in any shape to think about it right now. Let's let it rest, O.K.?" Don said.

Billy nodded. "O.K. But just looking at it quickly, I'd say here is where you're going to find—whatever." He tapped the map where Don had marked the red oval. "And look here, too, where the line you drew passes through the circle. See. It runs directly east-west," he said, pointing to the compass rose on the edge of the map. "It could indicate a direction more than a location. We'll have to check it out in the field some time."

"But not tonight," Don said hastily. "I want you to get your ass home. Are you O.K. to drive?"

"Course I can," Billy said. He stood up stiffly and picked up his wooden box. "I'm sorry about the window," he said. "If you stop by the store, I'll give you a new pane of glass free of charge."

"Don't worry about it," Don said. "As long as you're feeling all right." He was souring on the whole idea, and the more Billy talked about it, the more he wished he'd just get out of the house.

"I'm O.K., honestly," Billy said. "And you won't have to go checking up on me, all right?"

Don nodded, surprised that, again, Billy seemed to have the uncanny ability to respond to his unspoken thoughts.

They walked into the kitchen, and Don snapped on the outside light for Billy. As Billy swung open the screen door though, he turned and nailed Don with his hawklike eyes. "Some evening, when you have some spare time, just give me a hoot, and we'll take a look around. Maybe do a bit of digging ourselves."

"I thought you said we shouldn't disturb anything out there—just in case," Don said.

Fishing his car keys from his pocket, Billy shrugged. "We won't go tearing the place apart. I just want to see if the dowsing pinpointed anything, that's all. So, like I said, give me a call some time."

Don nodded, but he was thinking: *The hell I will! Swinging pendulums! Skeletal hands! I've had more than enough of this nonsense!*

He walked Billy to his car and, after making sure he really was well enough to drive home, watched as he backed around and drove off into the night.

A dull, gnawing worry came over him as he started back to the house as if something—a dark, nameless pressing *something*—was reaching out of the darkness toward him. He made himself a second cup of tea and sat at the kitchen table, waiting for Jan to get home. While he sat there, cradling the warm cup in his hands, he couldn't shake the feeling that the—*something*—wasn't just out there in the night; it was here inside the house, too!

He suddenly tensed when he thought about Beth.

Why hadn't she come when he called for help?

Taking the steps two at a time, he ran up to her bedroom and looked in on her. She was sound asleep, her body seemingly rigid beneath the blankets. Her hand, he saw, was clutching the wooden doll, and soft moonlight washed her face a powdery blue. She was smiling as she slept.

But as he eased the door shut, Don was suddenly struck by something Billy had said yesterday. Hadn't he mentioned that part of the Indian ceremonies involved carved wooden figures? What if that old doll

Beth had found *hadn't* been his mother's when she was a child living in this house? What if the doll, like the hand he had found, was *much* older?

Shaking his head, he tried to dismiss the thought as merely an overreaction from the strain of the evening, but, even after Jan had come home and they had washed up and tucked themselves into bed together, he couldn't stop wondering just how old that doll really was.

Chapter Ten

The Site

I

Don was mowing the lawn when Jan called him to the telephone. He killed the engine and went up to the house. The screen door slammed shut behind him, and he was wiping his face on a dishtowel as she handed him the receiver.

"Some guy named Mitchell," she said, raising an eyebrow.

Don tossed the towel into the laundry room and took the phone, barely able to pant out the word, "Hello."

"Mr. Inman. Roger Mitchell here. I've been trying to reach you for the past few days. I'm glad I finally caught you."

"What's up?" Don asked. After the dowsing experiment with Billy, he wasn't so sure he even wanted to hear what Mitchell had to say.

"Well, you see," Mitchell said, "I've spoken to quite

a few of my associates and shown them that hand of yours, and quite frankly the archaeological community is stumped."

"How so?" Don asked. He signaled to Jan to get him a glass of water, and she did him the extra service of dropping a couple of ice cubes into it before handing it him.

"For one thing," Mitchell said, "I've had estimates anywhere from fifty years to two thousand years."

Don snickered. "It should fit in there somewhere," he said, taking a long gulp.

Mitchell missed the joke and continued, sounding all business. "We'll know more once the carbon-dating results are in, of course. As I may have explained, the equipment is booked up quite a bit in advance, so I'm not exactly sure when that will be."

"No hurry, I suppose," Don said.

"None at all," Mitchell said, "but I wanted to know if I could drop by this Thursday and have a look around."

"Just a sec," Don said. Cupping the phone with his hand, he said to Jan, "The guy from the university wants to come out on Thursday and check the property."

"Is this about that hand?" she said, frowning.

Don nodded, and Jan shrugged as if she couldn't care less when they came.

"Thursday will be all right with me. About what time?"

He could hear Mitchell flipping the pages of his calendar. "I should think we'd be there sometime before noon. I might want to be there on Friday as well in case anything interesting turns up."

"I don't see any problems there," Don said. "You won't be—you know—digging the place up or anything, will you?"

Mitchell replied, "No. Of course not. We might dig a test hole or two but nothing major."

Looking at Jan, Don said, "It looks like your garden will survive."

She didn't laugh, and Don started getting upset that first Mitchell and now Jan—*no one*—was laughing at his jokes.

"You know, while I have you on the line, I was wondering about something."

"What's on your mind?" Mitchell asked, and again, as in Mitchell's office, Don felt like a dutiful graduate student seeking knowledge from the professor. It must be something in his tone of voice, Don thought.

"Well, now—" he began, feeling a wave of embarrassment. He considered not even mentioning that night with Billy, but, on the other hand, he wanted a professional opinion on what had happened. He decided he'd leave out the bit about Billy's seizure. No need to go into that!

"A neighbor of mine, an Indian as a matter of fact, came over a night or two ago. He dowsed the property."

"Are you putting in a new well?" Mitchell asked.

Don almost laughed, thinking this might be Mitchell's attempt at a joke. "No," he said as straight as he could, "I had told him about the hand and that you thought it might be ancient, and he wanted to see if dowsing the land got any results. The weird thing is the only place he got any real activity was pretty much where I found the buried hand."

Mitchell snickered, and Don thought angrily that he was getting the laughs in the wrong places.

"His dowsing pendulum inscribed a circle that comes to about thirty or thirty-five feet in diameter, and I found the hand within that circle. The other response he got was a straight line that cut the circle just about in half. The line runs east-west, pretty much in line with the sunrise and sunset."

There was a long pause at the other end of the line, and Don could just imagine Mitchell, feet propped up on his messy desk as he sucked vigorously on his unlit pipe. Finally, Mitchell said, "Is that a fact?"

Don continued to explain that the dowsing had been done on a map of the field, so there couldn't have been any hints to tip Billy off. He also told Mitchell that he thought the coincidence of having a reaction almost in the exact spot where he had found the hand was at least a little bit interesting.

"Coincidence, that's the key word here," Mitchell said, scoffing. "I hope you don't take any of this seriously."

Don ran his fingers through his sweat-soaked hair and sighed. The more he considered it, the more it seemed at least worth pursuing. Maybe it all boiled down to a question of attitudes. Don liked Billy. He found him a bit tough to get to know, but his intuitive sense told him that basically Billy was all right. And when he was honest with himself, he had to admit that he hadn't really cared for Mitchell. He seemed a nice enough guy, but his colorless lack of humor and his rather pompous nature didn't do anything for Don.

"What we had," Don said, keeping his voice low and even, "was a quite intense reaction, and—well, I was curious what you thought about the whole thing, dowsing and all."

"In a word," Mitchell said, "I think it's hogwash. It's pseudoscientific, psychic bullshit."

"Please, don't hold back your opinion," Don said, unable not to smile. "Be candid." He waited for Mitchell to laugh and, when he didn't, he continued.

326

"Anyway, I wanted to suggest that maybe, when you come out here, we could dig in a few of the spots where the dowsing got some reaction."

"I suspect it'd be a waste of time," Mitchell replied. "If you're so curious about this, I'd suggest you do the digging on your own, but I'd also add that the indications are that this might be a significant archaeological site. I'd hate to see it destroyed by amateur tampering."

Don opened his mouth, about to reply to that, but he decided to let it pass.

"Dowsing, in my opinion, is for crackpots if you'll excuse my bluntness. If it's results you want, on Thursday, I'll be accompanied by Desmond Patterson, of the Maine Archaeological Society. He's probably the most respected man in Maine when it comes to Paleolithic Indian sites."

"He's more than welcome," Don said. His ears were burning from the embarrassment of being put down, and he wondered why he felt so defensive about Billy Blackshoe's dowsing.

"Again, though, Mr. Inman, I know I can't tell you not to do whatever you want on your own property, but it would be best if you didn't tamper with anything out there in the field, at least not until we've had a chance to take a look at it."

Don was bristling, but he simply said, "Thursday, before noon. See you then," and hung up. He made eye contact with Jan, who instantly communicated that she had absolutely no desire to talk about Prof. Mitchell, dowsing, buried hands, or *any* of it; so he refilled his water glass and went outside to sit on the steps before finishing the lawn. He missed Max, wishing he were lying there at his feet so he could rub him behind his ears. Max would have listened to what was bothering him.

And what was bothering him, even more so after talking with Mitchell, was that he wanted to dig in the spots marked by the red felt-tipped pen on the surveyor's map of his land. Mitchell was full of professional snobbery, and Billy was full of old stories and superstitions he had heard from his grandfather. The facts, he thought, were buried right out there in the field. He might be skeptical of the results Billy got, but he wanted to check them out—without Billy *or* Mitchell being involved.

He leaned back on his elbows on the steps and looked out over the field, suddenly excited by the prospect of what might be out there. An Indian gravesite? Eino Kivinen's grave? Maybe even something valuable. Like those divers off the Florida Keys last year, he might find a cache of gold or jewels.

But the only image that came to mind was a withered, blackened hand, its fingers hooked into stiff claws. Shuddering, he let his breath out slowly, but it caught in his throat. He took a long swallow of cold water, but that didn't help. A cool drink in the shade certainly wasn't enough to remove the image of the mummified hand that seemed to be moving, reaching out to him from the buried darkness.

II

He finished the lawn two hours later. The sun was a dull red ball in the hazy sky, and the humid air clung to his skin as close as his sweat-soaked shirt. Streaks of sweat cut tracks through the dirt on his face and neck. Don was nursing a can of beer as he strolled out behind the barn where Beth was brushing Goblin. He called to her, and she looked at him, smiling widely. Goblin stamped her foot and snorted as though impatient at the break in her brushing.

"I'm going to take a quick shower and then drive Mom in for a job interview," he said. "Will you be all right here for an hour or two?"

"Sure," Beth replied, turning her attention back to the horse.

"We might stop off at the hardware store and get the insulation I need for the attic, too," Don said. He couldn't push aside the vague unease he felt, and he found his gaze kept shifting to Goblin's moistm brown eyes.

"We'll be fine," Beth said, sounding slightly impatient.

"Another thing," Don said, before turning to go. "I don't want you riding when we're not around."

"Dad. For crying out loud, Goblin and I—"

"I said, *no riding*. Understand?"

"Yup," Beth said sullenly. Her shoulders slumped a little, and she looked longingly at her father, but she knew he wouldn't relent.

Unable to shake the feeling that Goblin had listened to—and understood—everything he had said, Don went into the house and showered. When he came out to the car, Jan was standing there, waiting. She was dressed to the hilt, wearing a dark-blue dress and jacket. "Very professional," Don said, coming around to her side of the car and swinging open the door.

"And *very* hot," Jan said, rolling her eyes.

The drive into town had long stretches of tense silence between them, and Don couldn't figure if it was because she was nervous about this interview with York Harbor Realty or if there was something she wanted to say but didn't dare.

Don told her he'd be back in an hour as he drove up to the reserved parking in front of the real estate office's front door. "And if—you know, things don't go so well," he said, looking around, "why don't I meet you over there at that restaurant? But things will go just great. You've got the job sewn up, if you ask me." He leaned over and gave her a kiss.

He watched as she strode up to the door, only glancing for a moment over her shoulder before entering. Then he drove over to the hardware store to check on the price of insulation. In a way, he was hoping Billy wasn't working; he still hadn't made up his mind what he thought about him and his dowsing.

As it turned out, Billy wasn't in; he was making a delivery. Don talked about types of insulation with an overweight salesman named Wilson, bought ten rolls of fiberglass batting, and, with a little help from Wilson, got six rolls into the car and strapped the other four onto the roof rack. Because of the wind resistance, he had to drive slowly, so it was just over an hour later that he pulled into York Harbor Realty's parking lot. Jan, looking wilted, was standing in the shade by the front door.

"Well?" Don asked, leaning across the seat to open the door for her.

Jan swung off her jacket and slid into the car. "Hard to tell," she said softly. Don slipped the car into gear and pulled slowly out onto the highway.

"So what happened? How'd it go?" he asked impatiently.

"I think I did O.K.," Jan said at last. "I don't want to get our hopes up or anything, but I think I did fine. Everyone I met seemed nice, and even the man who interviewed me the most—Frank Johnson, I think his name was—said he knew my old boss."

"He knows Benford? Oh, great! They probably drink and whore together at conventions," Don said.

Jan didn't reply. She sat, staring straight ahead at the road as they drove toward home. As they came up the driveway, they saw Beth, sitting on the stairs by the kitchen door. Her legs were bouncing excitedly, and she was running toward them before Don had a chance to park the car.

"Mrs. Remy called and asked if I wanted to go to the movies with Krissy. Can I? It's wicked hot! And the theater will be air-conditioned."

"You've taken care of Goblin?" Don asked, glancing toward the barn. "She's brushed and fed, and you made *sure* the stall door was closed?"

"Yes! Yes! Yes! Can I go? They said they were leaving right away."

"What are you going to see?" Don asked.

"We haven't decided yet. There's tons of good movies!"

"Get going," Jan said, waving her hand feebly in front of her face. Before she could say more, Beth was dashing toward the house and the phone. As Don and Jan slowly got out of the car, Jan mumbled something about setting up a lawn chair in the shower and just sitting there for the afternoon.

Louise and Krissy Remy drove up fifteen minutes later. Jan instructed Beth to be home by five o'clock, but, when she protested, saying the movie probably wouldn't even be out before then, they agreed on six o'clock. So with Beth gone and Jan taking it easy, Don figured this would give him a chance to get started on the attic. Even with the heat, he didn't think it'd take more than an afternoon to lay the batts. He backed the car over the grass up to the front door, and, one by one, lugged the rolls of insulation up the stairs and into the attic.

By the time he had all ten rolls up there, sweat was stinging his eyes, and tiny threads of fiberglass gnawed at his arms and neck. The job suddenly looked much larger, once he started shifting around the junk in the attic and lifting up the few loose floorboards to open up the bays.

The July heat hammered the roof, filling the attic with a haze. Being in the attic made Don think, for the first time in a long while, about Aune's diary. He thought that maybe he should give Susan a call that evening to see how she was doing translating the book.

Don worked steadily, ripping up the floorboards, laying out the fiberglass, and cutting it to fit. He would only cut loose with a string of curses when he had to move something particularly heavy or when a rusted nail just wouldn't give. The work would have gone even faster if the bays had been standard width. The mask he wore to keep from breathing dust and fiberglass particles made him sweat all the more. He was convinced that, after only an hour or two, he had sweated off at least five pounds.

He came downstairs for a break when he figured he had half the work done. Jan was sleeping on the couch with the fan pointed directly on her. "I can *smell* how hard you've been working," she said sleepily when Don leaned over and gave her a kiss.

"Umm. Man work like bull—man smell like bull," he said, smiling. He glanced at his watch and said, "I was up there longer than I realized. Beth should be getting home soon, don't you think?"

Jan shook her head sleepily, smacking her lips, and made no effort to bring her head up from the pillow. Don walked into the kitchen, feeling itchy all over from the fiberglass. He was running the water to get it cold when he looked out and saw the Remys's station wagon, parked in the shade of the barn.

"What the—?" He was going to call out to Jan, but he realized she had been sleeping, and, even if she had been awake, she probably wouldn't have heard the car over the sound of the fan. Don took a few quick gulps of water and went out into the dooryard. As he came around the side of the barn, he saw Krissy and her mother, standing by the paddock gate. Beth was sitting on top of Goblin, walking her in a tight circle across the paddock. A wide smile split her sunburned face, but it quickly melted when she saw her father's expression.

"Pun'kin," he said, a mixture of greeting and rebuke.

Louise Remy made a mousy squeak of surprise and turned to face him. Don greeted her and Krissy, then watched as Beth cantered over to the fence.

Louise drew back, looking nervously at Goblin. "We got back just a little while ago," she said. "Beth wanted us to see her horse."

"Well," Don said, giving Beth a steady stare, "we generally don't let her take Goblin out unless either Jan or I know about it."

Beth shifted in the saddle and looked down at the ground, her smile now completely gone.

"But I suppose it's O.K.," Don continued, "since you were here."

"Me?" Louise said, her hand fluttering like a bird at her throat. "I don't know the first *thing* about horses. Krissy rides some, but me? No, never!"

"Well, Beth does just fine," Don said, addressing Louise. Then looking at Beth, he added, "But I sure would appreciate it if you'd let me know before you do. Understand?"

"I'm sorry, Dad," Beth said sullenly. "Can Krissy have a ride now?"

Don shrugged. "It's up to her mother."

Louise shook her head and put her hand protectively on her daughter's shoulder. "Oh, not today. Maybe some other time. We have to be getting on home now. Pa will be wanting his supper."

Krissy looked at her mother but didn't say aloud the plea that was written all over her face. Louise started backing away from the fence, her eyes fastened on Goblin. "Some time when Mr. Inman has the time," she said, still trying to mollify Krissy. "Beth and her folks'll be having supper soon, too."

Don almost laughed at the way she grasped excuses the way a gambler grabs poker chips.

"Anyway, thanks for taking me to the movie," Beth said, still sitting on Goblin. She leaned forward and rubbed the horse's nose. Goblin nickered softly as though speaking to her.

"We'll have to do it again soon," Louise said, giving Don the impression that even this was an excuse so Krissy wouldn't ride. Don walked with them around the barn to their car, and, as they drove off, Beth waved her hand and called out, "See yah!"

Once they were gone, Don went back to the paddock and was about to start in with his scolding, but Beth cut him off. "I know. I know," she said as she swung down out of the saddle. "I shouldn't have done it. I was just showing off a little, I guess, but jeez, really, it was O.K. Goblin would never hurt *anybody*!"

All Don could think about was the bloody, lumpy mass that had been Max before Goblin's hoofs got through with him. "Well," he said, fighting back the sudden wave of fear he felt. "I don't think it'd be such a good idea to let Krissy ride—at least not when I'm not around. O.K.?"

Beth nodded. "O.K." She led Goblin back to the stall, and Don went into the house for a quick shower. Now that he had stopped working, he figured he could finish the insulation in the attic when the weather was a little cooler. He walked into the kitchen, toweling his hair dry just as Jan was serving

334

up hamburgers and peas.

After supper, Don and Jan sat on the kitchen steps, watching the sun lowering in the hazy sky, while Beth—who knew she had stretched her limits riding Goblin without permission—did the dishes. Don had made a comment about how guilt had its own rewards, but Jan hadn't laughed.

Jan finally went inside, irritated by the steady strafing of mosquitoes, and Don, figuring there was still an hour or so of daylight left, decided he'd ignore Mitchell's "suggestion" that he not do any digging in the field. He went into the house for the surveyor's map he and Billy had dowsed on and told Jan what he planned to do. She merely threatened reprisals if he messed with her garden and left him to do whatever he wanted to do.

He got a shovel from the barn and walked out into the field well past the garden. Spreading the map out on the ground and holding it down on four corners with small stones, he lined up the compass rose with the setting sun. For several minutes he studied the map, constantly glancing at the land to gauge distances. Then he stood and began pacing off certain lengths. He marked several spots by removing a clump of turf. Finally satisfied, he was ready to begin digging to see just how good Billy's dowsing really was.

Just before he started digging, he glanced up at the house and saw someone in the bedroom window, looking out at him. He waved, thinking it was Jan just making sure he didn't mess with the garden, but she didn't wave back. The reflection on the glass made her figure indistinct.

Don snickered at himself, surprised that he took any of Billy's dowsing seriously, but, with a resigned shrug, he placed the blade of the shovel on the ground and stepped down on it. He turned over the first scoop of earth. A nightcrawler, cut in half by the shovel, twisted in the loose clumps of dirt. After several more shovelfuls, he had reached a depth of about two feet and discovered nothing more than several fist-sized stones. Feeling more than ever the fool, he scooped the dirt back into the hole and stamped it flat.

Looking at the map again and trusting it less, he surveyed the field and paced out several giant steps in another direction. The sun was dropping in the western sky, and crickets chirred loudly. The grass was a soggy, muted gray where he placed the shovel, and, when he stepped down on the shovel, the metal scraped against a stone with a teeth-chattering clang. He was thrown off balance and almost fell.

"Jeez!" he muttered, wiping his hands on his pants, "so there's rocks in a New England field. No surprise there."

He probed the ground with the shovel tip for the edge of the stone and was actually surprised when he at last found it. The buried stone seemed to be at least five feet long, as best as he could tell; it might have been several rocks, maybe even a buried stone wall. But whatever, there *seemed* to be—well, something!

And this was the spot where Billy's pendulum had shown the most activity, so if there was anything here—

Don shook his head and laughed aloud at himself. He leaned over and began scooping away dirt until he had exposed the edge of the stone. He then tried to wedge up the end of it, but no matter how hard he tried, the stone wouldn't budge. Finally, he gave up and re-covered it. The sky was darkening now, so he decided he'd try one more spot and then call it a day. As far as he was concerned, he was batting zero.

Squinting at the map in the deepening darkness, he

tried to get an exact fix on the center of the circle the pendulum had inscribed. He paced off the distance and, as the first few stars twinkled overhead, started to dig not more than eight or ten feet from where he had first hit stone.

Other than a few more rocks, he turned up nothing, maybe a few earthworms, but he couldn't see much in the gathering darkness anyway. But on the second try, the shovel tip grated against stone. The rasping sound set his teeth on edge, and he swore softly and stood back, realizing that he was bathed in sweat. He forced himself to breathe slowly and evenly, all the while wondering if it was worth going up to the house for a flashlight.

He thought about how foolish the whole thing was and was going to stop, but he felt compelled to continue. He stuck the shovel tip into the ground, probing for the stone, and, when he found it, he began searching again by feel for the edge. He glanced over to where he had first dug and wondered if, by some chance, this stone was the same one he had exposed earlier. If it was, then it was one hell of a big slab of stone.

As he worked, repeatedly jabbing the tip of the shovel into the ground, he realized that the stone was—or seemed to be—a perfectly flat slab, lying like a table top six or seven inches beneath the grass. If he was right and this was one piece of stone, then in all likelihood it was a buried ledge of granite. He continued probing the soil though, and eventually concluded that the stone—whatever it was—was a rectangle, roughly nine feet by six. If it wasn't a ledge, then it might be a long-buried and forgotten granite slab from Toivo Kivinen's quarry.

Working more from feel than anything else, Don knelt and began digging with his hands to expose some of the rock. He wondered if this was it—if Billy's dowsing plumb bob had just indicated the buried stone in the field. "Big deal," he muttered, as he clawed the soil away.

The stone he exposed had an unaccountable smoothness, and again the image of a buried table top came to mind. Considering the way Billy's lead weight had swung so wildly—enough to go shooting through the dining room window!—this didn't seem to be much of a find.

Don looked up at the house and saw the windows glowing with warm yellow light in the early summer night. All around him, the field was buzzing with insect sounds. Overhead, he could see the flittering silhouettes of bats.

But when he looked down at the ground where he was working, a sudden chill came over him. Where his fingers had dug into the cool soil, flecks of mica glittered like starlight, and, when he found the edge of the buried rock, he felt a sudden rush as though he were perched on the edge of a cliff, looking over a long drop. The ground seemed to fall away suddenly, and, uttering a low whimper, Don braced himself, desperately trying to hold on.

He lurched to his feet, almost tripping over the shovel as he scrambled away. He was filled with the sudden rush of fear that this, too, might be one of his nightmares. Looking frantically up at the house, he half-expected to see it telescoping in and out of range as waves of vertigo churned in his head. He staggered back from where he had been digging, wanting to scream, but there was only enough air in his lungs to utter a low, strangled cry.

He picked up the shovel and map and started to run toward the house. The map flapped in his back pocket like a broken wing. The tingling sensation that there was something behind him—*following* him—grew increasingly stronger, but he couldn't bring himself to turn around and look. The light in the window over the kitchen sink held his eye like a lighthouse beacon as he ran.

He was conscious only of the slap-slap of his feet on the ground, and the strong sense that *something* was following him as swiftly and silently as a shadow, and cold and deadly!

Slamming open the kitchen door, he just about collapsed into a chair. His hand, still clutching the shovel, was cramped and aching. He jumped, startled, when Jan called out.

"Don? 'S that you?"

"Uh, yeah," he managed to say. His throat was tight and threatened to cut off his words. He sat trembling, facing the screen door, expecting to see—*something* out there, framed against the night. All he could see was the peaked roof of the barn and the sprinkling of stars beyond, and only peaceful night sounds filtered through the screen, but still he couldn't keep his hands from shaking.

"How'd it go out there?" Jan asked, coming into the kitchen with an empty coffee cup. Don could hear muffled voices from the TV in the living room.

"Just—uh, just turned up a few stones, that's all," he said, his voice sounding jittery—at least to his ears. He blinked as his eyes adjusted to the bright light of the kitchen.

Jan put her cup in the sink and filled it with water. "If it was rocks you wanted, I found enough for both of us when I planted the garden."

"Yeah, but—" Don began, but he felt suddenly foolish. He had let his nerves get the better of him and had run up to the house like a ten year old with the boogeyman hot on his trail. If there was anything to

Billy's dowsing or *any* of that psychic bullshit, it was because people let themselves get sucked into it, let their imagination run away with them—just as he had.

Jan looked at him and shook her head. "The least you could do is not drag that dirty shovel into my clean kitchen," she said with a scolding shake of her head. "Didn't your mother teach you *anything*?"

"Sorry," Don said, and he went to the kitchen door slowly to put the shovel outside. One small part of his mind chattered wildly that, as soon as he opened the door, *something* would reach out of the darkness and grab him. He placed the shovel on the doorstep and quickly snapped his arm back into the house.

"And you ought to take a shower before you go to bed," Jan said before walking back into the living room.

III

First thing in the morning Don went back out to the field. In the morning light, the few clumps of earth he had turned up looked pitifully small, and the whole area looked about as threatening as a Sunday School picnic. He still felt an edge of nervousness when he looked at the small bit of exposed granite, but he saw it now for what it was: just some buried stone, maybe a ledge, maybe a forgotten slab from the quarry—nothing more.

Using his foot, he filled in the hole and walked back up to the house. He had work to finish in the attic and sure as hell couldn't afford to waste time digging holes in the ground!

Back in the attic, Don continued rolling out the insulation and stuffing it into the bays. The attic still held the coolness from the night, so the work went much better than it had the day before. No sweat dripping down and stinging his eyes.

Just before ten o'clock, the phone rang. The sound instantly reminded Don that he had forgotten to call Susan last night. As he started down the stairs, Jan called up to him that Dr. Mitchell had called to say that he and some other professor would be by within the hour. She muttered something else that he couldn't quite make out.

Don went back to work, picking up the pace because he wanted to have the job done before Mitchell got there, but, with four bays still left to fill, he heard a car come up the driveway. Brushing himself off, Don started down the attic steps, thinking to himself how much he missed Max's warning barks. The dust from the car was still swirling in the air when Don, wiping his face with a handtowel, came outside and greeted the men. Jan made a point of keeping herself busy and not coming outside.

Don shook hands first with Mitchell and then was introduced to Dr. Desmond Patterson, director of the Maine Archaeological Society in Augusta, and Paul Spencer, a senior from the University of Southern Maine majoring in archaeology and spending the summer on a work-study project with Mitchell. Don noticed the pile of surveying and excavating equipment in the back of the university car-pool station wagon.

"So," Patterson said, shading his eyes and scanning the field, "this is the spot."

Mitchell looked around and indicated the far end of the field, near the line of trees. "That mound over there might prove to be interesting," he said solemnly.

Patterson snorted. "We'll have to have a look-see."

"Where do you want to set up first?" Spencer asked. He had the tailgate down and was already unloading the equipment. He took out the tripod, adjusted the legs, then carefully placed a battered wooden box on the ground and took out the transit. He hummed what Don recognized as a Bruce Springsteen song as he screwed a telescopic device onto the tripod.

"What say we just take a look around?" Patterson said, and Spencer nodded.

"Did you get any dating results on the hand yet?" Don asked.

Mitchell shook his head. "No. The lab in Cambridge is backed up for more than six months."

"Archaeology is a profession for the patient," Patterson said without making eye contact with Don. "First off, I want you to show me exactly where you found that hand."

Don took them over to the garden and pointed to where, as best as he could remember, the Rototiller had turned up the copper-sheeted hand. Patterson muttered something about the site being rather unremarkable and then led the way as they walked up to the crest of the hill.

"That must flow into the swamp we saw along Route One, wouldn't you say?" Mitchell asked, pointing to the alder-lined stream in the gully.

"I've heard someone in town refer to it as Whippoorwill Swamp," Don said, "but from what I've seen of it, it isn't much of a body of water."

"Not now it isn't," Patterson snapped, "but one or two thousand years ago, it might have been a lake. If this stream is what's left of a free-flowing river, and with the ocean so near, this high ground here might have been very attractive to local Indians for a campsite or whatever."

Don didn't like the way Patterson didn't look at him when he spoke; it made him not trust him.

Spencer, the dutiful student the same as Don had felt like when he had spoken with Mitchell earlier, was busily scribbling notes in a small spiral-bound notebook.

"In fact," Patterson continued, "that mound I noticed over there might well prove to be a shell heap."

Don had to force himself not to point out that Mitchell had been the first to comment on the mound. Instead, he simply asked, "Why are shell heaps so important?"

"Basically, the shell heaps are the Indians' dumps," Patterson said. "We find all sorts of discarded materials—broken pottery, arrow heads, any number of things. The shells preserve the artifacts from the usual decomposition that would result from burial in soil."

"So, basically, you still think that hand I found was Indian," Don said.

"We can't jump to any conclusions," Patterson said. He glanced at Mitchell, who was puffing on his unlit pipe. "But the copper sheet and the beadwork do indicate that, and now seeing the land, I'd say it increases the probability. What do you say, Roger?"

Mitchell was still scanning the property. "If you look at the crest over there," he said, pointing fairly close to where Don had been digging the night before, "I'd even go so far as to suggest that it looks almost unnatural, the way it's built up."

Don was shocked that he had never noticed it before, but then again he hadn't been looking for it before. There was no doubt about it; just past the crest of the hill, there was a slight rise as though a rounded, rectangular area of the field had risen above the general level of the field.

Patterson nodded agreement. "Paul, why don't you get the sledge hammer and a few stakes?"

Without a word, Spencer ran to the station wagon

343

and got what had been requested. He trailed along behind the men as they walked slowly across the field, discussing the possibilities of the site.

When they got to where Don had done a bit of digging, Mitchell kicked the freshly turned earth with the toe of his boot. "So," he said, looking at Don, "you didn't take my advice after all."

Don shrugged but, before he said anything, he remembered some other advice he had been given; Billy had told him that, if indeed this was some kind of sacred Indian ground, Don should make sure no one disturbed the place. He shivered, hoping nobody noticed.

Mitchell knelt down and, clearing away the loose dirt, exposed the smooth surface of granite. Don pointed out that the stone was right where they had said the hill looked "unnatural," but, as he examined it, Mitchell suggested that the rock was no more than a piece of exposed ledge, which could account for the artificial look of the slope.

"This is the spot you told me about, isn't it?" Mitchell said, looking up at Don. "This is the place where your friend, the dowser, said he detected something?"

Don nodded, feeling a wave of embarrassment, and he looked at Patterson, trying to gauge his reaction.

Mitchell straightened up and brushed off his knees. "I said before, I wouldn't put any stock into this dowsing. If it was truly scientific, it would be repeatable by anyone, not just the few who, as dowsers are so fond of saying, 'have the knack.'"

"But the results were—interesting," Don said.

The four of them started down the hill toward the road. At the foot of the driveway, they stopped and looked back up the gently rising crest. Spencer, tired of carrying the hammer and the armload of wooden stakes, put his load down, leaned back against the slanted stone post, and closed his eyes.

"I *do* think there might be something to what the dowser found," Don said, not willing to let the discussion drop. "You can call it foolishness or just a hunch, but I think there might be something important buried up there."

"Really?" Patterson said, cocking one eyebrow.

At least, Don thought, he's looking at me directly!

"Don't you ever play hunches?" Don asked, pressing. "I mean, in the field—how do you know where to dig?"

Patterson frowned. "By careful, scientific observation," he said evenly. "There are certain indications here, several of which, I might add, are obvious to the trained eye. We look for certain land forms, signs that might have made the land attractive to the natives."

"But don't you ever make an educated guess, based on a—a *feeling* that a certain spot is right?"

"Sure," Mitchell interjected, "I'm sure that sometimes—I know I can't always articulate why I think a site might be rewarding. The only real test is to dig, and I suggest we start at that mound out by the edge of the field."

Patterson, Mitchell, and Don started to walk over, but, when they looked back, they saw Spencer was still leaning back against the stone gatepost, his eyes closed and a blissful smile on his face.

"Paul?" Mitchell said. "Are you coming with us?"

Spencer remained immobile, but, when Mitchell called his name a second time, he shook his head and opened his eyes, looking around slightly dazed as though he had just woken up.

"Are you feeling all right?" Mitchell asked. He was concerned that perhaps the hot sun had started getting to the boy.

"Yeah," Spencer said, "I'm O.K." He was shaking his head as though he had water in one ear. He stood up slowly, finding it necessary to lean against the stone post. Don noticed a curious slouch to the boy's shoulders that he hadn't noticed before.

"I was just kind of dozing, I guess," Spencer said. "It was just the heat or something."

"You can daydream on someone else's time," Patterson said firmly, "but not when you're working for me."

Spencer nodded and sluggishly pushed himself away from the gatepost. Hefting his load of wooden stakes, he followed the men out onto the heat-hazed field.

The boredom of the job began to settle in as Don listened to their talk about grids, baselines, and land profiles. Rather than tag along, he offered to go up to the house for a jug of ice water if they'd like. They took a short break to down several glasses of water and then went back to work.

The afternoon moved slowly, and heat wafted over the field in sodden waves. Don spent much of the time sitting in the shade by the house, watching the men as they marked off areas and dug several test holes. At one point Beth came out and asked if she could ride Goblin up along the road toward the quarry. Don was glad she asked for permission and helped her saddle up. He told her to make sure she stayed away from where the men were working, and, with a dry clumping of hoofs, she rode off behind the house.

IV

When Don went up to the house to refill the water jug for Mitchell and the others, he found Jan leaning

346

over the sink and looking out at the field.

"Have they done anything so far?" she asked, her mouth twisting into a crooked smile. "As far as I can see, they've spent most of the time wandering back and forth, just talking. Do they really get paid for this?"

Don smiled. "Right there's our tax dollars at work," he said. He got a handful of ice cubes from the freezer and dropped them into the jug, then ran the water to fill it.

"Well, I just don't like this," Jan said. "It makes me kind of nervous with them out there."

Don could tell by her tone that she meant it, but he figured no matter what he said, she wouldn't be satisfied until they left. He took the water out to them and watched them work for a while longer. As Patterson had said, "archaeology is a job for the patient," and Don just didn't feel the thrill of exploration and discovery he had expected to feel. He left them to go back into the attic and finish doing the insulation.

The work went smoothly, if a bit too hot, and he finished in a little over an hour. When he came back downstairs, Jan was weeding in the garden. He figured it was more to protect her garden from Mitchell than of necessity; not much of what she had planted was what could be called thriving.

He went outside and was starting across the driveway to speak with Jan when, out of the corner of his eye, he saw Beth, sitting on the front steps, her chin resting in her hands.

"Hey, Punk, how was your ride?" he asked, coming over to her.

Beth looked at him and shrugged. "O.K.," she said sullenly.

"You got Goblin settled in the stall?"

"She's in the paddock," she answered, then quickly

added, "And I made *sure* the gate was locked."

"So why the long face?" he asked as he took a seat beside her on the steps.

She shifted to one side to make room for him and shrugged, her face twisting up. Don could see the muscles along her jaw working as she ground her teeth, and, looking down, he saw that she was holding her wooden doll in one hand.

"I can tell something's bothering you," he said gently, "so tell me about it."

She shook her head sharply but said nothing.

"Is it anything to do with Goblin?"

Again she shook her head. Her eyes slowly shifted toward the field, and, when Don followed her gaze, he saw Patterson, standing in the field, waving his hand over his head and shouting something—he couldn't hear what at this distance—to Mitchell, who was peering through the transit.

"Those men out there?" Don asked.

"Umm," she said. She was sitting rigidly, staring at Patterson with an unwavering gaze.

Don clicked his tongue. "You're worse than your mother, you know that? She keeps bitch—ah, complaining about them, too, saying she's afraid they'll dig up her garden."

"They shouldn't be out there," she said, and her voice was so even and strong it made Don feel uncomfortable.

"It's just for a—"

"They *shouldn't* be *digging* out there!"

She turned and looked at her father, and her eyes softened, but only slightly. "What do they think they'll find?"

Don leaned back and scratched under his chin. He was feeling itchy and sticky with sweat and wanted nothing more than a nice cold shower—maybe even a trip up to the quarry if Jan and Beth were willing.

"I don't know what," he said, sighing. "I don't think *they* know until they find it, but they think there might be something to do with Indians around here, and they want to check it out. That's all."

"I just don't think it's right," Beth said.

Don looked at her closely, and for a moment her body seemed to shimmer as though she was far away, and curtains of heat wafted between them. A surprised sound came involuntarily from his throat, and he was left with the impression that, for the fraction of a second, he could see right through her body.

Beth had shifted her gaze out to the field again, and, without looking at her father, she nodded her head and said solemnly, "I thought so."

Don felt the tendons in his neck go wire-tight, and, fighting back a wave of panic, he muttered, "Pun-'kin," as he placed his hand on her shoulder.

The effect of his touch was startling. Beth jolted to her feet as though electricity had passed between them. She looked at her father, her eyes wide and flashing. "They should just leave him alone!" she shouted in a voice strangely not her own; it sounded twisted like an old woman's voice.

Don saw that her arms and legs were shaking with tremors of violent, suppressed rage. He stood and held her, wrapping his arms around her and holding her as tightly as he could. She looked up at him, blinking her eyes and trying to focus. Don had the weird sensation that she didn't recognize him.

"Beth. Pun'kin," he said, cooing. "What do you say we go inside and have a soda or something? I think the heat's getting to both of us."

She felt limp, wilted in his arms, and she let him guide her toward the door.

"Maybe we can give Krissy a call. See if she wants

to come over this evening to ride Goblin with you."

Beth nodded, but her gaze was fixed on the men in the field. "Someone should tell them," she whispered, just loud enough so Don could hear. "Someone should tell them to make sure they leave him alone."

V

Don was shocked that Louise Remy actually agreed to letting Krissy come over to ride with Beth, with the stipulation, of course, that Don would watch them the whole time. He and Beth were just finishing drinking their Pepsis when Krissy showed up at the door. The three of them went to the barn, and Don and Krissy watched as Beth saddled up Goblin.

After a few turns around the paddock, Beth dismounted and led Goblin over to where they waited. It made Don feel good to see the way Beth controlled the horse so confidently. He thought the responsibility of caring for the animal had helped her mature into quite a capable person, and he felt pride watching her "introduce," as she put it, Krissy to Goblin. He was also glad that her anger—or whatever she had felt about the men working in the field—had passed.

"Well, here you go, Krissy," Beth said as she handed the reins to her friend.

Krissy held the reins as though they were her lifeline. She walked slowly to the left side of the horse. "Hi yah, Goblin," she whispered as she lifted her foot to the stirrup.

Goblin suddenly drew back and snorted, and Krissy jumped back with a squeal.

"Don't move fast like that," Beth said. "And don't act afraid. I thought your dad said you had done a lot of riding."

Krissy frowned. "I'm just not used to her. That's

all."

"She can tell if you're afraid," Beth said.

Krissy forced a smile and said, "What if I *am* afraid?"

"Don't be."

After taking a moment to stroke the horse's muzzle, Krissy lifted her foot to the stirrup and swung up onto the horse. Her worried frown dissolved into a wide grin as she wiggled, adjusting her seat in the saddle. No matter how many times she had ridden, she was always astounded by how *big* horses are.

"There you go," Beth said, and she looked at her father, smiling.

Krissy clicked her tongue and started Goblin off at a slow walk. She kept glancing at Beth to make sure she was doing all right, but the longer she was in the saddle, the more confident she got.

Don placed his hand on Beth's shoulder and gave her a gentle squeeze. "You having fun?" he asked. He was glad he didn't feel any of the muscular tension she had had earlier.

Beth nodded, keeping a steady gaze on Krissy.

"Do you like Krissy?"

"Umm," Beth said. "She's O.K."

Don nodded. He could see it coming already—that same lack of communication he was beginning to think was characteristic of all girls approaching their teens.

"Well, while you and Krissy are riding, I'm going over to see how those guys are doing." He could see that they were digging in the area where he had uncovered the flat stone the day before, and he was curious to see what they thought about it.

Beth shot a quick, harsh look at the archaeologists, then nodded. "Yeah. We'll be O.K." The evenness in her voice sounded forced.

351

"Keep an eye on Krissy," he said and turned to go. As he approached the men, he saw that there were several bones arrayed on the ground.

"This is really quite interesting," Mitchell said, looking up at Don.

"What? Those bones?"

Mitchell shook his head and wiped the sheen of sweat from his forehead with a red bandanna. "No. Those are just cow bones. We found them in that mound along with a few Clovis points—arrowheads. No, I mean this—this stone."

Between the three of them, they had exposed nearly the whole surface of stone, and it was just as Don had expected, large and flat like a buried table top. It measured nearly nine feet by six.

Patterson was inspecting the edge of the stone, gently brushing dirt from the groove that ran along the outer edge, making a rectangle, rounded at the corners and slightly smaller than the stone slab. At one point, Don noticed, at the "bottom" of the table, the grooves met and formed what looked like a funnel, running off the edge of the stone.

"This is really quite peculiar," Patterson said, more to himself than to anyone else. He looked up at Don when he walked over beside him, casting his shadow over Patterson's work area.

"What have you got?" Don asked. He couldn't dispel the idea that the stone slab *was* a table for some giant from another age.

Patterson scratched behind his ear and took a deep breath. "I'll be jiggered, but I'm not really sure."

Don glanced at Mitchell and thought he detected a slight smile at Patterson's confession.

"I'll tell you one thing, though," Patterson said gruffly. "We've got one hell of a big stone, and it most certainly *isn't* a protruding ledge. This groove carved on the edge here—" He whisked clean a small section, then ran his index finger along it. "It wasn't the result of splitting the stone from the ledge. It was purposely carved into the stone."

Don nodded, feeling a deep satisfaction that his "hunch" and Billy's dowsing had hit pay dirt. *Coincidence?* he wondered—well, they'd have to do some more digging and find out for sure.

"So?" Don asked. "What is it? Who carved the stone?"

"Show him, Paul," Patterson said, huffing as he stood up and brushed off his knees. He stepped off the stone and onto the grass. Spencer put down the small shovel which he was using to probe the side of the stone and stepped onto the stone. He eased himself down until he was lying flat on his back with his arms and legs extended.

"You will notice," Patterson said, "that his wrists and ankles just touch each of the rounded corners of the groove. The funnel is centered between his feet."

"And?" Don said, confused.

"What we seem to have here," Mitchell said, "is what we rather unprofessionally call a 'sacrificial stone,' like the one at Mystery Hill in New Hampshire."

Don shook his head. "I've never heard of that," he said. In spite of the heat, he felt a chill dance between his shoulder blades.

"A sacrificial stone—or table," Patterson said, after clearing his throat. "An archaeologist in Portugal has excavated over thirty such stones in Europe. This, to my knowledge, is only the second ever found in the New World."

Don was confused, but he enjoyed the stuffy archaeologist's mystification.

"The speculation is that such stones were used by

prehistoric Indians for human sacrifice," Mitchell said, indicating Spencer, who was still spread-eagle on the stone. "The channel here was used to direct the flow of blood, and at the bottom here it was presumably collected in a cup or whatever for ceremonial use."

"Human sacrifice?" Don said, his throat suddenly dry.

The demonstration over, Spencer got up, brushed off the seat of his pants, and without a word went back to his work.

"Of course," Mitchell said, "There's no way of knowing for certain. Even when such stones have been found associated with burial sites in Europe, we can't be positive human sacrifice was involved. That it fits a human body might be coincidental."

"Oh, you mean it's just some inspired guesswork, is that it?" Don asked, unable to let the jab go by.

Flustered, Patterson looked down at the stone. "Such stones could have been for entirely innocent purposes. We'll have to dig down along the sides to see how far down it goes. This could be a capstone to a grave site."

"But do you think there's a connection between this stone and the hand I found?" Don asked. He looked steadily at Mitchell. "You said yourself that the hand, wrapped with beads and in a copper sheet as it was, seemed ceremonial."

Mitchell looked first at Patterson, then at the stone table, then back at Don. "We can't know *anything* until we've had a chance to excavate, and that, really, was the only purpose we had today—to determine if that was the case here."

"So you *do* intend to excavate?" Don asked.

Mitchell's eyebrows shot up. "Most certainly if you're willing to allow us. The hand you found raised certain questions. What we've found today only raised more complex questions."

Don scrunched down and ran his hand over the flat surface of the stone, feeling its gritty texture. The smell of freshly turned earth filled his nostrils, making him dizzy. "Well, I'd like to know when you'd start and exactly what you'd do. How much all of this will entail."

"We can't even consider starting until sometime next spring or summer," Patterson said. "We both have commitments this summer, and Roger is on sabbatical next year." He shrugged and clapped his hands.

"I'd want to spend some time first to do a complete survey of your property, get a detailed land profile. Then, after we set up a grid, we'll begin to dig. How far we go down depends on what we find and at what level we find it."

Don whistled between his teeth and shook his head. He was thinking about how Jan would react to this. An afternoon was one thing, but a major archaeological dig was quite another.

"I suppose on the bright side," Don said, "we can expect to have an accurate dating on the mummified hand by then. It sounds as though a full-scale dig is a pretty big commitment."

"It certainly is," Patterson said. "It would take us at least two summers. Probably more."

"Hi, Daddy," Beth called out from behind them. They all turned and saw her riding toward them. Krissy followed several paces behind.

"Hey, how's it going, Punk?" Don called out, waving. He was just about to tell her not to bring Goblin too close to where they had been digging when the horse suddenly jolted to a stop. Beth almost rocketed over Goblin's head.

"Hey! Whoa!" Don shouted, running over to her. "You all right?"

Beth straightened up in the saddle and nodded. She clicked her tongue and snapped the reins while Goblin pranced sideways.

"What is it, girl?" Beth said, leaning close to the horse's ear and stroking her side. "What's the matter?" She looked at her father, a worried frown creasing her brow. "What's the matter with her?"

"I don't know," Don said as he reached for the reins. He got Goblin to stop prancing, but, when he gave the reins a sharp tug, trying to lead her forward, the horse balked. Her hoofs stayed firmly on the ground as though planted. A low, threatening nicker sounded in her throat.

"She's never acted like this before," Beth said.

Don was pulling on the reins, trying to lead Goblin forward, but she just wouldn't budge. He backed her up and led her in a wide circle, but, every time he tried to get her to go toward the men, she stopped again. No amount of coaxing would get her to move forward, but, whenever he tried leading her to the side, she followed docilely.

"I can't understand why she'd doing this," Beth said, looking around frantically.

"It's probably the men digging here that's making her nervous," Don said, masking the concern he felt. "Maybe—you know—like donkeys sometimes just won't move? Maybe she's just getting stubborn."

Spencer shielded his eyes and looked up at them. "You know, the old-timers say that horses won't go on any ground that's unsafe—like in a graveyard. Maybe that's it; the ground here isn't safe."

"I don't know," Beth said, almost in tears.

"Why don't you and Krissy take Goblin back to the barn? She's had enough for today anyway," Don said.

He was thinking how strange it was that Goblin had stopped the same distance from the stone slab each time he had tried to lead her forward. It was as though some invisible barrier had stopped her each time. Maybe there was more to Spencer's suggestion than he realized.

Beth guided Goblin around and, once they were facing the barn, she jabbed her heels into the horse's flanks. Goblin took off, jostling Beth and kicking up clouds of dust as she ran.

The sun was setting behind the house as Patterson, Mitchell, and Spencer began packing up their equipment. Patterson warned Don repeatedly about not doing any digging near the "table stone," as he now referred to it, on his own. Once the car was loaded, Mitchell took one last look around the property. When he looked down at the end of the driveway, he suddenly gasped, letting his mouth hang open.

"That stone post down there," he said, pointing to the leaning gatepost. "Christ, I'm amazed I didn't think of it sooner."

"What?" Don asked, looking at the stone, now nearly lost in the early evening shadows.

"It might not be a gatepost at all," Mitchell said. "Speaking of the Neolithic sites in Europe made me think—that stone might well be a menhir."

"A what?"

"A menhir. A standing stone. Like the ones in Europe," Mitchell said. "I'm shocked I didn't think of it sooner. A menhir is a single, standing stone usually found associated with prehistoric Celtic stone circles and such."

"Is there anything special about them?" Don asked. As he looked at the stone, all he could remember was that, on the day they had first arrived in St. Ann's and just as they were turning into the driveway,

Beth had started choking and, when they got her out of the car, she had sat with her back leaning against the stone.

"Of course," Mitchell said, "like Stonehenge and all the other Neolithic sites, we don't really know what they were used for, but, in Europe, menhirs are often referred to as 'tingle stones.' Supposedly anyone who is psychically sensitive gets a, I don't know, a sort of pins-and-needles sensation when they touch a menhir. In rare cases, people have reported that merely touching a menhir has triggered a seizure much like an epileptic seizure."

Don looked at Mitchell and had to swallow hard before he could speak; his mind replayed that afternoon when Beth had nearly choked on her own vomit. "Of course," he said, "you don't put much faith in such nonsense."

Mitchell snorted and shook his head. "Of course not. I'm a scientist."

As Don watched the university motor-pool car rattle down the driveway, he was filled with conflicting thoughts. He, like Mitchell, had never put much stock in anything related to the parapsychic, but the discoveries they had made in the field—coincidence or not—seemed to vindicate Billy's map dowsing.

With starlight sprinkled overhead, Don stood in the dooryard long after the men were gone. He was thinking about the day's events, the buried table stone, the menhir at the foot of the driveway, and the mummified hand he had found. Somehow, he was positive they were all connected, and the one thing that gnawed at his mind was the conviction that the line Goblin wouldn't cross in the field *had* to correspond with the circle Billy's pendulum had inscribed on the map.

The more he thought about it, the more convinced

he became, and, as he walked up to the house, he resolved that he would ignore Patterson's request not to do any digging on his own. If there *were* answers buried out there in the field and if this wasn't just his imagination running away with him like a horse out of control, he was going to find them—no matter *what* he had to do.

Chapter Eleven

Coiled Serpent

I

Two days after Mitchell and Patterson had done their bit of digging in the field, Don received a package in the afternoon mail. It was wrapped in an old Shaw's supermarket bag and tied with thick, brown twine. The return address was from Susan.

As he carried the package up to the house, Don wondered what might be inside. He tried to break the string but it was too strong. In the kitchen he sliced it with a steak knife and tore the paper open to find Aune's leather-bound diary. He had all but forgotten about it.

In the front was a letter and, sitting down at the kitchen table, Don read:

Dear Donnie,

Here it is although it's not much. I guess my Finnish isn't what it used to be because I couldn't make too much sense of the diary. I translated what I could (though I did photocopy the whole thing and—if I get time!—I'll do some more). I got less than half but figured I'd send it along for now.

I suppose telling you in a letter isn't the best way, but Tom and I are getting a divorce. I figure you more than half-suspected that, anyway, but that's mostly why I haven't been in touch (much less done this translation for you). We haven't been doing very well together for years, and I finally had the guts to tell him I wanted a divorce. I don't have time to think. (Of course, I also spend *a lot* of time in the hospital with Grammy! Taking care of her has put *a lot* of stress on us, too! She's not doing any better, sad to say. You should come visit more often.) Anyway, the book pretty much explains itself—it's a record of her dreams—kind of like a journal. Some of it is really weird (one night I had quite a nightmare!), but I think it's my translation more than the dreams. Then again—who knows? Say "hi" to Jan and Beth for me. (I hope her hornet stings are all healed up by now.) So don't get all freaked out or anything about the divorce. I mean, it's been coming for a long time. I'll give you a call—maybe even come up for a visit— when I have a chance.

Take care.

Love,
Sue

"A divorce!" Don said, sitting back and looking out the window. "Shit!" Perhaps the biggest shock was realizing how wrong he had been about Susan. If *anyone* seemed completely secure in her marriage, it was Susan.

Don's hands shook as he hefted the journal and pronounced, as best he could, the title.

"*Tama on Minun Uni Kirja*—This is my Dream Book." Susan had written and translated beneath the title on the cover. The book felt heavier than he had remembered as he leafed through the pages. There were five sheets of paper stuck into the back, the translation Susan had done along with the pages numbered for reference. Don got a can of Pepsi from the refrigerator and sat down to read.

Aune had apparently begun the journal shortly after she married Toivo, long before they had moved to St. Ann's. Don skimmed over the first several entries, noting only that Susan had been right; the dreams, or her translations, anyway, were fragmentary at best—at times almost incoherent. Don knew, from the times when he tried to keep a record of his own dreams, that nothing ever captured their eerie, shifting quality.

Don skipped to the few dreams Susan had translated from after Aune had moved to Maine. Aune never referred directly to the move north, but Don inferred it from the dates. Just about the time when Aune's son, Eino died, there was a sudden shift in the tone of the dreams; they began to be filled with violent, horrifying images. Even with the dilution of translation, one or two of the dreams spread goose bumps over his arms.

One dream in particular related so specifically to Eino's death that Don half-suspected Susan of making it up just to give him a fright. Or maybe this was the one that had given her the nightmare. His voice shook as he read aloud.

February 12th, 1921—A dark hole in the ground. I was in the snow, digging. There was deep snow everywhere, but I think I was digging a garden. Scraped away snow and dirt and found a large rock—

Don's throat clamped shut as the image of the table stone came to mind. Had Aune know about the stone? he wondered, or was this just some bizarre coincidence?

I clawed at the dirt and snow, and found the rock was a coffin—a big coffin. I wiped my hands on my dress (or apron?) Dirt was thick and wet. Clumps. When I looked back at the coffin, I saw a snake, wrapped around it, looking at me. Big snake! Circle snake!

(I don't know exactly what she means here by "circle" snake—I think she means "coiled" snake—Sue)

Snake looked at me, and I was dizzy—almost fell. Eyes were black holes. They didn't blink! I tried to run, but my legs were freezing. The snake followed. I could feel it behind me—all around me—trying to circle me. Circle snake! Be careful! Beware! The stone!

Don's hands were shaking as he put the typewritten pages down. Rubbing his cheeks, he stared up at the ceiling and whispered, "Holy Shit!"

Another coincidence, or—like Billy's dowsing—was there more to this than just some crazy ramblings?

He quickly flipped through the journal and found the original entry. The vague sense of unease he had been feeling while he read Susan's translation suddenly exploded. The last words in Finnish were *Varokaa kivia*.

"So." Don muttered, shutting the book and placing it on the table. "So that's what *varokaa kivia* means—beware the stone!"

Don had never felt more alone and vulnerable—Jan had taken Beth to Portland, and Max was dead. Even the bright sunshine streaming through the kitchen window didn't help. He stared at the journal, not knowing whether to read more or start a fire in the fireplace and burn it.

Maybe that would solve everything, he thought, glancing up at where Jan kept wooden matches to light the stove when the pilot went out. Burn the journal, and that'd be the end of it!

But something else made him want to read and know more. If there were answers to what was going on—how the buried hand, the table stone, his nightmares, Eino Kivinen's death, and Billy Blackshoe's dowsing all connected—they just might be in that dream book.

Slowly, with trembling hands, Don flipped the book open to the last entry he had read. Scanning the page, he saw the words *varokaa kivia* written three more times in two other entries. Beware the stone! The words that meant circle (or coiled) serpent were repeated six times.

Uttering a low moan, Don stood and kicked back the chair. He began pacing back and forth across the kitchen floor, letting his eyes rest only briefly on the journal every time he walked past it.

"*Varokaa kivia*," he whispered softly, slapping a fist into a open palm on each syllable. "*Varokaa kivia.*"

His mind was clattering like a machine suddenly

and frantically out of control. Words and images blurred in his mind, and he had a curious sensation of lightness in his belly that almost made him giddy.

"Kivia! Kivia!" he repeated several times, and finally it hit him. *Kivia*, the Finnish word for stone, was also part of Aune's last name, Kivinen. There had to be a connection!

He grabbed the phone and held it cradled to his ear as he flipped through the phone book for Billy Blackshoe's number. "He'll know what to do," he whispered as he dialed and listened to the phone ring once—twice—three times.

"Yeah, hello," Billy said, and Don let out his breath slowly before responding.

"Billy, it's Don—Don Inman."

"My paleface friend," Billy said with a chuckle. "What can I do for you? You didn't wear out your lawn mower, did you?"

"Billy," Don said, almost gasping. "We've got to talk."

"I'm listening," Billy said, and listen he did while Don told him about what the archaeologists had uncovered in the field and what he had read in Aune's journal. It took Don nearly five minutes to get it all out, and by the time he was through, his throat felt as though it were on fire.

"I told you what I thought about that," Billy said once Don had stopped. "I said that if that was sacred ground, it would be protected. The worst thing you could do was let some palefaces dig around there."

Don felt suddenly flustered. "I—I didn't know what to do," he said. "I mean, I thought the dowsing you did was interesting, but I didn't take it seriously—until now! It looks to me that the table stone they uncovered is right where your dowsing pendulum showed the most activity."

"And like I told you," Billy said, "if you mess around with it, you're asking for trouble."

"How?" Don snapped. *"What kind of trouble?"*

There was a long pause on Billy's end of the line as he considered his answer. "Because," he said at last, "if there is a spirit guarding the spot, it will do anything—control anyone or destroy anyone—in order to protect the grave site—or whatever is there."

"That's what you think it is?" Don asked. "A grave?"

Billy chuckled. "I don't know and I don't *want* to know. You asked my opinion and I gave it to you. And you apparently ignored it because you let those pale-faces dig on your land."

"Then maybe we should do it," Don said, suddenly excited. "You and I. It's my property, and you—being an Indian—maybe you'll know what we've got here."

Billy laughed out loud. "Don, my curiosity is up, make no mistake about that; it has been ever since I got that reaction when dowsing that night at your house. There's *something* there—something powerful—but I'm sure not going to mess with it."

"Who's better qualified, you or those guys from the university?"

Billy paused, and Don could imagine the seesawing his mind was going through.

"I'm not qualified," Billy said. "I've heard stories and legends from my grandfather; that doesn't make me an expert."

"Those guys from the university aren't any better," Don said. The receiver was hot against his ear. "They said your dowsing was hogwash, and they were wrong. You and I know there's something there, and I think we should check it out before they can come back and screw things up."

"If all white men were as tenacious as you, no wonder my people lost," Billy said, but his laugh, Don could tell, disguised his real feelings thinly.

"So you'll help me with the digging?" Don asked. When Billy didn't reply, he pressed on. "I don't know what it is, but there's something—something really strange going on around here, and if digging up this stone can help solve it, then that's what I plan to do."

"You're a fool, you know," Billy said.

"I'm not the one they call 'Wingnut.'"

"O.K., you honey-tongued son-of-a-bitch," Billy said. "Give me a buzz some evening after work, and I'll come over—if only to watch you do the work."

II

It was a little before midnight, and the night was filled with the song of crickets. Mark Herman, followed closely by his friend Frankie Doyle, crept silently across the front yard up to the Inmans' house. They could hear the sharp call of nighthawks circling overhead.

Ever since the night he had watched the Inmans from the hayloft window, he had jerked off twice, sometimes three times a day while replaying the scene in his memory. Tonight was the first chance he had had to get out again, and, because Frankie hadn't believed his story, he had brought him along. He knew it was too much to hope for a repeat performance, but he was willing to give it a try, even in spite of the goddamned bats and that crazy horse!

Both boys flattened out against the side of the house like commandos, breathing in fast gulps after the run across the grass. All the lights downstairs were off, and Mark's only hope was that the family wasn't asleep yet.

"This is bull shit, I hope you realize," Frankie said, huffing. He was more than a tad overweight, with the kind of physique that would lend itself splendidly to a beer gut in early adulthood.

"You'll see," Mark hissed, and he began edging along the house, past the dining room window to underneath the kitchen window.

"Even if you *did* see something," Frankie panted, "it's too late tonight. Everyone's asleep in there."

"Shut up and stop complaining," Mark said. He crouched by the edge of the house, coiling his legs beneath him in preparation for the dash from the house to the barn.

"The only thing you saw in that barn was a pile of horseshit," Frankie said at his ear. "You ain't seen—"

"Sshh," Mark hissed. He had heard something from around the house, and, peering around the edge, he saw the screen door opening slowly. He pushed Frankie back, and Frankie fell to the ground with a grunt.

"Hey, man! What the—"

"Will you be quiet?" Mark whispered, cupping his hand over Frankie's mouth. "Someone's coming outside."

"Oh, fuck. They must've heard us," Frankie sputtered. He was trying to get back on his feet both quickly and quietly, which for his size was impossible. He opted for the "fast."

Mark grabbed Frankie's shirt collar before he had a

chance to bolt and make sure whoever was coming outside saw them. He held Frankie up against the wall and stared into his fear-widened eyes.

"You just keep your mouth shut, and we'll be all right. Understand?"

Frankie nodded his head vigorously.

They listened tensely as the spring on the screen door stretched open. There was a short pause—during which they both held their breaths—and then the spring twanged, and the door swung shut, slamming like a rifle shot. They heard soft, shuffling footsteps, and, edging slowly around the corner of the house, Mark saw a small figure gliding across the driveway.

Frankie finally got up his courage enough to peer around the edge of the house too, and, when he saw the figure washed in hazy blue moonlight, he gasped.

"I knew it," he said, his voice trembling. "I should've listened to my brother. This place is fucking *haunted*."

Mark waved his hand to Frankie to shut up. He watched as the figure moved out over the field, nightgown shimmering and hair streaked with a nearly phosphorescent light.

"Keep your fucking mouth shut, will yah?" he snarled. "It's just the kid who lives here. Looks like she's sleepwalking or something."

The expression on Beth's face had unsettled Mark. He had seen her only briefly on the day he and his father had delivered the bales of hay, but then she had seemed to be a bright, young kid—but kind of snotty, he thought. Now, in the dark, her face looked incredibly old—an illusion from the moonlight; but her expression was so fixed, so vacant, Mark was sure she wouldn't notice him even if he shouted and jumped out in front of her.

"What the hell is she doing?" Frankie asked, looking at Beth from behind the protection of Mark's body. His hands gripped Mark's shoulders and squeezed. He, too, could see that there was something weird about this kid.

They watched as Beth went into the field, moving slowly, almost mechanically. Mark had the brief impression that her legs were locked at the knees, as though she were made of wood.

"Christ, she's weird," Frankie said. "Let's get the fuck out of here. This is giving me the creeps."

"Hold your ass," Mark snarled.

Beth walked past the garden and up to the crest of the hill so her figure was dark against the starry sky. The moon cast her shadow like an inkstain at her feet. Tilting her head back, she looked up at the sky. Mark tried not to imagine the dead, fish-eyed stare she must have.

"She's a real weirdo," Frankie hissed.

Mark nodded, wondering what she was looking for. It took him a moment to register the sound above the loud cricket song, but after a while he realized that Beth was muttering in a low voice. He cocked his ear, trying to hear, but couldn't distinguish what she was saying.

"I'm gonna boogie," Frankie said, but he froze when Mark grabbed his arm.

"I said *hold your ass*, you chicken! If we don't see the old man and lady banging away, maybe she'll get excited and take off her nightie or somethin'."

"Big deal," Frankie said. "You're weird, you know that?"

Mark snickered and turned to look at him. "You

370

didn't seem all that reluctant to come here tonight."

"Yeah, but that was to see them screw. I don't give a damn about no little girl."

Mark chuckled softly to himself. He was still trying to make out what Beth was saying. Her voice rose louder, but the words sounded funny, as though maybe they weren't in English.

Beth started swaying from side to side, her hands raised over her head and sweeping back and forth in a lazy circle. But there was something about her, Mark thought, that was neither gentle nor beautiful; there was a savage undercurrent that emanated from her like waves of energy. Even Frankie seemed to feel it when he finally stopped squawking and listened.

Suddenly, Beth dropped to her knees, and, with her arms still raised over her head, she suddenly clenched her left hand into a fist and brought it down to the ground once—twice—three times. It looked as though she were holding a knife and stabbing something, but her hand was empty, and there was only bare ground in front of her.

"Christ on a cross," Mark muttered, fascinated. Beth's incoherent mumblings were steadily growing louder, and she was grunting with a near-obscene pleasure each time she brought her hand down. He thought it must have been an illusion, but each time Beth's hand hit the ground, he heard—he *thought* he heard—a low rumbling sound.

"It looks like she's trying to kill someone," Frankie said. "Come on. Let's get the hell outta here."

Mark didn't reply; he couldn't stop watching. Beth raised her hand up several more times and brought it down—thump—thump!—*thump*! Then, as though she were suddenly exhausted, she slumped forward, her head hanging down. She looked as though she was about to collapse.

"Think we should see what's the matter with her?" Mark asked, looking over his shoulder at Frankie.

Frankie shook his head violently. "No way, José! I ain't going near her. She's a nutcase."

"Maybe she's sick or something," Mark said, but even as he said it, he thought—for once—Frankie was right; just leave her alone!

They clung to the shadows of the house, watching as Beth shook her shoulders like a dog who had just gotten out of the water. She straightened up, turned, and started slowly back to the house. With the moonlight on her face, both boys could see her blank, unseeing stare. Frankie whimpered when he saw the dead gleam in her eyes. She passed within ten feet of them and didn't even seem to notice.

"She's a fucking zombie," Mark whispered as Beth mounted the steps, opened the door, and went inside. The door twanged shut, and, when it did, the whole night seemed in some odd way to return to normal, as though, as soon as she was back in the house, a dark haze had cleared or a cloud had passed uncovering the moon.

"I've had enough for one night," Frankie said. He could see by the luminous dial of his watch that it was well after midnight. "If my mom ever finds out I was out after bedtime, I'll be dead meat."

"You don't want to go up into the loft?" Mark asked. He was still staring at the kitchen door, wondering if Beth had gone upstairs or was sitting zombielike in the darkened house.

"Give me a break, huh?" Frankie said, and he started down the driveway toward the road.

Mark watched him go, but, when he saw Frankie, no more than a black silhouette under the streetlight, he started running to catch up with him. For the second time tonight—some kind of record, he thought—Frankie had been right; nothing else was going to happen here tonight. Of course, he would never admit to Frankie—or anyone else—that what they had seen that night had scared the living shit out of him!

"Hold on, Frankie," he called out as he sprinted toward the road. "Wait for me."

III

Jan knew it would hurt, but she didn't hesitate for a second as she drew back her foot and landed a solid kick on the front tire of the car. It made a satisfyingly dead thump, but the tire was just as flat as it had been when she came out of *The Rusty Anchor*.

She had driven to Ogunquit to get her last paycheck, which Dale had repeatedly forgotten to send to her. Because Sally had said he was out and wouldn't be back until closing time, she had waited until ten o'clock before coming into town. She and Don had spent the whole day painting the dining room woodwork, so she was tired and moody to begin with; having to face Dale only made it worse because, again, she had to face the conflicting feelings she still had about him.

She turned and looked at the darkened restaurant when she heard the back door open. "Must be a slow leak," Dale said, stroking his mustache as he walked over and knelt to study the flat tire.

"No shit, Sherlock," Jan said, glaring at him. She

373

knelt down beside him and slapped her hand on the tire.

"Is there a spare in the trunk?" Dale asked. He held his hand out to her, and she dropped the car keys into his palm. After he had opened the trunk, he found Jan's second piece of bad news; the spare was flat, too.

"Oh, just great," Jan groaned. She glanced at her watch, wondering if Don would start worrying when she didn't come right back home; she had told him she'd be gone only an hour.

"You don't happen to have AAA, do you?" Dale asked, slamming the trunk shut.

Jan shook her head. "No, we don't," She was conscious of the emphasis she had put on the word, *we*.

Dale went back to the front of the car and, kneeling, ran his hand along the tread. "New tire. Somebody didn't mount this right." Looking at Jan, he added, "We could either take the spare up to the all-night service station on the turnpike, or I could give you a ride home."

Jan shook her head, cringing at the picture of Dale Jackman driving her home after she was an hour or two overdue. "Uhh, let's try the service station first," she said.

Dale stood up and, shrugging, said, "Let's go back inside and give 'em a call. Maybe they'll send someone out."

The ad in the yellow pages said they provided twenty-four-hour service, but when Jan called, she was told they couldn't send anyone out. Her temper flared as the station attendant said several times that it was the road man's night off. No matter how many times Jan grilled him, asking why they advertised twenty-four-hour service when they didn't provide it, the station attendant just said that there was nothing he could do. She hung up on him.

Jan dialed home next, but the line was busy, so they went back outside. Dale jacked the car up, took off the flat, and put it in the trunk of his Jag, and they drove to the turnpike where a boy with stringy blond hair and a severe case of acne took nearly an hour to do the ten-minute job of resealing the tire. Dale offered to pay for it, but Jan refused.

Nearly two hours later, they were back at *The Rusty Anchor*'s parking lot. Dale rolled up the sleeves of his shirt and expertly replaced the tire. When he was finished, he lowered the car, replaced the jack, and kicked the hubcap back on. "Well, I guess that about does it," he said.

Jan nodded and smiled, feeling that saying thanks wasn't quite enough; his willingness to help, in spite of the cool tension between them, genuinely touched her. She shifted nervously from foot to foot, glancing from Dale to the car and back to Dale.

"I honestly appreciate your help," she said. She spent a moment fishing in her purse for her keys until Dale pointed out that they were still sticking out of the trunk lock.

"It's after midnight," Dale said, "maybe you ought to come in and give your husband a call so he won't worry. Maybe in payment, you could sit and have a drink with me."

Jan considered for a moment and then agreed. "Why not?" she said. "We deserve it, after this night." She surprised herself when she hooked onto Dale's proffered arm and they strolled back into the dark restaurant.

She got a busy signal again when she dialed, and, figuring Don was trying to call her, she hung up and joined Dale, who was sitting comfortably in one of the booths.

"I figured you wanted a rosé," he said, indicating the full glass on the table. "Most women are rosé drinkers."

Jan bristled but kept it to herself, considering how strange it was that her opinion of him could swing so fast from one pole to the other. "Rosé is just fine," she said, raising her glass to take a sip.

"Here's to—"

"To friends being there when you need them," Jan said and took a sip.

"Amen to that," Dale said, smiling. He eyed her over the rim of his glass as he drank.

Jan found she had to turn away, unable to maintain eye contact with him for long. She saw warmth in his eyes and wondered if that was all. Was there something more? Was he waiting for a signal? The attraction she felt for him was like a low-level electric current tingling through her.

Maybe it's just the wine, she thought.

"Summer's more than half gone now," Dale said, surveying the deserted restaurant, empty booths, and stools lit only by the rotating glow of a Budweiser sign.

"How's the summer season been for you?" Jan asked.

Dale shrugged. "Not what I expected—but then again, it never is. What are you up to these days?"

Jan focused on her wine as she spoke. "I've been applying around to a few real estate agencies, but nothing's turned up yet." She looked up, and the warm glow in Dale's eyes had—it *seemed* to have—intensified. "How's my replacement—what's her name? Wendy? How's she working out?"

Dale snorted and took a sip of wine. "She didn't last long. I *had* to fire her after she showed up for work one day too stoned even to walk, just about."

"But not before you got her into bed, I'll bet," Jan said.

Dale laughed. "Do you want to know something?" he asked.

Jan tried to look away, but his gaze held her. She thought for an instant of the way snakes were supposed to hypnotize their victims before they strike as Dale's unblinking stare bored into her.

"Tell me," Jan said. "What?"

"For the life of me, I cannot figure you out." He reached across the table and covered her hand with both of his. "I can't, you know, read you like I can most women, but it seems to me amazing that you can resist jumping into the sack with me."

Jan flushed and forced a short laugh. "Come on, Dale. Give me a break."

"I'm serious," he said, leaning toward her and squeezing her hand. His eyes were suffused with dim light, sparkling moistly. "I've actually gotten a complex about this. How in the hell can you resist my charm?"

Jan's chuckle twisted into a nervous titter. She looked him squarely in the eyes and wondered why she *didn't*. He was attractive and obviously experienced—maybe a bit egoistical, but so what? No, it was obviously something about her, either guilt or a sense of obligation to Don.

"For God's sake, Dale," she said, softly. "I'm a married woman with a kid. When you have your choice of just about any pretty single girl in town, I just—"

"That's just it," Dale snapped. "They're *girls*, not women—like you."

"Come on," Jan said. "You know what I mean." Her hand was feeling uncomfortably hot, and she tried to pull it away, but Dale held it tightly.

"But you don't know what *I* mean, do you?" Dale said, pressing. "You think I'm just putting you on, that I just want one more notch in my belt, is that it?"

Jan shrugged, sensing a warm rush in her stomach. How far will this go? she wondered. How far will I *let* it go?

"The only reason I hired you in the first place was because, right from the first time I saw you, I felt a—"

"A hard-on," Jan said quickly, and they both burst out laughing.

But Dale's laughter and smile melted quickly into an earnest expression as he let go of her hand, sat back, and stared out the window, genuinely exasperated. "No—not that," he said. "I felt a—an attraction, like something just clicked in my head."

Jan resisted the temptation of saying the "click" must have been in his pants.

"It was like—like—I don't know." Dale shook his head. "I was thinking you could—could . . ." He leaned his head back against the booth and sighed.

This is wrong, Jan thought. This is crazy and wrong, but it's real! She reached across the table and took Dale by the hand, feeling it warm and moist in her grip.

"Dale," was all she said, and he knew that this was it. He had won. Rising slowly from the booth, he came around to her side, tilted her head back, and planted a warm, lingering kiss on her mouth.

It's wrong and it's crazy, Jan thought, but she offered no resistance as Dale pushed the table aside and eased her down onto the padded seat, running his hands over the length of her body. Slowly, he unbuttoned her blouse and slid down her skirt. She raised her hands and began unbuckling his belt, feeling the tight muscles of his stomach.

So different from the way Don feels, she thought, only a little angry at herself for making the comparison. Closing her eyes, she rolled her head from side to side as Dale gently eased into her. Then she was lost in warm, embracing darkness.

When it was over, Jan was thinking that it had been short and a bit uncomfortable on the booth seat, but good—very good. They were putting their clothes back on in silence when the sudden shrill ringing of the telephone startled them both.

"Oh, damn!" Jan said as an icy ball hit her stomach. She looked at Dale, frightened. "That's got to be Don!" She was wearing just her skirt and bra as she ran to answer the phone.

"Hello?" she said, her voice tight, as though she had just swallowed alum.

"Jan? What the hell are you still doing there?" Don asked, and she registered the frantic edge in his voice. "I've been waiting for you to get home."

"I got a flat tire in the parking lot," she stammered. "I just got it fixed, but I tried to call. The line was busy. The spare was flat, too. I know I should've—"

"Jan," Don said again. The flat tone of his voice

cut like a blade through her confused rush of excuses.

He knows! she thought. Somehow, God almighty, he *knows*!

"Susan called from the hospital," Don said, his voice still strangely flat. "Aune died about an hour ago."

It felt as though a tight fist had just hit her in the stomach. It was crazy to think so, but she drew some kind of connection between her cheating on Don for the first time in her life and Aune's death.

"Ohh—gee," she said stupidly. "That's too bad."

"Well, it's been a long time coming," Don said. "And I suppose, in the long run, it's a blessing as they say. I never could understand why people said that—until now."

Jan could tell that his voice was close to breaking.

"And I've been worried about you, too," he said. "I thought you'd be home hours ago."

"Like I said—"

"The funeral's planned for Friday, in Gloucester," Don said.

Dale, now dressed, came over and placed his hands on Jan's hips, pulling her toward him. He mouthed the words, "Is everything all right?"

Jan shook away from his hold and said, "It really is too bad, but, like you say, it's probably for the best."

"So you'll be coming right along now?" Don asked.

"Yeah," she replied, "the tire's all fixed now." She felt suddenly embarrassed, standing in the middle of the restaurant, wearing just a skirt and bra. "I had just come back into the restaurant to give you a call to say I was on my way."

"Is Dale there?" Don asked.

As far as she could tell, trying to ignore the waves of

guilt, there wasn't the slightest trace of suspicion in his voice.

"Uhh, no," she said. "Bill, the cook, was still around, doing some cleanup. I'm sorry about your Gram."

"Yeah, well—You just be careful driving home, O.K.?"

"O.K.," she answered, thinking she need a long, slow drive home so she could consider and absorb her—*cheating*. The word stuck in her mind like a hook in a gilled fish. She hung up and went back to the booth to get her blouse.

Dale followed her, and, while she finished dressing, he refilled her glass with wine and held it out to her. She shook her head and reached for her purse.

"Do you want to talk?" Dale asked after she told him the news.

Jan shook her head and started for the door. "Not now—and probably not later," she said.

"You mean that's it?" Dale asked, astounded. "You're not going to see me again?"

They walked through the kitchen to the back door. Walking out into the parking lot, she looked back at Dale, framed in the doorway, and sadly shook her head. Speaking softly, she said, "Let's just look on tonight like we got what we wanted, not what we needed." And with that she was gone.

IV

"Ah, the beauty of wood," the voice from behind Don said as he drove the splitting maul through a piece of maple. The two pieces seemed almost to pop apart before the maul hit them. Over his shoulder,

Don saw Billy Blackshoe standing in the shadow of the barn.

He nodded a silent greeting, not appreciating the interruption of his thoughts. All night and all day, ever since Susan had told him Aune had died, he had been dwelling on what Susan had said were her final words. Just before she died, she had opened her eyes, as though terror-stricken and had screamed in Finnish: "Tell them to get out!"

Leaving the maul stuck in the chopping block, Don peeled off his shirt and, walking over to Billy, wiped the sweat from his forehead.

"They say that's the beauty of heating with wood," Billy said. "It heats you twice; when you cut it and when you burn it." He gave Don a cockeyed grin.

"*This* kind of heat doesn't do you a bit of good in July," Don said.

"I don't know about that," Billy said, poking at the slight bulge above Don's belt. "Looks like you could sweat out a pound or two—unless you're saving it up for winter."

Don tried to smile but was sensitive about the weight he had gained and not lost since he had quit smoking. "I suppose so," he said, weakly. "Anyway, what brings you out this way?"

Billy grinned. "I figured you might have tried calling me, but I was away, visiting my sister, over in Cooper Falls."

Don decided not to mention that he hadn't tried to reach him, but he knew why Billy was here.

"So—now that the 'professionals' have had their crack at it," Billy said, rubbing his hands together, "what say you and I do a bit of digging?"

Remembering the seizure Billy had had on the

night they had dowsed, Don hesitated. He looked out over the field but was unable to see the spot where Mitchell had exposed the table stone. He wiped the sweat from his face and said, "Well, I did want to get this wood taken care of first. And tomorrow I—" He stopped himself when he was about to tell Billy that Aune had died and her funeral was in Massachusetts the next day.

Billy chuckled. "First it's you trying to convince me; now it's me trying to convince you. Come on. Let's just drift over and take a look."

Don nodded, and they started toward the site. When they were by the barn door, Billy suggested he grab a shovel, "just in case"; and Don did. When they got to the site, Billy stood at the narrow end of the table stone, looking down at it with his hands on his hips.

"You know," he said, inhaling deeply, "it sure is satisfying to find out that the point we marked on the map proved to be where this is located."

"You sound like you didn't expect it to work," Don said. He was leaning his elbow on the shovel handle, resting.

Billy shrugged, and, when he replied, he never took his gaze away from the exposed slab of stone. "I never said dowsing works all the time." He seemed about to say more, but a curiously blank expression washed across his face.

Suddenly he shook his head and, shivering, looked at Don. "Jumped-up Jesus H. Christ! Don't you *feel* that?" He looked at Don with such wide-eyed intensity Don knew he wasn't faking it.

"What?" Don asked, looking around. He saw nothing but the peaceful stretch of grass waving in the wind. Hazy sunlight burned the ground a drying yellow.

Billy bounced up and down on his toes several times. "The ground," he said, his voice low. "It seemed for a minute there like it sort of—vibrated. Curious thing, ain't it?"

Don watched Billy carefully, fearful that he might have somehow triggered another seizure. "No, I—ahh—"

"Don't look at me like that, O.K.?" Billy said. "I ain't having a fit or anything. I definitely felt something. There's a lot of energy here. No wonder the plumb bob shot off the tripod like it did. Whew!"

"I don't feel a thing," Don said stupidly, feeling like a kid with a booger stuck on his face.

"I wouldn't even need to dowse here. I can feel it crackling all around me. Here, look." He held out his hand, and Don watched as subtle tremors rippled the muscles and skin of the back of Billy's hand. He had the impression there were worms or snakes crawling just beneath the skin surface.

"Are you *sure* you're feeling O.K.?" Don asked.

Billy nodded and closed his eyes. Holding his hands straight out, palms down, he slowly started walking around the edge of the table stone. Don cast a nervous glance up at the house, hoping desperately Jan wasn't watching this display.

"I can feel it," Billy said softly. "I can feel it tingling in the air like a charge." He took a deep, noisy breath and exhaled slowly through his nose. "Something's here—and I ain't exactly sure it's entirely good."

"What? What do you mean?"

Eyes still closed, Billy shrugged. "Don't know, for

sure—Something, though. Curious thing, ain't it? It's like—like—" He shook his head and opened his eyes, letting his hands and shoulders drop.

"I don't know," he said, stepping back. "I know it wasn't just this stone, here. There's more. It's like the stone you've uncovered is the focal point, but there's more—*much* more—buried here than just this."

"Do you think you want to dowse out here in the field?" Don asked, and, as soon as he said it, he regretted it.

"I don't have to," Billy said. Pointing to the table stone, he said, "Whatever you're looking for— whether it's your uncle's grave or someone's else's— it's right here, under this stone. It's strong medicine."

They were silent for several minutes as Billy walked around the exposed stone, studying it from several angles. He knelt and ran his fingers along the carved groove along the edge of the stone. Finally, he pointed to the top of the stone, the end opposite the funnellike opening Mitchell said might have been used to collect the blood of a sacrificial victim. He said, "I want you to dig right there."

"What for?" Don asked, hefting the shovel. He tried not to admit to himself that the whole thing was giving him the creeps. He would have like nothing better than to get back to chopping wood.

"I want to see if there's anything on the side of the table stone," Billy said.

Don smiled at his use of the word he and Mitchell had adopted for the stone, and he wondered if he had ever used it to describe the stone to Billy. Sighing deeply, Don began to dig, and, within half an hour, he had gone down a good five feet along the side of one of the stones supporting the table stone.

"Do you have any idea how far down this goes?" he asked, wiping sweat from his forehead as he looked up at Billy, who stood nearby, watching.

"We'll find out by digging."

Don snorted. "I should be putting this kind of sweat into my woodpile."

Billy pointed at the hole he had dug and said, "This is much more exciting. Keep at it."

While he was working, Jan came out of the house and walked over to them. She said she was going into town to get a few groceries and, after a quick kiss, she went to the car. Don and Billy watched as she backed around Billy's car and drove off.

"I'm not sure it's going to get any better," Billy said, and Don noticed the dreamy edge in his voice.

"Huh? What do you mean?"

Billy shook his head and smiled, watching the dust of the departed car settle slowly like a smoggy haze.

Don grunted and went back to work. After digging down another foot and widening the trench he had dug enough so he could kneel down, he threw the shovel onto the grass and boosted himself out of the hole.

"Lord have mercy," he said, collapsing onto the ground and covering his eyes with his arms. "I feel like I've been digging my own grave."

"Don't you ever—*ever* talk like that!" Billy snapped, turning on him with an angry glare."

Don sat up, confused. "Hey, I—"

"Don't *ever*! Do you understand?"

"Sure," Don said, nodding. "No sweat."

"There's *something* here—something not entirely good. Talk like that could only—just be careful, O.K.?" Billy said. The tone in his voice made Don take a nervous look around.

"O.K.—O.K.," he said, too exhausted to argue.

"Now," Billy said as he jumped into the trench, "let me take a look here." Billy's hands moved over the dirt-crusted stone as if they had a life of their own. Eyes closed and brow furrowed, he looked to Don like a blind person reading Braille.

"It's here. I know it is," Billy muttered as he clawed at the side of the stone, sweeping his hands back and forth. Small clots of dirt fell onto his shoes with the sound of rain.

"Ah-hah!" Billy said triumphantly. "Here it is!" He opened his eyes and peered closely at the stone. Don came closer, leaning over the edge of the trench, inhaling the fresh-dug earth smell. He watched Billy's blackened fingers clean away the dirt from the stone. A cool rush of fear and excitement swept through him when he saw that Billy was exposing a design carved into the stone.

"What is it?" Don asked after a sharp intake of air.

"This," Billy said simply. He moved to one side so Don could see, very faintly, a spiral design—a rough graphic of a whirlpool. "Curious thing, ain't it?"

"Holy shit," Don muttered.

Billy traced the deeply carved design with his fingertip. "It's an Indian sign for a well—the spiral serpent."

Don gasped and had to fight a wave of dizziness that almost knocked him over. The words from Aune's dream journal came rushing into his mind with an audible swoosh: *the circle snake—the coiled serpent*!

"It's the well, the spiral, the labyrinth," Billy said.

His voice had a strange hollowness that frightened Don still more. He looked at Don, his eyes blinking rapidly as though he fought back tears. "A variation on the labyrinth, anyway. The symbol is quite common around the world, and it's generally taken to signify a well—or a hole in the ground, the home of the sleeping serpent. Sometimes it means a grave."

"Jesus Christ," Don managed to say, but that was all. His mind was in turmoil, trying to sort out everything, wondering how much—and even *how*—he would begin to explain it all to Billy.

"When the line is curled like this," Billy said, "the serpent is asleep. You may know he's there, but he's not dangerous—not *too* dangerous, anyway. There should be—"

His voice drifted off as he started scraping away the dirt below the design. After a few minutes' work, he grunted and moved back, pointing out to Don the other design he had exposed.

"Three parallel lines," Billy said, his voice constricted. Don saw the wave pattern that was carved into the stone below the spiral.

"So?" Don said.

There was a strange, childish expression on Billy's face when he looked at Don. He clambered out of the trench and stood up, brushing his hands on the seat of his pants.

"Some thing—some things are best left alone, at rest," he said as backed slowly away from the table stone.

"What the hell are talking about?" Don said, almost shouting.

"Those carvings! That's what I'm talking about. They represent the serpent both sleeping and waking. That wavy pattern is the serpent *uncoiled*!" He stroked his chin thoughtfully, nodding his head up and down. "Both are also symbols for water. Maybe that's why I was able to dowse them and why the pendulum reacted so violently. I don't know."

"Who would use symbols like this?" Don asked, almost frantic. "I mean, who might have carved them on this stone?"

"Indians. No doubt," Billy said, looking down at the exposed flank of the table stone. He suddenly shivered involuntarily.

"Hey, come on," Don said, looking at Billy's blanched face. "You've been in the sun too long. You look like you could use a beer."

Billy smiled weakly and started walking with Don to the house. "Something stronger, if you have it," he said.

Part Three

August, 1986

. . . Let the earth hide thee!
Thy bones are marrowless, thy blood is cold;
Thou hast no speculation in those eyes
Which thou dost glare with!

> *Macbeth, III, iv, 93-96*
> —Shakespeare

. . . Beware! Beware!
His flashing eyes, his floating hair!
Weave a circle round him twice,
And close your eyes with hold dread.

> —Coleridge

Chapter Twelve

"Curious thing, though, ain't it?"

I

They got back from Aune's funeral in Massachusetts earlier than they had expected. Smelling of lemon-scented Handi-Wipes, they were all hot, tired of driving, and gritty from the road. Don had been extremely uncomfortable all day from being at a funeral—which always unnerved him—and from being dressed up. He had never enjoyed wearing a jacket and tie, but only recently had begun to take that as a sign of character.

While Don took a long, cold shower, Jan went upstairs to change. Beth lay down on the couch to watch TV but was asleep before Don got out of the shower. The only thing missing, Don thought as he walked into the kitchen half-dressed, his towel draped Arab-fashion over his head, was Max, whining and scampering, glad that they were home.

The sudden ringing of the telephone startled him, but Jan answered it upstairs before he got a chance to.

He sat down at the table and towel-dried his hair, waiting for Jan to come downstairs. Finished with the towel, he tossed it into the laundry room and began combing his hair. When he was finished and Jan still hadn't come downstairs, his curiosity got him. He glanced over his shoulder and, seeing no one there, went over to the phone and silently picked it up.

"—time, I told you. I can't," Jan's voice said.

Still unable to shake the sensation of being watched, Don cupped his hand over the receiver and looked at the doorway.

"Can't? Or don't want to, Jan," the voice at the other end of the line said. Don didn't recognize who it was.

Don heard a long, exasperated sigh from Jan.

"I don't have to beg, you know," the man's voice said. "There are plenty of others around, but it's you I want."

Jan sighed again and said slowly and evenly, "Look, Dale, what happened, happened, and there's nothing either of us can do about it. But that's all it was, nothing more."

"Please, Jan," the man's voice said. The tone of desperate pleading irritated Don, but his guilt at eavesdropping finally forced him to hang up, cradling the receiver carefully so they wouldn't know he had been listening.

Don sat back down at the table, his mind whirling. Anger and guilt swept through him like a riptide. All he knew was that, if Dale had called to ask Jan back to work—well, there was just a little too much of the tone of a jilted lover in his voice to satisfy Don. He stared blankly out the window, wondering if what he had heard and how he had interpreted it was for real or—maybe like the coincidences involved with the buried hand—something he was imagining.

Jan's footsteps on the stairs made him sit up straight. He looked at her as she walked into the kitchen, shoulders erect.

"Do you want some coffee?" she asked. "I'll brew some if you'd like."

"Why not," Don said. He thought he detected just a hint of tightness in her voice. She took the coffeepot and filled it with water before scooping coffee into the basket.

"So, ahh, who was that on the phone?" Don asked, trying to sound casual.

This time, there was no doubt in his mind; she froze for an instant like a rabbit caught in the glare of headlights. "That was—ahh, that was Dale," she said, putting the pot on the burner and turning the stove on.

Right so far, Don thought. "What'd he want?" he asked.

Jan shrugged, busying herself with getting cups, sugar, and milk on the table. "He said he was short-handed and wanted to know if I'd come in for the night, just to help out."

"Really?"

Jan tried to look directly at him but was unable to. "Yeah—I told him to go stick it."

Don nodded. "I'll bet you did," he said, smiling but still watching her for signs of guilt. The idea that she could even have considered cheating on him was, well, impossible to accept. He and Jan were tight, maybe even tighter than they had been when they first got married. She wouldn't—she *couldn't* . . .

"I've seen all I want to see of *The Rusty Anchor* and Dale Jackman," Jan said bitterly. The coffee began to perk, and Jan turned the gas flame down to half.

"You know," Don said, sitting back in his chair,

trying to appear relaxed, "because we got back so much earlier than we expected, I thought I might give Billy a call—see if he wanted to dig a little more out there in the field."

Jan shook her head and clicked her tongue. "Don't you think you've done enough out there for a while?"

"I don't know," Don replied, He was still studying her, trying to fathom the possibility of her cheating, but it was as though she had a wall around her that he couldn't pierce, and he began to wonder just how long that wall—that distance between them—had been there. Perhaps longer than he had realized.

"You said yesterday he was a little freaked out by some carving or something you found on one of the stones," Jan said.

"I'm counting on his curiosity to get the better of him," Don said. He stood up and went to the phone. When he picked it up, he noticed that the receiver was still warm from when he had been listening to Jan and Dale. Quickly, he dialed Billy's number, and, on the third ring, Billy answered.

"Hello, Don," he said.

Caught off-guard, Don shook his head and chuckled. "How in the world did you know it was me?" he asked.

"Just a hunch," Billy said. "Actually, I just visited my sister, and I don't get all that many phone calls. I figured you'd give me a buzz. You want me to come over, so we can take another look at that stone of yours?"

"You should know," Don replied. He was finally beginning to accept Billy's sometimes uncanny intuition.

"I'll drop by in an hour or so," Billy said. "Let everyone get settled after the funeral. See you then."

"Yeah," Don said, and he hung up the phone

slowly. He was *positive* he hadn't mentioned to Billy where he had been today.

II

Billy drove up just after five o'clock and stepped from his rattletrap truck, dressed in a white shirt and green chinos. His black hair, as shiny as a wet raven's wing, was pulled back into a tight ponytail. Don, who had been sitting on the steps waiting for him, walked over to meet him.

"Can I get you something to drink?" Don asked, but Billy shook his head. They turned and together went to the barn where Don picked up his shovel. Then they walked over to the exposed table stone, each of them keeping his own and respecting the other's silence. Don was struck by Billy's unnatural seriousness.

They looked down into the trench Don had dug at the head of the stone, but the mounded dirt cast a shadow that obscured their view of the coiled and wavy carvings. Don felt a surge of dizziness as though he were standing and looking over a long drop. He stepped back, hoping his reaction didn't show.

What was it about this place? he wondered. It seemed to attract him and repel him at the same time, and it seemed to have a weird effect on Billy, too.

"The last couple of days I've done a bit of reading," Billy said solemnly. "You know, to fill in some of the details."

"And—?" Don's dizziness was waning, but it was still there—like a swift underground stream just waiting to burst out at the weakest point in the surface.

Billy shrugged. "I didn't learn a whole hell of a lot. Not much I didn't already know. Facts are few when you're dealing with prehistoric sites. What I think—

what I *know* we've got here is a burial chamber. Those dudes from the university might call it a megalithic cairn. It's like places like Stonehenge in Europe."

Don shook his head. "I thought Stonehenge and places like that were used for primitive astronomical observation or something."

"They may have been lined up to face certain directions because of the symbolism of the solstice and equinox—you know, sunrise symbolizes birth, and sunset symbolizes death and, maybe, rebirth. There's evidence there were burial customs involved, too. One writer, name of Watson, suggested that stone circles were built along force-field lines—that there was some connection between the stones and ideas about life after death. It's possible, if there is some kind of electromagnetic force involved, that's what dowsing might be responding to."

Don scanned the field slowly. "Sounds like some of that psychic stuff you were talking about. Do you mean you're suggesting this isn't the only stone buried here? That there might be a whole buried stone circle, like Stonehenge?"

Billy frowned as he looked down at the table stone. "Might be; might not be. That's one thing I want to do, check the map and see where I got some activity dowsing. There might be a pattern there that we just didn't see before. But look—" Billy turned and faced where the sun was lowering behind the barn. "Have you ever noticed where the sun rises and sets?"

Don waved his hand in the direction of the street, toward the end of the driveway. "It rises from there. I know because it always shines in the kitchen window early in the morning. It sets in that direction." He pointed out behind the barn and house, toward the fringe of woods in the direction of the quarry.

"And," Billy said, pointing down at the table stone, "look at the way this lies. If you take into account that we're just a month or so past the summer solstice, it looks to me like this is in a perfect east-west line."

"And," Don said, "the head, where those serpent symbols are carved, is toward the west, and the foot is toward the east."

Billy snagged Don by the shoulder and gave him a piercing look. "And why do you call it the 'head' of the stone? Why not just call it the top or the edge?"

"I don't know," Don said. It just seems as though, somehow, that's the—head."

"The side with the carvings!" Billy said, slapping his fist into his open hand. "As though somehow the carvings of the serpent, uncoiling, gaining power, are connected with the setting sun, which has always been a symbol of death."

Don couldn't help but laugh at Billy's earnestness. "Alignment like this could just be a coincidence," he said.

Shielding his eyes from the lowering sun, he followed a line back to the top of the table stone. The glancing sunlight made the surface of the stone appear roughly textured, almost alive; and, as he looked at the stone, he imagined how Mitchell's assistant, Paul, had lain down spread-eagle to demonstrate how a sacrificial victim might have been placed.

"Just take a good look at this crest here," Billy said, "and think about almost any graveyard in New England. They're almost always placed on hilltops, with a good view. Think about it. Why do we do that? Why bury our dead up on a hill? So they can be closer to the sky, maybe? A wider view of the horizon?"

Don shook his heads. The sound of crickets in the field grew louder, and a trace of a breeze lifted his hair.

"This is a perfect spot for a burial ground," Billy said. "It's high, got a good view of the valley right down to where the town is. This place here," he said, indicating the table stone, "might not be the only grave site. The whole field could be filled with the bones of my ancestors."

Don's throat had suddenly gone dry, and he was afraid the words wouldn't even come out when he spoke. "They—umm—the bones would have decomposed by now," he said dryly. "They couldn't last long in the acidic soil."

"Like the hand you found?" Billy said. "Now look at the channel carved around the edge of the table stone. There's nothing on record to indicate prehistoric Maine Indians practiced human sacrifice, but there's nothing to indicate they *didn't*, either. Maybe, when a great chief died, members of his family or some of his close friends chose to follow him to the happy hunting ground. That's one possibility. Maybe they used the stone to sacrifice the person whose spirit would then guard the sacred ground."

Don was shaking his head slowly from side to side. "I don't think a lot of your logic would hold up to too much scrutiny."

Billy regarded him with a perfectly deadpan face. "We may not be talking about logical things here. There may be no clear answers here, but that doesn't mean the answers *aren't* here. Maybe we have to find the logic *they* used when they carved and buried this stone."

"And you have no idea what for?" Don asked, unable to resist the shiver that coursed up his spine.

Billy smiled. "We can find out," he said. "You must have some blocks of wood we can use. Look at the table stone. It's just resting on four stones. Let's try to get the top off and see what's inside. See if it's a hollow chamber or—whatever."

Don stepped back as another wave of dizziness churned up inside him. "I don't know," he stammered. "You were the one who said we shouldn't disturb it, you know."

As clearly as if she stood beside him, he heard Aune Kivinen's voice say, *"Varokaa kivia"*—beware the stone!

"There must be some kind of chamber inside, right?" Billy said. "And it will have more answers inside than we've got now. If it were in my yard, I'd be damned curious."

"Oh, I'm curious all right," Don said. "I'm just not convinced we should tamper with it. When Mitchell and the others come back next year, we can find out what's inside."

Billy scrunched down and let his hand move slowly over an edge of the table stone. The motion made a rough, scratching sound. "Maybe there's nothing to it at all," he said. "I mean, after all, this *is* the twentieth century, and our superstitions are supposed to have been conquered by science. And even if they're not, maybe my being 'of the blood,' as they say, will make it O.K. with the spirits."

"God, you make it sound like the place is haunted or something," Don said. "I just don't want to disturb it in case there are some valuable artifacts there. It'd be a shame to ruin anything."

"Look, Don, we can jawbone about it until the sun sets, or we can do something. Good Lord, where's your curiosity?"

Don pondered for a moment; then he turned and walked to the barn with Billy following close behind. Silently they loaded the wheelbarrow with five thick timbers, another shovel, and a crowbar, and wheeled it back down to the site. Don dumped everything onto the ground with a clatter.

Billy jumped down into the trench and ran his hand along the seam where the table stone rested on the supporting blocks. "I know this son-of-a-gun must be heavy, but I think if we get the right leverage, we can get it up enough to brace it. It's worth a try."

"Maybe we should wait until tomorrow," Don said. "Get an early start. If this *is* a grave, I'm not so sure I enjoy the prospect of opening it just as it's getting dark."

Billy looked up at him, grinning. "No sense of adventure, huh? Hand me the crow," he said. He reached up, and Don gave it to him, grateful that, at least this time, Billy was willing to do some of the muscle work.

Hefting the crowbar, Billy leaned to one side and jabbed the iron tip under the edge of the stone. The bar rang and sent tiny sparks flying, but every time Billy thought he had an edge and leaned his weight onto it, the bar would snap out.

"Are you gonna stand there all day gawking at me, or are you gonna give me a hand?" he said, looking up at Don.

Don hesitated a moment, thinking that this was the second time today he had been looking down into a grave; then he stepped down into the trench, aware of the moldly earth smell.

At first he had no more luck than Billy had had. It seemed almost as if the stone were repelling the crowbar—like two identical poles of magnets. But after several more attempts, he finally worked the tip under the edge. He and Billy both dropped their weight onto the bar, and with a throaty, grinding sound, the table stone lifted an inch or two.

"This mother's—heavier—than—I—thought," Billy said between grunts. His face was infused with blood, and small purple splotches stood out on his cheeks. Don remembered how Billy's face had looked the night of the dowsing when he had had the seizure, and his apprehension grew. He knew they shouldn't be doing this, but he didn't try to dissuade Billy any more.

"I—don't want—to get a—damn hernia—from this," Don said. He eased up on the bar, and the stone slammed back into place. When he tried to remove the crowbar, Don found that it was trapped by the stone.

Billy scrambled out of the trench and returned with two of the wooden blocks. "Let's give it another try, but this time with some leverage. Remember, they say with a fulcrum in the right place, a two year old could move the world. We just haven't found the right place yet." He placed one of the blocks under the crowbar and held it while he pushed down on the bar.

Don was just as willing to give up and wait until next spring when Mitchell would return with enough help, experience, and equipment. Let them do the sweating, he thought, but when Billy continued to press down on the bar, Don added his weight, too.

"Be—ready to—grab that—other—block," Billy grunted as the stone rose with a grating sound. "Wait—till there's—room—enough."

The stone went up easily this time; maybe because they were experienced with its weight, Don thought. A long black slit appeared below the table stone, and, as they pushed steadily down on the crowbar, the gap widened.

"Ready?" Billy asked. "Can—you get—that—other block?"

Don kept as much weight on the bar as he could while reaching for the wooden block. The stone started to drop, but once Don had the block, Billy heaved down hard, and Don jammed the block in under the stone.

"There!" Billy said as he took pressure off the crowbar. The stone crunched down on the wood like giant teeth, but the gap remained.

"Well, well, well," Billy said. "What do you think?"

He bent down and peered into the blackness inside the chamber. A cloying, rotten smell struck him full in the face, and he turned away, gagging.

Don held his hand in the opening and felt a cool, moist draft swirling out.

"It's been closed a hell of a long time," Billy said, bringing his face back to the opening but ready for the smell this time. "It's pretty rank in there."

"You know," Don said, "if we build the fulcrum point up there, on the edge of the trench, we could probably move the stone a lot easier."

"I was thinking the same thing," Billy replied.

"Great minds think alike."

"—And fools seldom differ," Billy added. "Come on. We can get some of those granite blocks out behind the barn, and we can build it up."

Don got out of the trench and, taking the wheelbarrow, started over to the barn, wondering how on earth Billy knew there were stone blocks out there.

He had taken maybe ten steps toward the barn when he heard Billy say to him, "Huh? What did you say?"

Don eased the wheelbarrow down, tossed his hands up, and shrugged "Nothing," he shouted. "I didn't say anything."

"Thought you said something," Billy said, bending down to look into the opening. Don could just see the top of his head above the pile of dirt.

When he came back, he handed one of the smaller

stones to Billy, who, with some effort, wedged it into the opening. Over where the ground was flatter, they made a low pile of stones. Using that as a fulcrum, they positioned the crowbar and found that either one of them could move the stone on his own.

They lifted the table stone several inches higher, piling up granite blocks at each stage to keep the stone up. Within another half-hour, they had raised the table stone high enough so someone—if he wanted to—could crawl inside the chamber. Both of them balked at the idea.

Exhausted and covered with sweat and dirt, they sat down on the grass and took a long look at their handiwork. The sun, slanting down behind the barn, cast long shadows over the field. The song of crickets rose in volume.

"I think that's enough—*more* than enough—for one day," Don said, collapsing onto his back with a groan. All he could think about, as he looked at the deepening blue vault overhead, was how nice a hot shower was going to feel on muscles he hadn't worked this hard in years.

Billy looked at him with genuine shock on his face. "Do you mean to tell me that after all this work you're not going to take a look inside?"

Don rolled onto one side and rotated his shoulder. "Do you mean to tell *me* that after all this work, I can't interest you in a cold beer?" he said. "This can wait till tomorrow."

"No, it can't," Billy said, sitting cross-legged as he stared at the slitted black opening. "You've got a funeral to go to in a couple of days, don't you?"

Don shook his head. "No. That was today. My grandmother died."

Billy nodded. "Oh, O.K. Well, then, why don't you scamper on up to the house and get a flashlight so we

405

can see what's in there? My curiosity's got me bad."

Don regarded him and then slowly rose to his feet. "Remember what curiosity did to the cat?" he said before walking to the house. He returned moments later, two beers in hand, and gave Billy the flashlight.

"Like you said, you're 'blood.' You can have the first peek."

"My curiosity needs a drink, first, though," Billy said, accepting the beer from Don and snapping the pop-top.

Don eased himself down onto the grass, and they both took long swallows of beer. It didn't take them long to finish their drinks. Billy put his empty on the grass, stood up, and, gripping the flashlight tightly, went over to the opening.

When he was near the stone, Billy snapped the flashlight on and directed the beam toward the opening. The blackness inside the chamber seemed almost to pulsate as though it had been in darkness for too long and didn't want to be in the light. He was leaning close, peering into the hole when the stone holding up the table stone made a low, crunching sound. White, powdered stone, looking like salt, sprinkled on the edge of the chamber.

Still sitting in the grass, Don made a sudden leap toward Billy.

"Watch out!" he shouted. He wasn't sure if the table stone shifted again or it just looked that way because of his movement.

"It'll hold," Billy said confidently, but there was some anxiety in the look he gave Don.

"Why don't we get some more stones and really block it open," Don said. He got down into the trench and, resting his hand on the table stone, decided that it was, indeed, securely supported.

"This won't take more 'n' a minute or two," Billy

said. He twisted his body to one side as he directed the beam of light into the chamber.

"Come on," Don said peevishly. "Take your look and get your damned head out of there."

The black opening seemed to swallow the light hungrily, and Don could smell the rotten stench wafting from inside. Maybe after the chamber aired out for a few days, he thought, he might want to stick his head inside and look around—but not until then.

Taking a deep breath, Billy ducked into the opening. He shifted from side to side, wriggling further into the narrow opening as he looked around. The table stone cast a thick shadow over Billy's back, and Don again thought he saw the heavy stone shift.

"Will you get out of there?" Don snapped, not even sure Billy could hear him with his head inside the chamber.

After a minute or two, Billy drew his head out into the open and inhaled noisily through his nostrils. "Sweet Jesus! It's dank in there!" he said, followed by a spasm of coughing.

"What did you see?" Don asked, grateful that Billy was no longer under the shadow of the stone.

"Not much, really," Billy replied, glancing at Don and then back at the opening. "From inside, it looks quite a bit larger than you'd expect—maybe eight by five feet, seven or eight feet down."

"Is there anything in there?" Don asked, still not feeling enough curiosity to stick his head inside. "Any relics or anything written on the walls?"

Billy cracked a wide smile. "No, and no uncoiled serpents, either." He stood there in the trench, contemplating the opening; then, placing his hands on the edge, he said, "I'm going inside."

"The hell you are," Don said. He snagged Billy by the shoulder and held him tightly. As if further proof were needed, the table stone again shifted slightly on the blocks, making a sound like a sleeper grinding his teeth. A steady breeze slithered through the grass with a soft, hissing sound, and the sun had lowered in the west behind a raft of hazy, yellow clouds.

Billy hitched one leg up onto the stone and swung one foot into the chamber. It made a curious visual effect because, once his leg was under the shadow of the stone, it completely disappeared into the blackness as though it had been cut off. Don shivered, realizing that there was no way he could talk Billy out of it.

"You're crazy, you know that?" Don said angrily. "First you tell me we shouldn't disturb the sacred ground, and then here you go, jumping down in there!"

"I never said I was consistent, did I?" Billy said, laughing.

Lying on his belly, Billy put one arm inside and then wriggled under the table stone. As he was bringing his other leg inside, his foot kicked one of the supporting stones. He and Don exchanged frightened glances, but, when nothing happened, they each let out a long sigh. Then, just as he was swinging his other leg inside, preparing to drop down, Don heard the sharp, crunching sound again.

He wondered frantically what he would do if the stone fell back into place once Billy was inside. In spite of himself, he laughed softly, thinking that then, at least, it would truly be an Indian burial ground.

Billy eased himself all the way under, hung for a moment on the edge, and then dropped inside the chamber. Don heard the soft thump as he hit the ground. He moved up close to the opening. It's blackness made the approaching night seem actually bright. He looked closely at the stones holding the table stone up; it was difficult to see, but he had the illusion that the granite blocks were squeezing down under the pressing weight.

"Will you hurry up and get the hell out of there?" he shouted, aware of the frantic edge in his voice.

"Take it easy," Billy said from inside the chamber, his voice muffled as though he were speaking from a great distance. "I just want to take a look—no, nothing really interesting here. It's pretty much like the inside of a cave, just bare stone walls and a dirt floor. There might be something buried here—"

"I don't give a damn if there's something buried there," Don said. "We can check it out later—after we get this damned stone off. Come on out now."

"All right, all right," Billy said. From out of the darkness, his hands reached up and gripped the edge of the stone; then his face appeared as he hoisted himself up.

"Aww, crap," he said angrily. "I had the flashlight in my pocket and it dropped out."

"Don't worry about it," Don said, as he tried to angle under the stone so he could help Billy climb up.

"Them professors might think it's an ancient relic. Start a whole 'flashlights of the gods' craze," Billy said. The laughter that followed hit him so hard he almost let go and fell back inside.

"Come on," Don said edgily. "I just want you to—"

The granite blocks suddenly shifted, and this time Don was positive it was no illusion. The table stone shifted several inches to one side.

"Jesus Christ," Don said, as he reached inside, caught hold of Billy's shoulders under the armpits, and started tugging. The grinding sound increased, and, when Don looked at one of the supporting granite blocks, he saw an edge of it dissolving like a sugar cube in the rain.

Billy's eyes widened, and he opened his mouth to say something, but the dank air of the chamber and his exertions made him cough instead. Digging his heels into the dirt, Don leaned back, pulling hard. Billy was scrambling, too, but to Don it felt as though someone was inside the chamber pulling Billy down. In spite of both their efforts, Billy was no more than a third of the way out.

"Come on, man," Don said, grunting as he pulled back, his feet digging for traction.

Billy said nothing; he riveted Don with a frightened, tortured stare. Again, Don was convinced that someone down inside, in the dark, was holding Billy back. The table stone shifted more. Billy looked as though he was trying to say something, but his mouth was an open, silent hole. A white froth spewed from his mouth.

"Oh my sweet Jesus," Don said in a whimper when he realized that Billy was having another seizure.

Then, with a sudden thunderlike boom, the supporting stones shot out as if an explosion had been touched off. Sharp-edged fragments of stone blasted out like shrapnel, dust swirled into the darkening sky, and the table stone dropped like a steel-jaw trap, crushing Billy.

In complete panic now, Don kept pulling on Billy's arms; then he scrambled out of the trench, grabbed the crowbar, and tried frantically to get the edge under the table stone. The metal rang against the stone, sending sparks flying.

In the last rational corner of his mind, he knew it was already too late for Billy, but he kept trying as Billy's eyes, bulging from their sockets, stared up at him, glistening. Gouts of blood shot from his nostrils, showering Don as he grabbed his friend's limp arm and pulled. Billy's unblinking stare held Don. His mouth moved, trying to form words, but only a streamer of blood and foam ran down his chin like drool.

Don fell back, collapsing on the edge of the trench. Cupping his hands to his mouth, he shouted up to the house for Jan as he watched, helplessly, as the weight of the stone bore down—down—crushing Billy. The gleam in Billy's eyes flickered and faded, and his body twitched as a cascade of blood foamed from his mouth, washed down the side of the stone, and soaked into the dark earth.

Tears stung Don's eyes as Jan ran across the field, immediately realizing what had happened. Like a zombie, Don sat back on the grass as Jan, in tears, held him close. All that rang in his memory was the sound of the stone, grinding down, crushing—and Aune Kivinen's voice repeating, *"Varokaa kivia . . . Varokaa kivia."*

III

Don and Jan didn't get to bed until well after two o'clock that morning. The local rescue unit came but, of course, it was too late for Billy "Wingnut" Blackshoe.

With the help of several volunteer firemen, they raised the table stone and got Billy's body out. As they were lowering the stone, it slid to one side, leaving a triangular gap at one corner—the corner at the bottom, where the carved channel became a spout—

—*for the flow of blood from the sacrificial victim*, Don thought grimly as he watched the ambulance disappear toward town, its red lights washing the night. The tears, stinging his eyes, made its lights shatter into rubies.

David Fahy, the chief of police, talked with Don for

over an hour, and finally satisfied that it was truly an accidental death—although he never seemed to fully understand what Don and Billy had been trying to do out there—he left. His blue lights flashed like summer lightning as he drove down the driveway slowly, through the knots of curious bystanders—"ambulance chasers," Jan kept calling them.

Even while there were still people out in the field, looking at the table stone and the thick, dried streak of blood on its side, Don and Jan went up to the house. Don seemed to be in a state of near shock, and he left it to Jan to explain to Beth what had happened. He sat at the kitchen table, staring blankly at the black rectangle of night that he could see out the kitchen window.

After Jan had Beth settled and asleep, she joined Don in the kitchen where they sat across from each other, mostly in silence. They drank three cups of coffee each and several times had to turn reporters away from their door, telling them that the only statements to be made would be found in Officer Fahy's report.

"You know one thing that's really weird?" Jan said. She glanced at the clock over the refrigerator and saw that it was well after one o'clock.

Don grunted, looking at her but not adjusting his focus; his eyes held a blue, watery stare.

"When I told Beth what had happened, she said something that—kind of bothered me."

"What was that?" Don asked, his voice curiously flat.

"She kind of whispered it," Jan said, holding her coffee cup with both hands, "so I wasn't exactly sure, but it sounded like she said, 'I could have told them.' What do you think she meant by that?"

Don had a sudden, frightening image of Beth,

staring at the blank, wooden face of her doll and speaking to it in whispers that only she seemed to understand.

"I—I have no idea," Don said, but the suspicion began to grow in his mind that Beth knew more than she was saying, that she, too, was somehow connected with this whole web of—whatever was going on.

"Well, I'm heading up to bed," Jan said, rising. She started to clear the table but decided to leave everything just where it was.

Don followed her up to bed, going through the paces of undressing and brushing his teeth automatically. His mind kept replaying the few clear memories he had of Billy Blackshoe, but, as he lay down in darkness, tears streamed from his eyes and soaked his pillow. Eventually he fell asleep—a thin, unsettled sleep but nowhere near as unsettled as Billy Blackshoe's sleep.

IV

"*It's burning!* Beth shouted. She raced over to the stove and turned the burner down, waving her hand frantically over the pan in which her father had been cooking scrambled eggs. A thin, brown collar had formed around the rim of the pan, and blue smoke rose like morning haze.

"Oh—*darn!*" Don sputtered. He grabbed the handle and skidded the pan onto the counter, almost knocking over his glass of juice. He shook his head with embarrassment. "I guess I just didn't have my mind on what I was doing," he said.

Beth sat down and waited while her father scooped the browned eggs onto three plates. The toast was already cold, and the coffee was just now starting to perk. Don handed one plate to Beth and then put his and Jan's plates onto the table. No matter how much he tried, he could never get a whole meal prepared all at once.

Beth looked sullenly at her breakfast and, Don thought, seemed about to cry. She speared a brown chunk of egg, popped it into her mouth, and chewed mechanically. Her face twisted up in near agony, and her eyes had a strangely unfocused look to them.

"Hey, there, Pun'kin. You don't look like you're feeling tiptop," Don said, leaning close to her and smiling even though he didn't feel like it. Billy Blackshoe had been dead for two days now; his funeral was this afternoon. Ever since the night Billy died, Don had found little reason to smile.

Beth choked down her mouthful of egg. "I—uh," she said, then hesitated. "I don't really feel too good."

"Is it, you know, about what happened to Billy?" Don asked. "I know it's kind of rough when stuff like that happens."

Beth shook her head and took another bite, but before she could say anything, Jan breezed into the kitchen, dressed in a sharp-looking blue skirt and jacket.

"Hey, what's the matter?" she asked, immediately sensing that something was wrong. Beth's gaze flickered in her mother's direction but never made direct contact. It seemed to Don that she couldn't quite control her eyes.

"She says she doesn't feel well," Don said, thinking that the dull yellow of the eggs seemed to match Beth's complexion.

Jan waved her hand in front of her face. "I won't either with all this smoke in here. Open a window, for crying out loud."

Don got up and slid the window over the sink up halfway, then opened the door to get a draft going.

Jan glanced at what was waiting for her on her plate and grimaced.

"So what's the matter, hon?" she asked. The coffee seemed to be done, so she poured herself a cup and took a small bite of toast.

Beth looked up at her mother and rubbed her stomach, her hand moving like faulty clockwork. "It hurts—down here."

Jan felt Beth's forehead and cheeks for a moment, then stroked her hair back. "You don't feel warm," she said. "Is it right here? In your stomach?"

"No," Beth said, looking down at her plate. "Lower."

Don caught the smile that twisted one corner of Jan's mouth, but her voice was steady and full of concern when she asked, "Do you think it might be your uterus?"

Beth shot a sidelong glance at her father, then nodded. "Umm. I think it might be."

"Ahh, I think it might be time for the old mother-daughter talk," Don said, moving toward the door. "I didn't really feel like eating, anyway."

Jan smiled at him and nodded as he went out to the barn to keep himself busy while she and Beth had a heart-to-heart talk about, as her mother had always referred to it, "becoming a woman."

An hour or so later, Jan came out and told him what was going on. Beth hadn't started her period yet, at least she wasn't bleeding, but she might be having some preliminary menstrual cramps.

"I have that interview this morning with the Beecher Agency," Jan said. "You should probably keep a pretty good eye on her. This isn't the first time we've had our little talk, but she might get a little nervous when she starts to bleed—if she starts today. It *is* a bit scary the first time it happens."

"You'll be back by one o'clock, won't you?" he said. "I really do want to make it to Billy's funeral at two."

Jan nodded, regarding him tight-lipped. She was careful not to say what was on her mind—that Billy's death had been senseless and foolish, all because Don wanted to poke around that buried stone. For the thousandth time, she wished to God they had never found that buried hand. *That's* what started all of this!

She walked out to the car, leaving Don pitching hay into Goblin's stall. Beth probably wouldn't be up to doing her chores today and, besides, he wanted to keep himself busy until it was time to get ready for the funeral.

Damn it! he thought angrily. He took the pitchfork and swung it around viciously, connecting solidly with one of the barn's support beams. The pitchfork handle snapped cleanly in half, and the three-tined fork whickered into the far corner of the barn.

V

Don arrived at St. Joseph's Church a good half-hour before Billy's funeral began. He hadn't gone to any of the visiting hours at the funeral home because he really had no connection with any of Billy's family or friends. He sat in the third pew from the back of the church, hands folded and eyes stinging as the priest delivered the eulogy.

Facing death up close twice in one week—first Aune, now Billy—filled him with morbid, disturbed thoughts. He felt that, somehow, there was more of a connection between the two deaths than he had realized, and he felt that he, and he *alone*, was the connection. Everyone else in the church had to deal only with Billy's death; he had a much deeper mystery to probe.

The hearse and slow-moving line of cars, their headlights glowing dimly in the bright sunshine, wended their way to Pine Haven Cemetery, and the mourners gathered in a semicircle around the freshly dug grave as the priest read the service for burial. A robin chirruped merrily from the grove of trees lining the cemetery. The heat of the day clung to Don's neck like a vise. He was impressed with how the priest looked so cool and comfortable in his heavy cassock— as though he were in a different environment.

Don tried to focus on that—on an aspect of life not darkened by death; but the fresh-turned earth and the gaping hole reminded him of the table stone and the burial chamber beneath. He remembered the stupid joke he had thought of when Billy had climbed into the chamber—that, if the stone fell now, the site would definitely be an Indian burial ground. The humor was gone now, leaving only the acid sting of sorrow.

Margaret—"Maggie," as Billy had told him only he could call his sister—held up well throughout the service, staring straight ahead, almost unblinking as she stoically tried to register her loss. Don knew, from the little Billy had told him, that he and his sister were close. That, too, was cause for regret—Don was nearly overwhelmed by a feeling of immense distance between himself and his sister, Susan.

He wondered if Margaret in any way blamed him for Billy's death. Farm accidents happen all the time—enough people get caught under a haymower or crushed to death by an overturned tractor—but the circumstances around Billy's death were just a bit too much out of the ordinary, and Don wondered what— if at all—Margaret thought about him.

417

The priest closed his book and extended his hand over the flower-draped coffin. He sprinkled a small amount of dirt onto the polished wood box while saying, "Ashes to ashes . . ." The coffin was gently lowered and disappeared into the dark hole.

When the priest was through, he stepped back, and the mourners started to drift away in small groups. Don saw the cemetery crew, sitting on their idling tractor, waiting at a discreet distance to fill in the grave. Don stared at the heap of flowers, then closed his eyes, and did the best he could to send up a prayer for Billy Blackshoe's soul. He ignored the tears that streamed down his cheeks.

"He liked you a lot, you know," a woman's voice said from behind him as he felt a light touch on his shoulder. "You're Don Inman, right?"

Turning, Don smiled weakly at Margaret, who regarded him with shimmering brown eyes and thin, pale lips.

"He was a good man," Don said, his voice choking. He took a tissue from his jacket pocket and wiped his eyes. "A *damn* good man!"

. Margaret nodded. "I know," she said, her face seemingly chiseled in a near-expressionless countenance. Her hair was pulled back in a braid, and her face was a haunting, feminine replica of Billy's.

"I'm going to miss him," Don said, groping for words. "I didn't know him all that long, but while I did . . ." He let his voice trail off.

Margaret nodded again. "He told me what you were doing—out there at your place—the buried stone and all." Her voice was threatening to break, but it never did.

A bitter taste flooded Don's mouth as he recalled asking Billy if he remembered what curiosity had done to the cat.

"I can't tell you how sorry I am that—that it happened like this," Don stammered. "I feel like I'm the one to blame. Your brother had a lot of living still to do."

Margaret's mouth opened, but nothing came out. The silence between them stung Don as he measured his loss against hers. Don was unable to look at her, so he let his gaze drift past the fresh grave to the trees that swung heavily in the muggy haze.

"I *do* hope you find something there," Margaret said softly, drawing Don's attention back.

He looked at her, eyebrows raised.

"Out at your place, I mean," Margaret said. "I hope Billy didn't—" Her voice suddenly broke, and a single tear spilled from her eye. "I hope he didn't die for nothing."

Don shook his head solemnly and looked over to where the minister stood with Margaret's two children. The younger, no more than three years old, was sitting in the shade, plucking clover.

"If you do, you know, find something," she continued, "maybe you could—I don't know—maybe do something as a memorial for my brother."

"I will," Don said, his voice rasping. "I will for sure." He gave her a quick, awkward hug, turned, and walked down the slope to his car.

Whatever could I do for him, he wondered, guilt and anger welling up inside him like trapped poison. He got into the car and drove off, feeling hot and scratchy from the heat. For the rest of the day, he was silent, working around the house. Throughout supper, Jan, although still angry at him for even beginning to poke around the site, kept a respectful silence.

"You know," Don said later that night as they were getting ready for bed, "I almost think he knew this was going to happen."

Sitting on the edge of the bed brushing her hair, Jan sighed. "With all this nonsense about Indian burial sites and dowsing and whatnot, somehow I'm not surprised you'd say something like that."

Don began pacing back and forth across the bedroom floor, slapping his fist into his open hand. "No, seriously. I mean it." He stopped by the window and looked out past the barn to where the table stone lay exposed in the field, glowing like bone in the moonlight. The opening that had been left when they had lifted the stone to remove Billy's body was a triangular black slash.

"I mentioned to you how he'd say things every once in a while—something totally out of the blue—and be *right*! Like how he knew Beth's name before I even told him we had a kid, and about getting a horse and some other things. It was like—"

"Things you forgot you told him," Jan snapped.

She put her hairbrush on the nightstand and swung her legs under the covers. Hand poised on the light switch, she said, "Are you coming to bed, or are you going to stand there, looking out the window all night?"

The light clicked off, and the room dropped into darkness, but Don didn't move from the window. "Do you know what he said to me—just before we started lifting that stone?"

"What?" Jan said, her voice strangely disembodied in the darkness.

"He said we should do it then because I had a funeral to go to in a day or two." Tears stung his eyes, making the image of the table stone blur and flicker.

"Come on, Don," Jan said. "None of this is doing you any good. Come to bed."

"But it was weird. I mean, it was like he knew, and he was trying to tell me."

Jan sighed. "He had just gotten confused about Aune's funeral, that's all. I'm sure you had mentioned that to him. Come on. Come to bed."

Don shook his head and wiped his eyes with the heel of his hand. "I don't think it was just that. I think somehow he knew, whether he knew it consciously or not."

Suddenly the hair at the nape of his neck tingled, and, for a moment, Don had the impression that there was someone outside in the dark, looking up at him in the window.

"The whole time we were working on it, too, I—" He stopped suddenly, wanting to back away from the window but for some reason not daring to move. He continued, his voice unsteady. "I had this weird feeling, too, like—you know—the way the air gets before a thunderstorm—all hollow, like."

Jan grunted a reply. Either she was falling asleep or she was faking it so he'd hurry to bed.

"There was this—this heavy, pressing feeling, like—like—oh! I don't know!"

Jan made no reply, but Don stayed at the window, looking out at the calm night. He still had the sensation that someone was outside, but, after waiting and watching, he was satisfied that it had only been his imagination. He made his way in the dark to the bed slowly and slid between the cool sheets.

By this time Jan was truly asleep. When he hugged her, trying to draw her closer, she moaned softly and rolled away from him. Don smiled sadly to himself and settled his head on the pillow, but sleep didn't come. Thoughts and memories of Wingnut filled his mind. After skimming the surface of sleep, he finally started to drift slowly down—down—and the dream began with a—

—*with a sound!*

—Something hummed, vibrated in the darkness with a throaty whoosh.

Don bolted up into a sitting position and looked around the dark room. A wash of moonlight lit the windowsill but did little to light the rest of the room. At first he thought it was blood rushing in his ears, but, just as he was about to settle back down, he heard it again—

—A low, thrumming sound—as though something whickered overhead, unseen in the dark.

A bat! Don thought with a sudden flood of panic. *Another damned bat!*

He was reaching over Jan's inert form to snap on the light when he saw—better from the corner of his eye than looking directly ahead—something at the foot of the bed. As he leaned forward in the dark, trying to resolve what it was, he also became aware that it was the source of the sound.

The covers slipped down as he leaned forward, and a rush of cool—*cold*—air spread goosebumps over his arms. There was someone—a person—standing at the foot of the bed!

"Beth?" Don said softly. His voice croaked in his throat, and the sound reminded him of the sound that had come out of Billy's throat as the table stone bore down on him.

"'S that you, Beth?"

As his eyes adjusted to the darkness, Don saw that the person standing there was too large to be Beth. Whoever it was had one arm up and was swunging it around in a wide circle. This, it seemed, was what was making the dull, vibrating sound.

"Who are you?" Don asked, his voice trembling. "What do you want?"

His ears prickled as the vibrating sound grew louder, swooping around and around with the tempo of the moving arm. Panic boiled like sour milk in Don's stomach when he finally distinguished the form of Billy Blackshoe at the foot of the bed. Over his head, he was swinging what looked like a flat piece of wood tied to the end of a long leather thong.

Cowering back, Don reached for the light switch, his fingers groping like mindless slugs. When he found the switch, he fully expected it not to work when he flicked it on so, when the room suddenly filled with yellow light, he let out a low whimper of pain. He choked back a scream when he saw—in the bright light—that the figure of Billy Blackshoe was still there!

Billy's eyes were glassy, staring blankly at a spot seemingly beyond Don as he shrank back from the horrid vision. The whooshing sound pulsated, keeping time with the rapid pace of Don's heart. Billy's face was rigid, like a marble statue, pasty white. Tattered streams of blood billowed from his nostrils like an insanely large Fu Manchu mustache. But it was the eyes—*the blank and staring eyes*—that held Don horrified.

Bile rose from Don's stomach as he licked his lips, trying to form words, hoping that, if he did, the vision would vanish—or else he would wake up.

This is a dream! his mind screamed. *This has to be a dream!*

Billy was dead and buried! He had been crushed to death, eviscerated and jacked up with embalming fluids. O.K., so the service had been a closed casket, and he hadn't actually *seen* the body, but this was *impossible*!

—Billy could *not* be standing here in the bedroom! He couldn't be—but he *was*!

Terror raged like a tornado within Don as Billy's jaw dropped open. His lifeless lips moved to speak, but instead of words a gush of blood poured out, its brilliant red standing out starkly against the pallid white skin. The bullroarer whistled more loudly over Billy's head as his arm tirelessly swung it around and around.

"Don—my friend—" Billy said, his voice gurgling thickly, the sound Dopplered by the swinging bullroarer.

Don leaned forward, tension bubbling inside him about to explode. He tried to speak, but his voice was choked off. The sharp taste of copper filled his mouth.

"Don—my friend—you know!" Billy said solemnly.

"What?" Don said, his voice squeaking. "*What* do I know?"

Billy rolled his eyes back until all Don could see were glistening whites, the color of ancient, cracked ivory. Billy's shirt—the shirt he had been wearing the night he had died, Don noticed—was sodden with blood that had begun to clot in stringy clumps. Slowly—slowly, Billy raised his empty hand and pointed it at Don.

"You—you already know what's there!"

"What is?" Don said frantically. "What is *where*?"

The trembling hand lowered slowly until the bony forefinger was pointing straight down. On the floor, a widening puddle of blood had stained the wooden floor and was flowing toward the bed. Billy was ankle-deep in the blood and he pointed downward and said, voice shaking, *"There!"*

Don shifted forward, holding his hands out, pleading. "What?—*what is it*?"

Billy slowly shook his head, a motion completely out of sync with the bullroarer swinging overhead. *"Curious thing, though, ain't it?"*

And with that, a hollow concussion filled the room. A spiral of flames shot up from the floor, engulfing the figure of Billy. The swinging bullroarer suddenly whipped around both of his hands and bound him at the wrists. The flames rose higher, and Don watched, horrified, as Billy's skin blackened and peeled back, exposing a grinning skull. Burning tendons twisted like dying snakes, and a ring of flowing blood framed Billy in a rippling rectangle.

The flames intensified, driving Don back as bright orange light flooded the room, casting crazily tilting shadows across the floor and walls. Then suddenly the light died, winking out of existence as if a switch had been thrown. The room was filled with a blackness that had more substance than air. Don jolted out of bed with a shriek.

"What the *Christ*!" Jan yelled, waking with a start and almost falling out of bed. She fumbled for the light switch.

Shaking as though racked by fever, Don squinted at the sudden burst as the light came on. He was trembling and slick with sweat, pacing back and forth across the bedroom floor.

"Jesus Christ, Don," Jan said sharply. "What's the matter?"

"I—I, uh, I guess I had another nightmare," he stammered. He was scratching, clawing at his throat, trying to relieve the burning he felt deep inside. The lurid image of Billy Blackshoe glowed in his memory like a Halloween poster.

At the foot of the bed, he looked down, expecting to see a thick mat of drying blood, but the floor was clean—no blood! no charred remains!

"It must've been a doozy," Jan said, easing back onto her pillow. "What time is it, anyway?"

Don glanced at the clock beside the bed. "Almost

five," he said, and he glanced out at the predawn gray in the sky.

That stone's out there! he thought, cringing at the memory of the nightmare. The ring of blood that had circled Billy, he suddenly realized, was shaped like the channel carved into the stone—to direct the flow of sacrificial blood!

Is that what the dream meant? he wondered. That Billy—just as maybe numerous prehistoric Indians—had been a sacrifice to the stone?

"Well?" Jan said, her voice thick with sleep, "are you coming back to bed?"

Don grunted, but, as Jan was reaching for the light switch, Don told her to wait while he went to the bathroom for a glass of water. He filled the glass and watched his pale reflection in the mirror as he gulped the water down.

"Or whiskey, if you have some," he said, forcing a smile before tiptoeing back into the bedroom.

Jan was already asleep, so he snapped the light off and slid into bed beside her. But in the darkness, he couldn't shake the gnawing sensation that there was someone—someone out there in the predawn, watching—watching.

Chapter Thirteen

Phouka

I

After breakfast the next morning, Jan left to do the grocery shopping for the week. Beth said that she was going over to Krissy Remy's after she had fed and watered Goblin. Once the house was quiet, Don, unable to concentrate on doing any work, decided to lie down on the couch. He wanted to nap, to make up for the loss of sleep the night before and, if not actually to sleep, at least to take some time to sort out the confused thoughts that lingered from his nightmare about Billy Blackshoe.

But unable to unwind after two hours, he admitted to himself what was bothering him; he wanted to dig some more around the tablestone. Yes, it was crazy—he knew it was—but he had, he thought, more than enough reasons. Curiosity was one reason, but he knew that alone wasn't enough. There was also a sense of responsibility—to Billy, if to nothing or no one else. Coupled with that was a dull sense of revenge. If the table stone was truly hiding some long-buried secret, he wanted to find out what—no matter what the cost.

He was also convinced that that was what Billy had meant—what *he*, Don, had meant, really—it was, after all, *his* dream. There was something out there, and he meant to discover what it was.

A strange sense of purpose seized him as he went to the barn and, shouldering a shovel and pickax, strode out to the table stone. He felt pulled in two directions at once; knowing that it would be wiser to leave the site alone until Mitchell and his crew could properly excavate it, but wanting—*having*—to find out what was down there *now*!

Once at the site, he dropped the tools and stared for a long time at the exposed granite slab. A wave of nausea hit him full in the gut when he saw the brick-red stain of Billy's blood—a wide, funnel-shaped streak running from the top edge of the stone to the earth. The remembered fragment of another dream crept into his mind—a towering stone, piercing the clouds and dripping with—

—No! Not blood!

He shivered, then, looking up at the sky, said, "Whatever's here, Billy, I'm going to find it—for both of us." The wind gusted briefly, swirling the dust until it looked like smoke around the stone.

Don started work by widening and deepening the trench that surrounded the stones that supported the table stone. And work, he found, was a remedy for the depressing thoughts that surrounded Billy's death. He threw scoop after scoop of dirt high over his shoulder, working feverishly to expose more and more of the buried stone structure.

He worked through the morning and into the afternoon, not bothering to stop for lunch. At one point, he took a short break and, looking up at the house, thought he saw Beth looking out at him from his bedroom window. When he waved to her, she drew back, and only then did he remember that she wasn't even home; she had left hours ago to go over to Krissy's and, as far as he knew, she hadn't come home yet.

By mid afternoon, he had three sides of the chamber exposed, having dug more than halfway down to the base. He couldn't bring himself to dig on the side where Billy's blood stained the stone. The trench was wide enough now so he could easily work at removing the soil.

The side with the carved serpents—sleeping and waking—proved to be the only side with any carvings; the rest of the structure was simply rough-cut granite. At last, exhausted and covered with sweat-streaked loam, he climbed out of the trench and sat on the mounded earth, staring at the table stone.

"Whatever your secrets are," he said, wiping the sweat from his forehead, "I'm gonna find 'em. You can bet on that!"

The triangular opening, left when the volunteers had removed Billy's body, finally drew his attention. He knew that his efforts working around the outside of the chamber had been an avoidance on his part. What was inside—*in* the grave—was what he looking for. He finally acknowledged that he would have to go down inside the chamber and look around. Just before he died, Billy had said there was nothing there, but he hadn't dug around inside. There might be something buried just below the floor of the chamber; maybe *that's* where the answers he sought were.

Muttering a low curse, he went up to the house to

get a flashlight. Beth, he found to his surprise, had come home and was sleeping on the couch. The house was eerily quiet, but he left her there, undisturbed, and went back to the site.

First he stood in the trench and peered into the dark opening without the light. The stench of rot was gone, but still the darkness inside the chamber made him dizzy. He aimed the flashlight at the opening and snapped it on, its beam slicing the blackness with a near-laserlike sharpness.

He brought his face closer to the opening and studied the inside of the four supporting stones. They were crusted with a gray, moldy growth, and, when Don reached his hand in and scraped the side, his fingers came away sticky with a foul-smelling pitch. On the near side he could see where the mold had been kicked away by Billy's efforts to get out of the chamber, and again waves of nausea swept through him.

The floor of the chamber was packed dirt, and Don could see evidence of Billy's having been there; his footprints showed clearly in the dirt. He couldn't be sure, but he thought there were other footprints there, too. First he dropped his shovel into the chamber; then he tucked the flashlight into his back pocket, gripped the edges of the opening, suspended himself over the dark hole, and taking a deep breath, let himself drop.

His knees buckled when he hit the floor with a muffled thud, and almost frantically he grabbed the flashlight and snapped it on. For the first few seconds, he had to fight back the choking claustrophobia. The dark, moldy walls of the chamber seemed to lean inward, threatening to crush him, and the rotten smell intensified. The small triangle of blue sky overhead looked impossibly distant, and he was filled with the fear that he might never see the sky again.

"The view from the grave," he said, and he surprised himself with the morbid chuckle that followed. The walls threw back his voice with an unsettling closeness, and he shivered when he remembered joking with Billy about their "digging their own grave."

After a few minutes though, he began to adjust to the closeness. Getting down onto his hand and knees, he started inspecting the place where the stones met the dirt floor. The hard-packed earth had a peculiar gritty feeling as he probed it with his fingers, and, using the tip of the shovel, he began digging down, fully expecting to hit solid rock—the bottom of the chamber.

But then at one end of the chamber—the "top" end as he thought of it—he found something buried about a foot below the surface. It wasn't the edge of the support stone; it was something else. He scooped the dirt away and before too long broke through the thin covering crust, exposing a rectangular stone, perhaps two feet by four, set in the ground. He cleared away enough dirt to expose the edges, and, by prying the tip of the shovel under the edge of the stone, he gradually started to work it loose.

It came up slowly, resisting his efforts through gravity and the dirt that quickly filled in the gap but eventually he got enough leverage on the stone and lifted it free. What he saw astonished him. On the floor of the chamber, long buried, was an opening going deeper down into the ground. There was a drop of perhaps five feet straight down and then what looked like a tunnel heading away from the chamber.

"Holy shit," Don muttered, inspecting the new opening in the glow of his flashlight.

He could see that the stone he had removed was one of at least two, maybe more, that blocked the opening of the tunnel. With just a bit more effort, he knew he could clear the opening enough so he could go down inside, if he wanted to.

Feeling strangely as though someone was watching him, he suddenly stood up and looked around. The triangle of sky above him was clear. The stone walls kept the silence of the centuries. Everything seemed to be fine, but somehow Don felt that he was violating something that perhaps should be left alone.

The fetid air of the chamber stuck in his throat like a fish bone, and he realized with a mind-numbing suddenness that a cold, clammy draft was coming up through the tunnel opening!

No one—not Mitchell, not Billy, not himself—had ever suspected that there might be a cave or tunnel beneath the chamber, and, as he looked down at the underground opening, Don got the idea that there might be more than one tunnel. The whole field could be honeycombed with tunnels! He knew an underground stream could carve out a vast network of caves, but at least this access to the tunnel was manmade. There was no doubting that!

And where does it go? he wondered, staring down into the opening. Maybe this was the answer he and Billy had been looking for. But, if it was, what had Billy meant, saying *he already knew what was there?*

Like a velvet glove, the air inside the chamber closed on his throat, and Don was filled with a sudden, sourceless panic. He wanted to go down further, to the next level, to follow the cave or tunnel, and to see where it went; but he also wanted very badly to get out of the chamber and under the open sky. The walls of the chamber were pressing in on him.

He pitched the shovel out of the chamber but, unwilling to be without light, left the flashlight on and stuck it into his front pocket before he jumped up to grip the edge of the opening. His feet scrambled and scraped at the side of the chamber, and his arms shook from the effort. But, as he pulled himself up, it also seemed as though the stuffy air of the chamber—the *grave!*—gripped his legs and tried to drag him down.

The image of Billy, trying to hoist himself out of the chamber as the table stone crushed down on him, filled Don's mind, and it surprised him that he didn't cry out in panic.

His head and shoulders came out into the open slowly, and he let out a low groan of relief when he finally could swing one leg up onto the edge of the stone.

"Christ on a cross!" he said as he swung his other leg clear. Leaning his head back, he took a deep, noisy breath of fresh air. The bright afternoon sunlight hurt his eyes, but the warmth only touched his skin. Still, beneath his skin, he felt the cold sensation of having been watched by something while he was in the chamber.

His nerves were singing, and his pulse made a soft whooshing sound in his ears. He was just about to move away from the opening when he registered a noise just below the threshold of awareness. It was a familiar sound—soft, muffled. It reminded him of—

—*Rats! Rats in the wall!*

Cocking his head to one side, trying to get a fix on the location, he made the connection. It was the same sound he had heard that day in the cellar just before Jan had called to him to come out and help her with the Rototiller, just before he had found the mummified hand!

Don glanced around, straining to hear the sound repeated. When it came again, a warm flood of fear filled him. The sound was coming from the opened chamber!

Don snorted a low laugh, trying to convince himself that it was his imagination. He had spooked himself down there and was hearing things. But when he came closer to the opening, he heard the faint rasping sound more clearly.

He jerked the flashlight from his pocket and directed the beam into the opening. There, in the hole he had discovered in the floor, he saw—thought he saw—a flicker of motion. The darkness shifted and thickened like a bloodstain as he watched, his throat burning as the dark tunnel mouth seemed to swallow the feeble ray of light. Something down there shifted and, flashing for an instant in the beam of light, he saw—

—Christ! No!

It had looked like thin, bony fingers, gripping the edge of the opening. As soon as his mind registered the image, he tried to convince himself that what he had seen was a loose clump of earth falling to the floor. The circle of light weaved over the smooth dirt floor, but, other than his and Billy's footprints, the chamber looked completely undisturbed.

Don watched the black opening in the chamber floor for several tense minutes, but the motion wasn't repeated, and, when he leaned his head into the chamber, he no longer heard the dull, rasping sound. When his hand began to hurt, he realized he was gripping the flashlight too tightly, so he gently backed away from the table stone and snapped off the light.

"Couldn't have been," he said hoarsely as he eased up out of the trench and onto the grass, keeping his eyes on the chamber opening the entire time. He wiped away the beads of sweat that formed on his brow and, with one last look behind, started toward the house at a rapid pace.

Imagination, pure and simple, he told himself repeatedly. He *knew* it was impossible for anyone to be down there. He hadn't seen a hand reaching up out of the tunnel; he hadn't heard any sounds from down there! It had been—it *had* to have been—a loosened clump of earth, falling to the floor. That was all!

There was no one down there! There *couldn't* be!

By the time Jan got home from shopping, he had convinced himself that, with the shock and grief over Billy's death, his imagination had been working full tilt. He also had become convinced that the only way to deal with whatever was down there was to explore further. In this dream, Billy had pointed downward and told him that that's where the answers were, and he was determined to find them!

II

Don had a teachers' meeting the next day, the first before the new school year began. He spent most of the day in conferences and small-group discussions at the high school. His first impressions, he was glad to find out, had been right. From the principal on down, the faculty at the school seemed like a dedicated bunch. After spending the past few days preoccupied with the table stone, mummified hands, and Billy's and Aune's funerals, it was somewhat of a relief to start planning for school, doing something familiar and concrete.

It was just after three o'clock that Don got home, and he found Jan busily weeding in the garden. Looking somewhat wilted after spending the good part of the day in classrooms that were not air-conditioned, Don walked over and gave her a hearty hug and kiss.

"So, how'd it go?" Jan asked, brushing dirt from her hands. "How do you think it's going to be?"

Don nodded his head with satisfaction. "It's going to be fine," he said. "I'll have to go in for a few days next week to start getting the shop set up. Today was more or less a getting-to-know-you day. Where's Beth?"

Jan's brow wrinkled as she hooked her thumb toward the barn. "She's, uh, taking Goblin for a 'spin,' as she put it."

"What—what's going on?" Don said, immediately picking up that something was happening.

"Well," Jan said, letting one corner of her mouth curl up into a smile, "your little girl's now a little woman."

Don clicked his tongue and shook his head from side to side. "So that's it, huh? That explains why she's been acting so tired lately."

Jan nodded. "She's been having cramps for the past few days, but the flow started this morning. At least that's when she told me about it."

"You said she was riding?" Don asked. "Where'd she go?"

As if in answer, the sound of distant hoofbeats drew their attention, and they saw Beth come riding around the corner of the barn, her hair streaming out behind her. Even at this distance, they could see the white flash of her smile when she saw her parents. She pulled the reins, directing Goblin toward them.

"Hey yah, Pun'kin," Don called out, waving.

The drumbeat of hoofs got louder, sounding like a distant roll of thunder, as Beth raced across the field. Goblin's hoofs threw up puffs of dust as she ran through the swishing grass. Then something happened and, before Don or Jan could put it all together, they were running toward Beth, shouting.

436

With a sudden, terrified whinny, Goblin had drawn up and was rearing back on her hind legs, her hoofs flashing in the sun like blades. Beth's smile had frozen into a rictus of fear once she realized she didn't have control of the horse.

Don was in the lead, running toward her, and, as soon as he realized that the exposed table stone separated them from Beth, a cold dash of fear hit his stomach.

What's happening? his mind screamed, cutting through the panic as he watched Beth struggle to gain control of Goblin. But Goblin wouldn't come under control; she reared back, neighing viciously as her feet pawed the air. Don struggled through the tall grass, feeling it tug at his legs as though he were running through knee-deep surf.

"Daddy!" Beth screeched as she pulled back hard on the reins. Her knees were locked to Goblin's sides, and she leaned forward, clinging to the horse's neck. "Daddy! Help me!"

Don ran around the table stone in a wide detour and came up as close as he dared to the horse, but, once he was there, he was not at all confident he could reach up and grab the horse's bridle.

"Hold on, Pun'kin," he shouted, darting toward the horse and then drawing back when Goblin reared back, seemingly turning on him. The expression of horror on Beth's face sent waves of panic through him. He glanced once over his shoulder and saw Jan, standing a safe distance away, her hands covering her mouth.

Tears streaked Beth's face as she slipped from side to side in the saddle, but she never let go. Dust and hayseed swirled up in a whirling funnel around Goblin. Every time Don tried to get close enough to make a grab for the bridle, Goblin would snort wickedly and turn on him, her hoofs flashing like knives. Foam flew from her mouth, splattering on the ground.

"Daddy! Help!" Beth shouted, her eyes wide with fear. She was jolted painfully every time Goblin's feet hit the ground.

"Just hold on. I'm—trying," Don said, as he circled around, trying to get on Goblin's blind side, but she sensed where he was every second and kept him at bay.

Suddenly Goblin whinnied as though in pain and, rearing way back, tossed Beth from the saddle. Before Don could react, Goblin turned and brought her hoofs down. Beth screamed with pain as one hoof raked down across her forehead, cutting to the bone. Blood spurted and ran, stinging, into her eyes. She spun once on her heels and fell face down onto the ground.

Frantic now, Don dashed to Beth, shielding her body with his as Goblin reared back threateningly. Choking on dust, he lifted Beth in his arms and, in a staggering run, started toward the nearest protection, the barn.

The thundering of hoofs behind him filled his ears, and spots of light danced in his vision as he raced across the field toward safety. When he was almost there and chanced missing his stride to look back, he was astonished to see Goblin, head down, calmly munching on grass several yards behind.

"God almighty!" Don muttered as he lay Beth on the ground and brushed her blood-matted hair from her eyes. Her face had the same dead-white pallor she had had their first day at the house when they had driven into the driveway and she had choked on her own vomit.

He leaned closely, listening for signs of life, and felt some relief when he heard a faint stirring of breath.

Her tongue was thrust out of her mouth, and she had bitten through it, leaving a small chunk dangling on her chin. A pink-tinged foam seeped from the corner of her mouth and ran down the side of her neck.

Don was whimpering as he untucked his shirt, tore off a strip of the shirttail, and began dabbing the wound on her forehead. He kept telling himself that scalp wounds always bleed profusely and looked worse than they really were. But he wondered why she was so limp in his arms. She couldn't be—

—No! She *can't* be dead!

Tears blurred his vision as Jan, confident now that Goblin had calmed down, came running over to them. Don put his ear to Beth's chest and listened to the faint thump-thump of her heart.

She's not dead! Not dead!

"Quick," he snapped to Jan. "Go call the rescue unit. Tell 'em to get over here pronto!"

Jan was halfway to the house before he had finished.

"Oh, God. Please, *please* don't let her die," he moaned as he rocked her in his arms. He looked across the field to where Goblin stood, head down, eating as though nothing had happened. If he had had a gun in his hands right now, he thought, he'd have no compunction about aiming it at Goblin's flank and pulling the trigger. None whatsoever!

Don heard the screen door open and, looking up, saw Jan running back toward them. Beth moaned softly and tossed her head to one side. Her face was still bleached white, but her breathing, though raspy, sounded stronger.

"How is she?" Jan asked, kneeling down next to Don and gently running her fingers over Beth's forehead.

Don looked at his wife wordlessly, trying to push

439

aside the thought that rose in his mind.

It *wasn't* true! Bad things didn't *have* to come in threes! First Aune, then Billy, but—*please, God*—not Beth!

They sat in the shade of the barn, watching Beth, not daring to move her any more. They constantly kept an eye on Goblin, afraid that whatever had possessed her the first time might get her a second time, and she would come charging toward them, ready to kill. But Goblin was now the docile mare she had always been. She wandered aimlessly around the field, casually eating grass and wildflowers.

Several minutes later, although the rescue unit still hadn't come, Beth's eyelids flickered open. She looked up at her father with a distant, milky stare. The whites of her eyes glistened like porcelain shot through with thin red veins. Her mouth tried to form a smile, but the pain of her wounds made her wince, and the dangling piece of tongue grotesquely warped her smile.

"I—my—my head hurts," she managed to say, her voice lisping because of her cut tongue. "Did I—fall or something?"

"Shush," Don said softly. "You took quite a tumble from Goblin, but you're going to be all right." He smiled down at her but, when he looked at Jan, his brow was wrinkled with concern.

"My head—and tongue—feels—I—I."

Her head slumped to one side, and she dropped off to sleep, her breath rattling loudly in her chest.

Please. Please, let her be all right!

With wailing siren and flashing red lights, the rescue unit arrived, and the crew expertly transferred Beth onto a stretcher and into the ambulance.

While a paramedic gave Beth a quick examination, Don walked out to where Goblin was grazing.

440

"Here, girl," he called soothingly, holding his hand out to the horse.

Goblin raised her head and looked at him, her eyes moist and calm, no longer flashing angry fire. It seemed to Don that the raging animal he had confronted had been another horse entirely, and he wondered what could have triggered such a reaction in the animal. Had something spooked her—perhaps a gopher in the grass, or—?

—No, not the stones! he thought. It couldn't have been the table stone!

But then he remembered the other time Beth had tried to lead Goblin out to the site, and the horse had balked like a stubborn mule when she had walked near the exposed stone.

He reached out and took the horse's bridle. Goblin nickered softly and affectionately nudged her head against his side.

"Easy there, girl," Don said, hoping the nervousness he felt didn't register. He was thinking that, at any moment, the horse might suddenly turn on him, rear back, and trample him. When he thought of Beth, lying on an ambulance stretcher, his anger boiled; he wished again that he had a rifle and could end it all for Goblin on the spot.

Instead, though, he led her slowly to the barn and put her in her stall. She seemed happy to be there and went over to the bucket of oats and began eating. Caught between confusion and rage, Don clenched his fists, shook his head, and went back outside to where the ambulance waited.

"You ready to go?" he asked Jan and then, crouching, climbed into the back of the ambulance after her. One of the crew shut the doors, and the rescue unit started down the driveway slowly.

The paramedic was still leaning over Beth, inspecting her injuries, but he reassured Don and Jan several times that, as far as he could see, there were no signs of serious injury. The cut on her forehead was certainly nasty but would heal easily. Only the tip of her tongue had been severed, and would need a few stitches. It might heal more slowly, but she certainly wouldn't have any lasting speech impediment. She might be in pain from the bang on the back of her head when she fell, but he promised them she'd be up and about in a day or two.

Don listened to the paramedic, but all the while his mind was focusing on the other things as well. He was still trying to figure out why Goblin had reacted as she had, and, as much as he tried to convince himself that it had been an animal in the grass or maybe a burr under her saddle, he couldn't shake the conviction that Goblin had gone wild because she had gotten too near to the table stone.

The ambulance arrived at York Community Hospital, and Beth was admitted quickly and efficiently. This surprised Don, who remembered how ridiculously slow the hospital in Rhode Island had been at the time when his appendix had come close to bursting. They knew Beth was in pain, but she put up a brave front as they wheeled her into the emergency examination room.

Don and Jan alternately sat and paced in the waiting room while Dr. Eldridge and an intern checked Beth over. Five minutes stretched into fifteen, then thirty. Neither one of them wanted to voice the concern that, for what the paramedic had described as "relatively minor injuries," the doctor seemed to be taking quite a long time.

Don got a Diet Pepsi to share with Jan and sat with a limp, outdated copy of *People* in his hand. He had to use an immense effort of will to dispel the morbid

442

associations he had between the antiseptic smell of the hospital and Aune's slow decline to death. He couldn't shake the thought that Beth, looking thin and fragile beneath the crisp white sheet on the stretcher, had reminded him too much of how Aune had looked during her last days.

"Mr. and Mrs. Inman?" the nurse at the receiving station called out.

Don and Jan went over to her.

"You're Mr. and Mrs. Inman?" the nurse asked, raising a suspicious brow.

Don held himself back from answering, No! I'm Santa, and this is Mrs. Claus! Instead, he nodded curtly.

"Dr. Eldridge wants to have a word with you. Follow me, please," the nurse said as she turned and started down the corridor.

"My daughter's all right, isn't she?" Jan asked, wire-taut tension in her voice.

Without breaking her stride, the nurse shrugged. "I wouldn't be able to tell you that," she said.

Don and Jan exchanged anxious looks as they walked into a small office at the far end of the corridor.

"Have a seat please," the nurse said. "Dr. Eldridge will be with you in a moment."

When Dr. Eldridge did show up several moments later, the frown he wore said more than the cheerful greeting and handshake he gave each of them.

"Well? How is she?" Don asked as the doctor rounded the corner of his desk and sat down. His leather chair creaked under his weight. He placed a manila folder on the desktop and folded his hands on top of it.

"Your daughter's doing just fine," he said, still smiling, but there was hesitation in his voice that bespoke, again, that perhaps everything *wasn't* all right.

"When can we see her?" Jan asked.

Dr. Eldridge raised his eyebrows and tilted his head to one side. "She's resting now," he said. "We gave her a shot of pent to knock her out while we stitched her tongue. The cut on her forehead will leave a scar, but it's really nothing to be concerned about."

"So when can we see her?" Jan repeated.

Dr. Eldridge rubbed his cheek with his hand and said, "I think, considering everything, tomorrow might be best."

"What do you mean tomorrow?" Jan shouted, almost rising from her chair. "I want to see her now."

"She's sleeping now, still under with the Pentathol," Dr. Eldridge said. "I'd like to keep her here at least for tonight."

"Why?" Jan snapped. Don looked at her and gave her a subtle signal to cool it.

"Frankly," the doctor said, looking back and forth between them, "I want to keep her under observation. She sustained a quite serious blow to the back of her head, and, frankly, I'm a bit concerned about possible brain damage."

"What?" Jan exploded. Don reached out and gripped her by the shoulder, giving her an affectionate, calming pat.

"I'd like to run an EEG," Dr. Eldridge said, "and take a few more x-rays of her skull. There was no sign of a fracture in the ones we got, but, well, I just want to be sure nothing's been overlooked." He rose from his chair, indicating that the discussion was concluded.

"There are a few papers to fill out at the front desk," he said as he swung the office door open and stood back for Don and Jan to leave.

"Can we see her a little bit later?" Don asked. He was holding Jan's arm just above the elbow.

Dr. Eldridge considered a moment, then nodded. "Why don't you fill out the papers and then go out for a bite to eat. She'll probably be awake in an hour or two, and you can visit her then."

"Damn right!" Jan snapped.

"Thank you," Don added, and, guiding Jan by the arm, he led her down the corridor to the front desk.

As it turned out, Beth was still too groggy to speak with them after supper. They sat by her bedside for nearly an hour watching her sleep then, realizing there was nothing else they could do, they headed home.

III

By seven-thirty the next morning, Don and Jan were back at the hospital, sitting in the same chairs in the waiting room. They each had a cup of coffee from the hospital cafeteria, but Don found his close to undrinkable. Jan seemed not to notice as she sat, staring out the window at the anemic morning sky.

They didn't know that Beth had had several seizures during the night, but Don knew something was wrong as soon as Dr. Eldridge opened the heavy oak door and walked briskly over to them, asking to speak with them in his office.

Don poured what was left of his coffee down the drain of the water cooler and followed the doctor and Jan down the corridor. As they walked past the doors lining the hall, he suddenly stumbled and, turning, stared into one of the rooms. He had seen someone from the corner of his eye; he could have *sworn* it was Aune Kivinen lying in bed, surrounded by an assortment of tubes and i.v.s.

"Impossible," he whispered to himself, and he saw an elderly woman—certainly *not* Aune Kivinen—roll her eyes toward him and smile. Don nodded a greeting to her and, resisting a shiver, caught up with Jan, who had shot him a "hurry up!" look.

Just someone who looks like her, he told himself. Nothing more. Aune's dead—dead and buried like Billy.

Dr. Eldridge opened his office for them, and they sat in the same chairs they had sat in yesterday. Dr. Eldridge eased the door shut and went behind his desk. He picked up the manila file that was lying on the desk and opened it, scanning it briefly before speaking.

After clearing his throat, he looked at each of them and said, "I guess there's no point in beating around the bush. Last night, after the Sodium Pentathol wore off, your daughter suffered several epileptic seizures."

"What?" Jan said, sitting forward.

Don slouched back in his chair as though defeated and muttered, "Oh, no!"

Dr. Eldridge's face softened into an almost pained expression as he regarded the report which had been written up by the attending physician during the night. The icy ball in Don's stomach seemed to be enlarging by the second. Jan looked at him with a frantic light in her eyes.

"At present, she is in a situation called *status epilepticus*—an extremely critical situation," Dr. Eldridge said solemnly.

"What—what the hell is that?" Don asked, unable to hold back the tears that welled in his eyes. Jan sat silently sobbing with her face in her hands.

"It's Latin for 'epileptic state.' What happens is the person suffers a series of *grand mal* epileptic seizures. The seizures come so closely on top of one another, it's as if there's no break between them. Apparently the blow to the back of her head triggered the seizures. We seem to have them under control now."

"What do you mean?" Jan asked, her face glistening with tears. "What do you mean 'under control'?"

"I mean," Dr. Eldridge said, "that we've administered an anticonvulsant and the seizures are no longer as severe as they were. The EEG shows that. Later today, I want to run through the family medical history with you, but can you tell me, have there ever been any incidents of epilepsy in either of your families?"

Jan and Don exchanged glances and shrugged. Shaking his head side to side, Don said, "None that we know of."

"I'll want your medical records from your family doctor, and of course I'll do a complete examination including brain x-rays and other tests, but the indications are that she has epilepsy. Had you noticed anything unusual about her recently?"

Jan muttered something under her breath, and Dr. Eldridge leaned forward. "What did you say?" he asked.

"I said, she had her first period recently," Jan said.

Dr. Eldridge nodded. "That was obvious, but I didn't realize she had just started menstruating. That could be significant. There are many cases of epilepsy first occurring in adolescence, but offhand, I'd say the blow to the back of her head is what triggered it. She might have had a predilection before that, but—"

"That goddamned horse!" Don said, smacking his hand with his fist.

"I told you we never should have gotten that for her," Jan said, glaring at him.

"That's not what we're here to discuss right now," Dr. Eldridge said calmly. "The most important thing for you to realize is that epilepsy is not a disease; it's a condition, and your daughter, once she's out of danger, can lead a perfectly normal life with proper medication. She's not mentally retarded in any way, and she—"

"But she can have more fits, right?" Jan asked sharply.

"They are not called 'fits,' " Dr. Eldridge said, slicing the air with his hands for emphasis. "They're 'seizures,' and reacting to this medical condition like someone from the Middle Ages is not going to help your daughter! You've got to understand, for Beth's sake, if not your own, that epilepsy is nothing to be ashamed of."

"Well, then," Don said calmly, looking at Jan and then at the doctor, "if it isn't a disease, what is it?"

Dr. Eldridge took a deep breath before speaking. "In medical terms, epilepsy is the outward manifestation of disturbed electrical activity in the brain. It may—and I emphasize the word *may*—be the symptom of a disease or a brain tumor. We have to do more tests to determine that, but I'd say, in this instance, you're daughter's seizures were triggered by a trauma to the head. I'll prescribe a mild dosage of Dilantin for her and, once she leaves the hospital, we'll see how she does."

"So how long can this—what did you call it?" Don asked.

"*Status epilepticus*," Dr. Eldridge said.

"How long can this continue without—problems?" Don asked. They all knew that what he wanted to know was, can this condition kill her? He looked at Jan, thinking he'd forever be haunted by the fearful gleam, like chips of blue ice, in her eyes.

Twisting his fingers together, Dr. Eldridge said, "I won't pull any punches; this is a critical medical condition. If the series of seizures doesn't break—within a day or two—" He looked long and hard at Jan and Don, judging their ability to handle the full truth. "There could be a chance of permanent brain damage. If it lasts too long, she could slip into a coma and eventually die."

"Oh my God!" Jan said.

She started to rise from her chair and then fell back. Don went over to her and hugged her tightly, patting her back to soothe the sobs that racked her body. After several minutes, she regained her composure enough to pull away from him and sit up straight. Her mouth, Don saw as he went back to his chair, was set in a tight grimace. He reached out and patted her hand, and she gripped his hand as though her life depended on maintaining the touch.

"We have her on oxygen and intravenous medication now and, as I said earlier, the severity of the seizures, at least, is declining."

Don shook his head, unable to hold back the tears. It was all crashing in on him—*everything*! First Aune, then Billy, and now Beth! He felt in his gut that this was it—this was the third horror—and somehow he felt entirely responsible for it all. Ever since they had moved to Maine, it had been one calamity after another. His breathing came in jerky gulps, and, as he squeezed Jan's hand, he had to fight the choking sensation that seemed to cut off his supply of air.

"How long—" he said, but his voice broke before he could continue. He swallowed and wiped his eyes with the back of his hand.

Dr. Eldridge shook his head sympathetically. "We can't say for sure. The incidence of *status epilepticus* is small, but if it continues through the night—" He shrugged helplessly. "The prognosis wouldn't be favorable."

"That goddamned horse!" Jan said, lowering her head and glaring at Don. "It's all because of that goddamned horse!"

Tears were streaming from her eyes and dripping from her chin. Dr. Eldridge handed her a box of tissues. She took several and wiped her eyes.

"Don't worry," Don said, his own vision blurring with tears, "I'll take care of it. We'll get rid of Goblin. Believe me." He wanted to go to her, to comfort her, but he felt as though the black curtain of his own misery separated them.

"What is of concern now," Dr. Eldridge said softly, "is your daughter's health."

"How could something like this happen?" Don asked, his voice breaking. "What could trigger something like this?"

Dr. Eldridge shrugged his shoulders as he tapped the end of a pencil on his desktop.

"We have no way of knowing," he said. "In spite of all our medical miracles, we still can't determine how something as simple as aspirin works to relieve headaches. Think of our brain activity, thoughts and emotions, as the weather all around the world. Epilepsy is like a storm, a hurricane, that can cause a great amount of damage. There are several contributing factors: Beth starting her period, the fall from the horse, even the shock of losing control of the horse. You told the admitting nurse she looked glassy-eyed before she fell, right?"

Don nodded. "She was scared out of her wits when Goblin started rearing up. Before that, she seemed all right, smiling and waving as she rode over to us."

"All we can do now," Dr. Eldridge said, "is hope and pray that she's strong enough to pull through this. I think her chances are pretty good. The medication

450

does seem to be having an effect. All we can do now is wait."

They left the doctor's office and took the elevator up to the fourth floor to the intensive care unit. Don thought the floor tilted at a sickening angle as they walked hand in hand down the corridor. The leaden silence between them hurt him almost as much as what had happened to Beth, and he felt helpless that he couldn't get inside Jan's veil of misery to help and comfort her.

Beth looked small and fragile in the bed where she lay, almost lost in a confusion of tubes, suspended bottles, and blinking monitors. The green sine waves on a circular screen were the first indication they had that she was indeed alive.

Jan broke down again as soon as she saw her daughter through the wire-meshed glass. She pressed her face into Don's shoulders, and her body shook with wrenching sobs.

Fighting back the sensation that he was looking at a corpse, Don hugged Jan closely while he regarded Beth. The image that rose in his mind was not of a twelve-year-old girl but of a ninety-two-year-old woman—Aune Kivinen. The similarity was enough to make bile rise into his throat, and he made a deep, whimpering sound as he watched the attending nurse make an adjustment on the i.v.

"Oh my God, Don," Jan said, her voice breaking. "How can she—she *be* like that?"

Blinking back his tears, he stroked her hair and whispered, "I don't know."

The wave patterns on the monitor remained steady, but it was Beth's face—her *face* that cut him to the marrow. Her expression had the quiet composure of a corpse. Her hand, resting on top of the sheets, looked as though it would simply dry up and blow away.

"I don't think it's doing us or her any good to stay here," Don said gently. He looked at their reflections in the screened window and for a moment had the impression that he and Jan had become ghosts, mere wraiths lurking in the hospital. He watched the window as the two wraiths turned slowly and started moving down the corridor.

IV

"You can sell her back to Stewart, can't you?" Jan asked. She was sitting at the breakfast table, looking at Don, as he paced back and forth across the kitchen floor. A full cup of coffee, now cold, was on the table in front of her; with her elbows on the table, her chin was cupped in her hands.

"I don't know," Don said, waving his hands in frustration. "I mean, I don't think I can very well call him up and say, 'Oh, hey, by the way, that horse you sold me is a killer.' And I sure don't relish the idea of his selling the horse to someone else, and then maybe hearing she's trampled another kid to death."

"For heaven's sake, Don. Nobody's died!" Jan snapped. "I mean, it's not like Goblin's some tiger who, now that she's tasted blood, is going to go on a rampage."

"How do you know?" Don yelled, slamming a fist against the countertop. "She's dangerous, and—and I'm not sure I want to take that kind of chance."

"Look, just give Hoss a call and see what he says," Jan said softly. Her face was pale, and her eyes were red-rimmed from crying all night after their visit to the hospital.

Don agreed and, after some prodding, Hoss said he would take Goblin back. He insisted on calling her Dobbin, but Don couldn't care less at this point. Don

452

wasn't surprised that, Yankee trader that he was, Hoss wanted to pay less than the amount he had sold her for, and, as frustrated as he was, Don readily agreed to a loss of a hundred and fifty dollars. How he'd explain it all to Beth—if she ever came out of the hospital—was a problem he'd have to deal with later.

"Just so long as that animal's out of here," he told Hoss, his voice edged with anger as though he held Hoss partly responsible for what had happened. He nodded, hung up the phone, and turned to Jan.

"Well?" she asked.

"He said he's on his way," Don said. "Damned good thing, too."

But any relief Don had felt quickly evaporated when he went out to the barn and saw that Goblin wasn't in her stall. The door leading to the stone corral was wide open. Don raced outside, around the side of the barn, and felt only slightly better when he saw Goblin grazing calmly near the corral gate.

"What! Do you have hands or something?" he asked, coming up to her but keeping the fence between them. "I'd like to know how you get those stall doors open."

Goblin looked at him, her brown eyes softly moist, and nickered. Don approached her, his hand extended as though he were holding a sugar cube.

"Come on now, girl. Easy there. Easy." He came up to the corral gate. Goblin's ears flicked, and her tail swished, sounding like tires on a wet road. She stamped her foot once, making dust swirl up like smoke.

Don kept one hand out in front of him as he eased the corral gate open. "Easy now—Come on, girl," he said.

Goblin watched him as he reached out for her halter, and she didn't react when his fingers closed on

453

the worn leather strap. Feeling confident, Don started to guide her back to the stall, but, with a sudden, furious whinny, Goblin pulled away from his grip and wrenched his shoulder. Don staggered forward and almost fell as Goblin pranced away from him.

"Come on, you goddamned animal," he growled, crouching to move toward her slowly but also to be ready to leap over the fence if he had to.

Goblin moved back and forth across the paddock, keeping tantalizingly out of his range. Every time he lurched to grab her, she darted away with a whinny that sounded strangely like laughter.

"Come on," Don said angrily. "I don't have all day."

When he made another grab for her, Goblin snorted, spraying him with foam from her mouth, but, instead of trotting away this time, she reared back. Her hoofs sliced the air over Don's head, and he had just enough time to dodge to one side before Goblin brought them down.

He started to run toward the stone wall, and Goblin charged him from behind. Don feinted to one side and then dashed to the other, but as he did, a hoof caught him on the shoulder, sending a bolt of pain down his arm. He staggered, his knees hitting the ground, then leaped over the fence. Goblin turned sharply. The dirt she kicked up splattered the stone wall like a spray of machine-gun bullets.

Don glanced at the open corral gate and started toward it, but it was as though Goblin could read his mind, and she ran full tilt for the opening. He knew he wouldn't make it in time to close the gate before she got out, so, timing it as precisely as he could, he ran out of the corral to grab the gate and jumped back into the corral, pulling the gate closed just as Goblin dashed out into the open field.

"Damn it!" he shouted, banging the gate with his clenched fist. He was safe, but she was out of the corral—free.

She pranced and pawed the ground in front of the gate. Her muzzle was dripping with white, bubbly foam, and her eyes now held a wild fire in their centers that truly frightened Don. She reared up several times and, charging the gate, brought her hoofs crashing down onto the wood, removing large chunks each time.

Don backed away toward the barn, considering whether or not he could make a dash for the house and safety. His biggest fear was that Jan would come outside to see what was keeping him, and Goblin would trample her. Yes, there was no doubt in his mind now; this animal *was* like a tiger that had tasted blood. She wanted him dead!

Goblin finally gave up her attack on the gate, and, with a loud snort, she turned and raced across the field toward the fringe of woods. Don watched her go, listening to the slowly receding thumping of hoofs. Once he knew she was far enough away and it was safe, he ran to the house.

In the kitchen, he hurriedly explained to Jan what had happened and, warning her to stay inside, he looked up the Remys' phone number in the book and dialed quickly. Louise Remy answered.

"Louise," he panted, realizing that they hadn't told the Remys anything about what had happened to Beth. "Is Earl home?"

"Uh, no," she replied. "He won't be home from the mill till 'round five o'clock. Is there something I can help you with?"

"I need a gun," Don said. "Do you have a rifle I can borrow?"

"You sound all worked up," Louise said. "Is something the matter?"

Don was still shaking from his encounter with Goblin, but he forced himself to slow down. "No, uhh, nothing's the matter. I've just been"—he scanned the ceiling trying to think of an excuse—"I've been having some trouble with a raccoon getting into the garden, and I wanted to see if I could get him tonight."

"Well, sure," Louise said, "we've got plenty of guns here. What were you thinking of?"

"A shotgun, I guess," Don said, regretting his lack of knowledge about guns. Whatever would you use to kill a horse? A .22 wouldn't have enough power, would it? A 4-10, or a 12 gauge? Maybe an M-16? Hell! He didn't know the difference.

"Well, why don't you wait until Earl—"

"I'd really like to pick it up now," Don said. "I've got—I've got some things to do later today, and I really want to make sure I have it for tonight before that critter does any more damage in the garden."

Jan was standing with her back against the sink, watching him with wide-eyed surprise.

"I can swing by right now, if it's O.K. with you."

"Sure," Louise said. "I suppose it'll be all right."

As he hung up the phone, Don looked at Jan. She placed a hand on his shoulder and gave him a level stare. "Why don't you sit down and take a breather? You look like you're about to have a coronary."

"I'm going to get that damned horse if it's the last thing I do," Don said sharply. "Could you give Hoss a call? Tell him to forget about coming for Goblin. That horse is going to be a glue-factory candidate before noon!"

Jan's face paled. "I don't know if I like the idea of you out there in the woods, hunting that horse," she said. "Not when she's acting so wild."

Don wordlessly turned and, grabbing the car keys, headed out the door, letting it slam shut and cutting off whatever else Jan had to say.

V

"I still think this is a bad idea," Jan said nervously. She was standing behind Don while he sat at the kitchen table inspecting the shotgun Louise Remy had loaned to him. At his elbow was a box of shells. Their brass caps caught and reflected the light of the kitchen. Don snapped open the chamber, slid in two shells, and snapped the gun shut.

"I mean, why not just let her go?" Jan asked. "If she comes back, we'll get her into the corral somehow. And if she doesn't come back—"

"No!" Don said, shaking his head. "No *ifs*! I'm not going to let an animal like that run loose." He hefted the gun, satisfied with the sense of power it gave him.

"But, Don, isn't there someone you can contact for help? The local game warden or state police or something?"

"Or maybe the National Guard, huh?" he said, smiling grimly. "No thanks. That horse turned on me. It was—weird. It was like she—like she *knew* what I was thinking, like she planned to lull me before trying to kill me. No, this is just between her and me!"

"Real macho stuff, huh? Have you been reading Hemingway lately?" Jan said sarcastically as she shook her head. "And how do you think any of this will help Beth, huh? Huh?"

Deflated for a moment, Don's shoulders drooped. "I don't know—for sure," he said, his voice husky with tension. "But I'm the one who has to do it."

He stood and put a handful of shells into his pocket. Then, shouldering the shotgun, he went to the door. Jan stopped him just before he left and planted a soft, wet kiss on his lips.

"Just be careful, O.K.?" she said softly.

He nodded and shouldered the screen door open. "Just make sure you stay inside," he said, "in case she comes back. Oh, and give Stewart a call. Tell him—tell him I've changed my mind about selling the horse back to him. Tell him I got a better offer."

Jan followed him out into the backyard and watched as he started off across the field. Just at the margin of the woods, he turned and waved, and then the dappled green of the trees swallowed him up.

It took no great skill to follow the route Goblin had gone. Don could easily discern where she had trampled through the underbrush. A low, tingling thrill coursed through his body as he entered the woods, feeling the coolness of the shadows on his skin. The thrill of the chase, he thought, the primitive glory of the hunt! He kept the shotgun cocked and at the ready as he walked briskly along the trampled path, confident that he would find Goblin in a matter of minutes.

His confidence, however, began to wane after more than two hours of tramping through the brush. As clear as Goblin's trail was on the whole, at times he lost it where she had run through a flat, open area. Apparently, the horse had doubled back on her trail several times, probably out of panic and confusion. Sometimes the trail was so confusing Don felt as though he were tracking more than one horse.

By mid afternoon, the humidity rose, and sweat ran down Don's face, stinging his eyes. In the emerald shadows of the trees, he circled around in a crazy pattern, weaving in and out of brush, through pine groves, high-bush blueberries, and thorn bushes that caught and ripped his clothes. His frustration and anger grew as the day got hotter. His clothes were sticking to him as with tiny suction cups.

All of his fantasies about the hunt and all hope of catching up with Goblin were gone after another two hours of forcing his way through the woods and definitely going around in circles. He was somewhere near the edge of Whippoorwill Swamp and was not entirely sure which direction was toward home when he stopped beside a gnarled oak to rest.

His breath came in burning gulps, and his hand ached from the steel-tight grip he had on the shotgun. A strange, rubbery sensation was creeping up the backs of his legs, and he was afraid the muscles would cramp up if he sat for too long.

Looking around, he tried to get his bearings. From the position of the sun, he guessed he was south, maybe southeast, of the house. He pushed aside the thought that he might have gotten himself lost, but, after following the confusion of several trails, it looked as though Goblin had taken off toward the swamp. Don wondered if he should continue the chase or, probably more sensibly, take Jan's advice and head home to call the game warden.

He pushed away from the tree and scanned the path, running in either direction. He could go on toward Whippoorwill Swamp, or he could turn back now. The surrounding woods were ominously quiet. Only the distant chirping of a bird and the gentle rustling of leaves broke the stillness.

Raising the shotgun to his shoulder, he sighted down the trail that led to Whippoorwill Swamp. Aiming at random targets, he imagined squeezing the trigger and feeling the solid kick of the gun as it spoke lead and smoke. With a shock and a sharp intake of breath, he realized he was looking down the barrel directly at Goblin. She seemed to have appeared quietly like the shadow of a cloud, from the surrounding woods, her sweat-sleek hide dappled with shadows. A thick lather rimmed her mouth.

"What the—" Don muttered, feeling a chill in his stomach, but, by the time he remembered the shotgun and squeezed the trigger, it was too late. With the deafening blast, she faded from sight, and the only evidence Don had that she really had been there was the distant drumming of her hoofs as she bolted down the trail.

But that decided it for Don; he knew he would have to follow her.

"Son-of-a-bitch!" he muttered, looking helplessly at the gun in his hands, as though it, not his aim, had been at fault. He snapped it open, shook out the spent shell and replaced it with another. He couldn't shake the impression that Goblin had been toying with him, taunting him with her gleaming eyes.

He started rapidly down the path with the shotgun raised almost to his shoulder, on the ready this time. He had been right, at least, about the swamp being nearby, and that made him a little less nervous about being lost. The path Goblin had taken led directly to the swamp and from there made a circumference of the dismal stretch of water. At least it was no problem following her footprints in the soggy earth.

Thigh-high ferns whipped against his legs as he followed quickly along Goblin's path. Long, slanting bars of light caught the surface of the open water. Checking his watch, Don saw that it was now past mid afternoon and he knew he'd have to head home if he didn't get Goblin soon, one way or another. He surely didn't want to be lost in the woods after dark.

The smell rising from the swamp, coupled with the

460

clinging humidity of the day, almost choked Don as he went down the trail. At first he couldn't place what the smell reminded him of, but, when he finally connected it with the smell inside the burial chamber, goose flesh spread over his arms. The association began to gnaw at his nerves, and he gripped the rifle tightly in his hands.

A sudden, sharp cry from behind made him stop short. Crouching, he started back down the trail. At the water's edge, dead tree trunks with thick algae collars stuck up, reminding him of the tall, black stones in his nightmare. The whirring sound of frogs and insects rose in a loud din masking all other sounds as he waited, tensed, for the sound to be repeated.

He lowered the shotgun from the crook of his arm and looked up. When the sound came again, he was able to get a fix on it and saw a small dot circling overhead against the blue of the sky. A hawk was lazily circling, riding the warm thermals that rose from the swamp. Don was so entranced by the bird's effortless gliding that he didn't register the thumping of Goblin's hoofs until it was almost too late.

"Motherfucker!" he just managed to shout as he turned and saw the dark mass of horse bearing down on him. His finger reflexively squeezed the trigger, and the shotgun barked, nearly jumping out of his hands. He dove to the side of the trail, and the concussion of air as Goblin raced by felt as though a train had just roared past. He stumbled and fell backward and ended up sitting in waist-deep stagnant water.

Goblin steamed down the trail and was just rounding the turn when Don lurched to his feet, raised the shotgun, and cracked off another round. He missed; he knew it as soon as he heard the buckshot ripping through the brush beside the trail.

"You goddamned . . . !" he shouted, shaking the gun over his head as he struggled to his feet. His pants made gross sucking sounds when he walked, and he kept wiping slimy gobs of muck from his face.

It wasn't until he was back on the trail, popping two fresh shells into the gun, that he realized something peculiar: Goblin had come at him from behind!

He bent over and studied the hoof prints in the muddy trail, trying to figure out how he had been fooled. After careful consideration, he decided the horse had veered off the trail and into the woods somewhere behind him. He must have been following tracks she had made earlier in the day.

He chanced to look up and saw that the hawk was gone. The buzzing sounds of the swamp rose again, following the interruption of the shots. Shivering and feeling foolish—but not foolish enough to get caught in the swamp after dark—Don started back for home.

With each step, his socks made squishing sounds, and his pants chafed his crotch, rubbing like cold hands on his thighs. He knew he'd be lucky if he didn't catch a cold from this, and he was glad Jan wasn't here to see how foolish he looked.

But there *was* someone there, he realized suddenly. He had followed the trail back along the margin of the swamp and was just starting up the wooded slope the same way he had come when he saw Goblin again. She stood at the crest of the hill, looking down at him with blazing eyes. Don was frozen by the malicious hatred he saw in her stare.

Impossible, he thought as he slowly raised his gun. Animals can't feel anger and hatred; those are human emotions! But that was the only way to describe how she regarded him as he took several strides up the slope toward her.

"You crazy killer!" he snarled, his lip curling as he brought the gun up. Goblin whinnied and stamped her foot, eyeing him with a look of impatience. Sunlight and shadow dappled her hide, making her hide appear to waver, seeming almost to blend into the trees.

Carefully, slowly, Don took aim and squeezed and trigger. The gun roared and kicked painfully back into his shoulder. He could hear the pellets tearing through the leaves, but Goblin didn't even flinch. She snorted loudly and shook her head, sending foam flying.

Then Goblin began to prance, her front feet kicking up clods of leaf mold and black dirt. She made a feint as though about to charge him. Don braced himself, took careful aim, and shot. The gun butt smacked his shoulder, and blue smoke swirled around his head, but, when he could see through the smoke up the slope, Goblin was gone as if she had never been there.

Don reloaded and started up the hill slowly, wondering if maybe he had been hallucinating. It seemed as though the horse, in keeping with her name, was able to appear first here, then there, then disappear like a phantom. He scanned the surrounding woods, expecting to see her charge from any direction without warning.

He knew that, whatever deadly game the horse was playing with him, he couldn't afford to be distracted. He had to get out of the woods and home before darkness fell. He vowed not to let Goblin distract him; if he saw her, he'd shoot to protect himself, but this was it. He wasn't going on any more wild chases.

The sun was slanting at a sharp angle through the trees as Don picked up the trail he thought led back to his property. Where had the time gone? he asked himself. He had left the house a little after eleven o'clock, after picking up the shotgun from Louise Remy. Trying to estimate the time, he would have said he had been in the woods no more than three hours, but here it was, almost dark. He could see purple fingers of clouds streaking the western sky. He couldn't shake the weird sensation that—somehow—he had lost several hours.

He followed the trail, always on the ready to hear the muffled thump of hoofs bearing down on him. But, after an hour of walking, Don had to admit that he was, in fact, lost. The woods should have opened up by now, if not onto his property, at least onto Hunter Hill Road. That road ran almost exactly north and south, and he, walking westward directly into the setting sun, should have hit it by now. Something was wrong—*seriously* wrong!

As the woods darkened, its shadow spreading like an inkstain, Don's nerves tingled. With failing sight, he relied increasingly on his ears to cut through the night sounds in the woods and to warn him if Goblin was coming. He was no longer the hunter, he knew; he was the hunted! If darkness came before he reached the road . . . Well, he didn't want to consider slashing through the woods at night.

The setting sun lined the tree limbs with fiery laciness, and shadows thickened as night sounds grew louder. Don continuously had to swat at mosquitoes buzzing furiously around his face and arms. The woods seemed to grow thicker and more tangled as he slashed aside underbrush with the butt of Earl's shotgun.

The sun was well down below the hills, and blackness embraced the woods when Don finally stumbled out onto the road. He tripped on the unseen lip of hardtop and fell, scraping his knees. It took him a minute or two to get his bearings, and then he realized with a shock that he was a good four miles further down the road than he had expected. He couldn't shake the feeling that not only had he somehow missed several hours of the day, but he had been mysteriously transported far from his destination.

As he started down the road that unrolled like a black ribbon in the night, he was suddenly aware that something was behind him. With a muffled grunt, he turned and saw Goblin, a hulking black shadow darker than the surrounding night at the edge of the road.

"Just leave me the hell alone, will you?" he shouted, and tears stung his eyes. He held the gun at the ready but thought that, provided he didn't aim it to shoot, maybe she would leave him alone.

"Go on!" he shouted, waving his arm over his head. "Get! Get out of here!"

Goblin moved to the center of the road and stood there, watching him impassively. In the dark, her coat seemed almost to glow with an eerie luminescence, and Don could see her flanks trembling with controlled tension. Then, without warning, she charged in a sudden clatter of hoofs.

Don dropped into the ditch beside the road and took aim at the rapidly approaching black mass. Quickly, he pulled the trigger once—twice. The shotgun spit fire and lead, and Don heard the pellets ricochet from the road. Still she came, her horseshoes setting off sparks from the road.

Fumbling in his pockets, Don realized with horror that he had used his last two shells. The horse charged down on him, casting a shadow that reached out for him.

Whimpering softly, Don waited to time his jump out of the animal's path at the right moment, but before she got to him, she veered back onto the center strip and disappeared down the road. Over the hissing of his breath, Don could hear the slowly fading clatter of hoofs.

Amazed to find he was still alive and not some bloody pulp on the road, Don got up and brushed his knees. He was cold, wet, aching, and hungry as he began the four-mile walk down Hunter Hill Road toward home.

"Some hunter," he muttered, snorting to himself. He knew Goblin was through tormenting him—at least for now. She was going to let him go—*for now,* he thought, unable to loosen the tightness that clutched at his throat.

Chapter Fourteen

"I want my doll!"

I

The next morning, every muscle and joint in Don's body ached: his shoulder from the recoil of the shotgun, his knees from falling on the road in the dark, his arms from thrashing through prickers and brush, his crotch from the chafing of the wet jeans. *Everything!* The only thing the hot shower had helped was his mood; it went from black to gray.

Jan seemed unusually edgy, too, as she bustled around in the kitchen, getting breakfast ready. She kept dropping silverware and knocking things over. When she spilled Don's orange juice, he made a lighthearted comment, but she smiled scornfully and went about her business.

"I'm not so sure we have to hurry, you know, to get to the hospital," Don said, once Jan finally sat down and they began to eat.

"What?" Jan shouted, glaring at him.

Don shrugged and pushed his eggs from one side of

the plate to the other.

"I don't know," he said softly. "I mean, it's really hard to just—just sit there, watching her. It's like it's some kind of—of deathwatch or something."

Jan's mouth tightened, and Don could see tears welling in her eyes. "It isn't," she said, sniffing. "It isn't like *that* at all."

"Hey, I know," Don said. He reached across the table to her, but she pulled away. "I know it isn't. It's just that, what with everything that's happened lately, I feel like I'm a wreck. And, truth to tell, Jan, you don't look so hot yourself. Have you looked in a mirror lately?"

She bristled, her jaw muscles flexing and unflexing. "It means a lot to me to be there," she said, dabbing her eyes with a paper napkin. "And I know it would to Beth, too, if she woke up and saw us there."

"I was thinking I might stay around the house today," Don said. "I've got a lot of work to do, and beside, I think maybe I should be here, you know, in case Goblin shows up or something."

"Goblin! huh!" Jan said, shaking her head. She got up, walked over to the sink, and looked out over the field. Her breakfast was untouched, and the eggs now looked cold and rubbery. "I hope you aren't planning on doing any digging out there today."

"I hadn't planned to," Don said, knowing it was at best a half-truth.

Jan turned and looked at him. Tears glistened on her cheeks, and she looked at least ten pounds thinner than she had only two days ago. Her skin was a pasty-white hue that seemed almost translucent. Dr. Eldridge had prescribed some tranquilizers for her, and Don thought maybe they were what was making her so irritable.

"Ever since you found that hand out there," she

said, her face tightening. "That *goddamned* hand!"

Don shivered as the memory of what he had thought he had seen down in the chamber—a hand, reaching around the edge of the opening. "Don't worry." he said, this time with a little more conviction in his voice. "I won't go down there."

"Good!" Jan snapped. "Leave it alone! None of this would have happened if you hadn't started poking around there in the first place!"

"Hey, come on," he said. He stood and came over to her, placing his hand on her shoulder. He could feel the muscles bunched with tension beneath her shirt. "Take it easy."

"It's true, though," Jan said, sniffing. "None of this would have happened. Beth wouldn't be in the hospital! Billy Blackshoe wouldn't be dead! And even Goblin. I think your digging out there affected her somehow."

Don laughed as he rubbed Jan's shoulder, trying to erase the tension.

"It's true," Jan repeated. "Ever since you found that hand, it's like you've been possessed by it, and — bottom line—it's left you with damned little time for me."

The smile on Don's lips slowly faded. "What do you mean?"

She stiffened and looked up at him, her jaw set with determination. "Maybe if you hadn't spent so much time wondering about that goddamned hand and what might be buried out there in the field, I'd feel as though you still loved me and I—" She dropped her gaze and, biting her lower lip, added, "And I'd feel as though I still loved you."

Oh, shit! Don thought, his face flushing. Here it comes!

"What are you saying?" he asked, his voice fighting

for control. He took his hand from her shoulder when he felt the grip involuntarily tighten. "What do you mean?"

"I'm saying that I can't take it anymore, that's what," Jan replied. Her tears had stopped flowing, but her eyes had a glazed look still that unnerved Don. "I can't take the pressure. I don't know if it's the move to Maine, what's happened to Beth, or what! All I know is that, ever since we moved here, you've been . . . different."

He looked at her and could see the artery in her neck pulsing rapidly beneath the skin. He knew there was more coming and waited patiently even though he felt about to explode.

"What pressure?" he asked, voice steady and low.

"All of it, for God's sake!" she snapped, hitting the countertop with her fist. "Everything! Goblin! Billy Blackshoe! Beth in the hospital! This stupid friggin' *house! Everything!*"

"It will all work out," Don said soothingly although, for the first time in his life, he felt the stirrings of more than a lingering doubt. "Beth'll get better; you'll see. And once school starts, you'll get a job that suits you, and we'll get into a routine. We'll be—"

"We *won't!*" Jan shouted, clenching her fists and shaking them in front of herself. "There aren't any openings in real estate around here, and I certainly won't go back to something like *The Rusty Anchor.* The only reason I *got* that job was because Dale Jackman was after me," she said sourly. "He gave me that job 'cause he thought he could get into into my pants, and—"

"And . . . ?" Don said, thinking, Oh, shit! This is it! He had a vivid mental image of all their plans for living in Maine flaking away like old paint from the

470

side of a barn. What was that old Japanese saying? When you speak of next year, the devils laugh.

Jan looked up at him, her lip trembling. "And . . . he did."

"Oh, dammit!" Don sputtered, suddenly feeling helpless.

He backed away from her and sat down in his chair at the breakfast table. He wanted to get up and run out of the house, run to Whippoorwill Swamp and *let* Goblin trample him, but his legs were too rubbery to support him. The silence between them as they eyed each other crackled like the air just before a thunderstorm.

"So," Don managed to say, his voice barely above a whisper. "How long have you been . . . uh."

He couldn't bring himself to say the words.

"Once," Jan said evenly. "Just once."

"Yeah," Don said, putting his face in his hands and shaking his head from side to side. "Yeah, sure."

"Honestly," Jan said. She started toward him and halted, then came up beside him, knelt down, and took his hand in hers. "Just once. I don't know why, for sure, but it meant nothing to me. Then or now."

Don looked at her, surprised at how strange, how distant she seemed, almost as though she were a different person. Maybe, he thought, his stomach dashed with coldness, he was seeing the real Jan for the first time in a long time. Maybe he *had* been taking her just for granted for too long.

"Then, why? Goddammit!" he said, tossed between rage and pain. "If it meant nothing, why'd you do it?"

Jan shook her head. "I don't know. It just happened. He'd been coming on to me since the day I applied. What can I say?"

Don pressed his palms against his throbbing tem-

471

ples. "Since before you started working there? And you knew it? So you must have wanted it. Maybe you *did* it so you could get the job."

Jan turned away, stung, and she began to cry again. "No. That wasn't it," she said, her voice jerking. "I did it because . . . because I wasn't sure if I loved you anymore. I'm *still* not sure if what there is between us can be called *love*. Habit, maybe. But he came on to me, and it felt good; it felt good, thinking that, even after seventeen years of marriage, I could still turn a guy on, that I was still sexy to someone."

"You're sexy to me," Don said although he felt pained. His voice sounded flat and emotionless to him. He wondered how she could possibly believe him. He kicked the chair back and, leaving her at the table, walked over to the door, staring out at the driveway. He felt it slipping away from him—all of it—his wife, his daughter, his whole life!

"We just don't seem to connect anymore," Jan said, running her hands through her hair. "You don't have time for me, what with everything you've been doing around the house here—"

"I've been trying to get this place ready for winter if you hadn't noticed," he said angrily. "I've been working my ass off to keep this family together."

Jan shook her head and said sadly, "What we used to have has been dead for so long we don't even miss it."

Don looked at her and softened, searching himself for the void he thought might be there, that definitely was there, now that he knew she had cheated on him. He began to doubt whether or not he could even make contact with his feelings for her; he felt anesthetized.

"Look, Jan," he said calmly. "We're both under a lot of strain right now, and I'm not sure this is the time to talk about this. I'm just as concerned about

Beth as you are, and Billy and Aune dying definitely affected me. You've got every right to be upset, and—"

"That's right!" Jan said. "I *am* upset, and I'm sick and tired of my life. If Dale Jackman can't change it for me, then maybe someone else can."

"Maybe *you* can," Don said. "Don't expect to find it in someone else if it isn't inside you! But I don't think now is the time to be talking about it, considering the stress we're under."

"I don't know," Jan said, wringing her hands in frustration. "I just . . . I don't know."

She broke down and covered her face with her hands, and in a second Don was beside her, holding her tightly to him and stroking her hair. They stood there embracing for a long time, neither one of them able to find the words to patch and heal the wounds they had found and made. Finally, sniffing, Jan pulled away and looked up at him.

"So," she said, voice trembling, "what do we do now?"

Her nose was running, and Don reached for a Kleenex from the counter.

"I don't know," he said, shrugging, "I guess—at least for now—we have to hang in there and work on it." He knew it couldn't possibly be that simple, but, at least for himself, he knew he was willing to try.

"If you say there's nothing between you and Dale, that it was a one-time thing—well, I believe you. I *have* to believe you. And I'll bet, eventually, I'll be able to get over it. Right now, the important thing is that, like you said, we're both here for Beth."

Jan looked at him and smiled, and he actually felt an element of warmth in the smile.

"And if, once Beth's better, you think—you know—that maybe you have to do something on your own, well . . ." He looked up at the ceiling and blinked away the tears that were forming. "We'll have to work on it. That's all."

Jan nodded stiffly and pulled away from him. "Umm. You're right. I *know* I've been pretty wired lately. What pissed me off was that you seemed so involved with other things, you hardly noticed what I was going through."

"I'll try harder," Don said. "Honest."

"O.K.," Jan replied. "Let's get ready and go to the hospital."

II

They didn't get to bed until after midnight. After sitting with Beth for most of the day—her condition, Dr. Eldridge said several times, was unchanged and at least that was not a bad sign—they had gone to eat in Portsmouth.

Don had suggested visiting Susan, but Jan cautioned that Susan and Tom had enough problems of their own. Once they got home, they talked and talked, as they hadn't in years. They talked about how so much of their time had been taken over by Beth, the move to Maine, their concern about jobs, and Don's seeming obsession about the burial site in the field—everything that had made them forget about each other. They agreed that they needed more time, just the two of them, to examine where they were with each other.

After a long, slow love-making, they settled down to sleep just before two o'clock in the morning. Jan drifted off first while Don lay in the dark, his hands clasped behind his head, enjoying pleasant thoughts as he drifted toward the edge of sleep. Twenty minutes later, he bolted up in bed with a tearing scream.

"Wha—? What is it?" Jan shrieked as she fumbled for the light switch.

Don squinted in the sudden brightness and ran his fingers through his sweat-drenched hair. The riveting terror of the dream still gripped him.

Jan put her hand on his chest and ran small circles around his nipple with her fingertip. "You're going to give me a complex about making love if that's how it's going to affect you." Her laughter was soft and easy, the way he remembered it from long ago.

"The dream I had," he said, his voice tightening. "What a doozy! Want to hear what it was?"

"I'm not so sure," Jan replied, still rubbing his chest.

"I was walking in the woods. It seemed like the same woods where I was chasing Goblin; I'm not sure. Anyway—" He suddenly shivered, clenching his hands into tight fists. "I can't believe my mind could come up with something like that. There was someone hanging—by his neck—from a tree."

"Oh, great!" Jan said. "Maybe you'd better save it till morning."

"It was raining," Don went on, heedless of her, "and this guy—a boy, I think—was swinging back and forth slowly. God, I can still hear the creaking sound the rope made, swinging back and forth, back and forth. I—I reached up to turn him around, to see who it was, and when I did, he—he looked at me with these weird eyes. It took me a minute to realize that he didn't have any eyelids."

"Oh, gross," Jan said, sounding exactly like Beth during her punk-imitation phase.

"His mouth was open, and when he spun around, the rain water that had collected in his mouth kind of spilled out, like drool. It poured over my hand, and, even in the dream, I could feel it, sticky and warm."

Jan shuddered and said, "Sounds like something out of a Bergman movie."

"But why the hell would I dream something like that?" Don asked, easing himself onto his elbows and looking intently at Jan. He wanted to get up and go over to the window for a breath of fresh air, but his legs felt too rubbery to support him.

"I haven't got the faintest idea," Jan said. She snuggled under the covers and closed her eyes. "Was it anyone you recognized?"

Don shook his head. "I don't know for sure. The face looked like he had been hanging there a while. It was kind of rotten. I thought he looked familiar, but I can't place him."

"Well, just try to forget about it. Go back to sleep." She snuggled deeper under the covers and smacked her lips.

"That isn't the worst of it, though," Don said softly.

"I don't want to hear it."

"The guy hanging there, he only had one hand, and I remember thinking in my dream: *How could someone with just one hand tie a hangman's noose to hang himself?*"

III

The night nurse was busy on her rounds, so, after adjusting Beth's i.v. flow and checking the monitors—no change—she had a quick cup of coffee before going to room 41B to check on Mr. Schroder, a cardiac patient. Had she been at Beth's bedside another thirty seconds, she would have noticed a remarkable increase in the spiked lines measuring Beth's theta waves.

The expression on Beth's face remained impassive,

476

the flaccid expression of a comatose patient, but suddenly her eyelids fluttered open. She stared around the room, trying to focus on something, and at last her eyes fixed on the acoustical ceiling tiles.

In terms of Dr. Eldridge's analogy of brain waves being like the weather, Beth was experiencing a force-ten hurricane. The disturbance lasted for just over two minutes. As it subsided, Beth shifted in her bed, closed her eyes, and settled back down to sleep. Her lips moved, and she spoke for the first time in days.

"Varokaa . . . varokaa kivia," she mumbled through parched lips. *"Varokaa kivia!"*

IV

The day dawned bright and beautiful, and, even though the temperature was heading up past seventy before breakfast, the humidity had broken so Mark Herman didn't dread today's haying as much as he had thought he might. At least now, he thought bitterly, it would be only a pain in the ass, not a *royal* pain in the ass! He finished his breakfast and rode with his father in the family combine out to the field.

Once they were ready to start, his father gave him the steering wheel and told him to "get a move on," so Mark rolled up and down the length of the field, glancing now and again at the shadowed figure of his father, sitting in the shade of the tree beside their house.

Mark rumbled deeply in his chest and sent a hayseed-speckled ball of spit sailing in his father's direction. "Useless—useless as tits on a bull," he muttered as he wiped the sweat from his forehead with his shirt sleeve. He smiled to himself for using the same expression his father used so often about him.

As he worked through the sweltering morning, sweat,

grime, and chaff covered his face and hands, but he didn't remove his long-sleeve shirt. Without it, the itch of the hay chaff would drive him crazy. "Crazy as a shit-house rat," Mark said, smiling again at another one of his father's gems of wisdom.

After years of helping his father hay the fields—he was just nine years old the first time his father turned over the steering wheel to him—he instinctively knew the sounds the baler made. And from the sound he heard now, he knew that something, probably some moisture in the hay, was clogging the chute. Of course, he wanted to get the damned job done, too, so he had been trying to pick up two windrows at a time, and he knew he shouldn't have tried that either. That might have had a little something to do with it, too. He dropped the gear into neutral and jumped down and cleared the auger housing before continuing the job.

Glancing up at the house, he saw that his father had gone off somewhere, probably inside for a shot of whiskey, Mark thought. Again he spat, and the glob of saliva landed on the engine housing where it bubbled and danced from the heat of the machine.

The combine rumbled to the far end of the field, and Mark turned around and started back up. He was surprised to see his father back under the tree, and he had been right. From the look of things, his father was taking swigs from a bottle filled with amber liquid.

"What I wouldn't give for a cold beer, myself," he said aloud.

The combine began to make the same loud, whining sound as before, and he knew there was more hay caught in the auger.

Swearing under his breath, Mark slipped the gear into neutral and jumped down again.

"You know," he said, addressing the figure in the shade of the tree, "if you spent half the fucking money you spend on drinking on a decent machine, this wouldn't happen."

His father obviously couldn't hear him over the chattering roar of the machine, but he must have seen that something was wrong. He had gotten up and started across the field toward Mark to see what the problem was.

Mark was leaning over, cleaning the auger blades when his father's voice spoke close behind him.

"How many times do I have to tell yah? Shut the goddamned thing off 'fore you put your hands in there," he snarled.

Mark glared over his shoulder at his father. "If I stopped this sucker, I'd spend the rest of the day tryin' to get it started. You know it don't start up good after it's heated."

"You're one stubborn son-of-a-bitch, you know that?" Frank Herman said to his son.

"I wonder where I got *that* from," Mark said, too softly for his father to hear.

His father reached up to turn the key to *off* but, as he did, his foot slipped. He fell forward and knocked the tractor into gear. The tractor lurched forward, throwing him to the ground, and, as he hit the ground hard enough to knock the wind out of him, he heard a sharp, piercing scream.

Without gas, the tractor soon sputtered to a stop. From the ground, Frank saw Mark twisting away from the machine and crumpling to the ground in a slow spiraling turn. He caught a glimpse of his son's face, and the expression of agony cut him to the quick. Mark was holding his hands close to his chest, and a trailing arc of blood shot out like a fountain.

"Holy shit, *Mark*!" he shouted as he scrambled to

his feet and raced over to the boy. Mark was face down on the ground, whimpering as his legs kicked and thrashed, digging deep divots in the ground.

As he knelt beside his son, a dull hammering filled Frank's chest.

"Fuck! Mark! What happened?" he said, shouting only inches from Mark's ear. The pool of blood seeping out on both sides of Mark told him it was bad—*real* bad!

He gripped Mark's shoulder and tried to roll him over, but the boy was twitching uncontrollably. A low, warbling sound—totally unhuman—came from Mark, but it seemed to be coming, not from his mouth, but from his chest.

Frank wasn't as strong as he used to be, and he finally gave up the effort of trying to roll Mark over. He stared at the side of his son's face, which looked chalky white beneath the grime. Mark's mouth opened and closed repeatedly, reminding Frank of the way a fish gulps out of water. Panic filled Frank Herman as he watched his boy struggle for breath.

"C'mon, boy. Tell me. How bad is it?" he asked, voice trembling. "C'mon, lemme see. Roll over."

Again, he tried to turn Mark over, and it was only with an immense effort that he finally succeeded. Mark's body was shaking violently, his legs jackknifing back and forth, his whole body twisting in pain. When Frank saw the bloody stump where Mark's hand used to be, he knew it all. What he had told the boy a thousand times would happen *had* happened: he'd left the baler in gear and his left hand, shirt sleeve probably, had gotten caught on the finger reel and been pulled into the auger. The auger had neatly sliced the hand off and shot it into the baling chamber.

Eyes bulging, Mark lay on his back, writhing as he

raised the stump of a wrist where his hand used to be. It was still jetting blood in spurts. His eyes rolled up and back, and he slumped into unconsciousness.

Whimpering a mixture of curses and pleas, Frank Herman did the only thing he could think to do; he tore off his shirt and used the sleeve as a tourniquet. His only thought was to save his son's life, not his hand. It never crossed his mind to try to find the hand for possible reattachment.

Frank's bony ribs popped out from beneath his pale skin as he hoisted Mark onto his shoulder and half-carried, half-dragged him toward the house. He had no idea whether Mark was dead or unconscious.

He got the boy up to the back door and then raced inside to call the emergency unit. When the rescue unit drove up, Frank was still bare chested and smeared with blood the color of dried ketchup. He watched helplessly as the volunteers expertly loaded Mark onto a stretcher and into the van. Frank was, himself, in a state of near shock as he got in and rode with Mark to the hospital. The news the paramedic gave him—that Mark was still alive—barely reached his awareness.

Patrick Clifford, Frank's closest neighbor but certainly not on the best terms with him, saw the activity and came into the yard just about the time the ambulance was pulling away. He watched the rescue unit depart, then quickly sized up what had happened. He decided the only neighborly thing to do— no matter how much of a pain-in-the-ass neighbor Frank Herman was—was to help finish the interrupted job so, with the help of his brother, he finished haying the Hermans' field.

Neither one of them realized that Mark's severed hand was still in the baler, and, when the hay bale dropped from the chute onto the ground, neither one

481

of them noticed the small splotch of blood on the hay. That was how Mark Herman's hand got lost, tightly bound into one of the hundreds of bales Frank would later store in the barn for winter feed.

V

A phone call at six-thirty in the morning means only one thing, Don thought as he fumbled for the receiver—trouble: either something's happened to Beth or someone's found Goblin.

" 'ello," he mumbled, smacking his lips and locking eyes with Jan, who was leaning close, trying to hear what was being said on the other end of the line.

"Oh, my God," he said, waking up fast and giving Jan a quick "thumbs up." He listened to the voice on the phone for a few seconds, a smile slowly spreading across his face. He nodded repeatedly, feeling a warmth spread through his body, a warmth that hadn't been there for days. At last, he nodded, said, "good-by," and hung up.

"That was Dr. Eldridge," he said after a dramatic pause, thinking you don't get many moments like this in any one life. "He said Beth's out of danger. She's no longer in *status epilepticus.*"

"Oh, thank heaven!" Jan said, collapsing back onto the bed and smiling widely. Her eyes immediately filled with tears.

"He said she was still very drowsy and pretty confused. You've got to remember, this is the first time she's realized she was in the hospital, and he had to explain a little bit why she was there. But he said the first thing she asked about was us and when could she see us."

They dressed within five minutes and ate toast and drank coffee as they drove to the hospital. For both of them, it was as if an immense, dark cloud had finally passed, and they chatted pleasantly and excitedly the whole way in. Don began to feel—to *really* feel—as though everything had finally turned around; everything was at last going to be all right, and they were going to get their second chance after all.

Their elevated moods dropped only slightly when they got to Beth's room and the nurse on duty told them that Beth was sleeping. They sat and watched her until Dr. Eldridge arrived and explained to them what had happened—that, according to the paper record, during the night Beth's brain-wave pattern had shown a remarkable surge of energy. He apparently liked similes and suggested that it was as though someone had used a car battery to light a flashlight. A short time after that, the night nurse heard Beth muttering, and then she opened her eyes and asked where her mother was.

Jan and Don were both teary-eyed with joy as the doctor filled in the details.

"She looks better—stronger," Jan said, smiling down at the sleeping girl.

"Her color's coming back, too," Don added. His eyes were continually drawn to the spiked wave patterns on the brain monitor. He had to take the doctor's word at face value that the brain activity was different, more normal; it looked as confusing as it always had.

When the nurse took Beth's pulse, Don couldn't help but notice how loosely Beth's arm flopped as if her arm muscles had turned to Silly Putty.

"She's a very lucky girl," Dr. Eldridge said before leaving. "Not too many of us get a second chance after something like this."

The nurse made a few notations on the clipboard at the foot of the bed and then left Jan and Don alone with their daughter. They each took a chair and moved close to the bed, holding hands as they watched Beth. Don kept thinking that Dr. Eldridge was right—they *were* lucky—all three of them were going to get a second chance.

A half-hour later, Beth began to stir, tossing her head from side to side and uttering a low groan. Jan leaned forward and placed her hand on Beth's shoulder, giving her a reassuring squeeze.

But Beth didn't wake up. Not at first. Her movements began to increase in intensity, and her fingers reached out, clawing the bedsheet into tight balls. Beneath the thin covers, her legs started to jolt. Dr. Eldridge's simile of the battery came into Don's mind, and he wondered if, maybe, the power had been turned up again, more than Beth needed or could stand.

"Is she having another fit?" Jan asked, her voice edged with fear. She looked from Beth to Don with wide eyes.

Don shook his head, confused as he studied the jerking motions Beth made. The high hum of the monitors didn't change in frequency, and he found that reassuring, but Beth's body was twitching with the abrupt motions that characterized a seizure.

Another seizure, Don thought as his panic increased, another seizure, and she could slip into a coma—maybe die!

Beth began to make strangled sounds in the back of her throat, and the trembling increased in intensity.

"Get someone," Jan said sharply, her mouth a thin, hard line.

Don dodged into the hallway and flagged a nurse, who came at a brisk trot to the room.

"She just started shaking," Jan said as she stepped aside so the nurse could get close to Beth. She rolled

Beth's eyelids back to check the dilation of the pupils, then made sure the i.v. was secure and stepped back. The tremors began to subside as though by magic.

"Well," the nurse said softly, "it seems to be passing now."

"What was it?" Don asked. "Another seizure?"

The nurse frowned as she glanced at the brain-wave printout. "It may have been, but, judging by this, it was just a muscle spasm."

"Over her whole body?" Don asked, suddenly mistrustful.

"After being in *status epilepticus* for as long as she was, her muscles are responding normally," the nurse said. "Like any other overstrained muscle, they'll contract now and again. It's nature's way of balancing things out. She might have such spasms for several weeks until she gets her full muscle tone back. There was nothing in her brain-wave pattern, at least that I could see, to indicate a seizure."

"Thank God," Jan said, but Don was less convinced. What was the difference between a muscle spasm over Beth's whole body and a seizure?

They all jumped when Beth suddenly spoke. "I want my doll! I want you to bring me my *doll*!" she yelled, her voice sounding raw with disuse.

They all looked at her, but Beth's eyes remained closed. "She's just talking in her sleep," the nurse said as she smoothed the bedsheets and adjusted Beth's head on the pillow.

Beth slept undisturbed, her face pale but relaxed. Dark circles ringed her eyes like smudges of ash. Her breathing was shallow but even, keeping time with the beep-beep of the monitors.

"What she needs more than anything else is rest," the nurse said.

Suddenly, Beth's head jerked to one side. Her eyes

snapped open and locked in a cold, fish-eyed stare onto her father. The tendons in her neck tightened, standing up like subcutaneous pencils as she spoke with great effort.

"Will you bring me my doll?" she said, her voice eerily hollow. *"I want my doll!"*

Don and Jan looked at each other, horrified. Don was almost staggered by a sudden rush of déjà vu— that this had happened before. Anxiety blossomed into stark fear as the déjá vu increased rather than subsided, lifting him up like an overpowering wave.

This has happened before! his mind screamed, and he watched the actions of Jan and the nurse, knowing what they would do before they did it. The nurse went up to Beth, leaning close as she rested her hand on Beth's forehead—

—Yes! He knew she would do that!

Jan stood beside the bed, her hands cupping her chin as she watched helplessly.

Don felt his face drain of blood and color. He moved in seeming slow motion to the foot of the bed, clinging tightly to the metal rail for support, commanding himself not to lose control. This hadn't happened, there was no way he could know that next, Beth would yell—

—*"Varokaa kivia!"* Beth screamed, raising her head from the pillow and making fiery eye contact with her father.

"Jesus Christ," Don said, his voice barely a whimper as he rushed forward and gathered Beth into his arms. She felt like a loose bundle of straw in his embrace except for the coiled energy that seemed to be hammering inside her body, seeking a way out, an escape.

"Take it easy, Pun'kin," he cooed into her ear as he stroked her hair. "Just take it easy."

Beth's mouth opened and closed several times, gulping in air as though it were water and she were drowning. After a few seconds that seemed like forever, she slumped back onto the bed. Don buried his face into the crook of Beth's neck, unable to stop the flood of tears. The two words Beth had spoken rang in his memory like the gong of a distant bell.

"She said that last night, too," the nurse said, sounding confused. "Or something like that. I was at the nurses' station so I didn't her clearly. I wasn't even sure if it was her or someone else. It's not uncommon for someone in her condition to ramble on quite a bit before she regains full consciousness."

Don rose slowly and stepped back, and the nurse readjusted the sheet under Beth's chin. Her eyes were closed, and her face was softened by sleep. Looking at her, Don found it difficult to believe that, seconds before, she had been wide-eyed and had spoken—

—*Varokaa kivia!*

How could she know those words? he wondered frantically.

Don looked at his daughter and was again nearly overwhelmed by the memory of how Aune Kivinen had looked, lying in her hospital bed—her deathbed as it turned out.

Maybe it was that, he thought; maybe it was just the family resemblance that had triggered his déjà vu which, thankfully, had passed. But even admitting that, he found it impossible to figure out how Beth could have known the Finnish words for *"beware the stones!"*

VI

After three more days in the hospital, Beth was showing what Dr. Eldridge called "remarkable" progress. Of course, he also told them it would be months—maybe even a full year—before they could determine conclusively how much, if any, brain damage she had suffered, but he was extremely hopeful.

"Hi yah, Punk'kin. How you feeling?" was Don's standard greeting every morning when he and Jan arrived. Then he would sit beside her bed and rub the back of her hand while Jan fussed around the room, adjusting the shades and arranging the flowers and cards.

"O.K.," Beth answered, her eyelids fluttering. Her throat made a thick, croaking sound, and the missing tongue tip made her voice lisp slightly.

"That's good," Don said. "I'm glad." The glazed yellow tinge to her eyes still bothered him, but he had to admit that she was looking better day by day. "If you keep doing as well as you've been doing, the doctor says you might be able to come home in another week or two."

"Neat," Beth said, but her voice was flat. Hiking herself up onto her elbows, she looked at her mother and said, "Did you bring my doll today?"

Don, expecting the same reaction Jan always gave—telling her they had forgotten it—was surprised when Jan opened her purse and extracted the stiff wooden figure slowly.

Beth's hand shot out, snatching it from her with near-blinding speed. Don sat there, mouth open, surprised that Jan had finally relented. They had talked about it and agreed to leave the thing home until Beth came home. He wondered what had made her change her mind.

The knuckles of Beth's hand whitened as she gripped the wooden figure, clutching it to her side. Her arm muscles tensed, trembling beneath the thin cotton sleeve of the hospital gown.

"Thanks," she said as she settled back onto the pillow. "Thanks a billion."

She held the doll up to her ear and smiled, nodding her head. Don couldn't shake the eerie sensation that she was listening to it talk to her.

"I'll bet you're getting pretty tired of daytime TV," Jan said, laughing. "Aren't all those soap operas garbage?"

Beth shrugged, still clutching the wooden doll. "Maybe you could bring my horse book in. I think I could read—a little, anyway. By the way, how's Goblin?"

Don and Jan exchanged quick glances that crackled like lightning.

"Uh, she's fine—just fine," Don said. The lie tasted sour on the back of his tongue.

"You've been feeding her and brushing her? And keeping her stall clean?" Beth asked.

Don nodded. "Every day," he replied.

Beth sank deeper into the pillow, and her eyes began to lose focus, as though she were dropping off to sleep.

"Well," she said, her voice drifting, "make sure you tell her—tell her—I'm sorry."

Jan and Don looked at each other again.

"Sorry for what?" Jan asked.

Beth's eyes were closed now, and her face was slowly going flaccid. "I don't know. I'm sorry. I guess I dreamed it, but I guess it's all O.K. I sorry, though, 'cause he said it had to be that way."

"What?"

"He said—sorry—we all have to die . . ."

"Who?" Don asked. "Who said that?"

Her statement sent a chilling wave through him. Who had to die?

"I think she's asleep," Jan whispered, rising to tuck

489

the covers under Beth's chin.

Don nodded and looked down at Beth's face. She tossed her head to one side, and, when she spoke, her voice was so muffled that Don wondered if he had actually heard what she had said.

"The man in my dreams," Beth said barely above a whisper. "He said everybody has to die." And then her breathing deepened as she sank deeper into sleep.

VII

One night, after a long vigil in the hospital, as Don and Jan lay on their sweat-soaked bed, the sheets tangled at their feet after an hour of satisfying sex, the sudden ringing of the telephone made them both jump.

"It's almost midnight," Jan said, glancing at the clock. "Who'd be calling this late?"

"I hope it's not the hospital," Don said, grabbing the receiver. "Hello."

"Mr. Inman?" the gravely voice on the phone said. "All Don knew was that it wasn't Dr. Eldridge, and he sighed with relief.

"Yes."

"This here's Frank Herman. Sorry to be callin' yah so late."

"What can I do for you, Mr. Herman?" Don said, nodding to Jan that everything was O.K. Maybe the old man had seen Goblin, he thought. Since the day she had run off, there hadn't been a sign of her, and, with Beth in the hospital, Don had been too busy to do much of anything about it.

"Maybe you could help," Frank Herman said. "It's my son—Mark. He's missin'."

"Missing? What do you mean?"

"You ain't heard what happened out here?" Frank

490

said edgily. "Probably not. Well, we was haying, and my boy lost his hand in the baler."

"His hand?" Don said, and, when he swallowed, it felt to Don as though a small glob of lava was working its way down his throat.

"Yup. His hand," Frank said matter-of-factly. "Clean off. He's been in the hospital for the last several days, but tonight he took off."

"Did you notify the police?" Don asked.

"Course I did. I ain't no fool. Soon's I found out. There's some guys checking 'round the hospital, but I figure he's heading back to home."

The receiver felt slick in Don's hand as he gazed at Jan and then stood up and wandered over the open bedroom window. He looked out at the calm, warm night, the moon coasting behind the distant trees.

"He was purty upset 'bout it all, losin' his hand," Frank continued.

Losin' his hand, Don's mind echoed.

"Doctor told me he wasn't doin' well 'bout it. I figured, maybe if he was headin' home, he might hole up somewhere. You know, stay close to home so's he could see when I left so—I don't know exactly." Frank's voice sounded tired and broken.

"Well," Don said, "I'll certainly keep an eye out for him. I—"

He broke off suddenly when he saw a vague flicker of motion outside. "Just a minute, Mr. Herman," Don said and, turning to Jan, signaled for her to turn off the light.

"What is it?" Frank Herman said. The bedroom plunged into darkness, and it took a few seconds for Don's eyes to adjust.

"I think I just saw someone outside my house, going up to the barn," Don said. He was straining to pierce the shadow cast by the barn.

"Is the downstairs door locked?" Jan asked nervously.

Don nodded. "I think so," he said as he leaned toward the window. He could hear Frank Herman's voice rattling in the phone, sounding like a bumblebee trapped in a Band-Aid box.

"Sorry. I guess it was nothing," Don said, putting the receiver to his ear but keeping his eyes on the yard outside. On the crest of the hill, the open excavation site lined with moonlight gaped like a wound. It hadn't been "nothing," and he knew it, but the last thing he wanted was Frank Herman involved.

"Well I'd 'preciate you callin' me if he shows up," Frank said.

Don was just about to say good-by and hang up when the shadows by the barn shifted. A slouched shape broke away from the side of the barn and dashed across the field. Whoever it was ran with a lurching gait, holding one arm close to his chest. Don's breath caught in his throat when the figure ran directly to the open chamber, and, without pausing, clambered into the night-stained hole.

"I—uh—I have to get going now, Mr. Herman," Don said, fighting to keep his voice steady. He questioned whether he had actually seen someone out there or whether he was so suggestible that he had imagined it because of what Frank Herman had told him.

"I'd 'preciate any help," Frank said and hung up, leaving Don with a buzzing dial tone. Without looking away from the window, Don handed the receiver to Jan, who hung it up.

"I want you to call the police," Don said. "No. Don't turn on the lights! Dial 0 and ask for the police. Tell them to get out here right away. I think we have a prowler."

Jan did what he told her, and all the while Don crouched at the window, not looking away for a moment from the open chamber. Hurriedly, Jan explained to the night dispatcher what was happening and then hung up.

"Come on over here," Don said, edging to the side of the window. "I want you to stay here, keep an eye on the site and let me know if you see anyone run from there. I'm going down to—"

"The hell you are," Jan snapped. "If someone's creeping around out there, I don't want *you* out there!"

"Do what I say," Don commanded, and Jan came over to the window and looked out into the night. Don quickly pulled on his jeans and, bare chested, went downstairs. Moving fast, he went to the kitchen and, leaning over the kitchen sink, looked out at the site. The mounds of earth from his excavating stood out starkly against the star-sprinkled sky.

Opening the cutlery drawer, he selected a long carving knife and gripped it tightly as he opened the kitchen door and stepped outside. If someone was out there, he sure as hell wasn't taking any chances. It might be Mark Herman, it might be someone else, it might be his imagination. Now he only wished he hadn't taken back Earl Remy's shotgun the day after Goblin got away.

A faint squeak on the steps was the only sound as he moved stealthily into the night. The air was soft and moist, but still his nipples stiffened as he walked barefoot across the driveway toward the excavation site. He walked in the shadow of the house as long as possible, glancing up to see Jan indistinct in the bedroom window before staring into the field.

Crouching low, he rounded the garden and cautiously approached the open site. His jeans cuffs were

493

soon soaked with dew as he walked closer to the black maw of the site. He had a brief, dreamlike sensation of being immobile as the black opening slid noiselessly across the ground toward him. He had to fight back the unnerving thought that the chamber would suddenly slide under his feet, and he would fall—fall down into a darkness darker than the night.

He was climbing slowly up the mound of dirt and just about to step onto the table stone when a flash of light swept across the field. He turned and saw a police cruiser jostling up the driveway. The cruiser's spinning blue lights created a weird strobe effect, reminding him of lightning flashes.

The cruiser stopped in a swirl of dust, and a door opened and shut. Flashlight beams sliced the night as two policemen walked toward him. Jan had obviously decided that it was all right to leave her post because the backyard floodlight came on. She stayed inside, though, obviously preferring to let the police handle the situation.

"You're Don Inman? Your wife called?" one of the policemen said as he approached the site. Don couldn't remember whether or not this man had been out to the house the night Billy Blackshoe died.

The glare of his flashlight blinded Don. He shielded his eyes and nodded.

"My name's Officer Lambert," the policeman said. "This is Patrolman Wallis. What seems to be the problem? She said something about a prowler."

Don was about to answer when he heard something that made him freeze. It was a familiar sound—a scuttling, scratching sound that seemed to be coming from the open chamber.

"In there," Don said, his voice wire tight as he pointed down into the opening. "I saw someone outside, by the barn, and then he ran over and

494

jumped in here."

He was pointing with the broad blade of the carving knife, and he suddenly realized how strange he must have looked: a half-naked man wielding a turkey carving knife from atop a pile of dirt. Great first impression!

Don was trying to ignore the scratching sound coming from the chamber. "I think someone's down there," he repeated.

Officer Lambert looked at him askance, then he jumped nimbly onto the table stone and directed his flashlight beam into the opening. Quickly he scanned the stone wall and hard-packed dirt floor.

"Well, there's no one in there now," he said, looking at Don with an expression that suggested he suspected this was all some strange practical joke.

"He was," Don said, finally finding enough nerve to step over onto the table stone with the policeman. "I saw him go in there, and, just when you drove up, I think I heard him inside. Maybe he went down into that tunnel down there."

Lambert looked into the chamber again, studying the tunnel opening Don had found before.

"He might have gone down there, but he'd have to be pretty damned desperate." He sniffed and drew back suddenly. "What *is* this place?" he said, crouching. "It smells like an open sewer."

The circular beam of light darted around inside the chamber, and Don drew close to have a look. The walls and floor appeared to be dry, but there was a ripe, moist smell that repulsed Don. The air down there seemed somehow denser, almost liquid as it subtly distorted the stone texture of the walls.

"Do you have any idea where that tunnel leads?" Lambert asked. There was still a note of skepticism in his voice as though he was waiting for the punch line.

Don shook his head. "I just discovered it a week or two ago. I haven't been down inside it."

"I wouldn't, either," Lambert said, shaking his head. "But there's no one in there now. Are you sure you saw someone?"

"I was positive," Don said, scratching his head. He quickly reviewed the sequence of events in his mind. What struck him as most odd was the way the person had run. It had been as if he was clenching his hand to his chest because he was in pain, and he had run with an odd motion of being off balance.

"Have you had trouble with prowlers before to-night?" Lambert asked. The other policeman had already gone back to the cruiser, and Don could hear the static of the radio as he reported back to the station.

Don and Lambert took several minutes to look around the site. A quick check of the dew-laden grass revealed only Don's and the two officers' footprints. As they walked back toward the driveway, Don knew the patrolmen had already written off the incident.

Not wanting to appear the complete fool, Don suggested that it might have been Mark Herman."

"Why him?" Lambert asked. He swung open the cruiser door and sat behind the wheel. He snapped off the revolving blue lights, to Don's relief.

"He lost his hand in a farming accident," Don said, "and I heard he was missing from the hospital."

"I know that," Lambert said, obviously getting irritated at Don.

"Maybe it was him, sneaking home or looking to hide out in my hayloft for a while."

"And then jumping down into that open chamber instead?" Lambert asked, shaking his head. "Look, Mr. Inman, may I suggest that what you saw was maybe an animal or a cloud going by the moon?

There's nobody down in that hole now, and we've been the only ones out there tonight. There weren't any other footprints. Head on back to bed."

He started the cruiser up but, before shutting the door, he added, "But if you *do* see someone—Mark Herman or anyone—don't hesitate to call us, O.K.?"

Don nodded. "O.K."

The policemen drove off, and Don went back to the house, making sure that both doors were locked. But, after he and Jan had settled back into bed, sleep didn't come. The image of a crouching runner played in his mind, darting back and forth, shifting, and suddenly jumping forward, face leering close, but the image was never clear enough for Don to see who it was.

VIII

Beth continued to improve rapidly, and Don and Jan spent the good part of every day at her bedside. She still looked pale and weak, but the muscle spasms had stopped, and the medication seemed to have the epilepsy under control. Dr. Eldridge expressed hope that the full extent of damage might be no more than a slight speech deficiency. With a solid P.T. program, she would quickly regain full motor control.

One evening when they got home from the hospital just before dark, they found a book propped up against the screen door. Two pieces of paper were folded in half and stuck inside.

"*Indian Earth Magic*," Jan said, reading the title over Don's shoulder. "Who would leave something like that for us? What does the note say?"

Don unfolded one of the sheets and read aloud, "Remember your promise. My brother was apparently reading this book the day before he died, and this sketch was inside, marking page one hundred and eight. Does it mean anything to you? Best wishes, Margaret."

"Margaret, huh?" Jan said with raised eyebrows. "And who might *she* be? And what's this about a promise?"

"She's Billy's sister," Don said. He unlocked the door and stepped into the kitchen, snapping on the light. He sat down at the kitchen table and spread the other piece of paper open, immediately recognizing a rough sketch of their property.

"What promise, though?" Jan said teasingly. "You and she didn't have a little thing going on the side, did you?"

"Of course not!" Don shouted, glaring at her. He shook his head and sat back, massaging his temples with his fingertips. At least, already, they could almost joke about what had happened between her and Dale—*almost*.

Jan backed off, waving her hands in the air. "O.K., O.K. Sorry," she said. "How about a cup of tea before bed?"

Don nodded absently as he studied Billy's sketchy map.

"Seriously, though," Jan said as she ran water to fill the teakettle, "what promise is she talking about?"

Don sighed, knowing before he said it what her reaction would be. "At Billy's funeral, she told me Billy had mentioned to her the digging we were doing in the field." He hitched his thumb in the direction of the window. "She—she made me promise that I'd find out what was in the chamber that had Billy so interested." He stopped himself short before he told her about the dream he had had of Billy's ghost, streaming blood and swinging a bullroarer.

"And—?" Jan said.

Don shrugged. "She seemed to think that it was her brother's curiosity about the chamber that caused his death and that—that he won't rest easy until I, or someone, can find out what's down there."

Don was grateful when the sudden, shrill whistle of the teakettle interrupted them. Jan was silent as she dropped tea bags into their cups and poured the water. She carried the two cups over to the table and sat down across from Don.

"Can't you just let it go?" she asked. "That—that *thing* out there gives me the creeps whenever I think about it. God"—she hugged herself and shivered— "when I just *think* about that hand we found." She took a sip of tea. "Anyway, that professor told you not to disturb the site, and look what happened when you did. Nothing's going to be of any good to Billy now."

Don nodded agreement. "I know I should just wait until the university people can come back, but . . ." He looked down at the book and the note from Margaret. "I don't know," he ended weakly.

They sat and drank their tea together and then went into the living room to watch some TV. Jan picked up some knitting—a sweater she had been working on for over six months now. Don had *Indian Earth Magic* and the notes from Margaret with him.

Settling back into his chair, Don opened and scanned the sheet with the roughly drawn map of his property. Billy had included things in the drawing that Don knew weren't out there.

In the middle of the field, just about where they had discovered the table stone and chamber, Billy had drawn a rough circle. At various points along the circle, he had marked X's. Radiating from the center of the table stone were several lines, running off the paper in all directions. One line, marked "summer solstice sunrise," ran from the table stone to the foot of the driveway. The stone post at the entrance had been marked "sunrise menhir."

Don was absorbed in his study of Billy's map, but he kept glancing at Jan to make sure she hadn't noticed what he was doing. He felt as guilty as a ten year old leafing through a copy of *Playboy*.

The line that marked the stone at the foot of the driveway continued off the sheet in the other direction, too. Billy had drawn a question mark at the opposite end with the words "summer solstice sunset."

The more he looked at the map, the more Don saw that, at least according to Billy's markings, the stones in his field took a configuration similar to Stonehenge. Of course, he knew there were no stones out there. But what if—what if the stones *were* there, buried beneath the surface?

A tingle of excitement ran through him as he picked up *Indian Earth Magic* and began reading the page Billy had marked.

"Goddamn," he muttered. When he had finished the page, he let out a slow breath and slouched back into his chair.

"Huh?" Jan said, barely distracted from the show she was watching.

"This book," Don said, thumping the cover with his index finger. "I can't believe what I just read."

Jan didn't look away from the TV, but her face expressed her exasperation. "I thought you said you were going to let it drop."

Don shook his head. "No, *you* said I was going to let it drop. I didn't. But listen to this—

" 'Professor Forstchen of Columbia University has even gone so far as to propose a Native American "Cult of the Dead," which may have practiced animal and possibly human sacrifice in association with burial grounds and other sacred places. The suggestion that the carved stone at Mystery Hill, in New Hampshire, was used for such sacrifices becomes more acceptable when considered in the light of other recent discoveries of stone structures bearing a remarkable resemblance to Celtic and Paleolithic stone structures in Europe. These—' "

"I'm really not interested," Jan said, letting her knitting drop into her lap and leveling a long, hard stare at Don.

"Just listen to this, and then I won't bug you with it any more, O.K.?"

Jan nodded but still wore a sour expression.

" 'These circles of standing stones have long been thought to have some connection with primitive astronomical observation, where their major axes indicate the rising and setting points of the summer and winter solstices.' "

Don looked at Jan, then held out to her the map Billy had drawn.

"Take a look at this, and then tell me what you think."

Jan took the briefest of glances at the paper, then handed it back to him without comment.

"Well," Don said, "he goes on about the stones being used for sighting the sunrise and sunset. The single standing stones are called 'menhirs.' Billy—or maybe it was Prof. Mitchell—one of them said that the stone at the end of the driveway was a menhir, and listen: 'Many people who are physically sensitive have reported an amazing variety of effects associated with menhirs—in Europe, called "tingle stones"—including anything ranging from mild dizziness and nausea to extreme physical reactions, such as fainting spells and seizures.' "

Jan stared at him but said nothing.

"Remember the day we came here? When we drove

into the driveway?"

Jan nodded, but her face was twisting with the effort not to admit to herself what she was thinking.

"As soon as we drove past that gatepost, Beth started choking on her vomit. Why didn't she get carsick earlier?"

"She did," Jan said softly, "right after we got on the road that morning."

"But she was fine the whole rest of the drive to Maine until we drove past that menhir," Don said emphatically. "So what if that stone was what triggered her getting sick?"

"I think you're letting your imagination get carried away with you," Jan said. She put her knitting aside, stood, and stretched her arms over her head. "I'm beat. I think I'm going to hit the sack. You coming to bed?"

Don sat in his chair, pondering the open book in his lap. "I'll bet that stone does line up with the sunrise," he said, more to himself than to Jan. "If Billy was right, and that stone *is* a menhir, then why not? Why *couldn't* it have triggered her reaction? Think about it for a minute. Hasn't Beth seemed different—really different—since we moved here?"

Jan shook her head and snickered. "Come on, Don," she said, "you're being ridiculous. She's been different, yes, but I think it might have more to do with growing up and moving away from her friends than it does with a stone gatepost."

"She's been diagnosed by experts," Don said. "She has epilepsy. They don't know why—because of body chemistry or brain damage or hormones or whatever. But if she was somehow tuned in to the energy of the menhir and the stone circle in the field, then— maybe . . ."

"You're really getting too carried away with all

this," Jan said, her voice shaking nervously.

"I'm going down there to take a look at it," Don said.

"Don't be ridiculous," Jan said. "It's almost midnight. Come on upstairs with me; I'll—"

Don shook his head, cutting her off. "It'll only take a minute. I want to have a look around." Before Jan could say anything else—even "good night"—he went out to the kitchen, got a flashlight, and went outside.

The night was filled with the heated buzzing of crickets, and there was just a hint of the autumn to come on the gentle night breeze that whispered like a snake through the grass. Keeping the oval of light just ahead of his feet, Don walked down the driveway toward the leaning stone post. He stopped about ten feet from the stone beneath the overhanging oak tree.

"Gatepost," he whispered, looking at the tall stone pillar. He wondered now why he had never noticed before how much it *didn't* look like a gatepost. It stood at least eight feet tall and was much thicker than a gatepost had to be. And there were no holes in it for the rails. The rounded, weathered knob at the top made it look thinner at the base.

Don ran his beam of light up and down the stone several times. He had the feeling that he had seen that exact same shape some place else—not just at the foot of the driveway, but—somewhere . . . But the memory was vague and shadowy, as though from a dream, and he dismissed it.

He approached the stone cautiously, tensed and expecting *something*—he didn't know what—to happen. If a bleached face were to suddenly loom out from behind the stone, skull face grinning, he felt he was ready. But it wasn't that; it was the mere presence of the stone itself that unnerved him, filling him with a dark, fathomless dread. He began to think that Jan

503

had been right: he was letting his imagination carry him away, and he was getting much too worked up about this nonsense.

"But if it *isn't* nonsense," he said softly, and his voice fluttered on the breeze. "It's got to be connected—somehow."

He studied the strangely cut stone for several minutes, and he felt as though he was really seeing it for the first time. Had anyone asked him before now what color the stone was, he would have said it was "just gray—like any piece of granite." But now he saw that the stone was swirled with subtle shades and, at least under the beam of the flashlight, it appeared to have a reddish tinge just below the surface—as though it had rusted over the years.

He was angry at the way his hand shook as he reached out slowly to touch the stone. He realized that he never had touched it, not since the day they had moved into the house. His fingertips brushed the cool, gritty surface, and he wasn't sure if he was relieved or upset that *nothing* happened as soon as he made contact.

No arcing flash of electricity.

No vibrating energy.

The only tingling he felt was in his own overexcited nerves. This was just a plain old piece of rock!

The rational part of his mind told him that it was foolish to think that stone circles and menhirs could have any effect on people, could channel and focus some vague, cosmic energy, just as the carved channel in the table stone was supposed to direct the flow of sacrificial blood.

It was bullshit! Pure and simple! he thought. The same nonsense Billy believed in that had earned him the nickname "Wingnut."

Don backed away from the stone and was thinking

of heading up to the house when an idea struck him. He approached the stone again, this time kneeling down and probing the ground where the stone was planted. Scooping away the turf, he dug down a few inches along the side of the stone until his fingers felt something—an indentation in the stone. Shining his light down, he gasped when he saw a spiral design carved into the side of the stone.

Sitting back on his heels, he let out a low, slow breath. "The spiral serpent!" he whispered, resisting the shiver that danced between his shoulder blades. Any doubts he might have had about a connection between this stone—this *menhir*—and the excavated table stone were now entirely gone.

He knew, even before he dug deeper, what he would find just below that design, and, with an energy bordering on frenzy, he started clawing the earth away from the base of the stone. Sure enough, down just a bit further, he uncovered another design—a wavy-line pattern.

"The uncoiled serpent," he said, and in his memory he heard Billy's voice saying: *The spiral is the serpent, coiled. The waves are the serpent, uncoiled.*

The dull apprehension he had sensed all night suddenly exploded in his chest. He grabbed the flashlight and scanned around him, certain that he was being watched. Somewhere in the night, eyes were watching him.

The night sounds seemed to intensify, and he was acutely aware of the hollow, rasping sound his breathing made. He looked all around and saw that he was alone, but, even as his initial fear subsided, he couldn't shake the feeling that out there, in the dark, someone—some*thing*—was watching. . . .

He tried to force himself to calm down, but the feeling wouldn't go away. The hairs on the nape of his neck danced as though electrified. Then, when the night breeze stirred the leaves of the oak overhead, he felt the presence lurking in the shadows of the tree above him!

Gripping the flashlight like the hilt of a sword, Don swung around and lanced the beam up into the branches. He was praying fervently that there would be nothing—no ambiguous shadow—*Please! Nothing!*

The oak leaves shuffled with a thick, leathery sound, and the shadows from his flashlight weaved and swayed. Of course, the tree was empty. Nothing— no one—was up there. But then . . . there, up on one of the uppermost branches, what was that? It seemed as though one of the patches of shadow was darker than the rest; it seemed to absorb the light.

Don moved to one side, straining to get a better view, but, as he moved, the darker-than-night shadow shifted as well. He was almost convinced that it was a piece of the night sky, but somehow this shadow seemed thicker, blacker, and Don sensed—or *thought* he sensed—a hateful weight pressing down on him from the tree.

The longer he looked, the more he became convinced that the shadow had taken on a human shape crouching in the branches. For a flickering moment, Don even thought he saw baleful green eyes, glaring down at him.

Keeping his eyes riveted upward, Don started to make his way to the driveway. He scrunched down, picked up a rock, cocked his arm back, and let it fly straight for the shadow. The rock whipped through the leaves, and Don waited, tensed, until he heard the stone plunk down on the grass. The peaceful sounds of the night were suddenly broken by a low, grumbling laugh.

Panic-stricken, Don turned and ran as fast as he

could toward the house. As he ran, fists clenched and arms moving like pistons, he fully expected to feel some clawed and vicious thing attach itself to his back and drag him down. He didn't dare glance over his shoulder—what if he tripped and fell?

He didn't slacken his pace until he made it to the doorstep. Then he drew to a stop and looked back down the driveway. There was nothing down there—nothing but the night, black and peaceful, filled with the night song of crickets and the breeze rustling in the grass.

Chapter Fifteen

Tunnels

I

At breakfast the next morning, Don thought Jan looked *too* drained—*too* run-down. He wondered if, perhaps, the tranquilizers Dr. Eldridge had prescribed for her were too potent, but he didn't say anything. It was probably him and the scare he had had last night down by the menhir—not her.

"You never told me what you found down there," Jan said as though reading his mind. She was buttering toast, and the knife was making rough, scraping sounds.

Don sipped his juice. The sourness made the hinges of his jaw sting. He tried to push aside the mental image of the black shape he had seen in the oak branches—"the watcher," as he had begun to think of it. He was pretty much convinced it had been his imagination, but still . . .

"You were sound asleep when I came in," he said. "Besides, I didn't think you were interested."

"I'm not," Jan said, and she sat down to eat. "Come on, let's get a move on so we can get to the hospital."

Looking nervously to one side, Don cleared his head. "Ahh. No. I was thinking I'd stay home today and get some work done." He took another sip of juice, swallowing with difficulty.

Jan sat back in her chair and regarded him silently for several seconds. "I know what you're thinking," she said, suddenly sitting forward. "You're planning on going down into that chamber, aren't you?"

Don considered a lie but then thought better of it. "I thought I—uhh—I might. Who knows? There might be a cache of gold and jewelry down there."

Jan shook her head and took a bite of toast. Her silence was worse than any accusation she could have made.

"Hey. Come on," Don said. "I don't have to be there in the hospital *every* day, for crying out loud. Beth's doing really well, and I'm—I'm curious as hell as to what might be there." He knew how silly he sounded, pleading with her like this.

Jan finished her toast with three bites, then stood, and went to the sink to rinse the crumbs from her plate. Turning back to face Don, she said nothing as she slowly wiped her hands on a dishtowel.

"Look, Jan. I have this—this feeling there's something down there—something *really* important. And as crazy as it sounds, I think it's all connected."

"What's all connected?" Jan asked, barely disguising the sarcasm in her voice.

"I know it sounds crazy," Don said, clenching his fists and shaking them. "But Billy was sure there was something out there. Some kind of energy he said he'd never felt before. I think what happened to Billy, and to Beth, and to Goblin, Aune's 'dream book'—a lot of the weird things that have been going on around here—have something to do with what's buried out there, and I want to get to the bottom of it."

"You have those people from the university who want to check the place out. Why not leave it at that?" Jan asked.

"Because—" Don said, and was unable to continue.

"That chamber—or whatever it is—has become an obsession with you. It's like something's got a hold on you, and you can't get away from it."

Don shivered when he pictured the mummified hand they had found; the blackened fingers slowly stretched, reaching for him in his imagination.

"It's that chamber," Don said weakly. "I feel like I owe it to Billy, and I have to find out what's down there, where that tunnel leads. Have you ever looked down in there?"

Jan shook her head. "No! And I don't intend to, either! I'm going to get dressed, and you should, too, if you're coming with me to see Beth."

Don shook his head. "I need a break from that damned hospital," he said.

Jan scowled. "Not as much as Beth does," she said before turning and going upstairs. Don took a flashlight from the cupboard and went out to the barn to get a shovel and pickax. He wasn't sure if he'd need them—or even if he'd be able to use them in the tunnel—but he wanted them on hand just in case. He waved to Jan as she got into the car and drove off. She gave him a quick little toot on the horn as she swung off the driveway and onto the road.

II

At the excavation site, Don paused and stared at the brick-red stain of Billy's blood on the side of the chamber. He considered washing it off, but somehow

510

that didn't seem right; it was as if he needed it there to spur him on. Besides, he thought, the next rain will take care of it.

He leaned into the opening, scanning it with his light first, and then dropped the shovel and pickax inside. He boosted himself up onto the edge of the triangular opening and lowered himself into the chamber.

A wave of dizziness tugged at him as he looked around at the stone walls. He attributed it to his excitement, but he couldn't deny the vague sense of uneasiness the thick stone walls gave him. The memory of someone—a crouching shadow—lurching across the field and jumping down into the opening only increased his tension.

He leaned the shovel and pickax against the stone wall and studied the tunnel opening. In spite of the uneasiness he felt, he knew he would follow that tunnel if he could. It looked as though he could fit in it by crawling on his hands and knees.

If this was, in fact, an ancient Indian grave, why was there an underground tunnel leading to it? Maybe it was a "speaking tube," as they were called in *Indian Earth Magic*—long, narrow tunnels used to magnify and echo the tribal priest's voice. Nothing like the old "voice out of the grave" to keep everyone nervous—and in line.

Another suggestion for the tunnel he had found in his reading was that it was somehow symbolic, a physical representation of the link between the grave and the underworld.

What had Mitchell said? Don thought. That this certainly raises more questions than it answers. Life was sometimes like that.

"The only way to find out," he said as he leaned over the opening of the tunnel, "is to go down in there and see." He held the flashlight in one hand and the shovel in the other. Taking a deep breath, grateful that the rotten stench had diminished somewhat, he started crawling into the opening.

The tunnel was narrow and ran straight back as far as he could see. The floor was hard-packed dirt, and the walls were constructed of closely fitted stones, with larger stones—some looking almost as large as the table stone—forming the ceiling. Their solidness helped relieve the tightening claustrophobia he felt from the darkness ahead and behind him. The flashlight beam seemed much too feeble.

His back brushed against the roof as he crawled along, and now and again the tunnel was so small he scraped his back hard enough to hurt. It strained his neck to keep looking ahead, so he kept his head down most of the time. Small rock and dirt slides that had sifted between the gaps in the stones clogged the passageway, but so far he didn't need the shovel to clear the way. Just as well, he thought, because in these cramped quarters he couldn't wield the tool very easily, anyway.

The air had a curious dryness to it—surprisingly so considering the moldy, rotten smell that had dominated the chamber until it had had a chance to air out. Even his smallest motions sent powdery dust swirling up in the cone of his flashlight beam. The overall impression he had of the tunnel was of brittleness and age—like desiccated bone.

He moved forward slowly, cautiously. It was difficult to estimate distance in such tight surroundings. Whenever he came to something blocking his way, he moved as little dirt and as few stones as he had to to get by. He certainly didn't want to take the chance of causing a dirt slide that could trap him.

The tunnel went straight back, and it took him

more than an hour to cover probably forty or fifty feet. Sweat broke out on his forehead, and he could already hear himself saying to Jan tonight, "Honey, get the Doan's."

At times, waves of claustrophobia swept over him, and it was only with incredible effort that he resisted the panicky feeling that there was someone or *something* ahead—maybe behind, just out of the reach of his light. He continually looked back, hoping there would be a place up ahead where he could turn around before heading back. He certainly didn't relish the idea of crawling backward the whole way; and now that he was so far in, he felt stupid for not having thought of that sooner.

The exertion of crawling down the tunnel and the swirling dust coating his throat made Don wish he had also thought ahead enough to bring something to drink. He was beginning to despair about the whole venture when, up ahead, he saw that the tunnel either ended or turned. He forged ahead, promising himself a cold beer when he finally got out of here.

It proved to be a turn in the tunnel, and, as Don rounded the corner, he was surprised and glad to see the ceiling was much higher—high enough, in fact, for him to stand up in a crouch and stretch his legs a bit. It helped—some—to relieve the ache of knotting muscles.

Another thing he forgot, he realized with some agitation, was a compass so he could estimate which direction the tunnel ran. The first stretch aimed obliquely toward the driveway, he thought; so now this turn must be headed toward the barn. In truth he was completely disoriented.

Glancing at his watch, he saw that it was already almost noon. He had been underground for nearly two hours, but it felt much shorter. It reminded him of how time had seemed somehow to compress the day he chased Goblin in Whippoorwill Swamp. But what surprised him was how much he had adjusted to the confinement of being underground. There was actually a measure of peace down here—something far removed from the idea of crawling into an open grave. A sense of adventure dominated any traces of uneasiness and claustrophobia, but he couldn't resist the fearful thought that it might be the result of breathing the thin air of the tunnel.

What if there were some poisonous underground gases seeping into the tunnel, he thought with a sudden flood of fear, but he pushed that thought aside as foolish.

"I'll bring a friggin' canary next time," he muttered as he sat back and stretched as best he could.

The construction of the tunnel for its whole length so far seemed to be the same—flat stone walls, dirt floor, and overlying stone slabs for the ceiling. Nowhere had he seen any carvings, much less Indian relics or bones. Dirt had funneled through numerous crannies between rocks, leaving hourglass designs on the floor that had been that way for—how long? he wondered. The sands of time. He hated disturbing them as he passed.

Don stretched his aching arms and legs as he considered whether he should head back now or push to the end. Jan wouldn't be home for at least another three hours—more, if she was angry at him for not going with her. Finally, he decided to follow the tunnel just a bit more before giving up for the day.

"So far, no treasure," he muttered, and then laughed softly. His voice, sounding distorted and faint, echoed in the tunnel. For a moment, he again had the sensation that he wasn't alone, but he passed it off as he started forward again.

Although the tunnel had widened at the turn, the ceiling again sloped down along the straight tunnel. Don was back on his hands and knees, pushing ahead with the bobbing light of his flashlight the only guide he had. Knowing he would at most only have to crawl backward to the turn made him feel a bit better about continuing.

His breath came in drier gulps, and its raspy echo took on a steady pattern that forced a rhythm to his movements. Occasionally he spoke his thoughts aloud, but the close echo took on an almost physical presence, so he stopped doing that. He began to wonder if the isolation and quiet were getting to him. When he came to a place where a particularly large boulder had shifted and now blocked the passageway, he started laughing as he pushed it out of his way.

The sound of his labored breathing filled the tunnel, but at one point he thought he heard something else—another sound from behind. He stopped and, leaning against the cool stone wall, listened tensely. The sound had been soft and husky—like laughter from behind a masking hand. But he at last dismissed it as dirt, long undisturbed, shifting in the darkness, the sound magnified by the tunnel.

From the turn in the corridor, he guessed he had gone another fifty feet or so when up ahead his flashlight beam illuminated a solid wall of stone blocking the way. Panting and sweating, he scrambled forward, thinking it might be another turn in the tunnel, but as he got closer he saw that it wasn't. The tunnel was sealed off!

"Just dandy!" he muttered, wiping his forehead on his sleeve. He played the circle of light over the blocking wall, hoping to find at least a crack where he could see beyond, but at last he had to admit that he had come to a dead end. The answer he had been looking for was that the tunnel went—*nowhere*!

The construction of the blocking wall looked exactly like the rest of the tunnel, so he was sure that whoever had built the tunnel had also blocked it off. But the thought that *something* lay beyond the wall nagged at him. He couldn't admit that this was the end of his exploration, and that the earth just might keep her buried secrets after all. That was too pat an answer.

Keeping his beam of light on the blocking wall, Don crawled up close and ran his fingers over the stones and into the joints between the stones. A fine grit covered everything, and, as he brushed the stones, his fingertips made soft, whispering sounds. The chalky dryness in his throat was getting worse, and he began to cough deeply in his chest.

Of all the stonework he had seen in the tunnel, this blocking wall seemed to be the most carefully done. The assorted sizes of stones fit together with the snugness of a jigsaw puzzle. And that was exactly how Don was beginning to think of this whole thing—as a jigsaw puzzle—with no solution.

He had his face close to the wall and was probing the stonework when the flashlight suddenly dimmed, glowing with a mellow orange—the orange of a humid day's sunset. At first mistrusting his eyes, Don looked back down the tunnel; then the truth of the situation hit him. The batteries in the flashlight were failing!

"Oh, damn!" he groaned. He shook the light, glancing fearfully at the tunnel behind him. The dark tube seemed to telescope, the blackness rushing toward him. "Come on. Come on," he grumbled, shaking the flashlight, but it was as though someone were slowly turning down a dimmer switch. The light faded down—down.

Don almost choked on his panic when he looked at

the bulb and watched the small coil inside glow fainter and fainter. . . .

And then it was gone.

The blackness of the tunnel swallowed him whole, and he was left with just the rapid sound of his breathing. By his best estimate, he had more than a hundred feet to crawl along to get back to the chamber and daylight. Like a stone-lined throat, the tunnel closed in on him until it felt as close as an extra layer of skin.

"Don't freak!" he cautioned himself aloud. "Just don't freak out!"

His voice sounded small and terrifyingly close in the thick darkness, yet it came back to him along the tunnel with a disorienting echo. He gripped the floor, resisting the rush of vertigo that made him feel as though he were floating in space, tumbling blindly backward.

He felt around for the way back, but somehow he had gotten turned around in the dark. He crawled forward and smashed his head against the blocking wall—at least he *thought* it was the blocking wall. He waved his hands in front of himself, and the flashlight hit a stone. He heard the lens break and glass tinkle to the floor.

"Just don't panic!" he whispered as he foundered around, feeling for the way back.

The tunnel threw back his words—"Panic— panic—panic."

At last he got his bearings and started crawling. He had no way of knowing how far he had gone, but he hadn't made it to the first turn by the time the voices started. At first he was convinced that he was imagining them—soft, corn-husk-dry mutterings, coming from both in front of him and behind him in the darkness. But when he stopped and listened, his body wire-taut, they didn't stop. They got louder!

Voices chattering like bats in the night were all around him, whispering, cursing him, taunting him in a language he didn't understand.

"No! *No!*" he shouted, pressing his fist hard against his face. His bladder wanted to explode from the pressure, and the hammering of his pulse in his ears nearly drowned out the voices. Nearly, but not quite. He could still hear them, all around in the dark.

It's a dream! his mind screamed frantically. This can't be real! *It's a goddamned dream!*

A soft drumming sound ran like a countercurrent beneath the voices, keeping the time with his raging heartbeat. Louder! Louder! The steady thump-thump of drums—heartbeats!—hoofbeats!

A sour taste flooded Don's mouth as he forced himself to break the immobility imposed by his fear. With a low whimper in his throat, he started to crawl again, trying to convince himself it was all a hallucination—an illusion of the darkness and the closeness of the tunnel.

Sensory deprivation! That's what it had to be! *Those voices and those drumbeats can't be real!*

Each time his panic threatened to overwhelm him, he held it in check by convincing himself that's what it was—just an illusion! He concentrated his mind on one thought: *Get the hell out of this tunnel!*

He couldn't see where he was going, and he kept careening off the stone walls as he scrambled down the tunnel. As he moved, the voices sounded as though they were definitely behind him now, receding into the black well he had left back there. He thought he could pick out certain sounds—words being repeated—but they were certainly no words he could understand.

In the darkness, he didn't see the turn in the

tunnel, so when he got to it, he went headlong into the wall, hitting his head with such force he saw tracer-bullet stars skim his vision. When he touched his forehead, his fingers came away sticky with blood.

If it were at all possible, the darkness of the tunnel grew even darker once he started down what he knew was the last half of the tunnel. The sounds were clearer—voices cursing, drumbeats thumping, heartbeats pounding, hooves beating. He scrambled frantically along the tunnel, unmindful of the cuts and scrapes on his hands and knees.

He knew it couldn't be far, now, to the chamber. It had to be just ahead. He was filled with the sudden fear that the tunnel had branches he hadn't noticed on his way in and, now in his effort to escape, he had missed the way out and would be trapped down here in the darkness forever!

Forever!

With the grating voices and drumbeats!

Hoofbeats!

But then the voices suddenly stopped, and the abruptness of their departure left Don's ears ringing in the silence. That seemed further proof to him that it hadn't been his imagination; that it *had* been real!

All he heard now was the steady hammering of his pulse, and, although he still wanted desperately to get out into the fresh air and open sky, there was a measure of relief that the voices no longer whispered to him in their strange language.

Taking a deep breath of dusty air, he crawled the rest of the way to the chamber with a calm determination. Even before he saw the diffused gray light up ahead—daylight!—his mind was busy convincing himself that it had, after all, been his imagination. What else could it have been?

"How could there be anything alive down here?" he

519

said aloud, and the natural, normal sound of his voice reassured him almost as much as the light he could see up ahead.

No voices! No drums! No hoofbeats!

When he saw the square opening of the tunnel clearly up ahead, he knew he was going to make it. His fear—nothing more than his fear of being trapped underground without a light, he told himself—peeled away like dried snakeskin.

He crawled through the tunnel mouth and collapsed in the relative openness of the chamber. He never would have thought he would have been so happy to be there again. Sitting up, leaning his back against the wall, he began to laugh, low and deep.

A shiver ran through him when he looked back at the tunnel, the dark maw yawning open like a mouth, pulling him toward it. Again the dizzy disorientation swept over him, and he had the momentary sensation that he was looking straight down into a well. He quickly looked up at the triangular opening, grateful to see the sky once again.

His breathing was ragged, rattling in his throat as he stood and stretched his arms freely over his head. He realized how much he had feared he would never be able to do that again. Sweat and blood mingled as they dripped from his forehead to the floor, leaving black dime-sized drops. As he brushed himself off, he thought he heard a sound—a soft, leathery laugh—but he convinced himself it was nothing more than the rustling of his clothes.

He realized that he had left his shovel back in the tunnel, by the blocking wall, but the last thing he intended to do was to go back for it. He figured the flashlight was no good anymore, so he left that in the chamber next to the pickax. Taking a deep breath, he swung his arms back and was just going to jump up to grab the edge of the chamber when a face loomed up over the opening, blocking out the sky.

With a loud shout, Don fell down and made a grab for the pickax.

"Christ! Don! What are you doing?" Jan asked, looking down at him through the opening. "You scared the crap out of me!"

Don looked up at her and forced a weak laugh. "Me? *I* scared of *you*?"

III

"You look like you've been through a war or something," Jan said later that afternoon as she daubed peroxide onto Don's numerous cuts and scrapes.

"It's close—ahh! That hurts! It's close quarters down there." He was leaning over the kitchen sink, staring out over the field while Jan worked on his back. The mellow, slanting sunlight was reassuring after spending so much time in the dark tunnel.

"You don't know what real fear is until you're in an underground tunnel and you lose your light."

"I hope you aren't planning to go back in there," Jan said, keeping her voice as moderate as she could. "I don't think there'd be too much of your back left if you did."

She smiled slightly, as though she enjoyed the pain he felt for his foolishness, each time he winced from the antiseptic.

"If I do—Ahh! Watch it, will you? I'll make sure I have extra batteries—a second flashlight with me. How was Beth feeling? You haven't really filled me in on what happened today."

Jan shrugged and poured more peroxide onto a fresh cotton ball.

"She's 'bout the same—getting a little bit better every day. She keeps complaining that she's going to leave the hospital looking like a blimp because of all the candy we've been giving her."

"Does Eldridge still think she can come home in a week or so?"

"He says so," Jan replied. "He keeps telling me he's never seen anyone make such a steady, fast recovery like she has."

"That's terrific," Don said as his gaze wandered to the mound of dirt that marked the open site.

"Oh," Jan said, lowering her voice, "when did you tell Beth you were doing some digging out there?"

"I did?" Don said, turning and looking at her.

"Umm. She said just before I left this afternoon that she didn't think it was a good idea for you to be—I think she said—'messing around' down there."

Don shook his head and scratched his chin. "I don't really remember mentioning it. Not recently, anyway."

Jan frowned. She screwed the top back onto the bottle of peroxide and put it on the counter. "I don't know where else she'd get the idea, then. She told me to tell you that you should stay out of the tunnel—that you might not like what you find down there."

"Oh? Really?" It took some effort for him to keep his voice calm, but Jan obviously picked up that what she had said bothered him.

"What is it?" she asked, nailing him with an intense stare. "You're acting like you're paranoid or something."

"Me? Paranoid? Why do you say that? Why does *everyone* say I'm paranoid?"

The joke was lame, he knew, and Jan didn't laugh.

"I saw a bumper sticker a couple of weeks ago, maybe I should get it," he said. "It read: 'The

Paranoids Are Out to Get Me!' "

"I don't think it's funny," Jan said, shaking her head. "I don't think it's anything to joke about."

"Umm," Don replied as he eased his shirt on over his raw skin. He didn't think it was funny, either. In his mind he was making connections, and he sure as hell didn't like where some of them led.

IV

"How late did you stay up last night?" Jan asked Don when he finally rolled out of bed a little after nine o'clock the next morning.

Rubbing his face with the flats of his hands, Don grunted something she couldn't quite make out. She sat down at the table opposite him and waited for him to focus on her.

"You left the blueprint out," she said. "What were you doing with it?"

"Just checking some things," Don said gruffly.

"It looks like you added some lines. Did you?" Jan asked.

"Umm. Yeah, I did," he replied. The last thing he wanted was her starting to nag at him this early. If she didn't like what he was doing out there, then why was she always asking him so damned many questions about it?

"What was that red line you drew? The one going from the site toward the house?"

"It's where the tunnel runs," he said. "At least where I think it runs. If there aren't any more turns, it looks like it runs right under the barn."

"You aren't planning on going back down there, are you?"

Don shrugged and, when it was obvious that Jan wasn't going to get him a cup of coffee, he got it for

523

himself. "I dunno," he said as he poured a big cupful, wishing it were a vat he could soak his head in. He knew he shouldn't have stayed up as late as he had—until past two A.M.

"I'd like to get an exact direction on the tunnel. Aren't you in the least bit curious?" He spooned sugar and poured milk into his coffee before leaning back against the countertop.

Jan shook her head. "Not in the least. And I hope you stay out of there, too."

"Why, because of what Beth said?" Don asked.

"No." Jan shook her head. "Not because of that. Because you look like you've been mauled by a bear or something. Look at your arms."

"Well, I won't go out there today, at least," Don said. He sipped at the coffee, but it was still too hot. "I was thinking of taking a break from my—my little exploration if only to give myself a chance to heal."

"Damn good thing," Jan said. She stood, pushing her chair back with her legs. "Are you coming with me to see Beth?"

Don nodded, but his gaze wandered again to the window and the field beyond. "But doesn't it make you wonder? I mean, someone actually built that whole thing out there. And that tunnel has to go *somewhere*. I'd like to know where."

Jan took one last gulp of her coffee and poured the rest down the sink.

"I did try to call Prof. Mitchell yesterday, to let him know what I found, but his secretary said he was out of town for a few weeks."

"That's all very interesting," Jan said, "but if you're coming with me to the hospital, you'd better get dressed fast. There's one thing, though . . ." She was standing in the doorway, looking down at her shoes like a nervous schoolgirl.

"What's that?" Don said.

Jan shook her head. "Uhh—yesterday, while you were fooling around down there in that chamber, I uhh . . ."

"Yes?"

Jan closed her eyes while she rubbed her forehead. "Well, Beth asked me how Goblin was doing, and I—"

"You *didn't*!"

Jan nodded. "I did. I *had* to tell her. I couldn't keep on pretending, and besides, she was going to find out sooner or later, anyway. I had to tell her we'd gotten rid of Goblin."

"Oh, great. Thanks a heap," Don growled. He began pacing the kitchen floor. "You didn't tell her I tried to shoot the damned horse, did you?"

Jan shook her head and chewed on the inside of her cheek.

"Of course not. I just told her we sold her back. And anyway, it wasn't like she drew it out of me. It was the way she asked, it was like—like she already knew Goblin was gone. She said she had a dream, that she saw Goblin running in the woods. And the weirdest thing was that she said it was all right. She wasn't mad at us about it. And she said that it didn't matter anyway; she knew Goblin would be there when she needed her."

Don shook his head in puzzlement. "What did she mean by that?"

Jan shrugged. "I don't know. But you want to know something else? The whole time she was talking to me about Goblin, she was holding onto that wooden doll of hers."

"I don't like that doll," Don snapped. "I didn't like it from the moment she found it. And don't you think, at her age, she's just a bit too old to be hanging onto dolls?"

"I don't know," Jan said. True, the way Beth clung to the doll bothered her, but what she wanted to tell Don was that the way he was getting so fanatical about exploring the site bothered her much more than any damned wooden doll!

"And I don't think a girl her age should even have dolls," Don said firmly. "I mean, don't you think it's about time she outgrew them?"

"No. Not really. Girls her age—and older—still play with dolls. I still had stuffed animals when I went to college."

Don bit his lower lip and shook his head. "Yeah, but this one's different. It's so—so . . ." He sighed deeply and looked up at the ceiling, wishing he could think of the right word.

"Honest to God, Don," Jan said, scowling. "You're acting so paranoid."

"Oh, no. Here we go again."

"So what's so wrong with it?" Jan asked, her voice rising.

Shaking his head slowly from side to side, Don took a deep breath. "That friggin' doll bothers me, that's what!"

"It's special to her," Jan said soothingly. "She found it the day we moved in, and it probably means something to her. She's had to deal with leaving her home and friends behind, and I think she clings to that doll because it represents a kind of security for her—like maybe the friends she doesn't have around here."

"There's Krissy Remy," Don snapped. "And when school starts, she'll meet plenty of kids."

Jan shrugged and looked away.

"Besides," Don said with a grunt. "That doll. She found it right after she got sick in the car."

"What do you mean by that?" Jan asked, her temper suddenly flaring.

"I mean that, what if she wasn't just carsick. What if that was the first time she had an epileptic seizure, and we just didn't recognize it. We talked about this before, but what if the menhir down by the driveway triggered that first seizure? Or maybe it was that doll!"

Jan snickered and moved to pick up her pocketbook. "Come on, let's cut out all this nonsense, O.K.? I don't want to be late getting there. First you say it's the menhir—that stupid stone at the end of the driveway—that caused it. Now you're suggesting that wooden doll had something to do with it, too?"

"All I'm saying," Don said, forcing calmness into his voice, "is that that doll gives me the willies. It bothers me the way she clings to it like an alcoholic clutches a fifth of whiskey. And it bothers me that she talks to it all the time and acts like the bloody thing answers her."

"You just don't understand little girls," Jan said. "Probably because you never were one."

"Thank God!" Don said, keeping his temper down only with effort. "But you just watch her sometime. She talks to it—whispers to it with it close to her mouth. And I swear, she acts like it answers her sometimes."

An expression of total amusement came over Jan's face. "We have to get a move on if we're going to make it in there today, but on the way home, I want to stop off in Ogunquit and see if I can find that *paranoid* bumper sticker for you."

V

They spent the whole day until well into the evening

with Beth. It bugged Don that the whole time they were there, Beth never touched or mentioned her wooden doll. The thought crossed his mind that she did that on purpose—that somehow she knew about the discussion he and Jan had had that morning and was ignoring the doll on purpose—to goad him. But—as Jan said on the drive home—that was just a bit *too* paranoid.

It was raining the next day, and again, Don decided not to go to the hospital to visit. He intended to putter around the house and finish up a few odds and ends he had left on hold. The work he had planned to do on the house had all been put aside after Beth's accident, so he still had plenty of painting and wallpapering to do in the living room and dining room.

To keep Jan happy, though, he decided first to put up the shelves in the pantry that Jan had been asking for. He got some of the wood left over from the repairs on Goblin's stall from the barn, gathered together the tools he needed, and set to work, first cleaning out the room, then measuring the wood to fit. Utility was uppermost in his mind for this job, and he planned the roughest of shelves, ignoring most of the detailed, finished-work advice he gave to his shop students.

Once he had determined the lengths for the sides, he plugged in his power saw, placed the first board between two chairs, and pressed the switch. The saw roared to life, its metal teeth chewing through the wood and spitting out sawdust. But the blade was no more than two or three inches into the wood when the power suddenly died. The saw stopped with a fading whine.

"Ahh, dammit!" Don said as he furiously pressed the switch several times. But the saw just made irritating clicking sounds, and Don realized he had blown a fuse.

"Just great. Just goddamned great!" he muttered.

He put the saw down and went into the kitchen to see if he could find a replacement fuse. The last he knew, there were some extras in the bottom drawer, and, after a bit of frantic searching, he found the box he was looking for. Without hesitation, he went to the cellar door, flicking the wall switch as he started down. The cellar light was also out, so in the semi-darkness of a rainy day, he went down the creaky stairs.

The cool dampness of the cellar embraced him like water as he descended to the hard-packed dirt floor. Rain splashed against the window with a steady, machine-gun-like drip. Silver ripples ran between pieces of grass plastered against the dirty pane like sweat-soaked hair. The runoff made a rhythmic drip-drip sound that had a peculiar lulling effect.

"Chinese water torture," Don said, walking past the workbench to the fuse box. Cobwebs swung lazily in the breeze of his passing. He snapped the fuse box cover open, quickly unscrewed the blown fuse, and put in the new one. As soon as he screwed it in, the light on the cellar stairs came on, but its weak, yellow glow did little to cut the gloom of the cellar. He couldn't help yawning as he swung the fuse box cover shut, and, before he started back up the stairs, he looked again at the rain falling outside the cellar window.

Mud was splashing up from beside the house, spattering the window, washing away some of the grass. As Don watched, he gradually became aware that the sound he heard—the splashing of water—wasn't coming just from the window. Looking around, he soon spotted the funnel-shaped stain on the wall next to the coal bin.

"Just what I needed," he said, clenching his fists in frustration. He went over to the coal bin, angry about the leak and concerned about how much damage to the foundation of the house might be involved. But when he started inspecting the wall, he saw something that made him forget entirely about the leak: his eyes fixed on the large stone in the foundation, the tall one that went from the floor to the ceiling.

"Jesus H.!" he said, his voice hushed as he stared at the stone. Although it was slightly smaller than the menhir at the foot of the driveway, there was no denying they looked like twins.

Coincidence? Don thought, but he shook his head, acknowledging that there had been too damned many coincidences lately. This stone was virtually identical to the menhir down by the road, and the recognition of that made his nerves tingle as he went close to the stone, but he couldn't bring himself to reach out and touch it.

The water leaking into the ceiling ran to the floor from roughly halfway up the wall. It made a throaty gurgling sound as it soaked into the dirt floor. Don felt a chilled clutching at his throat when he realized that the waterstain reminded him of something else. It looked quite a bit—*too much*—like the stain of Billy Blackshoe's blood on the table stone!

He felt an impulse to run—to go upstairs, get back to making Jan's shelves, and just forget about everything—the water leak, the stone in the wall, the blood—

—No! Not blood!

There was no doubt in his mind that this was another menhir. Either Toivo Kivinen or whoever had built the house had used a menhir from the field as part of the foundation, or the foundation had been built around and included the stone as it had stood in the field!

His hand shook as he neared the stone and reached out to touch it. Slowly, slowly he brought his fingers closer . . . closer. As soon as he touched the cold, gritty surface of the stone, a sudden jolt ran up his arm, numbing the nerves right up to his neck. With a grunt of surprise, Don spun away from the stone, clenching his arm close to his chest.

"This is insane!" he muttered, backing away from the stone but keeping his eyes fixed on it as though he expected it to tumble forward suddenly and crush him.

The leak in the wall gurgled and dripped as Don leaned back against his rickety workbench, eyeing the menhir. Suddenly, he reached behind himself and snatched up a rusted screwdriver. Nervously gnawing his lower lip, he approached the stone again.

If there was a leak in the foundation, he thought, then he had to investigate. The shock he had gotten hadn't really come from the stone; that was impossible, and he knew it. He was tense; he was wound up tighter than a Timex. His arm muscles had just had a spasm; that was all. Still, as he reached out to feel the stone again, he was ready for the jolt—if it came.

But it didn't. His fingers touched the stone, and all he felt was cold, damp rock. Setting to work quickly, he used the screwdriver to start prying out the ancient mortar from between the stones where the stain originated. The old mortar was soft, puttylike. It fell to the floor with a dull, plopping sound. As he worked, the more mortar he removed, the more freely the water ran down the wall and soaked into the floor.

While he worked at scraping away the deteriorating mortar, Don wondered how much of the foundation was in such bad condition. Probably all of it, and he would no doubt be wise—next summer at the latest—

to repoint the whole cellar wall. But for now, he had to find out how much damage this leak had caused.

The point of the screwdriver jabbed and pecked at the joints between the stones. The metal made sharp, rasping sounds that reminded Don of someone breathing with difficulty. Try as he might, he couldn't push aside the sensation that his wasn't the only labored breathing in the cellar but, whenever he looked around, of course he was alone.

When he had cleared all around one of the smaller stones, he pried the stone forward, using the old screwdriver now as a pinch bar. At first the stone stayed where it was, solid and fixed, but then, suddenly, it shifted forward. Grabbing at it with his fingers, he pulled back on it until it ground forward, making a gritty sound. Suddenly the weight shifted forward, exposing a long, black crack in the wall.

"God almighty!" Don said, when he brought his face close to the crack and realized that it was an opening. There was open space in behind there! He could feel a damp draft blowing out from behind the wall, washing over his face like a cold wave.

He worked more eagerly now, trying to get the stone free. The only way there could be a draft from behind that wall, he realized, was if there was—a sealed-off, long-forgotten room or—

—*A tunnel!*

The thought hit him with almost as much force as the jolt he had gotten when he first touched the menhir.

A tunnel! The tunnel he had been exploring underground had been heading toward the barn, but with one more turn—with *one more turn*—it would be heading directly toward the house!

As he pondered this, Don couldn't decide if he felt more excitement or more fear at the prospect. The only thing he was sure of, as he worked to get the stone free from the wall, was that he *had* to explore further. No matter what Jan or anyone else said about it, he *had* to find out!

Bathed with sweat and shaking with excitement, Don stepped back for a moment and surveyed his work so far. His shirt clung to him like strands of kelp, and he shivered when he thought about what might be behind the cellar wall.

As he studied the stones that made up the wall, at first he couldn't see a pattern to them; they looked like just any assortment of granite blocks used to make a foundation. But the longer he looked at the wall, the more he began to see what *might* be a pattern. The menhir marked one side of what looked like a doorway, narrow at the top and wider at the bottom, that had been filled in with blocks of stone.

Don wondered why he had never noticed the pattern before. Now that he realized it was there, it was so damned obvious! One stone had been set horizontally near the top, just below the floor joist, and the stones filling the doorway slanted inward. The arrangement reminded Don of entrances he had seen in pictures of Egyptian tombs.

He ran upstairs and out to the barn to get the pinch bar he had used down in the chamber and tunnel beneath the table stone. The waterstain was to the left of the embedded menhir, inside the doorway, and, because the mortar there was dissolving, Don started working there. If he could just get that first stone out, he was sure the rest of the blocking stones would follow easily. As best as he could judge, there was support in the right places, and the whole wall wouldn't collapse when he removed the stones.

But as hard as he tried, the stone wouldn't come out any further, so he set to work removing the mortar from around the surrounding stones. Within half an hour, he had cleaned away mortar from around six stones, and he tried again to free one stone. Just one, that was all he needed. All he wanted was a peek behind the wall.

Prying with the pinch bar and straining until his pulse hammered in his ears, he finally got another one of the stones to move. It scraped loudly as it shifted forward inch by inch. Don's breathing came in ragged gulps of damp air, and he felt as though there were a fungus growing in his lungs, cutting off his oxygen.

The stone resisted, but Don found just the right angles, and after a while he had enough of an edge sticking out so he could grab onto it and pull. With a deep rumble, the stone came out further and further, and then it suddenly dropped into his hands, making him stagger as he slowly lowered it to the floor.

"Hot damn!" he shouted with joy as he stared at the black opening in the wall. He was grateful that the whole thing didn't cave in. Dizzy with excitement, he came up close to the opening. From the gaping hole came a sluggish breeze that carried a choking, familiar aroma of decay.

It was now a matter of a few minutes to chip away more of the mortar and remove two more stones. Before too long, Don had an opening in the cellar wall that he could have easily climbed through—except he didn't have a flashlight! His only light was lying on the tunnel floor, broken.

He cursed himself for not immediately getting another flashlight. He should have known, dammit!

There were candles upstairs in the dining room, which Jan kept in case of a power outage, but he didn't relish the prospect of entering the tunnel, maybe following it for a way, and then having the draft snuff the candle out. No, sir! He wasn't going to be left underground without a light again!

A bone-deep chill gripped him as he regarded the opening. He knew, even without looking, that this was no sealed-off root cellar; it *had* to be the other end of the tunnel from the burial chamber. Intuition told him that. Or maybe, he thought with a chuckle, he was beginning to develop some of that sixth sense Billy had talked so much about.

Cautiously Don stuck his head into the opening, peering into the blackness that swirled liquidly in front of his eyes. The dripping water that had caused the leak ran down the inside of the opening, and the ground both inside and outside the cellar wall was squishy.

By the little light that came from the cellar, Don could see that behind the wall there was another room—or tunnel—but how far back it extended he could not determine. One thing he did notice, though, was that the stonework looked remarkably similar to the stonework in the tunnel he had followed from the burial chamber.

"This *has* to be where it comes out," he said, his voice hushed with awe. "One more turn, and here we'd be!"

He was torn by two conflicting impulses: one was to begin now, tearing down the wall to see if, indeed, this was the other end of the tunnel; the other was to replace the stones he had removed and do what Jan had been saying for so long—just forget about the whole damned thing!

But how could he forget all about it?

He reached into the opening and ran his hand along the inside of the wall. The stones were wet and, when he withdrew his hand, it was sticky with foul-smelling slime.

Don backed away from the opening, tossing about

in his mind what he should do. He didn't expect Jan home for another couple of hours, but, if he spent the day digging down in the cellar, he'd be hard put to explain why he hadn't gotten any other work—even something as simple as a few shelves—done.

His face was slick with sweat and grit as he pondered his new discovery. Without a light, it would be ridiculous to go in there, but then again, how could he be expected to go upstairs and blithely work on the shelves for Jan with something like *this* down here?

The only answer was to get a flashlight, so he hurried upstairs, cleaned himself up, slung on his raincoat, and walked briskly downtown to the local hardware store. He paid more than he cared to for two heavy-duty flashlights, but, purchase in hand, he ran most of the way back to the house, wondering what the clerk at the store must have thought of him, rushing in and out of the store, disheveled and dripping wet.

Before going into the opening, though, Don got several beams from the barn and made rough supports for the wall just in case the leak in the wall had eroded the mortar and the supporting stones weren't strong enough. It took him a little more than an hour to cobble together several braces, and, once they were in place, he removed a few more stones—just enough to make an opening so he could easily get in behind the cellar wall.

He took one of the flashlights and threaded his belt through the handle. With the second light in one hand and a pinch bar in the other, he wedged himself headfirst through the narrow opening and into what proved to be a long, narrow tunnel.

His light beam danced over the walls, floor, and ceiling of the tunnel as he pulled one leg and then the other in under him. Any thoughts that this wasn't an extension of the underground tunnel were immediately removed when he saw that the stonework was indeed identical in construction.

The tunnel took a sharp turn to the left. The wall directly opposite the opening he had made was one of the tunnel walls; the other was an extension of his cellar wall, stretching off into a swelling darkness. The floor of the tunnel slanted downward, and the runoff from the leak made the dirt mucky.

With a dry swallow but feeling secure with two lights, Don started down the tunnel. There were fewer dirt and rock slides than he had encountered in the other one, and there was even a bit more room, so he made rapid progress.

All around him, the darkness pressed in, rubbing against him like some dark animal. The thin beam of light pointing ahead, lighting his way, seemed to diminish. Looking behind, Don saw the dull, gray opening leading back into the cellar get dimmer and finally disappear.

After about thirty feet, the tunnel jagged to the right; then after fifty feet or so, it hooked to the left. Don felt certain that the tunnel turned in exactly the direction it had to in order to link up with the tunnel from the chamber. The further he went, the drier the air became, and he cursed himself again for not having the foresight to bring along something to drink.

At the left-turning junction, Don stopped to rest, lying down on the floor and stretching his cramped legs. In spite of the dry air, he was bathed in sweat, and his breathing was labored. It was damned good to stretch, and he felt no hurry to explore.

As he leaned with his back against the stone wall, he noticed something peculiar about the wall at the junction. The stone in the corner, just where the tunnel turned, looked as though it had been carved. Its shape, although smaller, suggested the form of the other two menhirs. This one, though, was shorter and squatter, and for the first time Don recognized the shape: it looked like a thick, erect penis.

"Underground porn," he said, chuckling softly to himself.

His laughter built, but he suddenly stopped when the sounds rebounding back along the dark tunnel reverberated with a hollow, sinister echo.

His nerves tingled as he shifted around and looked back the way he had come. For a moment, he had had the impression that there was more than his laughter echoing in the tunnel, but he dismissed the idea as a trick of the twisting tunnel. He got back onto his hands and knees and started scrambling down the tunnel again.

The further he went, the more the tingling sensation in his body grew. He thought it might have something to do with restricting his blood flow and getting pins and needles. Or maybe he was hyperventilating from the excitement.

Or maybe, he thought, he was tingling with the "energy flow" Billy had told him he had detected in the field. Intuitively, he felt that Billy *had* been onto something about the table stone, and the thought crossed his mind that Billy had died as a result of what he had learned. But that, he told himself, was paranoid—as Jan said. It was easy to imagine all sorts of weird things in the cramped quarters of the tunnel.

From the left turn, he went another forty feet or so, and then the tunnel started to curve gently, first to the right and then to the left, so he was unable to see very far ahead. Another thought struck him—that the pattern of the tunnel, with all its twists and turns, resembled the track of a crawling snake—

—The serpent, uncoiled!

Billy Blackshoe's words rang like a bell in his memory.

After another curve, Don saw with a sudden shock of disappointment that he was stopped again. Ahead was another stone wall, sealing off the tunnel!

For an instant, he had the feeling of déjà vu, looking at the blocking wall. As he scrambled up close to the stone blockage, he wondered if this was a different wall or if it was merely the other side of the one he had already encountered. He twisted around to a sitting position and looked at the closely fitted stones, his anger and frustration building.

He had the pinch bar with him, and he could have tried to remove one or more of the stones, but he wasn't sure how much support the ceiling received from the blocking wall. Probably none, he figured, looking up at the huge slabs that formed the ceiling, but then again there was absolutely no sense taking chances. If the tunnel caved in and sealed him in there, the only sign of where he had died would be a sinkhole somewhere in the field near Jan's garden. Not much of an end to look forward to, he decided.

Fatigue made his muscles ache and his joints burn as he sat crouched over, studying the blocking wall. His throat was as parched as though he had been in the hot sun for the last several hours. He decided that the best thing to do would be to come back here with enough timbers to support the ceiling—tomorrow, if not later today. Right now, all he had on his mind was a long, hot shower, so he started back along the tunnel toward the cellar.

He had crawled no more than ten feet, though, when he suddenly stopped and looked back at the blocking wall. He had heard—or *thought* he had heard—the sharp rasp of metal against stone. It hadn't been either his flashlight or the pinch bar, he was sure. The sound seemed to have come from behind him—from *behind* the blocking wall.

"No way," he whispered, running the oval of light over the stones. There were no gaps between the stones through which he could see, but when he crawled back and leaned his face close to the wall, he heard it again—unmistakably. Once—sharp and clanging—he heard the sound of metal banging against stone.

Don shrank back, staring horrified at the blocking wall. Fear and apprehension bubbled up inside him like a black soup, and he had to force himself not to cry out. He wanted to break down that damned wall and see what was behind it, what could possibly have made that sound. Was it that prowler he had seen several nights ago?

He chuckled softly, imagining himself turning Hulk-green and hammering the stones to dust with his bare fists. He *had* to get through that blocking wall to find out!

Crouching in the darkness, he listened tensely for the sound to be repeated, but after several minutes he was sure it wouldn't be. The utter silence of the tunnel grew so thick, like the darkness, it seemed to ripple. Finally, he started back toward the cellar, running through his mind several possibilities of what could have made the sound. Once, when he was maybe halfway back, he thought he heard something—a low whisper like a breeze blowing through pines, but he dismissed it.

Back in the cellar and able to stand and stretch, rational explanations arose. The draft in the tunnel, rushing along the curves, made what he had thought were soft whisperings. If there was a hole somewhere in the tunnel that he hadn't noticed, maybe it was where an animal had burrowed in, and that would explain the scratching sounds he had heard. The clang of metal on stone had to have been from him, inadvertently knocking his flashlight or pinch bar against the stone walls.

As he went upstairs to get to work on the shelves, these explanations seemed to satisfy him—for now. But he was still determined—obsessed—to go back in there, brace the ceiling, and tear through that blocking wall. He sensed that the two tunnels were connected, but he had to prove it to himself. He *had* to do that much at least—if not for himself, then for Billy Blackshoe.

Chapter Sixteen

Homecoming

I

"Don, we have to talk," Jan said, walking into the living room and sitting down next to him on the couch. Supper was over, the dishes were washed and put away, and Don had been reading when the phone had rung. Dr. Eldridge had given them the good news that Beth would be able to come home the day after tomorrow.

"This isn't anything about Dale Jackman, I hope," he said, holding his place in *Indian Earth Magic* with his index finger.

Jan obviously didn't see the humor in his remark and shook her head solemnly. "No, it's not," she replied. There was that tight edge in her voice that signaled to Don that she meant it—this was serious.

"What about?" he said, shutting the book and placing it on the coffee table.

Jan looked away from him to the blank TV screen. A shimmering film came over her eyes.

"Honey! What is it?" Don asked, leaning toward her and placing his hand on her shoulder. He could feel her shaking. "Come on, tell me. What is it?"

"You," she said simply, and she followed it with

loud sniff.

"Me? What about me?"

Jan looked at him, and he could tell it was only with an effort that she held herself back. "You know damn well 'what about.' How you've been acting lately."

Don started to protest, but she cut him off.

"I mean about that burial site and the tunnel. God almighty! I can't believe you spent the whole day today, tearing out the cellar wall so you could get at that tunnel!"

Don shifted uneasily, keeping his eyes fastened on her.

"I don't think it's good, not good at all, the way you're poking around down there." Her voice was as tight as a twisted piano wire.

"It's interesting," Don said weakly. "I find the whole thing pretty fascinating, and besides it gives me something else to do besides stewing about what happened to Beth."

"That isn't it at *all,* and you know it!" Jan snapped. He could feel her tensing up beneath his touch. "Beth's been improving steadily, and you talked to Dr. Eldridge just now. He said the anticonvulsant drugs she's taking are working. There's nothing to worry about as far as she's concerned."

"Then what's the problem?"

"You're so obsessed by the whole thing!" Unable to remain seated, she stood and began pacing the floor back and forth.

"Look, Jan, I—"

"I want you to promise me one thing, Don," she said, suddenly turning on him.

Don shrank back and ran his fingers through his hair. "Uh, sure. What?"

"I want you to promise me that, once Beth comes home, you won't go out there—you won't even *men-*

tion it! I want you to go out tomorrow morning and fill it in. That's what I want."

"I can't do that," Don said, shaking his head slowly. "No way."

"Can't you see what it's doing to you?" Jan asked, her voice frayed. "It's all you ever talk about. You talk more about that burial site than you do about Beth. Day and night, that's all you ever *think* about!" Her shoulders suddenly slouched, and she collapsed into the chair, clenching her fists.

Don was shaking his head rapidly from side to side. "No. Not at all," he said as evenly as he could manage. "I'll grant you I've been a little involved with it, but I think it's pretty exciting. I mean, that we actually might have an Indian burial site on our—"

"If you go down into that tunnel one more time," Jan said through clenched teeth, "One more time, I'll—I'll . . ." Her voice faded slowly, and they locked eyes.

"One more day," Don said softly. His throat felt as dry as the air in the tunnel. "That's all I need. One more day to—"

"No!"

"Yes!" he shouted. He slammed his hand onto the couch cushion, raising a puff of dust. "You obviously don't appreciate how much this means to me, but I have to. I want to brace the ceiling and take down that wall. I *have* to see what's behind that wall."

"That's exactly what I'm talking about," Jan said just as loudly. "This thing has—it's like it's taken over your mind or something."

"I have to see what's behind that wall," Don repeated, lowering his voice but still speaking emphatically. "Just one more day."

"You can't at least wait until next spring when those university people come back?"

Don shook his head from side to side. "No. I want to do it now."

"Well, you won't—not once Beth's home!" Jan snapped.

Don was shaking his head. "I won't need to. If she's coming home the day after tomorrow, I'll be done with it tomorrow. I wish you could see how important it is to me."

"As important as our marriage?" Jan asked sharply.

Don shook his head. "Of course not. You know that I—"

"If you go down into that chamber or that tunnel once more," she said, fighting to control her voice. "I mean it. I'll—I'll leave you." With that, she turned and ran upstairs, her feet clomping on each step.

Don wanted to follow after her—to apologize, to explain, to work it out—but he didn't move. He sat there on the couch, his anger smoldering like a banked fire.

Considering the strain they had been under the past month or so, he wasn't surprised that she would have a flare-up like that. If anything, it was overdue. He still wanted to blame the medication she was taking, but for the last day or two she hadn't touched her sedatives, so maybe her nerves were a bit jangled. By morning she'll have cooled off and forgotten all about it, he thought, picking up his book again and leafing though the pages.

The rain had stopped just after sunset, and a warm breeze wafted in the window blowing the living room curtains. Don sat and listened while Jan got ready for bed, and, when he heard the bed springs creak under her weight, he went into the kitchen and got a can of Pabst from the refrigerator. Coming back into the living room, he moved his chair over to the open window and settled down, listening to the whirring sound of crickets.

In spite of his hot shower, his shoulders and back still ached from being so confined in the tunnel. The beer was half gone when he placed it and his book on the floor beside his chair and leaned back, courting sleep.

Before long he was sound asleep. His hand dropped down and knocked the beer can over. It gurgled its contents onto the rug in a bearded foam. Don was just barely aware of the bubbling sound as he dropped off to sleep.

But the sleep was neither comforting nor deep.

—He suddenly found himself standing in the living room. The first thing he noticed was that all of the furniture had been removed. Almost all. There was something—a large wooden box set on two saw-horses—in the middle of the living room. It was too dark in the room for him to see clearly, so—

—He approached the object, his feet sliding over the carpet with a dull scuffing sound. He saw that the object was a coffin set up in the living room. Shafts of moonlight filtered through the lace curtains and glimmered on the polished mahogany and metal. Reaching out—

—He was surprised that he could see his hands. Something in his mind registered that it was odd to be able to see his hands in his dream. His fingers looked old and white like curdled milk as he reached out and touched the wood. A numbing chill ran up his arms to his shoulders, feeling as though ice picks had been driven straight to the bone. The polished wood felt like ice, and the cold reflection of the moon gave the wood an eerie depth as though the wood were no more than a transparent membrane covering something deeper—much deeper.

—He leaned forward and saw his face reflected in the wood, its outline distorted by the curved surface. He suddenly pulled back, whimpering softly when the coffin lid rose slowly. It sounded like a rusty nail being pulled slowly—steadily from ancient wood. Nothing he could see was opening the coffin—no bony hand pushing up from inside—but the lid swung wide open as if in welcome. He was filled with the blinding fear that this coffin was—

—his!

—He saw solid, impenetrable darkness beneath the coffin lid—the depths of infinity. But, as he watched, the blackness thinned, and he could see that the coffin was occupied. As his sight resolved the figure, he fully expected to see himself, reposed in the sleep of death. A low, strangled gasp escaped him when, instead, he saw Beth, lying with a frozen smile on her waxy face. Her eyes were shut, and her hands were folded across her chest. No motion of breath stirred the white lace dress she was wearing, but it seemed as if her eyelids were fluttering from the effort of keeping her eyes closed. His nerves stretched, tingling, and then—

—He heard a voice, distant and hollow, muttering, "No . . . no." Anger and fear coiled like twin snakes in his chest as he looked down on his dead daughter. He suddenly jumped back when Beth's eyes snapped open. Somehow, he had expected that—it was straight out of any dozen horror movies.

Expected? he wondered. *How can you expect something in a dream?*

—He came up close to Beth, staring down at her limpid eyes as though gazing into a deep well. He wondered if it had all been a mistake—that Beth wasn't dead after all. Her eyes held his, and it was—

—How long? Minutes? Hours? before he realized

that her mouth was moving in an effort to speak.

—He said, softly, "What is it, Pun'kin? Tell me what's wrong?" But Beth's head twisted from side to side, her jaws working to move but remaining shut as though clamped tightly against her will by some outside force. The tendons in her neck stood out sharply, trembling and twitching as her lips twisted to force out her words.

—He screamed and staggered back, almost falling, when Beth's mouth at last opened, and a twisting knot of corpse-white worms spilled out onto her chest. The thick, ropy mass seemed to have no end as it poured from Beth's mouth, unwinding itself over her dress, filling her coffin. The worms fell with a sickening plop-plop onto the carpeted floor.

—He jackknifed into a sitting position in his chair and, opening his eyes, stared at the gently wafting lace curtains. The living room was silent except for his ragged breathing. It gave him only a small measure of relief when he looked and saw that all the living room furniture was in place. No coffin!

Covering his face with his hands, he whimpered softly, trying to forget the dream, but he was unable to stop the slow-motion replay of white worms spilling from Beth's mouth and plopping onto the floor.

II

The next day Don gave up the idea of going back into the tunnel. Instead, he went with Jan to the hospital and they spent the day with Beth. She was thrilled about being able to go home the next day, and they had all they could do to convince her that she couldn't leave today.

When they weren't visiting with her, they were with Dr. Eldridge reviewing the necessary precautions to take with her at home. They also made arrangements for Beth's physical therapy to get tone back into her long unused muscles. They left for home well after visiting hours.

"You know," Jan said as they were walking out to their car, "in all the time we've been in Maine, we've never driven over to see Susan and her family."

The mere mention of Susan reminded Don of Aune's *Dream Book* and the portions Susan had translated of it. With everything else that had been going on, he had completely forgotten about it. The last thing Susan had said was that, because she and Tom were having marital problems, she didn't think she'd be able to translate any more of it—at least for a while. He wondered if she might have gotten more of it done and just hadn't had a chance to send it to him.

"Why don't we find a pay phone, and I'll give her a call?" he said. They got into the car and drove through downtown York looking for a phone booth. They found one on the corner by the police station, and Don parked next to the curb, got out, dropped a quarter into the slot, and dialed Susan's number.

Jan waited in the car, and the longer Don was on the phone with Susan, the more she realized they wouldn't be driving down for a visit. The overhead light in the booth cast a harsh shadow over Don's face, and Jan was shocked at how gaunt and tired he looked. His expression, too, seemed lifeless. She watched as he nodded and hung up the phone.

"Well?" Jan asked as Don returned to the car and slid in behind the steering wheel.

He shook his head. "Tonight wouldn't be a good night for a visit," he said hollowly.

"Is there a problem?"

Don nodded, biting at his lower lip. "Yeah. There's a problem. Tom's been giving her a real hassle about the kids."

"That's awful," Jan said, looking straight out the car window. "I wonder why she didn't let us know. I mean, maybe there was something we could have done."

Don shrugged and started up the car just as a police cruiser pulled out of the station driveway and swung past them, the officer slowing to check them out.

"I asked her—you know—what could we do. She said she was working on it herself and really didn't want me to get involved."

Jan clicked her tongue. "Well, she shouldn't feel that way. I mean, we may not be all that close, but what's a family for if not to pull together when you need it?"

Don shifted the car into gear and pulled out onto the road. "She's always been my big sister," he said softly, "and I kind of think she doesn't, you know, want to admit that she might need—I don't know—emotional support or something from me."

Jan was still shaking her head. "Well, maybe she just doesn't realize what families are for."

"Umm," Don said, concentrating on his driving. He was mulling over in his mind his conversation with Susan, and he was wishing he had at least mentioned Aune's journal. Now that, thanks to Billy Blackshoe and his own efforts, he had started exploring, he couldn't help but think there were more answers locked up in that book. Again, he wished to God that he knew enough Finnish to read and translate the rest of the journal.

When they got back to the house, they were both exhausted and, frankly, quite apprehensive about Beth's homecoming. They found that they had little to say to each other, so, after a quick supper of hot dogs and a salad, they went to bed. After the nightmare of last night, Don was more than a little apprehensive about what might sneak into his dreams tonight, but both he and Jan slept peacefully until well after dawn.

Shortly after eight o'clock, they got up, had a hurried breakfast, and drove to the hospital. Each of them was occupied with his or her own thoughts and expectations about the day, and Don, at least, was grateful for that; a good part of his mind was still planning how he would brace the tunnel ceiling so he could remove the blocking wall. Jan, he thought, might be right after all: he *was* a bit too preoccupied with the site. But he honestly felt that, once he had broken through that wall, that would be the end of it.

Checking Beth out of the hospital took longer than they had anticipated, much longer than necessary. While Don was busy filling out release forms, Beth sat in a wheelchair in the waiting room with Jan, who kept a close watch over her. Several times she spoke, but when Jan asked her to repeat what she had said, Beth would simply shake her head and say, "It's not important."

When Don rejoined them, he noticed, with some concern, that Beth was clinging to her wooden doll. When he asked if he could put it into the suitcase with her other things, she hugged the doll close to her body and protested loudly. Her left hand had such a tight grip on the doll her knuckles were turning white.

—*Milky white*, Don thought, and the image of the cascading worms filled his mind.

—*Corpse white!*

Several nurses and orderlies stopped to say good-by to Beth while she and Jan waited for Don to bring the car around. It was late morning, almost noon, when they finally rolled her out into the sunshine. It was a clumsy operation, getting her out of the wheelchair and into the back seat, but before long they were heading north on Route One again toward St. Ann's, toward home.

"I'm glad you're feeling so much better," Jan said, looking into the back seat of the car. For the first time in a long time, she was surprised not to see Max there, too, with his head in Beth's lap.

Beth smiled weakly, squinting from the bright daylight. Her body looked flaccid, and she swayed from side to side as the car took the curves of the road.

"I just wish Goblin was there when I got home. Don't you?" Beth said.

Don looked at her in the rear-view mirror and was surprised to see her addressing her wooden doll. The faded inkspot eyes seemed to look back at him, glaring. Beth's face looked washed of emotion, blank—too much like the expression she had had in his dream. He shivered, remembering the coiling worms . . .

"But it'll be good to get back home, won't it, honey?" Jan asked.

"I s'pose," Beth said, keeping her eyes fixed straight ahead.

The drive up Route One went swiftly, and before long they were turning left onto Mountain Road, heading toward St. Ann's. Sun glinting from storefront windows hurt Don's eyes as he slowed and took the turn onto Hunter Hill Road. He felt a growing uneasiness as they approached the house. Not really a déjà vu; more like the icy memory of déjà vu. When the car crested the last rise, and he saw the turn into the driveway ahead, he felt a sudden panic.

What if, he wondered frantically when they drove past the menhir at the foot of the driveway, the stone triggered another seizure? Without realizing it, he eased off the gas, slowing the car.

"What's the matter?" Jan asked casually.

Don shook his head and blinked his eyes.

"Is something the matter?"

The menhir! his mind screamed. That goddamned menhir! Was it all in his imagination, or was there really some kind of power to that tilted stone?

He glanced at Jan and forced a smile. As he slowed for the turn into the driveway, he kept his eyes fastened to the rear view, watching Beth—watching and waiting for—what? Some kind of reaction?

What if it triggers another seizure? he thought again with bowel-twisting apprehension. What if . . . ?

They drove under the dappled shade of the oak and approached the leaning stone post. To Don, even in the bright August sunlight, it looked somehow charged with power, seething with an energy searching for an outlet. He looked back at Beth in the mirror and what he saw filled his gut with an icy tingle. She was looking—staring—out the window at the stone, and she was smiling and nodding her head. Her wooden doll was pressed tightly against her ear.

Don was still staring at Beth's sinister grin. Her lips were pulled back, exposing the top row of teeth like feral fangs. She shifted her gaze, locking him with her eyes—

—*like in the dream!*

—blank, milky pools that didn't reflect back the light they caught.

He wanted to say something to Jan, something simple and trivial to break the spell, but Beth's unrelenting gaze held him just as a snake is supposed to be able to hypnotize a bird. His voice felt trapped in the back of his throat.

Beth's smile widened, and then her lips began to move as though she was trying to speak. The image of

553

her mouth, opening to disgorge a twisting mass of worms, filled him with terror.

"Don!" Jan suddenly screamed. Her shout broke the lock Beth's eyes had on him. He looked ahead and saw that they were heading off the driveway, straight for the menhir.

"God!" Don cried out. He was positive he had already driven past the stone and was halfway up the driveway—at least that's what it had felt like, but now he had to pull hard on the steering wheel to avoid hitting the stone. He hit the brakes hard, and gravel splattered against the underside of the car. The car swung back onto the driveway, and then the engine died.

It took several tries to get the car started again, but at last they drove up into the shade of the barn, and Don stopped the car.

"What in heaven's name were you trying to do back there, kill us all?" Jan swung open her door and stepped out of the car.

Don shook his head, rubbing his forehead with his hand. "I dunno," he muttered. "I just kind of drifted."

"You'll have us *all* back in the hospital at this rate," Jan snapped.

Don was still shaking his head as though dazed. He couldn't remove the image of Beth's eyes from his mind. He had to force himself to glance at her. But, when he did, he saw that she looked normal now— nothing more than what she was: a little girl returning home from the hospital, a bit weak, maybe, and just a bit shaken up by the near accident, but that was all. Her eyes no longer had that eerie deadness to them.

"I—um—I thought I saw something in the road back there," he said as he opened his door and came over to open Beth's. He looked back down at the foot of the driveway, unable to resist the shudder that shook him.

"Well it's not worth wrecking the car for, is it?" Jan asked sharply.

"Course not," he said. He scooped Beth up off the seat and was about to carry her up to the house, but, when she protested, he put her on the ground and let her walk by herself. Jan walked along beside her, gently holding her elbow to guide her.

Don snapped open the back of the car and took out the two suitcases. Jan had brought home most of the flowers from Beth's room, so he unloaded these, too. He worked slowly, emptying the car, trying to collect his thoughts.

What had made him nearly run off the road and almost smash into the menhir? It was as if he had suddenly blanked out or flip-flopped out of time, thinking he was halfway up the driveway and then suddenly realizing he wasn't! Had something forced him? It had seemed for an instant as though the menhir had leaned forward, anticipating the crash, wanting to crush him!

Probably nothing at all, he thought to himself. Nothing at all. A bit of psychic indigestion left over from that dream the other night. That's all.

The evil gleam in Beth's eyes had been nothing more that her excitement at seeing her home for the first time in weeks. His sense that he had already driven past the menhir and was heading up the driveway was just his anticipation of getting Beth home and set up comfortably in her room.

"That's *all* it was," he said, aloud this time, but, as he hefted a suitcase in each hand and started toward the house, the thought nagged at his mind that that might *not* be all—not by a long shot!

III

Beth spent the rest of the day lying on the couch watching reruns of *The Brady Bunch* and *I Dream of Jeannie*, and dozing off now and again. Jan commented that the amount of TV she had watched in the hospital probably did her more harm than anything else. Whenever Don or Jan asked her a question, she replied in short, clipped words, and her gaze seldom wavered from the flickering images on the TV. When it did, it was to look, almost lovingly, at the stiff wooden figure she held tightly in her left hand.

Over the next four or five days, an odd sort of tension began to build in the house. Other than meals and making sure she took her medication, Beth didn't need much attention. She had exercised some in the hospital, so she certainly wasn't bedridden. She could go to the bathroom unassisted and went upstairs to her room on her own to get a few books in case she felt like reading, but mostly she sat on the couch, watching the television.

When Don and Jan sat down together, in the kitchen so they wouldn't disturb Beth, they found that they had little to say to each other—other than the obvious about how Beth was feeling and doing. After supper, while Beth dozed on the couch, Jan peeked in on her one more time.

"She's fine in there," she said to Don, who was staring into the bottom of his empty coffee cup. She went to the door and took her car keys from the nail. "I think I'm going to go for a drive," she said. "This whole thing is getting to be quite a strain. I need to get away for a bit."

"It's too bad we can't get someone to come over and keep an eye on her, so we can both get out," Don said, glancing out at the darkness. He thought, as soon as

556

he said it, that the Remys probably would have been willing to sit with Beth while she rested on the couch. But, with Jan going out, he thought of something else he'd like to do—something he felt he had put off for too long.

"Is there anything you want while I'm out?" Jan asked, standing in the doorway, jingling her keys in her hand.

Don shook his head. "Uhh, no. I guess not."

"I'll be back in a bit," Jan said, and then she was gone. Don sat at the kitchen table, listening as the car started up and pulled away. He got up and rinsed his cup at the sink, careful not to let it clatter when he put it into the drying rack.

For a long time he leaned his elbows on the sink and stared out the window at the field. In the darkness, the mounds of earth where he had excavated the table stone looked weathered and much smaller than he remembered them. It seemed like months—years—since he and Billy had worked out here, but Billy had died less than a month ago.

He tiptoed into the living room and looked in on Beth. She was still asleep, her face lit a ghostly blue from the TV. Don walked over and looked down at her, studying the relaxed features of her face. She looked peaceful, and he realized that she hadn't looked like that all day; there had been a hard edge to her expression. He hoped now it was gone for good. An experience like the one she had been through could permanently sour anyone's personality, and he hoped she would come bouncing back from it better than ever.

Her nostrils dilated gently as she breathed evenly and deeply. With a deep measure of relief, he saw there was no trace of the sinister dead face of his dream. *This* was his Pun'kin.

His stomach tightened when he noticed the steady stare of the wooden doll peeking out at him from between Beth's folded fingers. Rising to the challenge, he stared back at the unblinking face, trying to stare it down. The beady black eyes seemed to bore into him.

He considered taking the doll away from her. It would be relatively easy to remove it from her grip, take it outside, and destroy the thing. He bent down and, flexing his fingers like an ace safe-cracker, started to reach for the doll. But just before he was about to grab it, Beth snorted and rolled over, covering the doll with her body.

"Damn!" Don said softly, stepping back. He knew he'd wake her if he tried now, and the doctor had said she'd need plenty of sleep. Besides, he wasn't sure he could quite bring himself to touch the thing, anyway!

Moving silently, he went over to the TV and snapped it off, keeping his eyes on Beth all the while to be sure she didn't wake up. Her breathing remained steady and deep. He took the afghan from the back of the couch and draped it over her.

"There—there, Pun'kin," he whispered, smiling down at her. She looked so small and fragile, he couldn't help but remember how she had looked as a baby, all cozy and cuddled in.

Don tiptoed out of the living room and into the hallway. He was heading toward the cellar door before he consciously realized where he was going and what he planned to do. But, he figured, with Beth safely sleeping and Jan out of the house, what better time to go back into the tunnel?

"One last time," he whispered as he swung the cellar door open and started down the stairs for the first time in nearly a week.

The air in the cellar was cool and moist, a welcome

relief from the heat of the day trapped upstairs. The cellar windows looked out on the night like polished black marble. He had brought some lumber in from the barn and cut them to the length he thought he would need, and now he set to work, tying them together so he could drag them along the tunnel to the blocking wall. With one of the flashlights in one hand, the other strapped to his belt, he pushed the timbers ahead of him, struggling to negotiate the narrow passageway.

He made his way slowly and painfully toward the blocking wall, taking only a short rest at the first turn in the tunnel. He knew he had to work fast so he would be out of there before Jan got home. In a little more than half an hour, he arrived at the blocking wall, his face and chest bathed in sweat.

As it turned out, the lengths he had cut were just about perfect. Using the butt end of the pinch bar, he wedged them into place to support the ceiling and began prying at the stones in the blocking wall. He left the flashlight on the floor, its beam directed at the place where he was feverishly working. He felt an intense need to break through the wall and just be done with it!

With the edge of the pinch bar, he probed the joints between the stones, hoping that age had loosened the mortar, but wherever he tried, the stones resisted almost as if the stones and the pinch bar were the repelling poles of magnets. As his frustration grew, he began to strike at the stones, and soon the tunnel was filled with the ringing of metal on stone. Sparks skittered like pinwheels onto the floor, and several nipped at his hands. The loud clang of metal hurt his ears, but that only increased his determination to break through the wall.

Working in such close quarters made it difficult for

him to bring much strength or leverage to the job. After more than half an hour of effort, the blocking wall still showed no sign of yielding. His shoulder muscles were knotting with pain, but he ignored that as he increased his frantic efforts to dislodge just one stone.

He drew back the pinch bar and shot it forward with jackhammer swiftness. Small nicks appeared in the stone, chips and sparks flew, but the wall remained—unmoving and unmovable!

"Goddamn it!" Don hissed between his teeth. The sweat coursing down his face made the numerous tiny cuts from rock chips sting. But he wouldn't give up; he *couldn't* give up! After several more violent attempts, he still hadn't breached the wall, and he sagged back against the tunnel wall, exhausted and frustrated. His breath felt like liquid fire racing through his throat.

He wiped the sweat from his eyes, took several deep breaths of the stale air in the tunnel, and studied the unyielding stone wall.

"You son-of-a-bitch!" he wailed as he shifted around and swung the pinch bar with every ounce of strength he had left. The metal scraped along the stone, shooting out sparks as it carved a deep scar across the stone face. One spark hit him in the eye, making him shout with pain, but that only increased his anger. The ceiling and walls of the tunnel seemed to suck in on him, filling him with a crushing fury.

These stones have been here for centuries, he thought. What the hell can one person do?

Finally, through his blinding fury and the swirling dust, he saw something, a small evidence of progress. Near the top of the wall, one of the stones looked as though it had slipped back. The stone below it, lit from below by the flashlight, cast a shadow over the bottom half of its surface, a shadow that he was positive hadn't been there before.

"Yes!" Don shouted as he ran his fingers along the newly exposed edge. "All right! I'm gonna get you now!"

Shaking his fists, he roared with laughter. The laughter reverberated down the tunnel, rebounding back and sounding like the insane giggle of a madman.

He wiped his sweaty hands on his pants legs and then leaned his full weight against the loose stone. He dug his toes into the tunnel floor, took a deep breath, held it, and pushed. He pushed until the tendons and veins in his arms stood out like thick wires beneath his skin. A palsy shook his body with the strain, but he kept pushing—pushing . . .

And finally he had to stop. He collapsed back on his heels, panting with exhaustion.

"What the hell does it take?" he wailed. The thought of trying a stick of dynamite and blowing the whole tunnel to Kingdom Come crossed his mind.

"What in the blazing hell does it take?"

His voice echoed back to him, and, as it faded and darkness closed around him, he thought he heard a dry, rattling laugh behind him. Wide-eyed, he turned and looked at the blocking wall, half-convinced that it was the stones, mocking him.

"You think you'll stop me, huh?" he said, his voice low and even but fighting for control. "You think you've got me, but dammit! you don't!" He crouched low and then, like a football player smashing into a practice dummy, he sprang at the wall. His feet kicked and scrambled as he pushed his entire weight against the stones.

When the stone finally did give, it went so easily Don at first thought he had lost his hold. He scraped down the side of the wall and sprawled onto the floor, banging his shoulder when he hit. He was only dimly conscious of the crunching sound the stone made as it slid back and fell to the floor behind the wall. He barely noticed the pain throbbing in his shoulder though, as he got up onto his hands and knees and looked into the dark opening in the wall. A wash of cold air funneled through the hole, chilling his sweat-drenched body.

"So much for you!" he said, smiling as he rubbed his bruised shoulder.

But his pleasure quickly faded, and he made a grab for his flashlight when he heard a soft, shuffling sound carried to him on the breeze shifting through the hole. He thought he could hear a low, deep laugh behind the wall.

Don's hand was shaking as he shined the light into the opening, but he could see little as the oval of light ran over the far wall of the tunnel. The sound continued, but it never got loud enough for him to be sure what it was or where it was coming from. It hovered on the edge of his hearing, hollow and tormenting. Was it really laughter, he wondered, or merely the wind echoing in the tunnel?

On hands and knees, he came up close to the opening and, holding the flashlight in front of himself, like a weapon, he peered inside. His breath came in hot gulps, burning his lungs.

The darkness beyond the blocking wall swallowed the light like water sinking into thirsty soil. Motes of dust swirled in the cone of light.

Inch by cautious inch, Don leaned further into the opening, amazed at what he saw. His ears prickled as he waited for the sound to either grow loud enough to be able to distinguish it or to fade entirely. But still it hung there, teasing him just beneath the rasping of his own breathing.

At first Don registered disappointment when he realized he had not broken through to the tunnel he had previously followed. He rested his chin on the edge of the opening as he regarded his discovery.

Beyond the blocking wall, the walls and ceiling of the tunnel were smeared with a thick coat of what looked like red clay. He could see the outlines of the stones beneath the red coating, but the overall impression was of looking into a large, beehive-shaped room, perhaps ten feet in diameter and about seven feet tall at its peaked center. The red clay had been applied to the walls and ceiling in sweeping swirls, and in several places Don could see handprints and other designs drawn into the clay when it was wet.

The whole thing reminded Don of pictures he had seen of prehistoric cave paintings. The handprints, he assumed, were the artist's signature. As he pointed his beam of light here and there inside the chamber, he couldn't shake the impression that he was looking into an opened carcass, and he wondered if that had been the intent of the chamber—to represent an internal organ.

"The heart of the earth," he whispered softly. Fascinated by the view, Don hurriedly removed three more stones from the wall—enough so he could easily enter the chamber.

When he put his head into the opening, debating whether or not to go inside, he saw something on the floor reflecting back the flashlight's beam. He leaned forward, trying to make out what it was, and he felt a wave of nausea when he finally recognized it. There on the floor were the shards of glass from his broken flashlight!

"Impossible," he said aloud, scanning the red-smeared walls. This wasn't the part of the tunnel where he had been before, he was positive of that! And he certainly had never seen red walls like this before! He twisted his body around, looking up at the ceiling and reached up. His hand touched the red clay on the walls, and, when he took his hand away, it was sticky, dripping with—

—*No! Not blood!*

His throat made strange clicking sounds as he brought his hand close to his face and looked at it, dripping with globs of red mud.

"No! *No!*" he screamed. The only thought that filled his mind was that he had to get out of there!

He was turning around, trying to twist out of the opening, afraid the swelling waves of panic would overwhelm him. His arm got caught on one of the stones, and to free himself he had to pull so hard that he wrenched his shoulder.

As he struggled, he heard—louder, now—what sounded like laughter, pressing close to him, all around him in the darkness of the red chamber. Just before he pulled his head back through the opening, he saw something move beneath him, between the opening and the floor. He tried to shine the flashlight down so he could see, but a jolt of pain suddenly shot through his arm. In terror, he shouted, but the sound was cut short as a bony hand reached up from the tunnel floor and closed its cold fingers around his throat.

IV

In the living room, Beth suddenly sat up on the couch. Her eyes were still closed as in sleep, and her face was blank and expressionless. Her left hand, clutching her wooden doll, was shaking violently, and she cocked her head to one side as though listening.

The only sound in the living room was the steady ticking of the clock on the mantel, but Beth suddenly nodded her head and with parched lips said, "Yes . . . I know . . . He's there now?"

Her body looked frail and withered under the afghan, and her breathing was no more than a shallow hiss.

"Yes . . ." she said, her voice sounding like tearing paper. "Yes, of course . . . I understand."

With a supple motion, she rose from the couch. The afghan slid to the floor at her feet, and she kicked it aside without looking. She clutched her doll tightly as she moved swiftly through the living room to the cellar door. Her eyes were still closed as she started down the steps. At the bottom of the stairs, she paused a moment and raised the doll to eye level. Cocking her head to one side, she seemed to be listening, then she nodded and went to the opening Don had made in the wall.

After propping her doll on the edge of the old coal bin, she bent down and picked up one of the stones her father had removed. Her knees buckled with the weight, but her face remained passive as, with a slow, steady tread, she carried the stone to the cellar wall and fit it snugly back into place.

Back and forth she went, lifting and replacing stones a girl her size would never have been able to budge, but she worked without apparent strain. Her shallow breathing never increased as she slowly worked at filling in the opening.

When the opening was nearly half-closed, she suddenly stopped, and turning one ear toward the gap that remained, she waited . . . listening. Suddenly a loud shout echoed along the tunnel, booming at her out of the darkness. She leaned closer to what was left of the gap, listening for the sound to be repeated, but all was silence.

Turning to the doll, she smiled and nodded. "I know," she said, her voice strangely lifeless. "It has to be this way." Then she went back to work, to complete what she had started.

V

Leathery fingers tightened their grip on Don's throat, cutting off both sound and air. He could feel the rancid yellow fingernails digging deeper into his throat as the powerful grip drew him, pulled him like a rag doll into the opening. His chest scraped painfully over the stones, and a pounding pressure began to build in his head. He could hear himself gagging, but the sound seemed distant.

He struggled to get free, kicking his legs wildly, but the clawed fingers wouldn't release him; they dug in and held with the tearing pain of pointed hooks. Again, dry laughter filled the red chamber.

In the struggle, Don had dropped the flashlight. The beam shot off at an oblique angle, focusing its circle of light onto the dripping red ceiling of the chamber. His shadow danced and twitched as the hand steadily pulled him into the opening. Suddenly a face loomed up out of the darkness, looking him straight in the eyes with its hollow stare.

Don nearly fainted as he looked at the horror that held him. Rotten flesh hung in loose strips from the face. The skin was gray and had the tattered texture of a hornets' nest. Ratty tufts of hair—long, black, braided hair—swung back and forth with the weight of beaded decorations. Don could see the skull beneath the decaying skin, twisting with worms.

But it was the eyes—*the eyes* that held him, burning into his bowels with an acidic, hateful glare. The eyelids were peeled back, exposing sickly yellow orbs. The night-deep pupils swelled and pulsated like fathomless wells, and the lipless mouth opened. With a fetid gust of breath, laughter rang out, filling the chamber and drowning out the sounds of the struggle.

Don increased his efforts to break free, placing his hands against the blocking wall and pushing back with everything he had. His feet scrambled wildly as the grip tightened. White points of light exploded in his vision, and Don could hear the tendons and bones in his neck crackling from the pressure.

The face came closer, almost touching Don's face, and, when the laughter stopped, deep, echoing words washed over him with the putrid breath.

"Defiler!" the skeletal face said. Its eyes tugged at Don's sanity stronger than the viselike grip. *"Defiler!"*

Don pulled back frantically and, as he did, he felt his foot hit something. The sound of metal clanging on stone rang out, and he realized that the pinch bar was close to his foot. Close enough to reach? he wondered. He reached down, feeling around blindly on the floor as his mind filled with swirling black.

"Defiler! Die!" the face said in deep, resonant tones. Flecks of foam streaked with blood flew from the snail-white tongue, burning where they had landed on Don's face. The hand and the eye pulled him further—further into the chamber.

Don could feel his strength ebbing as he was drawn into the darkness.

Better to die, he thought, than face this, but still his hand felt for the pinch bar—and got it! His fingers curled around the reassuring iron, his last hope for life. Slowly he raised the bar and, with what little strength he had left, slammed it point first into the grinning face.

The pinch bar glanced off the side of the creature's head, removing a wide swath of rotten flesh and hair. The creature reeled back, and the grip on Don's throat loosened enough for him to pull back and break the hold. He sucked air into his lungs and collapsed against the tunnel wall.

A roar of insane rage filled the tunnel. Don fumbled to release the backup flashlight from his belt. He snapped it on and directed the beam into the opening. Dimly, he could see a flurry of activity. He knew he should get out of there fast, but something held him, fascinating him.

The face suddenly filled the opening, and the bony hand reached out, grasping wildly. The jaw dropped open, and again the voice rang out, *"Defiler! Die!"*

Suddenly aware of the pinch bar in his other hand, Don swung as hard as he could at the face. He missed, and the bar struck stone, sending a shower of sparks flying. The face faded back into the darkness. His pain and panic told Don to move.

Keeping his eyes and flashlight beam fixed on the opening, he started to back slowly away from the wall. If it wasn't for the pain racking his throat and arms, he might have been able to convince himself that none of this was real, but, as he started back down the tunnel, he was ready for just about anything to happen. Even so, he couldn't help shouting when he saw a withered hand—with no arm attacked—skitter spiderlike through the opening, its dagger-sharp fingernails clicking on the stone.

Don swung again with the pinch bar, this time hitting the hand with a solid blow. Two gnarled fingers separated from the hand and shattered on the dirt floor. As they did, a loud shriek of rage and pain filled the tunnel.

"Defiler! Die!" the dust-dry throat rattled from

behind the wall.

"Get the fuck back where you belong," Don yelled. When he swung again at the severed hand, the remaining fingers curled around the iron bar and jerked it from his grasp. Don barely had time to duck as the bar shot out of the darkness and clanged against the wall behind him, removing a fist-sized chunk of rock.

Don snatched the pinch bar from the floor and, with the flashlight in his other hand, started down the corridor on his hands and knees. He knew without looking back that the thing was climbing through the opening, and his only hope was to get back to the cellar and wall the horror in where it belonged.

He felt like a pinball as he careened off the tunnel walls in his wild flight. The gut-wrenching fear that the thing had cleared the wall and was close behind drove him on. Below the sounds of his own frantic flight, he thought he heard rough scraping sounds, getting louder—closer. Laughter rumbling like thunder followed him down the tunnel.

His hands and knees were dripping with blood as he took the turn and followed the tunnel back. Panic and exhaustion threatened to sap him of strength, but he knew that, if he stopped, he would die. That thing back there would catch him and choke the life from him. The horror that *he* might become like it, become the next guardian in a succession of guardians, filled him with fear. He followed the weaving beam of light from his flashlight.

Dust filled his throat and, when he coughed and spit, he thought the saliva was tinged with pink.

—*No! Not blood!*

The creature was close behind, of that he was sure, so he redoubled his efforts to reach the cellar. His only hope now was that he would have time to fill in the gap. If not . . .

After going what he *knew* had to be more than halfway down the last stretch of the tunnel, he began to wonder why he didn't see light up ahead, filtering through the opening. He knew he had left the cellar light on, so where was it? Why couldn't he see it?

The scuttling sound behind him grew louder, reaching out from behind, threatening to snag his foot—hold him—draw him back.

With a frigid, mind-numbing shock, Don saw ahead that the tunnel dead-ended. There was no opening back into the cellar. Had he taken a wrong turn? he wondered, as sweat stung his eyes. He knew, in the small corner of what logical mind he had left, that that couldn't have happened. There were no other tunnels branching off from the one he had taken.

With the scuttling sound drawing closer, he quickly scanned the wall and at last saw what had happened. Someone had filled the gap with the stones he had removed. Only one small hole remained to be filled.

Don raised himself from the tunnel floor, bruised and exhausted, and looked out through the opening. With a jolting shock, he saw Beth, bent over, carrying one of the last stones over to the wall.

"For God's sake, Beth!" he screamed, slamming his fists onto the wall. "Beth! Get me out of here!"

His voice bounced back from the cold stone, hitting his ears with a dull thud.

Beth seemed not to hear as she hefted the stone into the opening and began to work it back into place. Don saw her face, eyes closed and mouth set in grim determination as she worked.

When dry laughter filled the tunnel, Don turned and shined the light back down the way he had come. Through the swirling dust of his hasty retreat, he saw a thin, crouching figure, glaring at him. Both arms were lacking hands, and the creature held out the stumps toward Don. At the creature's feet, the smashed hand with two missing fingers moved under its own volition, its earth-caked fingernails clicking like rat's teeth.

"Beth! Beth! What are you doing?" Don shouted as he slammed his elbow against the stone.

She had picked up another stone and was carrying it over to the wall. The stone made a loud grating sound as she slid it into place, cutting off the little light from the cellar that still trickled into the tunnel.

Gripping the pinch bar in his sweat-slick hand, Don pressed back against the blocking stones. He kept his flashlight focused on the crouching figure, which hung back, seemingly afraid of the light. The hand skittered on the ground like a mad crab, making vicious grabs at him.

"Defiler!" the creature rasped. *"Die!"*

"Beth! Please, Beth! Let me out of here!" Don cried. His throat felt as though it had been sandpapered. The pinch bar clanged on the stone as he dug his heels into the dirt floor and pressed his weight back.

The creature shifted forward, coiling its legs under it as though preparing to leap at him. Don held the pinch bar, ready to strike out if necessary, all the while concentrating on pushing back . . . pushing back against the wall. Then, with a sudden backward push, Don felt the wall give way, and he tumbled backward into the cellar, rocks tumbling all around him as the wall caved in.

Scrambling to his feet, he glared at Beth, who stood there, holding one more stone—the last one—in her hands.

"What the hell are you doing?" he shouted, but

then he pushed her aside and ran to his workbench. Sweeping the tools onto the floor, he manhandled the table over to the wall and, tilting it on edge, wedged it over the opening. He got it firmly into place and was starting to brace it with stones—stones that had almost sealed his grave, he thought—when he felt an enormous pressure slam against it from the other side.

"Help me! Beth! Don't just stand there!" he yelled. Beth opened her eyes, but she just stood there, looking blankly at him, as though she didn't even recognize him.

From the tunnel, the creature hammered on the table. The wood sagged and threatened to splinter, but Don kept his shoulder against the table, and it held. He hurriedly stacked up several stones, and after a while he had the workbench secured. When he was sure the creature couldn't knock it down, he put the remaining blocks of stone against the workbench and then turned to Beth.

"What the hell were you doing?" he shouted. He grabbed her by the shoulders and gave her a firm shake. "I could have been killed in there!"

Beth's expression slowly altered, and, when she made eye contact with her father, she registered dim recognition. He eased his grip on her, glancing behind him at the pile of rubble blocking the tunnel mouth. The workbench no longer shook from the pounding from the other side, but he could still hear, just on the threshold of hearing, low laughter.

When he asked her again what she had been doing his voice had at last lost its shrieking steel quality.

"I told you what he said,' Beth replied, her voice halting. "I told you in the hospital that he said we all had to die."

"Who did, for God's sake? Who said that?"

"Him," Beth answered faintly, looking past her

father toward the coal bin. Don spun around and looked at the coal bin, his eyes locking onto the steady glare of the wooden doll.

"What the hell are you talking about?"

"He told me to put the stones back into the wall, Beth said weakly. "He said you had defiled the grave, and you had to pay for it."

Don's eyes widened madly as he looked at the doll. Damned if it didn't look like that painted slash of a mouth was *grinning*! He started for it, hand outstretched, but Beth dodged past him and snatched the doll up.

"Don't! Don't you *dare* touch him!" she shrieked, hugging the stiff figure to her thin chest. She twisted away from her father, shielding the doll with her body.

"Give it to me, Pun'kin," Don said as evenly as possible although his pulse almost choked him. "I just want to—"

"Stand back!"

"Come on, Beth. Give me the doll!" Don commanded. "I just want to look at him."

Beth backed away from him as he moved toward her, holding his hand palm up to her.

"You can't," she said, whimpering.

"Give it to me."

She looked at him, her eyes glistening with anger and fear. Then, nodding, she slowly extended her hand with the doll.

"There, now. See?" he said gently. "I just want to—ahh! Jesus Christ!"

A sudden, needle-sharp pain jabbed at the base of his thumb. Involuntarily he dropped the doll and, looking at his hand, saw a thin streamer of blood curling down to his wrist. At first he thought he had gotten a splinter from the toy, but, when he looked at the wound, he saw that a small circle of skin had been removed—as if he had been bitten!

With a sudden, loud cry, Beth dove to the floor and grabbed the doll, hugging it to her chest. Don looked at it and saw blood—*his* blood running from the doll's widening grin.

Without a word, he lunged at Beth and tore the doll from her grasp, careful to grab it from behind so it couldn't bite him again. The wooden figure felt like a steel cable as it twisted in his hand, trying to break free.

"We're getting out of here," Don said, panting. Guiding Beth by the elbow, he took her, practically dragged her, up the stairs. The wooden figure nearly burst out of his hand, but he grasped it tightly as they went through the kitchen and out the door to the barn.

Don now knew what he had to do; he had to destroy the doll as he should have when they had first found it. However it was connected with the burial site, he knew that—somehow—it focused the energy of the guardian spirit, and the only way to ensure an end to that was to destroy it—*burn* it!

"Go over there and wait," Don said, shoving Beth in the direction of the garden. She collapsed on the ground and sat there, watching him as tears rolled down her cheeks.

"Please, Daddy," she wailed. "Give him back to me."

But Don ignored her cries as he went to the barn for the can of gasoline he kept for the lawn mower. All the while, the wooden doll wiggled and squirmed in his grip, trying to free itself.

VI

The moon had risen, and rafts of clouds drifting in

from the west were highlighted in silver as Jan drove up the driveway. Her headlights washed over Beth, who was sitting huddled in the field next to the garden. As she hit the brakes and the car skidded to a stop, she saw Don come running out of the barn with a gasoline can in his hand.

"Don," she yelled as she jumped out of the car and ran toward Beth. "What on earth is going on?" She was so concerned about Beth, she barely registered the expression of stark terror on his face.

"This!" Don shouted. He shook something he was clutching in his hand close to her face. It took her a moment to realize it was Beth's doll. In the darkness, the bloody smear on the doll's mouth looked like ink.

"Beth shouldn't be out at night," Jan said sharply. "The doctor said she needed rest."

"This goddamned thing *bit* me!" Don yelled. The hand holding the doll shook as though he was fighting to control it. He put the can of gasoline on the ground and held up his wounded hand for Jan to see.

"Don't be ridiculous," Jan said, half-suspecting a joke. "What's going on?" Beth stood up and, shivering, huddled close to her mother.

"It's no joke," Don said more calmly, but there was still a fevered gleam in his eyes that unnerved her. She wondered if he had completely flipped out.

"I'll tell you one thing, though," he said. "You were right. I should never have gone down into that tunnel."

"Did you go down there again?"

Don nodded, his body coiling with tension.

"What did you find?" Jan asked. She patted Beth on the shoulder.

"It's more what found me," he answered with a hollow laugh. Bending down, he picked up the can of gasoline while still holding the doll at arm's length.

The figure continued to flex and twist in his grip, and he was afraid it might break loose at any moment.

"Don—Are you sure you're . . . all right?" Jan asked, her fear for his sanity mounting by the second. "Come on. Let's take Beth up to the house and cool down."

"Not yet!" he snapped, shaking the gasoline and making it slosh. "Not yet. I have to take care of this, first. You stay with Beth. This will only take me a minute."

"The doll?" Jan asked incredulously. "What are you going to do with the doll?"

"The goddamned thing bit me, Jan!" he yelled. Then, without another word, he started across the field toward the table stone. His fingers felt stiff as though frostbitten as he unscrewed the can top. Still holding the doll at arm's length, he doused the table stone with gasoline. With what was left in the can, he soaked the doll, drenching his hand as well. He fished a book of matches from his pocket, lit one, and touched off the rest of the pack. Flames burst into an orange blossom.

"You want a sacrifice?" he shouted. "Here you go!" He tossed the burning matches onto the table stone, and flames shot up into the night sky. After waiting only a second or two, he threw the doll into the center of the swirling fire.

It might have been his imagination, but he was sure he heard a long, wailing scream as the wooden figure twisted and curled on the flaming table stone. Don stepped back from the raging heat and watched the tangled pillar of smoke rise, lit from below by a horrid orange.

"No! Daddy! No!" Beth shrieked as the sheet of flames billowed up from the hole in the ground. She broke free from her mother and dashed across the field, stumbling on the uneven ground. Falling down at her father's feet, she hugged his knees and looked up at him, pleadingly. Her face was lit a ghastly orange from the fire.

"Please, Daddy! Get him out of there!" she wailed. "Save him!"

Don only looked at the fire and smiled, satisfied by the charred lump forming in the center of the table stone. "It's over," he said softly, letting his hand brush across the top of Beth's head.

Jan walked over to them slowly, wearing an expression of mixed surprise and concern. The flames in the excavation site spun and raged, and Don watched, fascinated. As he gazed into the flames, he thought he saw the blackened figure expand until it covered the table stone—a human form lying spread-eagle. The image lasted only a moment; then it was gone.

Jan knelt down beside Beth and hugged her tightly. When Don looked at them—his family—all he saw was the orange flames, dancing madly in Beth's moist eyes.

Hypnotized by the fire, Don at first didn't register the low rumbling sound that had begun to shake the ground. It wasn't until a sudden jolt of the ground knocked him down that he looked, horrified, at Jan.

"Is it an earthquake?" she asked. He read her lips more than heard her as the thundering sound increased in intensity, shaking the ground like a dusty rug.

Thick, oily flames lit their faces, giving them a ghostly, masklike definition. Then, with a loud boom, sparks corkscrewed into the air. Don hugged the ground, fighting back the nauseating sensation that the ground was tilting.

"What the devil?" he shouted. He pointed to where a section of ground had sagged inward and, as they watched, a deep depression angled across the field. His first thought was that the ground was shifting along a natural fault line, but he suddenly realized that the underground tunnel was caving in, marking the field with a deep trench.

The flames from the table stone shot even higher into the sky, illuminating the field with an unnatural glow as thick as paint. They watched, horror-struck, as the dark line, slowly folding into the earth, caved in a portion of their driveway as it headed toward their house.

"Sweet mother of Jesus," Jan murmured, barely heard above the rumbling of the earth.

Don lurched to his feet and started running toward the house. He leaped over a portion of the trench and was halfway there when the violent pitching of the earth threw him off balance. He fell face down onto the ground.

"What the hell is happening?" he heard Jan scream. When he looked back, he saw Beth and Jan, huddled together and watching, terrified.

"I don't know!" he shouted, staggering back onto his feet. "Something gave way. The whole tunnel's caving in. I—"

His words were cut off as the concussion of a thunderous explosion bowled him over again. The shock wave hit him like an iron fist in the stomach. Looking up, he saw the explosion ripping through the house, engulfing it in flames. Glass and burning timbers shot into the night sky and showered down all around him. He heard Jan scream his name several times, but her voice came from the darkness behind him, sounding impossibly far away.

Scrambling to his feet again, he backed away from the hammering heat as the fire stripped the house to its frame. Jan's face, lit by the blaze, loomed up out of the darkness, floating apparently bodiless. He ran to her, calling her name.

"Are you all right? Beth? You're all right?" he asked frantically. His throat felt as though he had been inhaling the flames.

Crouching in the field to avoid the blasting heat, Jan nodded as she stroked Beth's shoulders. "We're O.K.," she said. "And you? You didn't get burned, did you?"

"I'm O.K.," he gasped. He looked at Beth, who sat in the grass, watching as the flames consumed their house. The fire gave her eyes a wicked gleam that unnerved him. When he touched her, he felt a deep tremor in her body—like the rumbling in the earth, he thought, suspecting she might be having another seizure.

"Pun'kin," he said, shielding her from the heat with his body. "You'll be all right." Hot tears ran down his face as Jan clung to the both of them.

"What in God's name did you do?" she asked. "Was there dynamite in the cellar or something?"

Don shook his head and looked over his shoulder at the house. "I don't know. I just don't know."

The shadow of the caved-in tunnel stood out like a black scar on the land. The old timbers of the house crackled and exploded like rifle shots while meteor sparks whistled through the thick smoke.

"Don! Look!" Jan said suddenly, fear tightening her throat. "Is there someone in the house?"

Don looked, but at first he could only see the skeleton of burning rafters and walls. But when he looked at where Jan was pointing, he saw—

—No! It couldn't be!

He saw a twisting human shape in the whirling flames.

"It can't be," he said, but he couldn't shake the

feeling that this was the creature that had stalked him in the tunnel. The figure raised its arms, and both appeared to be without hands.

Impossible! Don's mind screamed.

"It's him!" Beth suddenly shouted almost joyfully. "He's there!"

The strobe-light flickering of the fire gave her face an eerie, tortured expression that made her look older than her age. Don gasped when he thought for a moment he was looking at the face of Aune Kivinen.

"He's still there!" she wailed, struggling to stand. "He's been waiting. Waiting for *me*!"

Jan tried to hold her back, saying softly, "There, there. Take it easy, honey."

But Beth spun out of her grasp, lurched to her feet, and started running toward the burning house before either Jan or Don could react.

Jan screamed, falling forward as she tried to tackle Beth. When she missed, Don sprang after her. Beth ran swiftly, gliding across the parched grass, giving Don the impression her feet never touched the ground. Don knew, even as he pounded after her, there was no way he was going to catch up with her. He struggled as he ran as though through waist-deep surf, his injuries and exhaustion wearing him down.

As Beth neared the house, exploding showers of sparks spun around her in a fiery whirlwind. Don heard a low, whistling sound that gradually built into a hollow, sinister laugh.

"No!" he screamed, falling to the ground, beaten down by the blast furnace heat. *"No! Beth! No!"*

He watched as she ran straight into the flames. As he crawled toward the house, a rippling wall of flame swept up, hiding her from his sight.

Looking back at Jan, who stood lonely and terribly small against the night sky, Don let out a cry that ripped his lungs.

She did it on purpose! his mind screamed. *She went into the fire on purpose!*

Looking at the burning house, dizzy and near fainting, he saw something—something he knew had to be imagination. Standing in the center of the holocaust were two figures, side by side. The fire twined around them in knots, shifting, flickering, and then fading.

"No!—Beth!—No!" he cried, collapsing face first in the grass. He could feel the heat singeing his hair; he could smell what smelled like burning flesh; and he was falling . . . falling.

He was barely conscious of the explosion that ripped the night, sending burning timbers cartwheeling through the air. One huge beam came crashing down, shattering the bones in his left leg and pinning him to the ground as the fire consumed his house.

VII

The Remys had seen the flames flickering above the treeline and had called the fire department. The volunteer firemen arrived, but of course it was too late to save the house. They pulled Don back out of the stifling heat and, amazed that he was still alive, radioed for an ambulance. The house was a charred ruin, with only a few timbers and the teetering chimney still standing. They hosed down the barn and managed to save that at least.

Huddling in the field, well out of harm's way, Louise Remy tried to soothe Jan, but once she realized the truth—that Beth was still in the burning house—she found she had little to say. Nothing could ease *that* loss, she knew, feeling the baby in her uterus give a solid kick.

The ambulance arrived, and both Jan and Don were driven off to the hospital to be checked, treated for burns, and, if necessary, sedated for shock.

The physician's assistant in the Emergency Room at York County Hospital swore he would never forget what Don said as they wheeled him in on the stretcher. His face was gashed and smeared with soot, and the fire had removed his eyebrows, giving him a shocking, skull-like look. His voice cracking like an old man's, he repeated over and over, "Did you see? He didn't have any hands! *He didn't have any hands!*"

Epilogue

October, 1987

Being asked what he thought of these things he answered it was an amazing and humbling Providence, but he understood nothing of it.
                    —*Records of Salem Witchcraft*
                        1864, Vol. II, p. 108

The courses are being fulfilled;
Those under the earth are alive;
Men long dead draw from their killers
Blood to answer blood.
                                    —*Sophocles*

October Rain

I

Life went on.

A year after the fire at the Inmans' house, things in St. Ann's, Maine, were pretty much the way they had been before the Inmans moved to town. Other people bought or built houses in town. Kids graduated from York High School and either went to work or off to college—usually to the University of Maine in Orono, but now and again someone would hit the Ivy League. Other folks either died or moved away, and of course there was always the summer influx of tourists, who hit the area like a spring flood tide that didn't ebb until Labor Day, leaving behind littered beaches and deserted shops.

Life went on.

Louise Remy had her baby, a boy, that September—almost exactly a month after the fire. They named him Michael. One day the next spring, Earl Remy was shooting black powder. A flash in the pan blew up in his face, blinding him in one eye. He took to wearing a black eyepatch and began calling Michael, "Matey."

Hank Wilson, who took over most of Billy Blackshoe's duties at the Trustworthy, had a stroke while shoveling snow one snappy February morning. He retired as soon as he was out of the hospital and moved to Orlando, Florida. He never told anyone, not even Laura, his wife, about the dream he had had the night before his stroke. He had seen Billy Blackshoe standing at the foot of his bed with blood gushing from his mouth.

Speaking of Billy Blackshoe, his sister, Margaret, got married for the second time, to a man from Tamworth, New Hampshire. Counting her husband's children from his first marriage and her own, they had four boys and one girl tearing through their house. With the money they received from Billy's will, they moved to Holland, Maine, and bought a nice house.

Life went on.

Frank Herman broke open that fateful bale of hay to feed the cows one January evening just after the first real blizzard of the new year. He found his son's severed hand, now shriveled to a bony claw with skin the color and texture of an old raisin. A week later, the embolism in his right lung blew out like a rotten bicycle-tire tube. He had been dead for five or more days before anyone found him.

Sometimes, life didn't go on.

Mark Herman was never heard from or seen again. Most people around town figured he had run off to get away from his drunken father. There was some pretty-well-founded talk around town that Frank made a habit of beating the boy—especially when he was "in his cups," as they say.

Goblin, also, was never seen again, but townsfolk had devised a more prosaic end for her; they figured she had died in the woods and coydogs, Maine's "new wolf," had eaten her.

Jan left Don in the first week of September and moved in with her parents in Hartford, Connecticut. She landed a very good job with Scoville Realty, but the loss of Beth had taken a drastic toll on her; she developed quite a dependence on antidepressants. She never contacted Don, and, whenever he called her, she would answer him with single-word comments. She seldom spoke about Beth, and he knew it was because she was still—would *always*—blame him for Beth's death.

Don was living in a twelve-by-sixty-foot trailer he had set up halfway between the road and the burned-out ruin of the house. The chimney continued to stand until the first blizzard of 1987. One neighbor had jokingly suggested that he salt and plow over the land where the house and table stone had been—a suggestion Don almost took. His burned-off eyebrows grew back, but the left one had a curious twist that gave him an expression of permanent surprise. Until the day he died, he would walk with a limp from the broken bones he had gotten the night of the fire.

Experts from Portland had come and combed through the wreckage of the house, sifting the ashes for answers as to *how* and *why*. They never found any and, strangely enough, they never found any of Beth's remains—no charred bones. There was some speculation that the fire had been hot enough to reduce even Beth's bones to ashes, but the experts insisted that a fire that hot would also have melted the stones in the foundation as well. Whatever, they never found any trace of Beth's body, and that *certainly* became the source of many town "tall tales."

Several months after the fire, Don received a package from his sister, Susan. It contained the rest of her translation of Aune's journal, which she had worked up from the photocopy she had kept. Reading them in the light of recent events, Don saw them—every one—as predictions and warnings about what would happen if he disturbed the Indian grave site. He became convinced that Aune's son, Eino, had been a victim of the guardian spirit, and that Aune had known it—but only through her dreams.

Susan told Don in the accompanying letter she had allowed Tom to move back home against her better judgment. She said they were giving their marriage an "honest" second shot, and Don earnestly wished them success.

Don didn't spend much time thinking or reading about stone circles or Paleolithic Indian sites. Of course, his blueprint of the property and Billy's copy of *Indian Earth Magic* had been destroyed in the fire. But one afternoon in late May—nearly a year after the fire—he went to the Registry of Deeds and got another map of the property. He hadn't been having any disturbing dreams, but there was still one thing nagging at the back of his mind.

When he returned home with the new map, he spread it out on the formica table in the kitchen and sketched in the location of the table stone. He had wanted to remove the menhir at the foot of the driveway, but—frankly—hadn't dared to. Starting at the menhir near the road, he drew a straight line through the table stone and off into the woods. If the menhir that stood at the foot of the driveway marked the summer solstice sunrise, he figured directly opposite it he would have to find another menhir, marking the solstice sunset.

But he didn't try to find the other menhir until one afternoon late in October, well over a year after the fire.

II

It was the last day of October, and a light drizzle had been falling all day, giving the fallen leaves an oily coating as Don started off into the woods. The same woods, he recalled, through which he had chased Goblin—*when?*

Over a year ago?

Over a lifetime ago!

Every nerve seemed alive and tingling as he walked into the woods, only casually looking for the standing stone, he told himself. Acorns falling from the oaks ripped like bullets through the browning leaves, hitting the earth with dull plops. Far off, the nerve-jangling song of a bluejay rang out. On rainy days his leg hurt more than usual, and, not far into the woods, he cursed himself for starting the search on such a crummy day. He could have waited for a warm, Indian summer day.

His eyes brimmed with tears whenever—and it was often—he thought about Beth . . . *Pun'kin.* He missed Jan, but he felt the vacuum of her being gone would eventually be filled. Maybe, maybe not. But *never* would he get over the pain of losing Beth. *Never!*

Don suddenly paused in his walk, looking around as though some primitive sense had warned him of danger. He looked back along the path he had come. He could see his footprints in the muddy trail. The feeling that something was wrong—*seriously* wrong—

twisted like a worm in his gut.

A sound, he thought, tensing and listening. It had been a sound!

He looked around, leaning forward to peer through the autumn-dead leaves and was shocked when he saw something—the top of a tall, narrow stone through a break in the trees. Maybe the menhir, he thought, feeling a flood of panic.

"Oh, no," he muttered, wishing he had never come out even as he started through the underbrush toward the stone. A subtle tingling in his hands warned him that this was, indeed, the other menhir.

He pushed through a tangled mass of dying puckerbrush and then jolted to a stop. At the top of the menhir was a carefully drilled, weather-rounded hole. Through that hole, a rope had been passed and tied off. The figure he saw dangling from the end of the rope filled him with the numbing terror of a nightmare remembered. Hanging, toes pointing downward not three inches from the ground, was the body of a boy—a young man. The rope made a low, creaking sound as the body swung slowly back and forth.

Feeling a strange sense of disorientation, Don walked slowly up to the body, his eyes carefully taking in the rotten clothes that hung in tatters from the corpse. He tried but was unable to avoid looking at the face, swollen and frog-belly white. The boy's tongue stuck out like a bloated black slug between tightly clamped teeth. The head was tilted back and the worm-hollowed eye sockets were staring up at the gray sky.

Don felt a shimmering shock pass through his body when he finally realized that it was Mark Herman hanging there: the boy who had helped him load hay into his hayloft, the boy who had lost his hand in a farming accident.

The rope continued to creak as the body slowly twisted around, and Don saw that the left hand was, indeed, missing. As the body turned, the head snapped against the taut rope and suddenly dropped, facing Don with a vacant, smiling grimace.

With a scream building in his chest, Don staggered back onto the path. His arms pinwheeled wildly as he fought to keep his balance, but the earth seemed to pitch and reel from side to side as he ran, as fast as he could, away from the corpse.

How could he have done that? he thought, his nerves threatening to unravel. How could someone with only one hand tie a hangman's noose?

Lurching and stumbling, he ran through the woods, fighting against the tearing brush as he raced toward his trailer, toward the safety of home. He wished he could forget the face that danced in his memory, forget the twisted glee he had seen on Mark's face. He told himself repeatedly that the face hadn't—it *couldn't*—have *smiled*!

Pain shot up his left leg with each pounding step, and just as the trailer came into view, Don's foot caught on an exposed root, and he went sprawling on the ground.

Lying face down in the mud, he began imagining that Mark's corpse had not only turned slowly on the end of the rope, but that something else had happened. The body had slowly raised its handless arm, pointing the stump accusingly at him.

Trying to calm his racing pulse and to find the strength to get up and run the rest of the way home, Don became conscious of a sound, faint and far off at first, but steadily growing louder. His head was spinning with blackness, and points of light spiraled across his vision as he turned, trying to find the source of the sound. What had at first sounded like his pulse pounding in his ears began to sound more and more like the pounding of hoofs—horse's hoofs—charging down on him from behind . . .